Cold
Iron

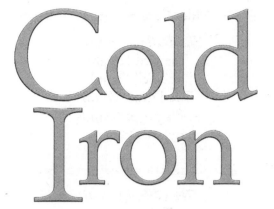

Cold Iron

Masters & Mages
Book One

MILES CAMERON

GOLLANCZ
LONDON

First published in Great Britain in 2018 by Gollancz
an imprint of the Orion Publishing Group Ltd
Carmelite House, 50 Victoria Embankment
London EC4Y 0DZ

An Hachette UK Company

1 3 5 7 9 10 8 6 4 2

Copyright © Miles Cameron 2018

A CIP catalogue record for this book is
available from the British Library.

ISBN (Hardback) 978 1 4072 5127 1
ISBN (Export Trade paperback) 978 1 473 21767 6
ISBN (eBook) 978 1 473 21769 0

Typeset at The Spartan Press Ltd,
Lymington, Hants

Printed and bound by CPI Group (UK) Ltd,
Croydon, CR0 4YY

www.gollancz.co.uk

Again, regarding principles, it is argued that they can be known through experiences, but this is both deceptive and fallacious, for experiences only have the force of establishing a universal principle by way of induction from many cases; and a universal principle never follows from an induction unless the induction includes every singular for the universal, which is impossible ... Let us assume that whenever you have sensed iron, you have sensed it to be hot. It is sure that by this reasoning you would judge the iron that you can see and all iron that exists, to be hot. And that would be a false judgement. Iron is often cold.

Tirase, *Questions on Metaphysiks*

Bactra

Liber

Iron

Circle

Prak

Praga

Rabe

Araho R.

Daka

Bastarna

Milla

Aquilea

Sulia

Geta

Krotiam

Sea

Bessinia

Abragos

The Chain

Sanatos

Devouych

Gortyn

Magua

The
WORLD

Prologue

It was late in the day when Syr Xenias di Brusias was ready to leave Volta. Almost everything that could go wrong had done so, and he was rushed and was prone, even after the life he'd led, to forget things, so he made himself stand by his fine riding horse in his two-stall city stable and review everything.

He still had not decided what to do by the time he mounted. He set himself in motion, mostly to avoid thinking too much.

His mare was delighted to be ridden; she'd been cooped up for as long as he had himself, and as soon as she was out in the street behind his house she was ready to trot, or more.

He kept her gait down because it was very important that he not be stopped. He was a little overdressed for a common wayfarer, in tall black boots all the way to his thighs and a black half-cloak and matching black hat full of black plumes, but he liked fine things and he lacked the time to change.

He was riding out of a maelstrom, and he needed to stay on the leading edge.

He could hear screams from the north, where the Ducal Palace was. He patted the sword at his hip with his bridle hand then he turned his horse at the first cross street — away from the palace of towering brick on the hillside, and down towards the river, the bridges, and the street of steelworkers where he had a commission to collect.

It struck him that if he collected the commission then he had made his choice; he would never be able to come back to Volta.

It also struck him that a violent political revolution could cover a great many dark deeds. There were already looters on the streets; two men passed him carrying a coffer, and neither looked up or caught his eye. The sound of breaking glass was almost as prevalent as the sound of screaming from the north.

He heard *gonnes* firing, and the snap of crossbows, and a sulphur reek floated past him and made his mare shy. There was the acrid reek of magik, too.

He let the mare trot, and her hooves struck sparks from the paving stones. Volta was one of the richest cities in the west, and it had fully paved streets and running water from the two great aqueducts, which was still nothing compared to the wonders of his home. The City.

Megara. Which he was about to help destroy.

Or not. He still couldn't decide.

The mare stopped abruptly. There was a corpse in the street, and the sound of steel crossing steel. He tugged at her reins, turned along an alley that ran across the back of the shops and emerged on the next broad, empty street, with tall houses tiled in red rising high enough to block the sun.

He looked right and left, but the street was empty. From long practice, his eyes rose, looking at rooflines and balconies above him, but nothing moved, and he gave the horse her head. They flew along the street, past the corner of violence, and down to the riverside, where he reined in and turned the mare into Steel Street, where the armourers were. He knew the shop well; Arnson and Egg, the two families on the gold-lettered sign, had made fine *gonnes* since the principle had first been developed far to the east.

He had a moment of doubt; the street seemed deserted.

But he saw a light burning, and smoke from the chimney, so he dismounted, tethered his horse to a hitching post and moved his dagger back along his belt from habit. Then he pounded at the door despite the darkening eve and the sounds of violence in the high town.

He heard footsteps.

'You came!' said young Arnson.

He pushed in beside the young man.

'I came for my *fusil*.'

The lad smiled. 'It is done.' He pointed at a leather case on the front bar. 'Pater is gone; he says it will be bad here. I'm to keep the doors locked and only eat food in the house.'

'Very wise.' The man paused to admire the case; the fine steel buckles made by hand and blued, and expert leather-work.

Then he took out the weapon.

'You made this?' he asked.

The young man grinned. 'I did, too. Pater helped with the lock; I'm not that dab with springs, yet. And I hired the leather-work.'

The boy was so pleased with himself that the man almost laughed.

He permitted himself a smile instead. 'And the compartment?'

'Just as you asked,' the young man said. 'Not in the weapon, neither.' He showed his visitor the cunning compartment built for keeping a secret.

'Superb,' the man in the black cloak said, and slammed his dagger into the young man's temple, killing him instantly. The blade emerged from the other temple with admirable precision, and the man in the black cloak supported the corpse all the way to the floor, stepping away from the flow of blood. Then he filled the secret compartment with his deadly secret, wearing gloves; one tiny jewel skittered away across the table and he tracked it down, picked it up with coal tongs from the fireplace, and put it in his belt-purse. Then he threw his gloves – fine, black gloves – in the fire, where they sparkled as if impregnated with gunpowder. He left, satisfied, leaving the shop door wide open to the looters already moving along the street like roaches.

But then he paused. The decision was made; there was no point in being sloppy or sentimental now. He took the tiny jewel from his purse using his handkerchief, covered his horse's head with his cloak, and tossed it back through the open door. It was so tiny he didn't even hear it hit the floor.

He led his horse away. Only after he counted one hundred paces did he trigger the jewel's *power*.

The house behind him seemed to swell for a moment. Then fire, white fire, blew from every window, the glass and horn panes exploding outwards, the shutters immolating, the door blowing off their hinges. It sounded like a crack of thunder, followed by a rushing of wind, and then the fire began to catch the other old houses in the row, even as the first house collapsed inwards in a roar of sparks and a burst of thick black smoke.

He mounted his mare, who didn't like the smell of blood on him or the sound or smell of smoke, and he used some of his *power* to cast an *occulta*. It didn't make him invisible; it merely compelled most people to look elsewhere.

He drew a second pair of gloves from his belt and tried not to acknowledge that he'd always intended this.

The killing.

The secret.

The compartment.

The fire.

The massacre to come.

He had a little difficulty at the bridge; angry, unpaid mercenaries were holding the near end, and they wanted money and no amount of magikal *compulsion* was going to fool them. So he paid, handing over one hundred gold sequins – almost five years' wages for a prosperous craftsman – as if it was his entire purse. They wanted to open his case, the case with the secret and the little *fusil*, and he prepared to fight them, but they lost interest.

There were more unpaid sell-swords in the streets of the lower town, and they were killing. He had to wonder if the duke was dead; and if he was, if the plan was still valid.

He considered changing sides.

Again.

To his enormous relief, there was no one on the Lonika Gate. He rode through unchallenged, and he was tempted to let the mare gallop; he needed to put time and distance between himself and Volta. The weight of his secret was tremendous; he flinched from it, trying to occupy his mind so that he would not think too carefully of what he was doing or what it would mean. He knew this would end his relationship with his wife.

Myra, his mistress, wouldn't care. She might prefer him alone. She wouldn't even understand.

But he understood all too well what it would mean.

All too well.

People were fleeing the violence; he passed a long line of carts in the winter fields. He rode aside at a barn, dismounted, and took off all his jewellery and his dagger belt, and put it all in his leather case. Sell-swords might search the case, but at least his rings wouldn't give him away. He put his beautiful black doublet in the case as well and pulled on a smock. It was not as cold here as it would be in the mountains, towards the barbaric Arnaut lands, but it was cold enough, and refugees trudged past him carrying beds and bedding, blankets and furniture.

Lonika was five days away; Megara three or four more days beyond. But he had a fast horse, and the money to buy remounts at Fosse and Lonika; as soon as he was free of all the violence, he'd eat up the ground. Nine days travel for a man on foot would be perhaps three for him. He could arrive exactly on schedule, if he was fast. Dark Night. The night the ignorant feared. The perfect night, or so the Servant said. That was not his problem. Delivering was his problem.

He had to make the Inn of Fosse in two days; he'd managed as much on other occasions.

There were soldiers ahead, stripping a wagonload of a poor merchant family as a mother cowered with her children and a man held his split scalp together. Five men in rusting armour threw the family's worldly goods into the mud, rooting for coins. Ten years of falling grain prices and increasingly violent weather had already stripped the countryside of coin and brought out the violence in people.

This was going to be worse.

He rode down a farm lane and well around the soldiers, and emerged on the turnpike into near darkness.

It was a major risk to travel in the dark. But he could see a farm-house on fire off to the west, and it seemed to him that the whole world had come apart, which gave him comfort for what he was choosing to do. The world might end, but it would be far away and he'd be very well paid. Rich, even. And he'd have Myra. And other entertainments.

He left Volta on fire behind him and rode through the night.

By morning he was just twenty leagues from the Inn of Fosse. He knew the road and the hills, and he was wary, because the Arnauts, although they hadn't made trouble in a generation, were a race of degenerate cattle thieves and sell-swords.

He climbed into the snow-clad hills, his horse tired and hungry, and he was watching the trees either side of the road. But when the road curved sharply into an ancient gully, he had no sight line, and the unpaid mercenaries had chosen their spot perfectly. They had a tree across the road, and he had no warning to turn aside or prepare a *working*, and he had to halt.

He loosened his sword in the scabbard and reached to unbuckle his *fusil.*

He never saw the crossbow bolt that hit him in the chest. It took him ugly hours to die.

Book One
Master of Arts

Knowledge is power...

A ranthur blew on his fingers and cleaned his quill on a scrap of linen. He was too tired to do his best work, and he took a deep breath while he looked through the small glass paned window in his gable. The glass window was the single greatest attraction in the long room that he shared with three other young men. They each had a gable with horn panes, seven storeys above the cobbled street, which allowed only a fraction of the winter sun to enter. Only the desk window had glass where a student could see to work.

His eye was caught by the sparkle of his talisman, a *kuria* crystal. He waved a hand over it, thinking he'd left it engaged when he was studying for his examination, cursing the waste and then regretting his curses, but the brilliance was only the natural sun tangled in the stone and not an emanation of *power*.

The room was bitterly cold. He glanced at his brazier and his bag of charcoal, counting his coins in his head. He'd bought some things for his mother: elegant ironwork, better than he could afford; fine paper for his sister, leather gloves for his father that he had made himself from expensive ibix leather. He didn't have the money to waste on charcoal.

It was also the last day of classes, and most shops would be closed and most of his tutors had already left.

He looked down at the lines he'd transcribed.

In the beginning there was darkness, and a void, and yet there was the mind of Sophia. And She said the word, and the word was Light, and light filled the whole of the heavens, and there was yet no earth, no water, no fire, no air. All was light.

He looked at the letters he had just formed. *Të gjitha është dritë* in the tongue of home. School – the Academy – so far had been little more than a pile of languages and a lot of writing. A little practical philosophy, and a very, very little magik. And even that little was more theory than practice.

He brushed back his unbound hair and tried not to curse; transcribing sacred words was not supposed to be accompanied by inattention and blasphemy. But it was a pleasure to write in his own tongue and not one of the dry, dead tongues that the Academy seemed to prefer, like Ellene, which drove him mad. He'd almost failed Ellene.

He'd almost failed everything. He hadn't, but it had been close.

He sighed and dipped his pen. He could see from the last fifteen characters and the dots over the vowels that his quill was beginning to fray and needed cutting, but he was in a hurry.

And She spoke into the void and there was light, but to the light She sang, and then there were the elements, air, and water, and fire and earth. And the word was song, and the song was the Song, and even as the elements distilled from the light, She desired other voices in Her song, and they joined Her. And there was polyphony, and harmony, and unity. And earth and fire made Earth, and air and water made the Sea; fire and air made the Stars, and earth and water the other planets, and each was a unity, and each was a living form amidst the Infinite; and the Void was not in opposition, but was filled, so that where there had been nothing, there was Everything.

He wrote, and breathed on his hands, dipped his quill, and wrote again. But when his next vowel had an unacceptably sloppy dot, he sat back, managed not to swear, and rummaged for his friend Kati's penknife. She was a student from Safi, a far-off land of burning deserts, and she had already left for home, sixteen days by ship and camel. Her parents were rich, and very demanding, but he envied her. She was going *home*.

She'd left him her penknife, a precious thing, sharp as a razor, just two inches of superb steel. He sat back and took a fresh quill from a tube of them, and cut it: a cut at the reverse angle to help with shape, a squeeze of the fingers to break the quill and form a slit, and then another deft slice to shape the nib. He rolled the quill in his fingers, liked the result, and used the knife to trim the feather to fit his hand, murmuring an invocation to the dead bird for the use of her quill and another to harden the tip. He dipped and tried it on a scrap of laid paper; the line was fine and steady. He went back to his work on vellum, copying out the opening chapter of *The Book of Wisdoms*.

He looked out of the window again and wondered if he was prevaricating. He had an eight-day journey home, and it was warm enough in the City. Arnaud, his Westerner mate, a Frankese from the other end of the world, claimed it was warmer outside than it was in the room. But the City was warm and comfortable in many ways, and the trip home was no little thing; he'd have to work as a deckhand to take a ship, and then he'd have to walk across half of Soulis, his home province, to reach his parents. He felt the temptation to stay – to write them a letter and then go to bed for a few days. He could get some scribal jobs and do more leather-work and use the money to eat his fill.

He could take some extra fencing lessons. He was in love with his sword, purchased in a used clothing market on a whim. With his rent money, because he was a fool. He smiled at the memory without regret, and eyed the blade where it hung on a peg meant for a book sack, by the human skull Daud had bought.

Why did I buy that sword?

It had been a foolish, impulsive purchase – a winter's savings gone in a few beats of his heart, as if he'd been laid under a *compulsion*. It wasn't even the kind of sword he thought he favoured...

He took the freshly cut pen back to his high desk by the cold window and settled himself. He had about a hundred and sixty more lines to copy, and then he could give his sister something truly beautiful for the Day after Darknight. First Sun. A holiday in almost every religion in the City and at home.

He wrote, and wrote. He paused a few times, ate a handful of nuts, breathed on his hands, and, with a wry look, threw some charcoal on the brazier. But he was no longer giving any thought to staying, and he began to write faster, his letters as precise as they would have been on an Academy project. He'd survived his first year at the Academy. He'd learned a few things.

And now he was going home.

It was almost dark when he prepared to make his way down to the docks which all but surrounded the City. He had a simple leather shoulder sack, a heavy cloak rolled and tied to it, and the sword – his most expensive possession and one that he wasn't sure he should even carry – on his waist belt with his purse.

He liked the sword, even though he wasn't very good with it. He wasn't sure it was completely legal for him to carry it outside the City, but it had, in just a few weeks, become a part of him. A symbol of the changes. An identity. Students were allowed swords by ancient privilege. Also, it wasn't an Arnaut sword, curved and razor sharp. It was a Byzas sword, an old one, with a complex hilt that seemed at odds with the simple, heavy blade.

If the sword was one outward sign, then so were his clothes – City clothes, nothing like what Arnauts wore: tight knit stockings and boots and a doublet with buttons to the throat. Arnauts, like Attians, wore baggy trousers and voluminous shirts and turbans or skullcaps or both. It occurred to Aranthur how much he would stick out at home, in his City clothes, with his City sword.

He grinned at his reflection in his room-mate's expensive mirror. With brown skin and green eyes, no one would ever mistake him for an aristocrat, but he was satisfied with what he saw, and he was tall and powerfully built, and size had advantages.

He settled the sword on his hip and imagined arriving home with it – imagined his father's annoyance, his mother's worry, his sister's admiration. He nodded, put the cover on his brazier to seal the fire, said a prayer to the Eagle, and walked down the steep steps of the ancient building in which he lived: six flights, and his sword tapping on every step.

He'd forgotten to return Kati's penknife. He paused on the stairs and swallowed a curse. But he was honest enough to admit that if he went back to return the knife to her room, he might just stay.

He went out into the afternoon air of the City instead.

The City was vast, a long peninsula riddled with alleys and criss-crossed with canals. Every street led to the sea in at least one direction, and some in both, and wharves full of ships bound to the whole of the known world waited at every pier. It was an aspect of the City that he loved above all others. But the Academy dominated the highest hill, and its precincts included not just the ancient, magnificent buildings of its founder, but the rows and rows of taverns, inns, and tall houses with crazy chimneys that had been built over a thousand years for the students and the masters, their fronts decorated with crazy patterns or magnificent frescoes, fresh or ancient. Most of those houses had glass windows, because students required light to read and write, and the winter sun reflected on glass and sparkled like ice; away to the north, at the top of the City, the Emperor's palace positively glittered with mosaics and the crystal dome of ten thousand panes that rose over his reception hall into a high point like a spire. And to the east, the Temple of Light dominated the waterfront like a mountain made by men. To the west, the rose marble 'Palace of the City' where the Great Assembly met and sat.

The sight never failed to make him breathe deeply and contemplate his own insignificance. Born a farm child in the distant Arnaut hills, the largest building he had known was the village's stone barn, and later the local lord's manor house where he had learned his letters and his first cantrips.

Even the deep woods he loved could not really rival the City.

At the base of his street, lined with tall houses and overshadowed by wooden galleries, balconies, and even bridges at the upper levels, he turned left, descending the hill towards the canals. There, on the first terrace, was the statue of the Founder: Tirase. He faced the statue, a little self-consciously, and made a reverence on one knee, the point of his scabbard catching on the cobblestones. Tirase gazed out over his Academy – a long, ascetic face, relieved by the obvious humour of his mouth and the ever so slightly raised eyebrow. He wore a simple long gown and he was pointing east. Theories abounded as to why.

Aranthur straightened. He revered Tirase; he was always aware that without the man's reforms, he would be tending milk cows in Soulis. He made a face and went down the marble steps. He'd never known the Academy to be so empty. He'd never been alone on the terrace before, and he had the odd feeling that his hero was watching him.

At the base of the steps he passed over the line of gold set in the ground that marked the Precinct. He paused at the shrine of the goddess Sophia and said a brief prayer, a simple invocation and request for blessing on his travel, and then he crossed the line.

As soon as he was out of the Academy he thought in terms of his own people, the People of the Eagle, the Arnauts. They were not *against* the one great Goddess of Wisdom that the educated preferred, but at home they tended to worship the Twelve, and especially the Eagle, the great god of the sky and of lightning, and his pantheon of brothers and sisters and lovers and enemies, and the Lady, who might or might not be Sophia. He wasn't sure he believed in the Eagle any more, but the Eagle was pinned to his thoughts in ways that gentle Sophia was not. His first weeks at the Academy had taught him to reflect on such things. He had a Magos who said the gods were nonsense invented for weak minds, and he had another who claimed that all *power* came from the goddess, and that only the most rigid adherence to her tenets would allow a student to master *power*. But here, walking along a canal no wider than the alleys above him, smelling the sea, he was a different young man. Although he was turned away roughly by the first ship he tried, the second ship was different. She was a small lugger whose owner was the captain, and Aranthur felt that the Eagle was with him; indeed, there was a carved eagle on the bow.

The ship was bound for the Gulf of Lonika, had need of a strong back, and when the captain heard he was a student at the Academy, the older man took him immediately.

'Can you master a wind?' he asked with a raised eyebrow.

'No, Master,' he said.

He wanted to add that he understood the principle – that in an emergency . . . Instead he touched his *kuria* and shook his head.

Farming taught you to keep your silence. So did the Academy. Farming also taught you to work hard.

The ship's master nodded.

'Good, a straight answer. What's your name, boy?' he asked, kindly enough.

'Aranthur,' said the young man. 'Aranthur Timos.'

'Arnaut?' the man asked.

'Yes, Master.'

The man tugged at his own beard and nodded.

'My wife's an Arnaut. Five days, and if you help us unload, five silver chalkes.'

The student bowed. 'At your service,' he said, and both men spat on their hands and shook.

Aranthur was no sailor, but he had grown up within two days' walk of the ocean and he'd been on a few ships. He didn't get sick, but he didn't really know how anything worked, either. He simply stood amidships all day waiting to be tasked, and the work wasn't too bad. They didn't overwork him, and he loved to stand on the deck just at the edge of darkness and watch the stars come up in the firmament, to say the prayers he'd learned at school and watch the sky as he had been taught for signs and portents. There was plenty to see: a meteor storm; a confusing flash in the heavens; the Eagle constellation, more gloriously laid out than he'd ever seen the nightly manifestation of his people's god.

The breeze was steady despite the onrush of winter, and even when snow fell on the ship, the wind didn't rise. They sighted land early in the morning of the fifth day. Before noon they were alongside a pier, and Aranthur was stripped to the waist despite the weather, throwing bags of grain grown in Atti from the hold up onto the deck. It was, at first, an excellent piece of exercise, and then it became dull. He turned his mind elsewhere, heaving sack after sack to the men above him, covered in sweat, and he did it until his arm muscles trembled with fatigue, but five silver crosses would transform his holidays and he was used to hard work. He lifted and threw, lifted and threw until his arms would barely function.

And then, suddenly, they were done. The sailors were as eager to go to their homes as Aranthur was to go to his, and after a couple of warm embraces, Aranthur was virtually alone. He was alone long enough to fear that the ship's master had forgotten to pay him, and then the older man came up the gangplank from the pier.

'You're a good worker,' he said. He handed over a small leather bag. 'Count it, lad. There are more thieves than honest men in this world, by Draxos.'

Aranthur opened the little purse. There were six silver chalkes and a tiny gold sequin.

'For my sins,' the ship's master said with a smile. 'Pray for me, will you, Student?'

Aranthur bowed. 'It is too much.'

The older man smiled bitterly. 'Bah. Perhaps. I got a fine price for the grain. Darknight is coming, eh? Best do a good deed. Take it, and eat well, and think of me.'

He nodded and stomped off to his cabin.

Aranthur went down the plank, shrugging into his wool cote and getting tangled in the knife he wore around his neck. He was cooling off rapidly, and he pulled on a hood, paused, and realised he had left his sword. Almost as if it had called out to him.

He stopped at a dockside tavern that looked faintly reputable and ate a good cuttlefish stew, black with squid's ink. Eating fish didn't trouble him, although he made the invocation to the spirit of the fish. It was a matter of debate among the learned as to whether fish had the spark or not. Aranthur grinned, thinking of how hot such debates could be, and how different theory was from a bowl of fish stew on a cold morning.

But the day was still young and even with a sequin in his purse, he didn't have the time or money to linger in Lonika.

Still, the men in the tavern – and they were all men – were talkative, and he listened. And then, in turn, the barkeep asked him where he had come from. The barkeep was eyeing his sword.

Aranthur was already wondering if the sword had been a mistake.

'Academy.' He was really quite proud of his status as a Student. In the City it didn't mean that much, but here . . .

One man actually tipped his hat. The others made faces.

'I saw a Lightbringer yesterday,' said the man who'd tipped his hat. 'Civil bloke. Very civil.'

'Very few students become Lightbringers,' Aranthur explained. 'I myself . . .'

The barkeep was still looking at his sword.

'Saw a swordsman yesterday,' he said. 'He was from the city. A Master.'

Aranthur nodded. 'I'm not a master of anything. I'm just a student going home for the Feast.'

'Oh, aye,' said the first man with a smile. 'Home?'

'In the hills,' Aranthur said.

'Oh, the hills,' a sailor muttered. He touched his knife and muttered, 'Mongrel.'

Coastal people were very fair, like Voltains in the west. Arnauts were a race of mongrels, all the shades of the earth. Aranthur himself was betwixt and between, like most of his people; he was green-eyed, but coloured like old wood.

But despite the hostility of the one sailor, the others wished him well. The idea that he was going home for the great feast made him more normal to them; a longshoreman patted him on the back. Another asked for a blessing. Aranthur had never given anyone except his sister a blessing before. But he swallowed, made the sign of the Eagle on his chest, and managed to say a prayer without faltering. The man grinned.

'You'll do,' he said, and went about his business.

Aranthur hoisted his pack and went out into the brisk air. He pointed his nose north and west, and began to walk. In ten minutes he was passing a statue of the Founder, and he paused and made his reverence.

A minute later he was approaching the landward gate. A pair of soldiers watched him and he had the uncomfortable knowledge that he held the focus of their attention because he had a sword.

The shorter one looked dangerous: a heavy mouth set in a frown; short as a *Jhugj*, the old folk of the hills. The taller one, seen closer, was a woman, wide-shouldered but slim. She had a fine steel breastplate and every inch of her was armoured in plain steel polished like a mirror. Her peaked armet made her appear taller. Her armour had bronze edgework, and she had a fine edge of scalloped red leather on her breastplate – worth a fortune. In the City, Aranthur had learned to notice such things.

The short man's face told Aranthur he was to be stopped, so he paused.

'Let me see your slicer.'

The man's voice was deep and rough. His maille was heavy, made up of rings of different sizes, and his leather-work spoke of money and hard use together. Aranthur did leather-work to fund his studies; he knew the good stuff when he saw it.

Aranthur took the sword out carefully and handed it pommel first to the guard.

'Stupid sword for a stripling,' he said. 'Too big for you. Steal it?'

'No, sir,' Aranthur said.

'Arnaut?'

'Yes, sir.' Aranthur nodded his head as if he was speaking to a Master at the Academy.

'Thieves and cut-throats,' the guard said. 'And you more of the same, I guess.'

'No, sir,' Aranthur said.

'I'll just keep your sword, honey,' the guard said. 'Strip that belt and give me the scabbard too.'

The short man was watching him; even in Aranthur's state of near panic, he noted that the powerful man was intent and careful, as if he, Aranthur, might be dangerous.

'Drek . . .' The woman's voice was deep, and had a cool dignity Aranthur wouldn't have expected in a guard.

'I have a writ,' Aranthur said, his voice rising. He tried to breathe, to practise the control he'd learned at the Academy. That sword represented every penny he'd saved . . .

'Let me see it.' The woman sounded bored.

Aranthur fumbled in his belt-purse, the feeling of panic rising, clouding his ability to find the thrice-damned fold of vellum.

He drew a breath and touched his *kuria*. Paused, accepted the calm, even if it was artificial.

The moment he touched the crystal, the woman stepped back and put a hand on her sword hilt.

Of course he'd put it in his coin purse. An inner pocket.

'Sorry,' he mumbled.

She kept her distance.

'You are a Magos?'

'Keep both hands where I can see 'em,' said the short, heavy guard. He drew and put the edge of his sword against Aranthur's throat all in one motion. 'You don't have a fuckin' writ.' He was grinning now. 'And you're wasting my time.'

Aranthur's fingers closed on it. The vellum was smooth and cold, and he extracted it, and held it out, the artificial calm of the talisman helping him.

The woman opened it with practised fingers, left handed, her right still on her sword hilt.

She looked at him with her head tilted slightly, as if he was something foreign to her.

'You are an Imperial Student?' she asked, her intonation putting the capitals on the words.

'Yes, ma'am,' he said.

'Oh, by the Lady, anyone can say . . .' The guard rolled his eyes, but the woman gave him one look and he was silent.

She nodded, folded Aranthur's writ and tapped it on the back of her sword hand.

'Give the boy his sword, Drek.'

Drek obeyed. He wasn't even surly, he just handed it over.

'Can't let everyone walk about armed,' he said.

Aranthur wanted to sheathe the sword easily, but his hands were shaking, and he fumbled with it for so long that the big guard reached over and slipped it home in the scabbard.

'Too long for you, boy,' he said. 'That hilt is old-fashioned...'

Aranthur nodded.

The woman scratched under her chin and looked out of the gate.

Aranthur was calming; he had enough control of his fear to note that the woman in the fine helmet was perhaps forty, and had a strong face and even features and looked like...

'That writ is for students learning to fight in the City,' she said. 'I'll pass you – you are a Student, after all. It might as well be tattooed on your head. But...'

She looked at him, and suddenly he saw that she was not a lowly gate-guard. She was someone else – someone reviewing the watch, or commanding the town. And that he was very, very lucky she had been here. She gave him a flick of her eyebrows. A quarter of a smile.

The big guard nodded. 'There's a lot of crap out there, Student,' he said. 'Where are you headed?'

'Home,' Aranthur said. 'The hills.'

The guard grunted, as if the hills made him uncomfortable.

'We hear there's fighting out west,' the woman said. 'Be careful.' She looked at him intently.

'Get a smaller sword,' the big man called after him.

Aranthur walked away, his cheeks burning, thankful and indignant by turns. As his feet crunched the new snow he heard the man say, 'Fluster him and see what he's made of...' and a moment later, 'I was *not* stealing his fucking sword, ma'am.'

The wine was good. That was about the best thing that could be said about his day, or the fact that he couldn't feel his feet.

Aranthur sat back on his stool and drank a little more. He had at least two days' walking ahead to get to his home village, high in the hills north of the Great Road, and less than four silver crosses left to pay his bills. He'd made it to the inn, and he had his sodden feet by a fire. And the wine was good. It tasted of home – or, he thought in his current mood of self-examination, was the wine merely good by association? Was he closer to home and forcing the taste of the wine to meet his expectations?

The inn was a fine one too – one Aranthur had known of almost from boyhood. Its stone walls had seen several sieges – most of them unsuccessful – and even its barns were stone. It lay directly on the Great Road from Volta to the City, and there was not another such inn – with post horses and decent wine – for two days in either direction. As a boy, Aranthur's father had gone down to the inn to buy mules and sell his olives and smoking leaf.

'Something happening out west,' the young man behind the bar said, seeing that Aranthur was considering another cup of wine.

Aranthur rose off his stool by the fire and smiled at him cautiously. They were not quite alone. There were three farmers hiding from the heavy snow, men like his father, and thus familiar and homey; and an old priest, an actual Lightbringer, and his acolyte, by the great bay window, sharing a book and quarrelling about the speed with which the pages should be turned. The man behind the bar was Aranthur's age, give or take a year, and he wanted company, although both were young enough that a year or two could be a gulf.

In the dimmer corner at the east end of the common room, an older man sat by himself, almost unmoving, a pitcher of what had to be cider untouched at his elbow.

'I saw too many soldiers on the road,' Aranthur admitted.

He walked to the counter, careful to keep his long sword from catching his cloak. He was still so cold and so wet that he hadn't stripped off his clothes, even though he was old enough to know better.

'Any trouble?' the young man asked. 'I'm Lecne, though almost everyone calls me Lec.'

'What would you like to be called?' asked Aranthur.

The young man smirked. 'Lecne.' He laughed. 'Lec seems so indecent.'

Aranthur paused, searching for the pun, and found it in Liote, the language of this village. But he was too slow.

'Hah, had you there. But you smoked it in time. You must be a Student.' Lecne had an easy smile.

Aranthur held out the hand that had been on his sword hilt and offered it to Lecne, who clasped it. Both men touched their foreheads and made the sun-sign.

Aranthur pointed mutely at the pitcher of wine on the bar.

Lecne shook his head and poured him a cup from a small barrel behind the counter.

'Try this.'

Aranthur hesitated. 'I can't afford it,' he admitted.

Lecne looked out of the great window that filled the front of the inn – an advertisement of its own, clear glass lavished on the building. Outside, snow fell like rain, and already the bottom row of panes of the magnificent window were covered by the stuff. Lecne held out the cup.

'Let me try my wit on you, friend,' he said. 'You are a student coming home from the City for High Holidays.'

Aranthur nodded.

'And then you will turn about and return to the City,' Lecne continued.

'Too true.'

'And like most students, while home, you will get money from your parents.' He smiled, lest his words be taken as an insult.

Aranthur smiled back to show he was not offended.

'You might easily be a student yourself.'

Lecne smiled crookedly. 'I would have liked to be one. But my father owns this fine pile of stones, and I expect, as he has no other male child, that I had best learn to run it. That said, I'm guessing that you are poor, but when you come back this way, you will be . . . less poor.'

Aranthur nodded. 'You are the very prince of philosophers, sir, and if you were not so soon to come into the possession of a fortune and a great responsibility, I'd suggest I might come and study with you.'

Lecne bowed slightly, to say that he appreciated the compliment and the way in which it was phrased, but his slight smile denounced any vanity.

'Pay me when you come back. I see you as a good investment, and to be honest, I haven't spoken to a boy – that is, a man – my own age since winter started.' He paused. 'And then there is your sword.'

Aranthur accepted the better wine.

'Indeed? My sword?'

'You have one,' Lecne asserted.

'I do,' Aranthur allowed.

'And you said you saw soldiers on the road,' Lecne reminded the student.

'They say there's been a *stasis* in Volta. A civil conflict.' He looked around, caught the odd gaze of the man in brown, and looked at Lecne. 'I was warned at Lonika, but I made it here. Alive, if a little cold.'

Lecne nodded. 'I have heard the same. The Tyrant murdered in front of the Temple. Fighting in the streets.' He leant close. 'A great fire. They say it was three days ago, and there was a *curse*, and . . .'

'A farmer said as much to me this morning, when he found me asleep in his haystack.'

He shrugged to indicate that anyone might have been in a haystack.

Lecne clearly felt the same. He grinned and waved a hand.

'And the soldiers?'

Aranthur had now been in the warmth of the inn's main room long enough to thaw a little. He let his wet cloak come off his shoulders and caught it on his arm, so that the other man could see that he was soaked to the waist.

'I hid in the woods. I had to cross a rivulet to lose them.'

The loss of the cloak also revealed the complex hilt of his sword: a cross guard embellished with two plain steel finger rings either side of the cutting edges, and a complex ring that linked them.

The innkeeper's son nodded, eyes on the sword.

'After your purse,' he agreed.

'And my sword.' Aranthur shrugged.

It had been the wrong thing to say – if he had a good sword, why hadn't he fought the soldiers? The question was on the other man's lips, and yet he was too polite to ask it.

A middle-aged woman in a fine wool gown appeared from the stairs at the rear of the main room and smiled at Lecne, who, from their shared ruddy brown hair and elegant, slim noses, had to be her son.

She bowed her head in Aranthur's direction.

'Mater, could you take this man's cloak and dry it?' Lecne said 'He's soaked. Had an encounter with soldiers. Syr Timos, this is my lady mother, Thania Cucina.'

Aranthur bowed again. 'I can take my wet things to the back. Although if I might be allowed to hang the cloak in the kitchen . . .'

'Will you stay the night?' the woman asked.

Behind her, Lecne gave a minute head nod. Aranthur surrendered to the luxury of a night in a warm bed, even if there were lice or bugs. He'd had two days' walking, and he'd slept hard, and his fingers ached all the time. It meant walking twelve hours tomorrow, though; he couldn't be caught in the open by Darknight.

'Yes, Despoina,' he said.

She grinned. 'Don't "despoina" me, young sir. I'm old enough to be your mother.'

Aranthur considered a touch of flirtation and decided she, or her son, might take offence. He was just getting the hang of flirtation – more humour than compliment, always a light touch. His room-mates had mocked his seriousness about everything, but then, how had they learned?

She flashed him a fine, if matronly, smile and took his cloak.

'I'll see it's properly baked. I assume you've been too cold to have bugs. I hate bugs.' She frowned. 'Where are you from?'

He bowed again – respect for elders was an essential part of the life of the student and the farmer.

'Wilios,' he said. 'A village on the Amynas river. Not so far from here.'

'Amynas,' she said. 'Does your family have vineyards?'

'Vineyards and four hundred olive trees. And we grow stock around the house.'

She made a face and moved her nose. Not everyone approved of stock – a cultivated weed that some people smoked and some chewed.

'Well – to each his own, I'm sure,' she said. 'I've never been as far as the Amynas, but we have the wine.'

'My father never sells our wine. Well, never out of town, anyway. But he's had his olive oil here. I came down once when I was young.'

'Child, you are still young to me. I must know your father, though I can't think of a man from Amynas with olive oil.'

A voice – a man's voice – came from the kitchen like a great argosy under full sail.

'Timos! Hagor Timos!'

The owner of the voice squeezed himself out of the kitchen and into the main room. He was tall enough to have to mind his head on the beams and wide enough to struggle with the door, and his face was almost perfectly round, despite which he clearly resembled the young man at the counter.

He had garlic in one hand and a very sharp knife in the other hand.

'Which makes you Mikal,' he said.

23

'Aranthur,' he said in near-perfect unison with Lecne.

The man shook his head. 'Don't know you,' he said equitably.

Aranthur raised his eyebrows. 'But I promise you, sir, that I am Aranthur, son of Hagor.'

Lecne's father nodded. 'I won't shake, given the garlic.'

He vanished as quickly as he'd appeared.

'And he's my pater,' Lecne said. 'Latif by name. Cucino, of course.'

Aranthur's magpie mind immediately delved into the complexity of Liote gender typing. The Academy had ruined him – he could now think about *anything*. But the new wine was good, and he raised his cup in appreciation.

'My thanks, Lecne.'

'I'll find you a room,' Lecne said.

'I can't afford aught beyond the common room floor,' Aranthur said quickly.

Lecne made a face and rubbed his nose.

'Bundle of clean straw, then?'

The floor temperature was more like that of ice than would promote sleep, and Aranthur nodded again.

'I would be your debtor.'

Lecne laughed. 'You will be, too! Pater's making a fine meal – almost High Holy Day. Dumplings with meat in butter. With grated cheese.'

Aranthur smiled. '*Knocci*,' he said.

A dish of home. The wine of home – the Liote accents and gentle manners of home. And eating a little meat wouldn't kill him.

Donna Cucina summoned her son to point at something in the yard, and Aranthur felt the weight of his sodden hose. He wanted out of them. He crossed the common room to where he'd placed his pack carefully by the open hearth – a hearth that vented not into a modern chimney like all but the very oldest houses in the City, but into an opening in the roof high above. Hams and cheeses hung in the smoke near the vent, at the end of the second floor balcony, and up there was a whole deer, gutted, hanging like some rotting criminal, and a whole pig carcass as well.

Aranthur took his buckler – a small round shield not much bigger than his hand – off the top of his pack. He'd tied it there because, being wood and metal, it was waterproof. He'd hoped it would keep the snow out of the simple tube of his soft pig's hide knapsack.

Perhaps it had, but the time Aranthur had spent lying in snowdrifts and crossing streams had negated its effectiveness. All the clothes in the tightly rolled bundle were wet through. The ache in his right shoulder was explained – the pack weighed far more than it ought due to all the water.

He steadied himself before he could curse. Cursing was weak.

'Avoid all mention of Darkness,' one teacher had said.

So be it.

'You are a swordsman?' asked a gentle voice behind him.

Aranthur rose from his crouch by the pack. The older man who had occupied the niche in the east wall was standing at the counter while Lecne cut him bread and ham. The older man was also wearing a sword. It had a broad blade and a simple cross-hilt. The grip had seen a fair amount of use.

Aranthur smiled carefully. Wearing a sword in public had certain consequences.

'I would not venture so far as swordsman,' he said. 'I am a Student in the City.'

The older man's clothes were very plain but very good. He wore plain brown, but it all matched and the cloth was expensive, and there were touches of elegance   brown ribbon at the cuffs, a fine standing collar that made the man's doublet look like an arming coat that a soldier might wear. But he had no jewels and a plain purse, and Aranthur was unsure of the man's status.

He bowed, nonetheless.

The older man narrowed his eyes.

'That was well said. Few men who wear swords are swordsmen, and, as the seer said, "humility is often the best scabbard".' He paused. 'I do not usually intrude on others, but I overheard you to say – my pardon – that you had trouble on the road.'

'Yes, syr. Soldiers, or bandits.'

'Often the same, in my experience.' The man in brown frowned. 'I am sorry to insist, Syr Student, but I am waiting for . . . guests of mine. From the west. They are late.'

Aranthur was fascinated by the man's careful manners.

'I wish I could be more helpful, syr, but I came from Lonika, from the east.'

'My thanks, nonetheless.' The man in brown looked for a moment at Aranthur's sword. 'That is quite old, isn't it?'

'I think so, syr. To be honest, I know little about it.'

The man in brown smiled slightly. 'A *javana*, or a bastard *javana*. Is it actually First Empire?' He looked carefully. 'Almost a *montante*.'

He reached out, as if such a motion was natural, and put his hand on the hilt.

Aranthur had the oddest feeling that the man could have killed him with his own sword. But he paused.

'My pardon, young syr. But I love swords. May I?'

'Of course, syr.'

The man in brown stepped back, and Aranthur drew the sword.

The man took it with a slight bow and walked to the great window, where the Lightbringer and the acolyte were reading together. He made a cut with it, and it hissed through the air.

One cut, and Aranthur knew him for a master. It was not a complicated movement; it was simple, and *perfect*.

He walked back. 'Remarkable. The blade is very old. This hilt, which is also old, is not its first hilt. You inherited it?'

'I purchased it,' Aranthur shrugged. 'In the night market.'

The man in brown laughed mirthlessly.

'I should spend more time in the night market, then,' he said. 'Perhaps, if there is time, you might let me draw the hilt and the pattern on the blade. You see the dragon's breath?'

He pointed at a series of formless patterns that ran down the central fuller and flowed like ripples of oil over the fuller almost to the cutting edges.

Aranthur smiled. 'I think it was the pattern that made me buy it.'

'Remarkable,' the man in brown said. 'Well. At least you are not a fool. Until later.'

He nodded, walked back to the bar and took his bread, cheese and ham, and sketched a bow without introducing himself – a trifle uncivil, but not so uncivil as to warrant offence.

Lecne's eyes followed the man for a moment and then met Aranthur's – and he grinned.

'What a rod,' he said.

Aranthur tried not to smile. But it was good to have an ally.

'Are you any good? With your sword?' Lecne asked. 'I mean – I don't mean...' He paused. 'Now I'm the rod. I've always wanted to take lessons.' He flushed when he spoke.

Aranthur laughed. 'As did I,' he allowed. 'It was the first thing I did when I reached the City.'

He could feel the older man's attention, but the niche was behind him and he knew that if he turned, someone would have to react. Two fist fights in the City and a warning from the Rector had convinced him to be careful in his interactions. But he was saved from further interaction by the sound of bells – dozens, if not hundreds of them, out in the snow.

'Company!' Donna Cucina called.

Beyond the window, they could see a coach, or a heavy travel wagon, indistinct in the snow.

Lecne made a face and started to pull on a heavy overshirt of new wool that hung behind the bar.

'We don't have an ostler just now,' he said.

Aranthur was already soaked to the waist.

'I'll go.'

He knew animals, and he could unharness a team, especially if the coachman helped.

Lecne looked at his mother, who, in one glance, told Aranthur that his place in her pecking order had just risen, and then smiled broadly.

'You're on, and thanks.'

He pulled the heavy wool shirt back off his head and tossed it to the student. Aranthur unbuckled his sword belt and handed it over the bar to Lecne, caught the shirt and pulled it on – and was instantly warmer.

Aranthur passed the table of farmers and the priest, who looked up. His acolyte was more senior than he had appeared – his own age or even older – and was shockingly handsome, with an aquiline nose, chiselled dark features and a shock of white-blond hair under his cowl.

Then Aranthur was out into the snow, and his first step into the deep stuff robbed his feet of all the warmth they'd accumulated in the last half an hour.

It was a heavy travel wagon, a wain with eight horses before it and four more in reserve behind – a monster rig. Aranthur went forward with all the courage of the volunteer. No one could possibly blame him if he made a mistake with the complex tack, and the thought bolstered him. He noted, too, that there were men out there in the snow – a surprising number, all mounted on big military horses and wearing armour. Behind, in the darkness, loomed another shape – *another* wain.

One of the high-sided wagon's side doors – it had four – opened suddenly. The inside seemed to be lined in fur, and it looked warm and incredibly rich, and the smell of incense wafted out on the cold air.

'Content yourself that I have not slit your throat, you whore,' said a voice that cut as sharply through the snow as the scent of incense. 'Perhaps you can ply your original trade here, my dear. At any rate, I won't have to listen to any more of your foolishness.'

A woman – Aranthur knew it immediately – fell to one knee in the snow. She was wearing a gown of silk, edged in fur, that showed more of her shoulders than was usual in the City and which was utterly impractical for the weather, despite the fur. She had short red-brown hair and a straight back and her voice dripped with contempt.

'You might pass me my cloak and my hat, my lord,' she said. 'Is my travelling case too much to ask for?'

He laughed nastily. Aranthur had an impression of bright white-gold hair, a long pale nose and a grating voice.

'Drive on!' he shouted, and slammed a stick of some sort against the roof of the wain.

His blow only served to dislodge some snow, which fell on his head. He cursed, using Darkness imagery that shocked even Aranthur, a student of the City. Still muttering blasphemous oaths, he pulled his door shut.

Aranthur could see that *power* was in use. The woman reeked of it.

She stood alone in the snow. Closer now, Aranthur could see that there were indeed armoured men on horseback all around the great travel wagon. Only a man of paramount importance – the Emperor, perhaps – had a wagon-carriage that big, and twenty knights to guard him on the road, with spare horses and a wagonload of supplies in the dark midwinter.

Aranthur had no real idea what was going on, although the entire tableau had passed in Liote, heavily accented the way Westerners from the Iron Ring spoke. Since he did not understand, he continued with his original plan and made his way to the front of the great wagon. Two men were perched high on the box, swaddled in heavy furs.

He began to climb the steps, even as the near driver cursed. As he did so, his backwards glance crossed with that of the woman. Her face was lost in darkness and distance, only a pale smudge with dark eyes, but he thought her beautiful, or the paleness suggested great beauty. Something sparkled in her hair as if she had an aura – a flare of red-gold—

'What the fuck, mate? He thinks we'll drive him all the way to the City?' The man paused, catching Aranthur's movements, and turned. 'Who're you then?'

'You want me to take your horses?'

Aranthur was still warm, and standing on the ladder to the drivers' seats was nice. It kept his feet out of the snow.

The nearer man looked back.

'What's the duke up to? He gave the drive on.'

'We need to change horses,' said the far man.

'Duke didn't say nothing 'bout changing horses,' said Near Man.

'Ain't ezactly duke any more either, is he?'

A small window opened behind Near Man's head – the travelling wagon had as much glass in it as the inn.

'Perhaps you missed my thumping on the roof, idiots,' a voice said. 'Drive on!'

'Your Grace, we have to change horses.'

'Change at Amkosa or Lonika,' said the voice. 'Now go.'

'You heard the man,' Far Man said.

Aranthur looked back along the wagon. The woman was still standing, her shoulders square, in the biting wind, watching him. Watching the wagon.

She must be very cold.

'I'll take her travelling case,' Aranthur said.

Near Man looked at him. 'What?'

'The duke's lady,' Aranthur said, stringing the story together in his head, a little surprised to hear what he was saying.

Near Man looked back, saw the woman, and started.

'Glorious Sun in the Heavens!'

Far Man twitched the reins, and the eight horses pricked up their ears. But they were horses – they could smell hay, and a barn, and warmth and food. They shuffled, but they did not push forward yet.

'Where in all the Dark hells are we, boy?'

'The Inn of Fosse,' Aranthur said, hoping he sounded as smug as

29

inn workers and ostlers always sounded to him. 'He said to hand down her case.'

It was a foolish risk to take, but his mind seemed to be running on its own, quickly and accurately.

Far Man twitched the reins again, and snapped a whip in the air.

The horses gave up their hope of food and leant into their traces, and the great wheels began to move, crunching the cold, dry snow.

Near Man got up out of his furs with a grunt and leapt up on the roof. The great wagon swayed as one wheel dropped into a particularly nasty rut and then righted itself, and Near Man slipped, cursed, and tugged at something.

The wagon was moving along now, as fast as a man could walk.

Near Man got a foot back over the seat and dropped a heavy leather portmanteau onto Aranthur's hands.

'Here's her case.' Then he tossed another. 'And she'd miss this one, I expect,' he said with a smile. 'I knew the duke would have her guts for garters. Tell her Lep the Wheel wished her well, eh, boy?'

Aranthur nodded. 'I will!' he shouted.

The wagon made a fair amount of noise – with half a dozen horses and six wheels and two drivers and all that tack, plus bells on the harness, and an axle that needed a man to look at it as it screeched like a *Zanash* and all.

He was keeping his place on the drivers' ladder with his weight, as he had a leather case in each hand. The wagon was starting to move faster still, and the snow was deep. For a moment, he was afraid that if he threw a case, it would vanish in the snow and be lost until spring. He wanted to serve the woman – serve her as best he could . . .

So he turned and jumped into the dark.

He landed in snow so deep that it went straight up to his crotch, as if a cold spike had been driven into his body from below.

The wagon passed him, moving away faster and faster. The cold cut through into his brain even as the cavalry troop went by, their red surcoats only visible in darkness because the wain had lanterns lit. Their captain had a fur-lined gown over his plate armour. He turned and looked at the young man in the snow, the man's heavy sallet gleaming with an eyeless menace in the near-perfect darkness. The knight didn't look human, somehow, and the hairs on the back of Aranthur's neck stood up even as the rest of him grew colder. Then the horsemen were gone in a clatter of steel-shod hooves and creaking, cold tack.

Why did I do that? Aranthur wondered suddenly.

He still had the two cases in his hands and he began to walk back in the darkness, pushing his way through the drifts. The inn was surprisingly far away – a stade or even more, and if it hadn't been well lit from within, he might have been afraid. It was *dark*. Almost the darkest night of the year, save two – well into the season when evil could triumph easily, or so his people thought.

Behind him, the lanterns on the travelling wagon vanished around a bend in the road, and he was alone, holding two heavy leather cases. He trudged into the wagon ruts where the snow was less deep, although there was water in one rut under the ice and his footing was uneven. The whole walk was difficult, cold, and . . .

Outside the inn, the woman stood in the snow as if the cold had no effect on her. She was staring at him, her lips moving softly.

Aranthur had an inkling, now, of what had just happened. He walked up to the woman, feet crunching on the more shallow snow of the inn yard.

'Despoina,' he said. He was prepared to remonstrate with her.

She coughed, and a little blood came out of the corner of her mouth before she threw her arms around him, and fainted.

His return with the woman in his arms threw the inn into a whirlwind of activity. As the value and cut of her gown had impressed Lecne's mother, she was taken away, warmed by a fire, fed a posset, and then passed up the steps into a private room. Women of several ages appeared as if by thaumaturgy, and went to tend her.

Aranthur went back into the snow once more to pick up the cases he'd dropped when she'd fainted. He carried them in, and then put them against the near wall, behind the priest and his acolyte, who both gave him civil nods.

The priest even stood.

'That was well done, especially at this time of year,' he said. 'When the Dark floods a man's mind and culls his thoughts.'

His young apprentice smiled. 'Tiy Drako,' he said.

Aranthur took his hand. 'Aranthur Timos.'

Drako was a noble name. A very old one from the City. Aranthur wondered if it was real, or something religious, the sort of name a man took when he became a monk or a priest.

'We're of a size,' Drako said. 'Since I wasn't brave enough to rescue the princess myself, perhaps I could loan you some dry hose and a shirt and braes?'

'He has more of them than he should,' the priest said with a forgiving smile. 'He could improve your condition and his own as well.'

Aranthur bowed to them both, and accepted.

'All my clothes are wet,' he admitted.

Drako had a fine leather pack in a dark orange leather with green trim – a nobleman's equipment, or a rich merchant's. The pack was a tube like a quiver, but larger, and had a matching cover that would keep out rain or snow. It was not the travelling kit of a holy man's disciple, vowed to poverty.

Aranthur rather admired it.

'My father was against my vocation,' Drako said. 'But in the end, he accepted and provided me with some good things. There – all I have is black.'

He handed over a pair of black hose in a wool so fine and soft that they made Aranthur feel warmer just looking at them, and a splendid linen shirt with embroidery and a crest – and initials.

L di D.

The acolyte saw the direction of his gaze and flushed.

'Ah, the vanity of my former life. Take it. Keep it. Lucca Tiy di Drako needs your prayers more than his soul needs the shirt!'

Aranthur protested, but the young man was insistent.

And something about Drako rang false. He explained too much. He was too charming, like a confidence trickster. But men said that Lightbringers could not be fooled, and no one sane would pretend to be one...

He took the dry clothes anyway, with a bow.

'Lecne!' he called.

The young man appeared from the kitchen.

'Pater's gone for the chirurgeon,' he said. 'She can't see and her head's pounding. She threw up.'

Aranthur thought he might know why and found it hard to spare any compassion, but he nodded.

'I need to change – and dry my clothes?'

Lecne grinned. 'Fair enough – if getting to carry that armful wasn't its own reward, eh?' He laughed. 'Sorry – she's so pretty! I hope that she recovers and spends a few weeks here. Where's the wagon?'

'Drove on.' Aranthur shrugged. 'Dumped me in the snow.' He indicated his clothes.

'Bastards.' Lecne beckoned Aranthur into the kitchen and showed him the great fireplace. 'All the women are seeing to the princess.'

Aranthur had his wet clothes off before his new friend finished talking. He was instantly warmer, and he padded about the hearth hanging his things on drying racks placed there for the purpose.

As he changed, he said, 'I'm not quite sure what happened. But the wain – there was at least one – drove on.' He looked at Lecne. 'A man pushed her out and told the driver to change horses at Amkosa.'

Lecne whistled. 'That's another twenty parasangs. In this snow? Almost Darknight? That's a bold rascal!'

Aranthur began to dress. 'I think it was the Duke of Volta,' he said.

Lecne's eyes widened. 'But—'

Donna Cucina's voice cut through the door and a bell rang.

'More visitors!' Lecne said cheerfully.

He passed back to the common room through the kitchen door, which had a small service window in it – really just a spy hole. Aranthur looked through for a moment and then went back to the kitchen fire. On the broad trestle table, a vast pile of *knocci* was already made, the dough broken up into spoonfuls. There was water on an enormous copper kettle over the fire. Steam was rising from it, but it was not aboil yet. The water smelled of oregano and something else, and it cleared his head.

Dry, and much warmer, he pulled on linen braes like breeches that buttoned at the waist, and thigh-high wool hose which would have laced prettily to a doublet, had he owned such a thing. In fact, in his tiny garret in the City, shared with the three other young men, he owned one, bought from a used-clothing seller and carefully mended. But it was not for a journey like this one, and he'd left it in his trunk. Instead, he laced the hose to his braes and tucked in the beautiful shirt. It was the finest shirt he'd ever worn – and that was saying something, as his mother's shirts were a byword.

Lecne returned with a great cow horn and handed it over.

'Grease for your shoes, or they'll be spoiled by the fire,' he said.

'Sun bless you,' Aranthur said. 'The water's almost boiled.'

Lecne shrugged. 'Pater will return soon enough – Master Sethre isn't far.'

He went back through the door even as the bell rang again. Aranthur took the grease and sat by the kitchen fire and began to spread it – it was good grease. Cow belly? Perhaps even goose fat. Something unctuous and fairly tolerable in smell.

'A fine inn,' he said aloud.

By the chimney hung the family talisman, a fair-sized *kuria* crystal. With a good crystal, a person of very little talent indeed could still summon fire, or warm air, or clean water. That the crystal was of uncommon size and clarity, and hung unguarded by the chimney, spoke volumes about the stability of the inn. And its wealth. It looked like it was rose-tinted; the best *kuria* was rose-coloured, and sometimes called 'Heart of the Gods' or 'Imperial Heart'. He touched it and felt its *power*, and took his hand away guiltily. *Kuria* crystal had become ever more expensive the last few years, and the rose crystals were almost never seen. Imperial Heart came from the Emperor's estates on Kius, an island in the south. Most of the other *kuria* crystal came from other countries, like Atti and Armea, in the East.

He began to work the grease into his boots – a pair of mid-calf walking boots with slightly curled toes, the most prestigious that he could afford, which was not much. Nonetheless, they were good boots, had lasted all of the week's walk and salt water too, and were likely to survive the journey home, although not in the same fine red-brown colour with which they'd started life.

He smiled. The brave new boots, now turning mud coloured, led him by some path of association to the woman he had carried in, who had smelled like . . . like the inside of a temple. Some exotic resin or perfume.

The crystal hanging by the fireplace glittered, and Aranthur smelled the perfume again, and the two came together.

She used power on me.

He was sure of it – as sure as a student of the same art could be. He could still taste it on his lips and feel it behind his eyes – the most potent piece of work he'd ever experienced.

She bent my will to get her travelling case, he thought to himself.

It was the only explanation that fitted the evidence. He remembered that feeling of absolute clarity as he went up the side of the wagon . . . Yes. A fine manipulation. So fine, and so puissant, that it had exhausted her and made her sick, just as his *Workings* Master warned could happen.

Who was she?

The man in the travelling wagon had been called the duke. The world abounded in dukes, but the most likely one was the Duke of Volta, who was reported dead three days before in a riot in his home city.

'*Ain't ezactly duke any more either, is he?*' Far Man had said.

Aranthur realised with a start that he wasn't hearing any sounds from the inn. He'd been working on his boots for a while now and Lecne had not reappeared.

Aranthur listened. He couldn't hear the drone of the farmers talking so he made his way to the door, feeling foolish, and looked through the tiny service window.

And ducked back.

Soldiers.

The kitchen was lit only by the fire, and was otherwise dark. Aranthur stood away from the service window and looked again, cautiously.

There were at least four of them. Angry. Demanding.

Aranthur didn't even think.

Off to his right there was a doorway he hadn't seen used. Aranthur made his way to it and, as he'd hoped, it led to the back stairway with a sort of alcove that also looked into the taproom from the far west wall. He leant his back against the wall and listened.

'. . . you're not understanding, boyo. I'll have wine, and my friends will all have wine, and then we'll have whatever else we fancy.'

The man's tone ill-suited his words – he sounded unsure of himself, a little wild, a little afraid.

Aranthur moved very carefully along the alcove. It was dark, and there was no light in the stairwell, which was no wider than one man's shoulders and curved sharply too. He moved so slowly he felt that he was a glacier in the mountains above his village, watching the people far below. He harmonised his breathing and began to sub-vocalise his ritual – carefully. So carefully. He raised *saar*, that infinitely difficult mist that hung at the edge of the immaterial world, the *Aulos* on which the Magi might write their will.

His ritual was all to focus his will – to enable him to keep in his head the balance of forces that would allow him to manipulate the material world. He fed the *saar* into his *working*...

'Doesn't this shithole have any women?' a skinny man in a rusted maille shirt asked. 'Wine!'

Aranthur could see the man's hand as he struck Lecne a glancing blow. He could also see that the man's gloves were red-brown with blood. Fairly fresh blood. His strength in his ritual wavered; his feeling of writing in fire, his favourite image, paled.

'I'll have to get m-m-more from the—'

The main door opened, letting a cold in, so cold that it almost snapped Aranthur out of his ritual trance. It was like a blow.

'An' who the fuck might you be?' another man said.

'It's my inn, and I might ask you the same,' said Don Cucino.

He was not visible to Aranthur, but he was moving forward – the door creaked.

'Not unless you want a foot of iron in yer guts,' said one of the soldiers. 'You don't ask, fuck. We ask. Where are the women? Where's the wine?'

Cucino was an innkeeper, not a choirboy.

'Keep a civil tongue and keep your blasphemy for your own Dark places,' he snapped.

He passed into Aranthur's sight. Behind him was a heavyset man with stooped shoulders and a deep scarlet hood – the near-universal sign of a medical professional.

Aranthur's ritual steadied.

Lecne said, 'Pater – they...' He paused.

'She's upstairs,' Don Cucino said to the chirurgeon, who attempted to pass the soldiers. But an arm was put out to bar his way.

'Who is?' asked one of the soldiers. 'No one goes anywhere.'

'No one gives orders in my inn but me,' the keeper said. 'Sit down and you will be served.'

'That's it, fuckwit,' said the nearest soldier.

He had a red cloak over his arm and a vicious, hooked scimitar that locals called a *storte* at his belt. He had the light eyes of a man either drunk or mad.

The soldier reached almost casually for his sword hilt.

Aranthur had a little direct experience of violence and men of violence, and he knew from riots in the city that once blood flowed, events took on an inexorable rhythm. As the soldier drew his *storte* and exposed the vicious blade, Aranthur took a careful gliding step towards the chimney corner where all his possessions were. He was not just willing. He was strangely *eager.*

The soldier raised his hand – and for a moment, it seemed so much bluster – but then, powered by fear or hatred or simply winter dark, he cut.

The blade struck the innkeeper's arm and cut it deeply – so deeply that his left hand dangled. Blood fountained and Don Cucino seemed to deflate.

Aranthur moved another step closer to his own sword and the buckler atop his pack. He was out of the shadows now, and his ritual was wavering again – the violence, the blood, the innkeeper's face, his own fear . . .

He lost his *working*. But he'd expected it, and he moved faster, with a sudden long step – shoeless, completely in contact with the smooth wood floor, balanced. He made a grab for the sword, which leant in its scabbard by the fireplace.

No one challenged him, because the man in the fine brown clothes rose to his feet. Aranthur caught only the end of the movement – it focused all of the soldiers in the room on him.

Lecne's hand was just going to his father's arm . . .

A second spurt of blood washed a table, and Don Cucino began to topple . . .

The man in brown put his right hand on his sword hilt. The motion was economical and not particularly fast. He had three men within his reach, all armed – one with his sword in hand, and the other two already reaching for their blades.

Aranthur's hand closed on his own sword hilt.

The innkeeper, staring at the ruin of his left arm in horrified fascination, fell forward onto a table already slicked with his own blood.

The man in brown drew.

The man who'd maimed the innkeeper raised his blade, a broad grin crossing his thin face, admiring his cut. Aranthur's attention was still on the man in brown. His draw was also a cut that rose through the entrails of the nearest soldier and finished over his head just in time to parry a desperate, tardy slash from the original attacker – so neatly timed that they might have practised it.

The man in brown pivoted on the balls of both feet and cut *down* with all the power in his hips, beheading the second man while he tried to draw his sword. But the same pivot powered his left arm to cross-draw a heavy-bladed dagger from behind his back, with which he continued to guard.

And then the room exploded into motion.

By ill luck the thin man, who wore a browned shirt of maille, was closest to Aranthur. Now he saw Aranthur's sword and he turned and lunged, focusing on the younger man as the acolyte rolled across the table, unarmed but game.

The soldier reached for Aranthur's still scabbarded sword. Acting on his training, Aranthur let him take the scabbard and pulled back his left leg, leaving the other man's cut to whistle past him. Then he leant back and pulled, the motion drawing his weapon free. Aranthur thrust without thinking or planning, simply committing to the attack as he'd learned it. He was, in fact, too eagerly terrified to think about his actions, and his motions seemed slow, as if his limbs were wrapped in string.

And then his sword was a hand span deep in the thin man's bicep, Aranthur's point penetrating right through the man's maille shirt.

His victim bellowed, tried to raise his arm and the pain stopped him.

Aranthur – still running off school lessons – rotated his hand from thumb up to thumb down, pushing outwards with his hand, so that he twisted the blade in the wound and ripped the sword out of the flesh and maille that trapped it. Someone was roaring – a huge shout that filled the taproom.

Tiy Drako hit the wounded man waist high.

The thin man fell, his hand clutching at his opened bicep. A piece of him flapped as he moved and his head struck one of the oak tables.

Behind him were two more soldiers, and one raised a crossbow...

Aranthur realised, in one beat of his heart, that the man in brown had somehow put all three of his assailants down. And the crossbow was pointed at him...

Aranthur was not well trained enough, nor agile enough, to cross the space. His hand was fully extended – he couldn't have thrown his sword, even if he'd thought of it. He saw the man in brown's eyes as he understood the imminence of death, and the anger this sparked.

The priest said a word, and there was a brilliant flash.

Aranthur flinched, blinded, and raised his sword.

'Stop fighting,' said a voice. It was a *working* and it was powerful, and Aranthur felt the *compulsion* and the flood of *saar*.

There was a flash – and a sharp *bang* like the sound a smith makes when he hits a piece of iron very hard.

The crossbowman dropped like a doll. The last soldier standing whimpered and dropped his sword.

The man in brown moved silently with a rolling gait like a sailor. He lunged, and his sword passed through the back of the soldier's head and emerged from his mouth like an obscene tongue. He, too, fell forward, head still supported by the blade that killed him, eyes open. His feet scrabbled madly on the floor as if he was trying to outrun death, his hips rising and falling in an obscene parody of life. The man in brown gave a fastidious turn of his hand and the dying man slipped off his blade and lay still.

Aranthur saw the woman from the snow on the balcony above. The chirurgeon was lying flat on the floor by the alcove like a summer solstice worshipper. She held a wand . . .

Aranthur understood. It was, in fact, a puffer. The tang of sulphur in the air was his evidence. As he thought this, he tried not to look down to the creeping pools of blood at his feet.

When he was a boy, he and his father had killed a deer. The first of many. The deer had bled out on snow – the red spreading, spreading . . .

At his feet – his unshod feet – the man he'd hit in the arm was writhing. Warm blood was soaking through the fine black hose that the acolyte had given him.

The man in brown was moving from downed man to downed man, finishing them with careful thrusts. The priest moved to stop him and the two men all but collided.

'None of your pious crap here,' the man snapped.

'On the contrary,' the priest said. Aranthur could tell that he was very angry. 'On the contrary, sir. You will stop killing immediately, or I will see what can be done.'

'Mumbo jumbo.' The man in brown raised his sword's point, leaving the last soldier alive. He stopped by Aranthur's shoulder.

'You've never fought before, have you?'

He sounded like an angry fishwife. His voice was shrewish, as if the idea that some young men avoided fighting for their lives annoyed him.

Aranthur was watching the wounded man. He'd made the mistake of meeting the man's eyes. The man's mouth opened and closed, and blood was *pouring* out of his arm.

'He'll bleed out in a few minutes,' the man in brown said. 'Or you could behave like a gentleman – like a *swordsman* – and either finish him or stop the bleeding. Ignore this fake. Be a man and put him down.'

Tiy Drako was nursing his own shoulder from the flying tackle he'd made, but he sat up.

'We must save him, of course,' he said.

The man in brown frowned. 'If he were mine, I'd kill him.' He looked Aranthur in the eye. 'Who teaches you, boy? That imposter Vladith?'

'Master Vladith is in fact my swordsmaster...'

Aranthur felt light-headed. The woman was looking at him, and she had a silver hairnet with pale jewels at the interstices of the net, and this drew his eye dangerously. He saw the fire in her aura again and wrenched his head away from the sight of her. The remnants of his own ritual were still singing in the recesses of his mind and he used them to build himself a shield. It was the first *occulta* he'd learned.

All in one beat of a man's heart.

Tiy was already on his knees by the downed man, digging his thumbs into the wound, trying to stop the blood.

'Sunrise!' he said. 'I can't stop it!'

Aranthur knelt by the man he'd hit and put a hand above the wound – and realised for the first time that he still had his sword in his hand. He put it down with too much emphasis.

Then he got both hands on the man's shoulder and pushed as hard as he could.

The flow of blood lessened immediately.

To his left, the chirurgeon was on the floor by Lecne's father. Aranthur dug his thumbs into the man's shoulder and the man screamed. Tiy was playing with a string – a loop of linen thread.

'You really are trying to save him,' the man in brown said. 'He'll hang, you know.'

'I won't send another man to the Dark tonight.'

Aranthur hadn't known what he was going to say until his mouth opened, but once he spoke, he was surer of himself.

The man in brown cut most of a wool shirt off the crossbowman and used the fabric to clean his sword. He bowed to the young woman above them, like a goddess in the theatre.

'I believe I owe you my life, Despoina.' Even his thanks were cautious.

She frowned. 'You sound none too pleased. And I think it was the Lightbringer's action that saved you.'

Her voice had a coolness that was very much at odds with her appearance.

Aranthur was scarcely aware of the exchange, because he and Tiy were fighting the man's body for his life.

'Why should I be pleased?' the man in brown asked. 'I failed myself and misjudged my adversaries.' He shrugged.

'You're welcome, I'm sure,' the woman said, her Liote pure the way Westerners spoke it. Then she stepped back from the balcony, even as Tiy Drako got his loop of linen into the blood and gristle.

'Hold on,' he said.

Aranthur could taste salt in his mouth. He was having a hard time not looking at the dying man or smelling the result of the man's voiding his gut and bladder in his agony. His heels were drumming on the floor.

'Slaves of Darkness!' the man in brown spat. 'Just kill him!'

A heavy staff struck the floor near Aranthur's head.

'Be silent,' the priest said. 'If the boys choose to save the man, what business is it of yours?'

The man in brown sheathed his sword and stepped back, offended as the priest knelt in the blood and began to sing tunelessly.

The three of them laboured together. Tiy and the priest knew their business. All Aranthur had to do was keep the thumbs of his two hands locked together until he was relieved. The two sang together in low voices.

Lecne burst in among them. 'Are you a healer, priest? Then for Sun's sake save my father.'

The priest neither looked up nor ceased his singing.

'My father is a good man. This man was a killer!' the young man said.

The singing went on.

'What kind of justice is this?' Lecne shouted. 'My father is dying and you are saving a murderer!'

The priest sat back on his heels, his face grey. He made the sign of the sun over the soldier's head.

'You can let go, now,' Tiy said softly.

Aranthur had trouble focusing and his hands were stuck together with the man's blood.

'I might ruin it,' he breathed.

'You can't ruin it,' Tiy said. 'He's dead.'

'Now will you come to my father?' Lecne begged.

'I will come,' Tiy said. 'My master has spent himself.'

'On the criminal!' Lecne spat.

The old priest slumped and hung his head.

Tiy Drako rose smoothly to his feet.

'We treat all men the same,' he said carefully. He was not yet as good as most priests at controlling his face and his voice.

'All men are not the same,' Lecne said.

'How wise of you,' Tiy said.

He went towards the huddle around the fallen innkeeper. The chirurgeon was working as fast as he was able, but he had no *power*, only craft. The woman stood in the alcove from which Aranthur had emerged, reloading her puffer from a small flask.

Aranthur got up off the floor slowly. Most of all, he wanted the blood off his hands and his feet. Without apparent volition, he began to move stiffly to the kitchens, where he knew there was hot water.

He found himself nose to nose with the woman with the shining hair. She had put her charge into the barrel of the deadly object and was winding the clockwork wheel that drove its spirit – or so he understood. She looked up at him from under her lashes.

He avoided her eyes.

'If you have the *power*,' he said quietly, 'you might *use* it.'

She winced. 'If I had any *saar* left, you think I'd use this cannon? You . . . ?'

'Yes,' he said savagely. 'I retrieved your cases under your *compulsion*.'

She looked away. 'I'm sorry.' She was not, in fact, sorry. 'Where are they, then?' she asked sweetly. 'More than one?'

He had to push past her. They were very close and he was aware of

42

her aura and aware, too, of the blood all over him. She smelled like a temple – incense, and a bitter tang like musk.

'You could help the innkeeper,' he said.

'I can't expend my reserve,' she said. 'I . . . overspent already. You are the boy who brought me in from the snow?'

The chirurgeon was shaking his head.

He nodded. 'Ah – you *burned* yourself?'

She nodded. 'Why did I tell you that?'

'*Can* you save the innkeeper?'

'Probably,' she admitted, not meeting his eyes.

He could smell her breath. She ate cloves.

'Can you channel?' he asked her.

She looked at him and gave a smile – a nasty little smile.

'Yes.'

'I have *power*. A little—'

'Sunlight, you're like a fucking customer. All right, sweetheart. Come.'

She grabbed his hand in a vice grip and dragged him over. Lecne was kneeling on one side of his father and the chirurgeon was holding his good hand mutely on the other side. Donna Cucina was sitting on her heels, praying.

'You asked for this, sweetie,' she said.

Everything went black.

Aranthur awoke in a bed. With a wool sheet under him and a fine, quilted double blanket atop.

He took a deep breath and the spike in his head made him whimper aloud. Outside the blanket, it was cold – cold enough that he could see his breath, and cold enough that he had slept with his head tucked in under the wool. He blinked at the sunlight coming in through a narrow window above him, and the sunlight made the pain in his head more intense. He found that he could control the pain by closing his eyes, and once he'd managed it, he found his mouth was paper dry. He'd no doubt been snoring. The other three students with whom he shared in the City complained about it constantly and mocked him as well.

Under his dry mouth was a taste of blood – coppery and full of bile. He almost gagged.

There was water by the bed: a handsome brown pitcher and a

matching cup. He mastered the spike in his head long enough to pour a cup – one of the most difficult exercises of his life – and drink it.

Exhausted, he pulled the blankets over his head and went back to sleep.

The sun was still filling the garret when he awoke a second time. Cautiously, he moved his head, and the pain there was nothing but an echo of the pain from earlier in the morning.

He took a deep breath, stretched, and rose. His head stayed on. In fact, he felt . . . solid. It occurred to him that he hadn't slept so long for . . . a year? Two?

He was naked. He usually slept naked, to save his threadbare shirts, but he had no memory of becoming naked, and he saw no sign of his clothes. He was in someone else's room. Cautious investigation suggested that it was Lecne's, shared with several other young men, almost like a barracks room. But the area at the end, under the narrow window, was clearly Lecne's. There were two heavy wooden chests barred in iron, and a much-repaired clothes press of ancient vintage.

'You alive?' Lecne called.

A sharply curving set of steps entered the attic room in the middle and Lecne's head appeared from the hole.

'Hello?'

The cold air was getting through the hours of sleep.

'I have no clothes,' Aranthur said.

Lecne laughed. 'Mater's washing all your stuff. Wear mine. Here!'

He bounced into the attic, ducking his head under the gable timbers with the ease of long practice. He threw open the clothes press with a violence that would not have pleased the last person to repair the drawers.

'It's all simple stuff,' he said with some embarrassment.

Aranthur started to dress and remembered his manners.

'How's your pater?' he asked.

He knew the answer had to be favourable – no young man whose father was dead would be as bouncy as Lecne was that morning.

Lecne looked at him as if a horn had grown from his head.

'You saved him,' he said. 'You and Donna Iralia. And the priest, I guess.' Seeing Aranthur's confusion, he said, 'You really don't remember?'

44

Aranthur shook his head, which proved unwise.

Lecne bubbled with enthusiasm.

'Iralia is really something!' he said. 'She did a ritual, but she used your . . . stuff, whatever the stuff is called. It was incredible! We could see this dark red light flowing out of you into Pater!' He danced around, and then said, 'And then the priest said that she didn't know much about healing and he came and did something – but still with your stuff.' He shrugged. 'Anyway, they pasted Pater's hand back on his arm. It's still there today!' He leant forward. 'So Mater's washing all your clothes and you can stay here for ever, I reckon.'

Aranthur smiled.

And thought of the big man dying on the floor.

It hit him like a blow in the gut, and for a moment, he thought he'd vomit.

'I killed someone,' he said.

Lecne nodded. 'Yeah, that was pretty amazing too. I'm sorry for what I said to the priest. But Pater was dying!'

Aranthur thought that he was looking at the other young man across a gulf of fire, so deep was the chasm between them. He sat up.

'I killed someone,' he said. He wondered what it meant for his *power*.

Lecne shrugged. 'He was a bad man. You helped us.' He grinned. 'Although the other man, Master Sparthos – he was incredible! He killed – what – three of the men? Four?' Aranthur nodded. 'Turns out he's a master swordsman from the City. I guess he's the best swordsman in the world.'

Aranthur had a sharp memory of the man in brown's face as the crossbow was levelled at him.

Anger. Failure.

'Anyway,' Lecne said, dismissing anyone's quibbles about the morality of the killing in one word. 'Cook's kept breakfast hot for you in the kitchen, and Mater wants to speak to you. So do some other people. Iralia has been asking for you since she woke up.'

Aranthur was dressed in Lecne's Liote clothes, very like Arnaut clothes – flowing trousers, light shoes, a shirt, and a red wool vest over a fustanella that had forty tiny buttons on the front and fitted at the shoulders but fell away to his knees like a giant wool bell. It was comfortable, warm, and rather dashing.

'That's my best coat,' Lecne confirmed. 'No, you wear it. You look good in it. I hope I look that good in it. Listen, can I ask you something?'

Aranthur smiled. 'Ask me anything.'

'Will you give me some sword lessons?'

Aranthur knelt beneath the window and said a very tardy prayer to the Sun. And then, because he was thinking in Liote, he said a prayer to the Eagle.

Thanks, source of light, for my life, and the lives of Lecne and his family. Take to your warmth the man I ... killed. The man I killed.

His mind skipped over the idea like a rock skipping across water.

To the Eagle he said, *Allow me the chance at glory, that I may return it to your splendour. Amen.*

He rose.

'Are you very religious?' Lecne asked.

Aranthur shrugged. 'At the Academy we go to temple every day.' He realised that was not an answer. He frowned. 'I'd say it was a habit, but I think the Sun became real to me when I began to work with ritual.' He met the other boy's eye. 'I'm not sure what I believe.' He looked around. 'Do you have cloth for a turban?'

Lecne laughed. 'We never wear them, but I can find you something.' He shrugged. 'There – you sound like me. I never know what I believe. Listen, will you give me sword lessons?'

Aranthur wrinkled his forehead in an attempt to fight the headache.

'I need to *go*, Lecne. I only have three weeks for holidays and I've already used more than one. And Darknight is *tomorrow night*. I was supposed to be home today.'

'Can you ride?' Lecne said.

Aranthur considered for a moment. 'Yes, all Arnauts can ride. Oh, not *that* well, but I have ridden my uncle's mare and mules for ploughing, and my *patur* had a horse when I was a boy. Before I went to school.'

'Come and eat,' Lecne said.

The two of them went down the stairs to the common room. The attic turned out to be a floor above the guest rooms, and for the first time Aranthur appreciated the sheer size of the inn. It had perhaps fifteen rooms along the balcony of the first floor, even if most of them were nothing more than a bed and a washstand.

The common room was abustle with activity. A party of merchants were being regaled by two maids with the events of the night before, while two older women washed at the bloodstains in front of the bar. The whole front window was ablaze with light, and the priest sat there with a scroll. His smile when he saw Aranthur was as bright as the sun behind him. Aranthur bowed his head in respect and followed his new friend through the alcove and into the kitchen.

Lecne's father lay on a settle between the great fireplace and the back door. He raised his head and managed a smile.

'Ah, my hero!' he said weakly. He raised his left hand and it gave a feeble twitch. The hand was, however, fully attached, and a red line ran almost halfway round it.

The chirurgeon was sitting by the bed. He smiled at Aranthur.

'It will probably never regain full mobility,' he said. He shrugged. 'But it is *there*.'

Aranthur was surrounded by praise and congratulations, which he attempted to refuse.

'You are too modest!' said Lecne's mother.

Aranthur shook his head. 'The praise should go to the lady. She performed the art – the *working*. I only provided—'

The chirurgeon was shaking his head.

'Boy, these are not educated people,' he said softly. 'And the lady is receiving as much praise.'

'You must be a great sorcerer!' Thania Cucina proclaimed, and made the sun sign with her hand.

The chirurgeon gave Aranthur another *just as I told you* glance and shook his head. 'Among the scholars, Donna, a "sorcerer" is a servant of the Dark. A master of Light is called a "Magos", or perhaps, if I am not too pedantic, a "Magas" in the case of our lady, and all together they are "Magi".'

Aranthur was none too sure of the doctor's etymology, but it seemed plausible.

'I am merely a new scholar.' Embarrassed by the continuing praise, he said, 'I really must start walking. I have twenty parasangs or more to go to reach my father's village.'

Lecne sat him down at the great table and two girls put plates in front of him – festival food: a massive plate of bacon and another of fried eggs, and a cup of pomegranate juice. The nearer girl lingered after putting down the plate of eggs.

'It's hot,' she said helpfully. And then, even more boldly, 'I'm Hasti.'

Hasti was short, lithe, and had large eyes – that was the only impression Aranthur could form. The morning was passing in a haze. He could not seem to see or hear anything properly.

Lecne was sitting across from him, taking bacon and nodding. His mother sat, and so did the chirurgeon, and the girls leant against the walls or settled on stools.

Lecne leant forward.

'I'm sorry I have to be so quick, but there are still travellers coming in. Remember yesterday we spoke of *stasis* in Volta?'

Aranthur nodded. 'And that was the Duke of Volta in the great wagon last night.'

Lecne nodded, as did his mother.

'And those soldiers were Voltains,' Lecne added. 'Two merchants who came in this morning say that one of their leaders – the sell-sword Cursini or maybe the Pennon Malconti – is fighting to take the city even now, or has taken it already – that the mob killed many of the old duke's soldiers and the rest fled. The traders say...'

Donna Cucina leant across the table and took Aranthur's hand.

'My sweet, my son is saying the west road is packed with refugees and vagabonds in this mortal cold. The traders are afraid to go west.' She shook her head. 'And we've already had all the Easterners we can take, the poor things. Too many refugees. What's the world coming to?' She frowned. 'Surely your own mother would want you to stay here until the trouble passes.'

Lecne gave his mother the look that adolescent boys give cautious mothers in all the great wheel of the world.

'All the soldiers had horses, Aranthur. We gathered them in last night and most of them had loot in their saddlebags – they'd pillaged something. Perhaps the duke's palace?' He grinned. 'We're giving Master Sparthos four horses and whatever is on them, and you two, if that suits you.' He grinned. 'I think that with two horses, you could ride home.'

'That's foolish and dangerous,' Donna Cucina said. 'There has been enough ill luck already, and this is the season of the Dark.'

Aranthur felt as if a new sun had risen.

Horses? Two horses?

He could ride from the City to home in a matter of days – could make home that very night, even with a late start.

'Come!' Lecne said. 'Let's look at the prizes.'

Aranthur – as a student – was in the habit of self-examination, and it was with some surprise that he went out to the inn's stone barn without a qualm for the man he'd killed. That is, the killing sat like a horror on his shoulders, and yet the thought of taking the dead man's belongings troubled him not at all. Among his people, dividing loot was a matter of course; what the gate guard at Lonika had said was very true. They were a tribe of thieves and killers and sell-swords, or had been in the past. Lately they were farmers on land that they'd stolen, or so people said.

The horses were not magnificent. They were a mismatched assembly of nags and brutes with a few smaller horses of much better colour and shape. The man in brown – Master Sparthos – was taking a brush to one small mare even as they entered, while another man, small and blond and very pale, curried another. The barn was not warm, but neither was it nearly as cold as the snowbound world outside, despite the immense vaulted ceilings. It was like a comfortable temple to animals, and smelled of horse and cow and pig and hay.

Master Sparthos looked up from his work and surprised Aranthur with a slight smile.

'I'm glad you survived, boy,' he said. 'A good day's work for a student, I'd say.'

He waved a hand at a dozen horses tied to posts in the central bay of the great barn.

Aranthur gave him a proper bow. 'I am honoured to know you, Magister.'

In the City, the absolute masters – three or four men and women whose work was beyond question the best from each guild – were honoured with the same title as the masters of divinity at the temple, and the masters and mistresses of the *Ars Magika* in the Studion of the Academy. Sparthos was not well known – Aranthur had never seen him, for example – but his name was famous. He was the paramount master of the sword in the City, and thus, to Aranthur, in the world.

Sparthos nodded, as such was only his due.

'How many horses are they giving you, boy?' he asked.

Aranthur bowed. 'Two, Magister.'

The master nodded, as if this seemed just to him.

'I have already made my choices. May I guide yours?'

Aranthur bowed again. 'I would be most pleased, Magister.'

The man in brown smiled thinly.

'I have taken one fine Nessan horse – this little mare. She is worth as much as all the rest, or most of the rest, but I'll leave her in this barn until the weather clears. She's unsuited to the snow, and too pretty to ride to death. But her sister is right there – almost as pretty. I recommend her, as long as your second choice is a nice practical plug like this gentleman, who seems solid, if a little old. I'd say he's seven or eight. He has some scars from the wars, to say he's got a good temper, and those heavy haunches promise work.'

The horse in question would never have won a beauty contest, but he was big and powerful.

'If my man, Cai, was bigger, I'd have taken him,' the magister added. 'But he's a pipsqueak and needs a little horse.'

'Any horse is better than walking, maestro,' the blond man said in Liote.

Lecne nodded. 'My lord has good horse sense, if I may say—'

'I'm not a lord, nor should you refer to me as one,' Sparthos said. 'My title is earned – I am the best sword in the world. Keep the word "lord" for those whose qualities are less obvious and more,' he smiled nastily, '*inherent.*'

Lecne smiled broadly. 'Ah, no offence meant, my lord – that is, Magister. A master swordsman! Of course – your fighting was brilliant!' He paused. 'I've always wanted to learn to use a sword.'

Magister Sparthos did not have a long nose – in fact, he had a nondescript face and a short, almost pug nose – and yet he managed to look down it with something very like disdain.

'Why?' he asked.

Lecne looked puzzled. 'I don't know. We have a sword, and I love the feel of it in my hand. And—'

'You are an innkeeper,' Magister Sparthos said. 'Take one of the *stortes* that the dead men left, and practise cutting with it – no one even needs to teach you. A strong arm with a *storte* will overcome any threat that might come to an inn.'

His contempt for the profession of innkeeping was obvious.

Lecne could not help but be stung, and Aranthur put his hand on the other young man's arm.

'When I come back, I'll give you a lesson,' he said.

The magister laughed. 'In the kingdom of the blind, the one-eyed man is king.' He laughed again, clearly pleased with himself.

Aranthur was not impressed with the man's manners, but after a review of the horses tied to various posts and pillars, he agreed with his suggestions and accounted himself fortunate to have two such fine animals. The Nessan was not, perhaps a pure breed – she was a little too big and her head was a little too square to be perfect. Her dam or her sire had been a Nessan, and the other parent had been a military horse, and the combination was very pleasing. She had nice manners and took food like a lady.

'I won't own you long,' Aranthur told her. 'You are *not* a student's horse.'

She had a fine, plain saddle on her and no bags. Lecne, who recovered quickly, told him that they'd all agreed that morning that each of them – the inn, the lady, the priest, the swordsman, and the student – would take their choice of horses and have whatever was on the horse as well.

'The swordsman took the two most heavily laden horses as his first choices,' Lecne said. 'And the acolyte, the one who's slumming? He said that all the stuff is loot from Volta.'

'So Master Sparthos passed on Ariadne because she had no loot,' Aranthur said.

Her saddle alone was worth all the fees for a month of classes – a light riding saddle. It had neither silver nor gold, but the leather was the best, and the stitching was very fine, with decorative whorls, all done doubled so that every pair of awl-cut holes had a heavy thread between them, instead of every other hole as cheaper harness and tack was made. In this Aranthur had an advantage – he worked in a leather-maker's shop from time to time. Any country boy or girl knew how to wield an awl and a needle, but in the city such skills were rarer. He could no more make a saddle than cast heavy magik, but he knew good work when he saw it.

The big military horse had an old and ill-used military saddle, high-backed and with a heavy base – the sort of saddle any horse might dread, more like a chair mounted on a horse's back. But there was a pack – a long cylinder – strapped to the back of the saddle, and a sort of truncated cone like an inverse dunce's cap hanging from one side of the pommel. The big horse was fretting, and Aranthur, who had grown up with animals, if not with horses, guessed the poor beast wanted rid of the heavy saddle.

Lecne poked him in the ribs, half in fun and half seriously.

'Would you choose?' he asked. 'The lady chooses next, and then the priest.'

Aranthur made a cursory transit of the other animals, but he'd already given his heart to the mare, and the conical leather case on the big brute held his attention. And the big brute... Aranthur already liked him. Something about how he held his head.

'I assume we can't look in the packs until we choose,' he said, more in banter than in earnest.

'That's right,' Lecne said.

There was another fine half-Nessan horse, but she was smaller yet and seemed timid, or perhaps merely tired. The rest of the military horses were tired plugs with most of their grace beaten out of them, vicious spur marks on their sides as semicircular white scars on bay horsehair, and badly tangled manes. Aranthur suspected – as a farmer – that most of them would clean up well enough with food and rest. As to plunder, the habit soldiers had of putting their stolen goods on the worst horses and riding the best meant that the two horses with the largest packs were sway-backed brutes.

The prospect of horse ownership opened vistas of ease and comfort to Aranthur: home every holiday and not once a year; the ability to take courier jobs in the City; even to get a place on a nobleman's staff for the summer. He suspected it would cost almost as much to keep a pair of horses in the City as he could make by owning them, but the whole idea was itself an adventure. Either way, he wanted the horses for themselves, and was uninterested in taking the goods – stolen goods, in fact, although he'd have had a hard time explaining how he thought all these things through.

In the end, he took the two horses recommended by the magister. He was a student, easily swayed by expert opinion, and the man in brown had, in fact, a good eye for horseflesh. As soon as he made his choice, he took the big gelding into a stall, tied him to a handy hook and unsaddled the poor brute, who all but shivered with pleasure. With iron resolution, he began to curry the horse, who needed care desperately, instead of rifling the pouches of the military saddle, opening the conical case, or the cylinder of new leather on the back of the saddle.

Magas Iralia came in next. Aranthur heard the higher music of her voice and the low response from the magister, and they laughed together. The sound made Aranthur curiously jealous. He tried to analyse that feeling and found nothing there but bottomless irrationality, but the feeling lingered through the whole of his new horse's rump and back legs. He decided to name his gelding Rasce, after a character in a play who behaved badly for comic effect, and Rasce seemed to accept the name in good part. He ate placidly from a manger full of valuable oats, and seemed at peace with the world.

The lady appeared outside Rasce's stall, and she leant against the door frame. It was the first time that Aranthur had fully given her his attention – or rather, sensing something was different, looked at her carefully. She was different this morning – she almost looked like a different young woman. Her silver hairnet was gone, and her fine silk gown, for one thing.

'Not so beautiful without my make-up, eh?' she asked.

Aranthur knew that some women painted their faces, but he'd never met one before. Since only courtesans, whores, actresses and queens did such things, his face flushed. He stammered something inadequate about her face and appearance that was so quiet he couldn't hear it himself.

She laughed. 'You are such a boy. I see you are in good health – no spiritual hangover this morning?'

He shrugged. 'A terrible headache when I awoke at sunrise. I didn't even pray.'

'I took too much,' she admitted. 'I even topped up my own reserve. You are very well provided with *saar*.' She smiled. 'And *sihr*.'

He shrugged. *Sihr* was the darker element of *power*. He knew he had it; all mages did. He didn't know what to make of her comment and he recombed an area of his new horse he'd already done. She confused him. She was younger than he'd thought the night before. Without her paint, she was likely closer to twenty-five than thirty-five, and her hair was rich and brown, no trace of red, her face narrow and delicate, her limbs long. In fact, she looked like the frescos of the fae folk in the Temple of the City – the Temple of Wisdom, Hagia Sophia.

'You used sorcery against me – when the duke first put you out of the wagon,' Aranthur said. He met her eye. 'Then you drained me of *power*,' he went on. 'Are you a Dark student, Donna?'

He hadn't meant to ask her that. In fact, until that morning, he hadn't fully believed that there were students of the Dark. It was a far nastier statement than he'd meant to make.

'Ouch,' she said. 'No.' She turned to walk away, and spoke without turning her head to look at him. 'Not everyone has nice fat rich parents to provide a Studion education, eh?' she spat. 'I came to *thank you* for my cases. And to *apologise* for using *saar* to manipulate you. I *know* it's wrong, but how was I to know you were a student? Or had *power*?' She looked at him and her look softened. 'Not that that makes it any better,' she said softly.

'You are welcome. My parents own a small farm in a village. My father is not the headman, nor are we the richest; until the land reforms, we were peasants. *Arnaut* peasants. I owe my place in the Studion to the whim of our local lord, and nothing more. I doubt I'm even the smartest boy in my village.' He shrugged, trying to be indifferent to her opinion, and mostly failing. 'And Lec the Wheel sent his regards, and said that he knew that the duke would have your guts for garters. What did he mean?'

'I do *not* serve the Darkness,' Iralia said.

She walked away before he could answer, and as he curried his Nessan, he thought of all the things he might have said. The best retort was *if you continue using* power *to manipulate people, you will serve Darkness*, but it was too wordy. And too pompous.

In fact, she'd done him no harm. The entire incident had been to his advantage, at least so far.

Count no man happy until he is dead seemed apt, from among the ancient sages.

But his Magos of Philosophy liked to say that too much idealism was the death of rationality.

'Look at the results,' he would declaim.

And in this case, none of her arts had injured him. And she was a user of *power*, and yet she had killed ruthlessly. And he had killed, and his *power* seemed intact...

He frowned, trying to get to the root of the causality. The duke was overthrown, she was his... mistress? And he abandoned her on the road as he fled – a lesson in astrology, really. Had he not looked at his stars? And she, deserted, had claimed her belongings – which were, in all likelihood, really hers. More so than the loot in the saddlebags of all the horses were the property of their new owners, anyway. He tossed it all around while the curry brush went round and round, and the old mud and horse sweat filled the air.

'Let me try this again,' she said from the doorway of the stall.

'Were you with the Duke of Volta?'

Aranthur wished he'd kept his mouth shut – she was making peace, and he was chasing the solution to a problem.

She winced. 'Yes. "With" being such a resonant word, full of . . . meaning.'

'I'm sorry. I'm trying to understand.' He tried smiling. 'I . . .'

He shook his head. He couldn't very well say, *I'm a peasant boy and we don't really understand how the upper classes operate.* It was an accurate statement, but not what he wanted to say.

'So the duke pushed you out in the snow, and you used art to get me to help you,' he said.

'Yes,' she admitted. 'You know,' she said, with a bitter smile, 'I have two sets of arts. In a warm room, surrounded by people, I can ask most people – most men – to fetch me wine, and they will, without asking themselves why.' Her eyes kindled, and she flashed him a smile.

He all but froze.

She nodded. 'Do you know that when you attempt a *compulsion* using *saar* . . .' She looked him in the eyes. Her eyes were deep and surprising, a livid blue that was like the sea on a bright summer day. 'I speak to you as a *scholar*, you understand?'

Aranthur was almost bowled over by her assumption of his knowledge. 'I'm not—'

'When you attempt a *compulsion*, it helps if your target already likes you, and it makes the *compulsion* much harder – and much more dangerous to both the caster and the target – if the target dislikes the caster. You understand? If I had asked you to help me, and you declined – even if you only declined because, say, of the press of your chores – then it would be very, very difficult for me to send my *compulsion*. Almost impossible, in fact.' She shook her head. 'And I was almost drained anyway. I said something in the wagon that I should not have.' She smiled at the false elegance of her own diction. 'I told the duke he was a coward. I'd been wearing myself out using my arts to keep him from simply killing me – oh, he was angry. He *is* a Dark-damned coward, by the Sun. If he spent the energy ruling Volta that he did on escape plans—'

'I don't understand. Were you his . . . ?'

She smiled, and it was an unpleasant smile.

'Mistress? Courtesan? Whore?' She shrugged. 'What would *you* do to be trained in the *Ars*?'

He winced.

She shook her head. 'I'm babbling. Listen, farm boy. I was a thirteen-year-old whore when my *power* came upon me. I am what I am, but I do not serve the Dark.'

'Babble more,' Tiy Drako said. He had his head and shoulders over the partition from the next stall, and now he leapt over, lithe, terribly graceful, and far more like an aristocrat than a priest. 'I think you're the most beautiful woman I've ever seen.'

'Are you sure you are a priest?' Iralia's tone was arch, but her eyes stayed on him. 'Is that your best line? Do you use it often?'

Aranthur had the strangest feeling that they knew each other.

Drako bowed – again, like an aristo and not like a priest, who would simply bow stiffly from the waist.

'Your wit cuts like a good sword, Donna. I cannot decide if I am a true priest, or not.' He smiled at Aranthur. 'My mentor is angry with me for tackling the man we killed.'

Aranthur nodded and held out his hand.

'I'm not. Without that . . .' He paused. 'Although I'm still . . . not happy . . . that I killed him – we killed him . . . What have you.'

'We tried to save him,' Drako said lightly. 'Surely that exculpates our sin?'

Aranthur thought of his Philosophy Magos and his comments about results, and bit his tongue.

'That's a fine beast,' Drako said, examining the small Nessen mare. 'I took a pack horse, myself. I would never have convinced my mentor to ride, even if he were considerably more lame than he is. I gave the innkeeper's son the goods in the bags.'

Iralia raised her eyebrows. 'Because you have no use for worldly wealth?'

He grinned at her. 'Something like that.'

The two of them locked eyes for a moment, and Aranthur went back to making careful strokes with the brushes.

'Just how bad a priest are you?' she asked, her voice suddenly lower.

'We're not celibate,' Tiy laughed. 'By we, I mean me. My mentor is, but he doesn't need to be.'

She smiled wickedly. 'If I understand the theology of the Sun it's possible that *he* does not need to be – but perhaps *you* do.' She smiled again, a dangerous smile, and turned. 'Aranthur, am I forgiven? I promise, if it is ever in my power, I'll do you a good turn. I can be a good friend.'

Aranthur bowed again. 'Yes.'

He wished he had something witty or elegant to say. He wished he was as quick as Drako, who was, in fact, smirking a little at his discomfiture.

Iralia walked away, her pattens clicking on the barn floor, and Drako laughed.

'Holy Sun rising in the east,' he said. 'It is like finding a gold Imperial in a dung heap.'

Aranthur kept working.

'My former self would have passed through the cold halls of hell for that face,' Drako said. 'At least for a week or two, or until my money ran out and my father reined me in.'

He fitted his shoulders into a corner of the stall and looked at Aranthur, trying to assess the impact of his words.

Aranthur could feel the weight of the other man's regard, but he kept the brush moving, changing direction with the grain of the mare's hide. She was beginning to gleam.

'You know what my father said when I told him I was going to become a priest?' Drako raised an eyebrow.

Aranthur looked up and met the man's eyes. He was smiling, but the words had clearly hurt him.

'He said, "This is one little fad I will not support." He thought my conversion was temporary. That I'd purge myself for two weeks and then be all the more self-indulgent for it.' Drako shrugged.

Aranthur was working on the legs now, and he wondered why the older man was telling him all this.

'I'd love to prove him wrong,' Drako said. 'If you'd just give me a little help here – I am confessing to being a worthless *daesia*. A little sympathy, and I can probably keep myself from following that *incredibly beautiful* young woman inside.' He laughed in self-mockery.

Aranthur looked up, and met his eye, and smiled.

'For the Sun's sake say something!' Drako said.

Aranthur giggled. He shook his head and rubbed some of the old dust and sweat off the brush by using it on the stable wall.

'I'm probably so green I don't even know what you're talking about,' he said. 'What's a *daesia*?'

'A man who lives to . . . I don't know. For pleasure. To lie with others,' Drako said with a wicked look. 'And gamble, and fight, and raise hell. A person who goes to plays and jeers at the playwright. Goes to temple and mocks the priest's hypocrisy. Goes to the brothel to find love. Fights duels. Writes poetry.' He laughed. 'Bad poetry.'

Aranthur shook his head.

'Sounds wonderful,' he said. 'Where do I sign up?'

Drako looked at him and his brow furrowed.

'You?'

Aranthur thought about what his Magi might say, but he could only laugh, because he was honest with himself, and he knew how instantly Iralia enflamed him.

'Only . . . I think I'd be terrible at it,' he said. 'Because I'd want to write good poetry, and that takes work, and I'd want to be a great swordsman, and that's a lifetime of study, and I'd want to prove the priests to be hypocrites, and that would get me arrested.' He laughed. 'Especially the last, because I'm a peasant, not an aristo.'

Drako fingered his hairy chin. He had the beginnings of the full beard that priests wore, and from its length, Aranthur estimated the other man had been an acolyte for about two months.

'What attracted you to your mentor?' he asked.

'Can't you just feel his holiness?' Drako asked.

Aranthur nodded. 'I can.'

Drako nodded. 'I've never met anyone like him. All my father's friends and their sons are landowners. Everything is about land and money.' He made a face. 'Marce Kurvenos is a Lightbringer. He lives it. He . . . He *talked* to me. He sat with me and got to know me, and he told me what I was and where I had failed myself and the way of the Sun.' Drako winced. 'See? Even in my spirituality, it's all about me.'

The mare shone like a bronze statue and the bigger gelding was contentedly munching the good, clean hay.

'I want to see what I got,' Aranthur admitted. 'I'm *not* an aristocrat.'

Drako laughed. 'You have nothing to say to my troubles?'

Aranthur looked at him. 'They're not like my troubles.'

He hadn't meant it to be funny. In fact, he'd meant to add a stinging rebuke about how rich boys playing at monks deserved whatever they got. Or maybe he only thought he'd deliver such a rebuke – there was something about the man calling himself Tiy Drako that was very, very easy to like.

But he roared with laughter. He put his hands on his knees, he laughed so hard.

'Oh, by the light of the new day, my friend, that was good – and well deserved. I will—' He laughed a while longer. 'I will eventually repeat that.' Then he stopped laughing. 'Let's see what you got in your bags. You make me wish we'd given our share to you. The inn's rich enough.'

Aranthur understood in a flash of insight: Drako had been waiting for him to open the cases all along. He frowned, filled with unaccustomed peasant suspicions – unaccustomed because he'd spent his first half-year at the Academy unlearning the habit of suspicion.

'Why do you want to see?' Aranthur asked.

Just for a moment, there was something hard in Drako's eye – something utterly at variance with the banter and the softness.

But the aristocrat smiled easily. 'I think the cone hides a *cannone* or a fine puffer. Something marvellous like that. I want to see it!'

Aranthur didn't think the acolyte meant him harm, but the mountebank was showing under the acolyte's façade.

Still, Aranthur wanted to see what was in the case too. He shrugged and opened it. It was smooth and beautifully made of heavy leather, carefully moulded into a shape a little like a leg of lamb prepared by a butcher, and it had a neatly fitted cover that was decorated with hair or fur – a very heavy, dark fur.

He opened the buckle, which was fine too – steel, but gilded and decorated with chasing. The little belt that went into the buckle had a metal end that was also decorated. Superb work.

Inside, the case was lined in chamois or buckskin, and nestled deep in it like a scroll in a tube was a heavy snaphaunce – like a puffer, but with a longer barrel. The stock was cunning – it could be placed against the shoulder or chest, or even held in one hand. The weapon appeared almost new, and the barrel was as long as his arm.

Drako whistled. 'That's beautiful. Deadly, too. Watch out – it's loaded.'

Aranthur flinched.

'Let me,' Drako said. 'Look – this is the pan cover – marvellous design. When you open the cock, the pan cover moves. Oh – I'd like to take this apart. See the powder in the pan?'

Aranthur found that he'd handed the acolyte the weapon without even thinking about it.

Their eyes met. But the acolyte's eyes were guileless, and the weapon remained unthreatening between them.

Aranthur understood the basic principles of firearms.

'I do,' he said. 'If that ignites from the sparks, it burns through the torch hole and lights the charge in the barrel.'

Drako dumped the contents of the pan into his hand. They were silvery grey – almost black; small kernels and flakes, all different.

'Very good. They teach this at the Academy?'

'Yes,' Aranthur said.

Set into the side of the case was a set of tools – very handsome tools: a turn screw and a small pair of pliers and a bullet mould and a bronze-headed hammer. There were bullets in a hard leather tube. Seeing the mallet, Drako put the pinkie of his left hand into the barrel – Aranthur wanted to cringe at his daring.

'Grooved. By the Sun! Let's try it!' He pointed at it. 'This is a fine weapon – something special. I can show you how to keep it clean. It won't thank you for mistreatment.'

Aranthur could not restrain himself from putting the butt to his shoulder. It was small, but he could get his head down.

'Oh, promise me we can shoot it!' Drako said.

'Of course!' Aranthur said.

The puffers and *cannones* that the scholars devised were among the most famous inventions of the City, even though the best ones were made in Volta and even further north.

But he noted that, despite the young aristocrat's excitement, he continued to pull things out of the case. He opened every little compartment, unscrewed the bronze tube that held the cast balls and poured them out on his hand, and held the powder horn up to the light.

He's looking for something.

Aranthur watched the other man go through the case and made no objection. He didn't really feel that the magnificent little weapon was his; he expected the aristocrat to seize it. So he watched somewhat fatalistically.

His little mare, Ariadne, shuffled and snorted, and Drako looked up and raised an eyebrow. Without a word, he replaced everything – the bullets in the tube, the tools in their little case, and everything went back into the leg-of-lamb holster.

'Sorry,' he said. 'I got carried away. Beautiful work. Let's look at the travelling case, shall we?'

Aranthur sat back and pushed the case over the straw.

'Be my guest.'

Drako was startled. 'No, no,' he protested. 'It's yours.'

'It belongs to a dead man. It's no more mine than any of the rest of this. You want to see it? Be my guest.' He paused, and then said, as lightly as he could manage, 'I owe you for the black hose. Go ahead.'

The case itself had a small coat of arms on it, and initials: X di B.

'Damn me.' Drako's voice changed. 'Syr X,' he said, and then, his mountebank voice changing, he laughed. 'How mysterious.' He gave Aranthur half a smile. 'Listen, open it. Just let me watch.'

It was a man's travel case – a *malle*. As soon as Aranthur opened it, he sat back on his heels. The case had a slight smell – spikenard or some other rare resin.

It struck him that this was *somebody's*. The carbine had no real owner – in fact, it looked to be new. But the *malle* was full of clothes, so tightly packed that a securing strap had been cinched tight inside. There were shirts, some fine and some full of patches and holes, and two pairs of fine, light shoes, and a whole suit – hose in pale pink, and a black doublet and matching short cloak. There was a ring – a simple man's ring in gold, with a black stone, tied to the securing strap. There was a closely wrapped man's belt, and a purse, and a dagger. And a book – Kafatia's *Consolations*, all done in neat scholar's calligraphy. And a roll of gold Imperials, ten of them. A fortune to an Arnaut peasant.

Aranthur could feel the man's death. It came at him suddenly, and he realised that he had felt it when he first opened the case. The man had been a merchant or a scholar – from Volta, he guessed. They'd killed him on the road for his horse and his case, which was redolent with the personality of the man – and his death. He'd been touching it when he died, or close by.

Drako put a hand on his shoulder.

'I'm no Magos,' he said, 'and I feel it too.'

'I can't take his clothes,' Aranthur said.

'They're as nice as mine. Let me get my Lightbringer and he'll exorcise the poor man. Summer Sun, something bloody nasty happened to leave this much . . . this much pain.' He put a hand on the case. 'Damn.'

His anguish sounded genuine, but Aranthur felt as if there was a great deal unsaid.

The old priest came and lit a censer. His exorcism rite was complex and involved two forms of incense and a trance, and Aranthur watched in fascination – though there was very little to see after the initial ritual.

Eventually the priest's eyes opened. He released a long sigh and rose stiffly from his cross-legged trance position. Except that Aranthur saw the priest focus first on his acolyte, and nod, and Drako's face registered a spasm of anger.

Then the old priest winced and smiled at Aranthur.

'I am not as young as I once was,' he said. 'You did well to ask me. They thought he had something more – and they tortured him for it.' He shook his head. 'He was already dying, with a crossbow bolt in him. Ugly, ugly, and then we killed them, anyway, so that their evil was itself for nothing.'

'You took no part in the killing,' Aranthur said.

'Did I not?' The old priest put a hand on Aranthur's head like a father with a very young child, and Aranthur, who at times had a very high opinion of himself, was humbled. 'I might have prevented it, but I failed. The *working* I intended to end the fight merely allowed a slaughter of the guilty. I certainly have blood on my hands.'

'Prevented it?' Aranthur asked.

Tiy Drako shook his head. 'He means that if we had taken other paths, we would not have allowed this event to occur.'

The Lightbringer turned, and his glare was frightening.

'I mean more than that, O all-knowing disciple,' the priest said with flat anger. 'Had I been more alert, I might, for example, have been on my feet and in among the soldiers so that they grew calmer and less violent. It is the duty of the Lightbringer to do good actively, and not accept a passive role. I should, at least, have been the first to die, insisting that they not harm any but me. But I was dozing, having read all day.'

'Surely—' Aranthur began.

The priest smiled. 'Young man, I'm a Lightbringer, not a fool. I do not pretend to perfection or enlightenment, nor do I try to convince you I have achieved any such state. I merely describe how, had I been nearer perfection, I might have behaved. Fear not! I do not accept responsibility for their deaths. I took no action to help them. Or hurt them. Unlike my disciple, who put one foot back on the path of violence, and who now stands here contemplating carnality.'

Drako looked as if he'd been struck.

The priest laughed. 'Is she more beautiful than your soul, my friend?'

'Forgive me, Lightbringer,' Drako begged.

Again the priest laughed. 'I? Forgive you? You have done nothing against me. It is against yourself you sin. I find her beautiful as well – I merely see her from a greater distance than you. Were I nearly perfect, I would see her only as a soul.'

'Yes.' Drako sounded more wistful than crestfallen.

The priest opened the case. The beautiful smell was still there, but it did not exert *aura*.

'Master, if something can receive spirit, or *aura*...' Aranthur knew that the *Ars Magika* and the houses of theology had different terms for almost everything. 'If the case can be imbued with the dead man's torment,' he went on, 'why can I not put a *working* into an object?'

The Lightbringer assumed a serious expression.

'You can,' he said.

Aranthur shook his head. 'I've been told that it is impossible.'

Lightbringer Kurvenos nodded and pursed his lips.

'Then why do you ask me?' he said softly.

'Because the spirit of the dead man was palpable in the case. I felt it. Tiy felt it. You exorcised it. Hence, it was there. Spirit or *aura* can be worked – manipulated. Thus...'

The priest nodded, obviously pleased.

'You must be someone's favourite student.' He fingered his long beard for a moment. 'I will tell you. I suspect otherwise you might be of the kind who will experiment, to the detriment of your soul and others. A servant of Darkness can create an object of great *power* by first manipulating a person – or an animal, although that is weaker – in a way that alters that person's aura to suit the needs of the Dark sorcerer. And then—'

'He kills his victim in the presence of the item.' Aranthur sat back on his heels and whistled. 'Ritual *sacrifice*.'

'Death is one of the strongest powers,' the old man said. 'Only in death can spirit be fused to dead matter.' He paused. 'Even that is not strictly true. The ancients had glyphs and sigils that could inscribe power on metal or stone. And some material objects are receptive to spirit: the *kuria* crystal; some metal alloys; surely you have heard of the Seven Swords . . . ?' He blinked. 'I wax pedantic.' He smiled.

Aranthur began to speak and paused.

'Ask,' said the priest. 'I am here for you, not for me.'

'Are there also Darkbringers?'

The old man shook his head. 'Some would have it so, with an endless procession of horrible conspiracies. But I have walked the world for seventy years and some, from the Outer Sea to the Assinia, and I have never met one. Men and women need no help from organised evil cults to be selfish and brutal – do they?'

Drako laughed ruefully. 'No, master.'

Master Kurvenos nodded. 'I confess that there are people who use the powers of Darkness to increase their *power*. Who, knowing the true path, turn their backs on it and go the other way, seduced by the lure of this world. Some even profess that there is only this world.' He shrugged. 'They are the ones who create artifacts such as you describe. Long ago, men made many artifacts; before that, the Dhadhi made more. There – I have told you something interesting, have I not?'

Aranthur shook his head. 'Incredible. Why have my Magi not told me this?'

Kurvenos smiled. 'Have you ever asked?' He waved his hand. 'Enjoy your new possessions. By liberating his spirit, you have made them truly yours.'

'What do I owe you, Master?' Aranthur asked.

The Lightbringer looked away.

Drako nodded. 'I will take care of that. A Lightbringer is above considerations of mere money. Or should be allowed to be.' He smiled. 'Two chalkes would do it, I think.' His smile widened to a grin. 'And a shot of your carbine!'

Aranthur realised that while the Lightbringer had been speaking, his

64

acolyte had laid everything in the case out on the clean straw and then had run his hands carefully over the inside. The man was still looking for something – looking meticulously.

But he hadn't found it. Whatever it was.

Aranthur considered challenging him. He thought of the Light-bringer, of the acolyte – of the possible ramifications.

Not worth it.

One thing you learned as an Arnaud peasant was when to take what was given and avoid conflict. Sometimes Aranthur managed to keep his mouth shut, and this was one such time.

So he repacked the case instead, carefully brushing straw from all the shirts. The acolyte knelt by him, helping him, and running his fingers over the doublet and hose. His attempts to be secretive were now revealed.

Or the man was just nosy.

Minutes later they were in the deep snow beyond the inn's yard and barns. Every step broke through the crust, so that both young men – and Lecne Cucino, who joined them on invitation – were wet to the crotch. But the cold didn't touch them, as they slogged back and forth to a stunted tree, setting an old board against it. Lecne took a shoeing hammer and put an old prayer card onto the board. He pointed at it – a woodcut of death with a sickle reaping the lives of men.

'Let's see if we can kill death,' he said.

The other two young men were silenced by the comment. Aranthur felt it was ill-omened, to say the least.

Still, in a few moments they had replaced the priming in the mechanism's spoon-shaped pan and shut the cunning little cover that seemed to operate on some internal spring and catch.

'Want me to do this?' Drako asked. 'I've shot a puffer.'

Aranthur almost gave way, and then changed his mind, although as a student he disliked the omen about death and the mechanism made him afraid. His hands were shaking.

He attempted to analyse his feelings, as the Magi taught, but his mind was a whirl of impressions and impulses, because it had been that kind of day.

He raised the weapon and put the butt carefully against his shoulder under Drako's shouted instructions to 'Keep it tight, tight!'

The weapon had a tiny ring on an equally tiny staff that folded up out of the stock to form a rear sight. It was simple enough to place the weapon's front sight – a tiny white ball of silver – in the rear sight's circle. He placed the white ball on the playing card of death and jerked the trigger bar.

The flat crack shocked him. So did the lack of movement from the carbine. Where he had expected a blow, he felt only a slight movement, as if the weapon was a living thing.

The three walked to the old tree. The board was untouched, but there was a hole a fist higher than the top of the board – two fists above the prayer card.

'Not bad,' Drako said. 'You pulled the bar too hard, and it lifted the barrel. Let me have a go.'

He showed the other two how to load the piece as he went, first putting a charge down the barrel from a small cow horn full of the silver-black powder, and then tamping it with the ram-stick under the barrel. Then he took one of the small round balls out of the pouch made for them and put it on the barrel. It was too big. But not very much too big – the ball went about half its own diameter into the barrel and stuck.

The other two young men came up to help. There was an odd tool in the case, like a ramming stick but only two inches long, set in an egg of polished bronze. But it didn't make sense.

'I can show you,' Iralia said.

They hadn't noticed her coming out, but there she was, sensibly clad in man's clothes, with high hose and boots.

Mutely, they handed her the weapon.

She took the bronze tool and placed the short ram-stick – which had a cupped end – on the ball, and pushed very hard, her mouth tightening with effort. The ball popped into the barrel. Then she took the longer ramming stick and placed it against the ball in the barrel, took the pretty little hammer, and drove the ball all the way down. She showed them that there was an engraved mark on the ramming stick to show that the ball had been driven all the way home.

'You shoot it,' Drako said. 'You loaded it.'

'Why, thank you!'

She raised the weapon, placed the short stock against her shoulder, and pulled the trigger bar in almost the same motion.

They all saw the card take the hit, and splinters exploded from the back of the board. The distant hills echoed the sound of the shot after some delay.

'Oh!' they all said, and then they applauded her.

'Not *just* a pretty face,' she said, mostly to Drako, who made a face at Aranthur as if to say *I never suggested otherwise.*

Drako had a remarkable quality, which came out as each of them loaded and shot the weapon several times. That is, he was content to allow Iralia to take over the loading. He did not press his knowledge.

Aranthur's third shot hit the card precisely, his lead ball obliterating death's skull face. All of them hit the card. Drako hit it every time.

Iralia smiled. 'I love the smell,' she said. 'I always have.'

The powder stank of sulphur like the public baths, the *thermi*, in the City, but with another tang, almost like salt.

'Now we clean it,' Drako said.

Iralia agreed. 'This is a very fine weapon – as good as mine. I even think I might be able to name the maker.' She examined the breech and the muzzle and then shook her head. 'Intriguing – a masterwork, and unsigned.'

Lecne nodded. 'I know nothing of puffers. Ha! That's not even true any more. I love you people. But I know workers. I bet it's the work of a journeyman as a try piece for his mastery. We have a superb copper kettle like that – nicest one we have.'

Drako nodded. 'I think you have something there.'

Iralia joined in. 'I suspect it's from a shop in Volta – you see how plain it is, and yet so elegant? Volta. You Byzas have to put flowers on everything, or the rising sun of the world, or the First Invocation or some pious saying. In Volta, they add nothing.'

Aranthur laughed. 'Perhaps the Byzas engravers are simply more skilled.'

Iralia gave him a look that might have been pity.

'You need to get out more often,' she said. 'But I mean no offence.'

'None taken,' Aranthur said. 'I am Arnaut, not Byzas.'

She flushed, and he wondered if he was cursed to always say the wrong thing to her.

Aranthur let the argument go. Even with a horse to carry him, he was aware that the morning was gone and the afternoon was pressing. The four of them went inside and under Drako's careful ministry, the weapon was opened. The complex mechanism was removed, and then the barrel, which hooked in and out of the breech and had two wedges held with pins.

Iralia brought her own puffer to the kitchen table.

'I think you know more about taking one of these apart than I ever learnt,' she said. 'I just shoot them.'

Drako asked the cook for boiling water and a little *rakka* oil. He took the barrel off Iralia's puffer and took both barrels out in the yard, where he poured boiling water through them, creating clouds of stinking steam. At first the water ran black, but after a moment it ran clear. Then he ran wads of tow – the combings of the flax crop – into the barrels and dried them, and oiled them.

Then he laid the mechanisms on the kitchen table with the cook's grudging permission.

'I call this part the lock,' he said. 'I suppose early ones – in my father's time – looked like door locks.'

He showed Iralia the inside of her lock, with brown rust and old grease and some black dirt or powder fouling.

'You could grow carrots in this,' Drako said, and smiled.

Iralia shrugged. 'Go ahead, smart boy. Show me how to clean it.'

Drako nodded. 'I will.'

He heated the lock a little, putting it on a brick in the fireplace, and then – before Iralia could protest – he poured boiling water over it. Immediately he picked it up with tongs and put it on the hearth.

'The water can't cause rust on the metal if it vanishes from heat,' he said.

Aranthur didn't think that his physical logic was sound – but practically, his actions worked. The lock was mostly clean, with a few brown streaks of rust. He took a wad of tow, balled it up and put some oil on it, and then pressed it into the ash at the edge of the hearth until the tow was almost grey. He used it to polish at the streaks of rust.

'A real gonner or an armourer could have it apart, and make the lock shine inside as well as out,' he said.

But when he was done, and had poured water over it again and then put the *rakka* oil over everything, the lock looked like a miracle in steel.

Iralia unbent as they cleaned. She helped Aranthur work on his carbine while Drako worked on her lock. Of course, the new carbine needed much less work, and Aranthur was afraid of its complexity – the inside of the lock was like a world in miniature. But before the clock on the wall counted the second hour, both weapons were clean and oiled, and Aranthur had fetched his sword, and cleaned and oiled it, too.

'Curious beast, that sword,' Drako said with a smile.

Iralia immediately loaded her puffer, and tucked it in her belt.

Aranthur grinned at all of them.

'I – really – have to go.' He looked around. 'I feel very fortunate that I have met you three. The last day has been . . .' He shook his head. 'Like something out of a story book.'

They all kissed him, even Iralia.

He picked up the carbine case and his new travel case, and carried them out to his new horse, feeling that it was all a little unreal. Then he saddled the heavier horse, checked the gelding's shoes, saw to it that his mare had food, and brought his horse round into the front of the inn.

Lecne was waiting – and so was Tiy Drako.

'I'm not slipping away without paying,' Aranthur said.

'You really don't seem the type,' Lecne said. 'You owe nothing. We are in your debt.'

Aranthur smiled. 'I accept, only because I'm a poor student. But I would like you to keep my mare for a few days – perhaps even a week. And I'll pay for her.'

He described the contents of the travel case and handed over four chalkes, the round silver coins of the Imperium.

Tiy smiled. 'Are you sure you aren't an aristocrat?'

Lecne took the coins. 'We could have a hard winter without Pater,' he said. 'I won't refuse good money when you have some. But you're welcome here when you don't, too.'

Drako nodded. 'I'm not a real priest, but that was well said, brother.'

Aranthur hugged each of them.

'I'll be back soon,' he said to Lecne.

'Come and visit me in the City,' he said to Tiy. Despite the aristocrat's search of his new possessions, he liked the man.

The acolyte stifled laughter and bowed his head.

'We're going the other way,' he said. 'But I imagine I'll make it back to Megara in time, and perhaps I'll visit you with my begging bowl, at that. If you're wealthy now.' He grinned.

'School,' Aranthur said. 'School will eat it all. Will you take the road with me?'

'My Lightbringer says it's a bad day to travel – so who knows? Perhaps I'll still be here when you return. But let me offer you a word of counsel.'

Aranthur stiffened.

'The *cannone* – in the city, it's illegal.' He shrugged. 'But possession of one qualifies you for the Selected Men.'

'Oh!' Aranthur said, with pleasure.

The Selected Men performed in all the great processions, and marched ahead of the guilds at festivals. They were part of the city militia.

Drako nodded. 'I have written you a letter to open a door or two. Please – no thanks required. Pray for me!'

Without another word, the acolyte handed him the letter, turned and went inside.

Aranthur hugged Lecne again.

Only later, when he was munching bread with oil on it, did it occurred to him that when he asked the Lightbringer if there were Darkbringers, the man had never answered. And Aranthur chewed, and thought, and he did not like his conclusions.

Riding was difficult and, initially, dangerous as well. No one had tried to dissuade him from riding towards Volta, and perhaps someone should have, because twice in the first parasang he encountered groups of soldiers. But he was wary, and they were on foot, and in both cases he and his excellent mount simply trotted into the frozen fields that flanked the road.

The second time, a more determined soldier loosed an arbalest, a very heavy crossbow, at him. He never saw the bolt, but the thud of the heavy metal bow sounded over the snowy fields, and his horse – clearly trained for war – gave a little curvet that almost threw him off.

After that, he rode wide. He began to worry for his friends at the inn, but they had the man in brown and numerous other travellers.

His luck was in – within an hour of leaving the road, he found a parallel path running through the trees two fields north of the road. In places it was impassable, but for two parasangs it ran reasonably clear and well off the road – which didn't prevent Aranthur from riding with caution. He had to, as his riding skills were relatively meagre and every stade increased his awareness of his own shortcomings.

When he could see the mountains that nestled his home village between his horse's ears, he gave a whoop of delight at his own navigation, and his horse dumped him in the snow. But the horse – better trained than his rider – then stopped and stood, head down, and waited. He got up, none the worse for his fall except for the cold and wet, and Lecne's best fustanella kept him warm and dry enough. He remounted – a more exciting operation in deep snow than he'd imagined – and he realised that he would never have caught Rasce if he had run. He spent long minutes rewinding his turban in the proper Arnaut way, and then he let the horse move forward.

Chastened, he rode even more cautiously until his path went down a steep slope. There, he dismounted, unsure of how to stay in the saddle. He and his mount picked their way very slowly down the slope in a series of self-imposed switchbacks. By the end Aranthur was as cold and wet as he had been arriving at the inn.

But at the base of the hill lay a winding road, paved once, hundreds of years before, with cobblestones. Now there were small trees growing through it and many pits under the snow. He knew it immediately as the ancient road that ran along the Amynas River, which he could hear, rushing in winter-flooded fury, down the gorge beyond the road. He was sharp enough not to whoop again. He knew where he was, and it was a dangerous place.

He noted the tracks in the slush and snow of the road, however. On the side path, he'd been alone, and the utter absence of tracks had lulled him into a feeling of safety. Here, it was different.

He drew and checked the carbine, feeling self-conscious – a fraud or an actor. He touched the hilt of his sword. Then he loosened the sword in its sheath and carefully mounted his horse. The touch of the hilt against his hand was oddly comforting, like a kind word from a teacher.

The sun was setting in the west, in a spectacular blaze of golden orange – but full dark was only an hour away.

Full dark on the darkest night of the year. In the village, they would be dancing in a great circle, holding the dark at bay.

He reconsidered, dismounted, and gave the horse a bite to eat from a nosebag. Then he put some water from his clay water bottle into the nosebag and the horse drank it greedily before it could leak out of the heavy linen.

'That's all I have,' he said.

His feet were numb and he was becoming afraid – of nothing. Of everything. He thought of Iralia's seductive attraction and how like Tiy Drako's charm it was, and wondered what the priest and the acolyte really wanted. He wondered if he had just played a small part in a larger story, or been made a fool of. It didn't matter, because it was Darknight, and he needed to get under cover. His horse was solid, and he got back into the saddle, turned his mount north, and they began to climb in a world suddenly bathed in the bloody red of a midwinter sunset.

An hour later, the last light of the sun was just a glow on the western sky. He was much higher now, and the air was much colder. The river splashed along mightily on his left side, and the dark woods of his childhood, heavy spruce and old, tall pine, pressed in on his right. He told himself that there should not be soldiers or deserters from the Volta troubles on *this* road, but he was aware that smugglers *to* Volta used it sometimes, and he was also aware that it had seen a great deal of traffic lately.

But his horse had heart, and strong muscles and a steady desire to get the day done, and kept plodding on. In the very last light of the failing day, Aranthur plucked up his courage and cantered along a flat stretch of road at the very top of the Syomansis Ridge, past the beehive-shaped tomb of the ancient ones. He was close to home. Indeed, when he lost his nerve and reined in, the road was broader and better defined – and he could see twinkling lights and smell smoke. Rasce pricked up his ears.

'You are a good soldier,' Aranthur whispered to his mount. The horse's ears moved again, and Aranthur laughed, his nerves fading as he neared his homestead. 'I should call you Soldier and not Rasce!'

Full dark sat on the fields like a gargoyle in the eaves of a great temple by the time he turned into his home village's side road. The howling of wolves across the valley where the Amynas flowed over fast through Combe, downstream from Wilios, made the night seem darker yet, but the snow reflected the starlight. It seemed bright enough, though the shadows tricked the eye everywhere.

It was Darknight and he was alone, out on the road. There wasn't another mortal to be seen and no one but a fool rode abroad on Darknight. He'd lost time and was out later than he'd imagined – he taxed himself with tarrying too long with his new friends and his fancy weapon.

In the field off to the right, four dark shapes began to pace him. He saw them from the corner of his eye, and Rasce knew they were there, too.

The Studion taught that wolves were not servants of the Dark – indeed, that no animal served any need but its own – but Aranthur had a farmer's sense of the animals. He feared them and was not wholly satisfied with the rational explanation. Still, although his right hand drew the carbine halfway from its case, he resisted the urge to shoot it at the pack. He was no more than two stades from home. When he finally turned into his father's lane, his heart soared – and his fears fell away. He pushed his carbine back into the case, and his mount, scenting a barn, began to trot.

The sound of horse's hooves in the lane – not so common in the dead of winter, on Darknight, in a mountain village – brought Hagor, his father, to the door with a spear in his hands. Behind Hagor, his younger sister Marta stood with her bow half-drawn, still dressed in her best from dancing against the dark. Light and warmth seemed to stream through the door. In heartbeats he was off his horse and locked in their embraces, passed from sister to mother, mother to father.

Rasce, forgotten, gave a snort.

'You're mad!' said Hagor, obviously impressed. 'You came home on Darknight?'

'For First Sun!' Aranthur said.

On its accustomed place on the small table that usually held the family gods and the household shrine there sat a sun disk, magnificently polished bronze. Above it four winged spirits blew trumpets as they coursed around and around, their wings driven by the rising hot air off six candles in a sacred hexagon. The First Sun shrine had been in his mother's family for generations, the work of some master artificer in the City from some long-forgotten holiday visit, or perhaps loot from some long-ago raid into more settled lands. The spirits had tiny bells that struck the sun's outstretched rays very softly as they rotated and gave a constant chime. Something about the sight made his eyes fill with tears.

Then he had to curry Rasce and bed him down, all the while telling

73

Marta that he was not stolen or rented but his very own. Then, with hot mulled wine in his hand, he had to tell the whole story again. He found that telling Mira, his mother, that he had killed a man and taken his horse was not nearly as heroic as he'd expected, and Mira's expression was forbidding.

'Why do you even *own* a sword?' Hagor asked. 'No—' He raised his hand, a powerful patriarch. 'Our boy's come back on Darknight, and we'll not take this any further. Let's be merry, and keep old cold winter away! And spite the Dark, as my grandfather liked to say.'

Long into the night, they sang hymns to the Sun, and farmers' songs, told riddles and played the games of childhood. Then each went to their favourite corner of their small house, and wrapped the little things they had prepared as presents.

Aranthur had his own notions. The work of his pen, the little missal with his careful capitals, went to Marta, along with the fine hairbrush he'd found in the travelling case, and all ten gold Imperials in a little bag to Hagor. For Mira he had the pair of bronze and iron spoons he'd bought in the market in the City – originally his only presents. One was a large dipper for serving soup, and the other a skimmer for taking the fat off – both implements that any good housewife could live without, but lovely to have. These were well made, the rivets attractive and decorative, the metal burnished.

And when the stars turned and the middle of night came and passed, Hagor blew out the last candle, and they sat in the darkness of the longest night, and said prayers. Different peoples celebrated the long night in different ways; some kept candles burning all night to the Lady, or the Sun. Or Coryn the Thunderer, or Draxos the Smith. But the Arnauts sat in darkness, and awaited the coming of the First Sun. They called it the Long Watch.

Lying in the attic trundle with his sister, Aranthur looked at the ceiling. Marta was already snoring and he smiled to hear it. He'd made it home.

In the morning, it was First Sun, the best day of the year to every child and still a delight to Aranthur. He awoke to the smell of his mother's cooking, full of spices – cinnamon and nutmeg and something wilder and sharper. And sugar, and bread, and meat, which he was forbidden at the Studion. Oregano and thyme.

Aranthur woke Marta and they went down into the main house. The attic was almost as cold as the outside air, and they dressed by the fire while Mira tended to two puddings in a pot and turned a pheasant over the coals. Aranthur looked at the matchlock over the fireplace: his grandfather's mounted silver weapon, now black with age, tarnish and old smoke.

'Is Uncle Theo coming?' Aranthur worked up the courage to ask.

The musket always made him think of Uncle Theodoros.

Marta made the *shush* sign.

Mira pursed her lips. 'No,' she said primly.

His father's brother was a drinker. It was a dark thread woven through their life: he would come to festivals drunk; he would embarrass himself; he would walk off, humiliated, promising never to do such a thing again. For part of Aranthur's childhood he had lived first in the house, and then in the barn.

For complex reasons having to do with swords and shooting the musket and various bows and crossbows, Aranthur liked him. Uncle Theo had carved a lot of wooden horsemen and toy swords. He'd been a playmate; he'd taught Aranthur to ambush his mates in a snowball war. His drinking wasn't the whole of him. Aranthur had a notion that his own love of the sword had come from his uncle, even if the Arnaut sword dance with its curved sabre and explosive leaping was as far removed from Master Vladith's lessons as Arnaut dancing was from the ballet of the Byzas.

But he let it go. He'd been foolish to ask his mother.

And when it was time to illuminate the sun disk, Aranthur grinned, held up a hand, reached inside himself, and cast the *volteia* of fire. Mira's gasp of astonishment was its own reward. Hagor had to stop and put the family's tiny *kuria* crystal back in its velvet box.

Hagor regarded him with a mixture of astonishment and amusement. 'You wanted to do that,' he said.

Aranthur grinned in triumph. 'Since I learned how, I imagined lighting the Sun on First Sun day.'

They all laughed together, and sat at the table for breakfast.

There was a saying in the City – '*No man is impressive to his horse, his tailor, or his wife*' and after a week at home, Aranthur wished to add *or his sister or his father.* His family was delighted by their presents and his talents, but then equally appalled at his relative wealth and its source. Every night brought on a debate concerning the morality of the thing and the implications.

On the fifth day, he was in the barn, moving hay. Despite the cold, he worked stripped to the waist, his pitchfork moving with precision. He was using the work to practise his footwork – his stance, the way his legs moved, the front leg with its foot always splayed off line like a dancer's – and for the same reason, his balance.

He was almost dancing, skimming the wooden floor of the hayloft. But he got the hay moved, as his father had asked. He thought that into the bargain he'd chop wood, so he went to the mountain of sawn wood behind the barn and began to chop. Chopping wood had been one of his favourite pastimes since he was old enough to be allowed to use an axe, and every piece he split with a single cut seemed a victory. He made a game of it, choosing tiny flaws and marks in the surface of the cut ends as a target and then cutting as close to that as he could manage – two handed and one handed. Sometimes he would step before he cut, and sometimes he would stand too close on purpose and make his cut backing away a pace.

Then he stacked the newly chopped wood on the low wooden wall his father had built across the front of the yard – a long wall of firewood. It was a family habit and Aranthur could stack the wood without conscious thought. He'd learned to cut firewood from his uncle. He wondered why Uncle Theo wasn't coming.

When he'd added twice the length of his body, as high as his waist, to the wooden wall, he stretched for a while, as his lower back was tired. Then he began to move bags of grain from the grain cellar to the heavy farm cart.

Hagor came in with a calf on his shoulders.

'Two more, born early and frozen,' he panted.

It was the first time Aranthur had fully appreciated that his father was getting older, was not as indestructibly strong as he had seemed in Aranthur's youth. But he ran out into the snow and followed Hagor's tracks through the olive groves and down the hillside. The snow was already melting – snow was never of very long duration there. He found the calves mired deep, almost newborn. One was very close to death, and the other seemed sprightly enough.

He thought he could carry them both. He got one over either

shoulder and began to plough through the drifts where the sun had not yet reached, consciously using his footwork to *push, glide* left and then *push, glide* right in a powerful zig-zag. After a few minutes the wind froze the sweat to him and the calves seemed to weigh more than full-grown horses. His muscles began to feel the strain. But the animals themselves were alive and warm, and he did his best to use his *power*. A ritual was difficult to invoke while moving and carrying things, but he did his best, focusing on his will and shoring it up.

He made it to the barn, and found Hagor warming the first calf with warm milk and two stones heated by the fire.

He grinned to see him. 'You are strong, son.' He took the weaker of the calves, breathed on it, saw its head move, and nodded. 'This one's for t' house,' he said. 'Whatever your *matur* says.'

They exchanged a grin. It was the first time his father had spoken to him in his old way since... Well, since the Byzas nobleman had come down the lane two summers back to inform his father that Aranthur had been chosen for the Studion.

'I miss you,' Hagor said. 'I'd forgotten how easy the work was with another man to do it.'

High praise in many ways.

'Go have some fun,' Hagor said. 'Don't just do work.'

Aranthur wanted to ask if his father was feeling well.

'Have fun?' he asked.

Hagor shrugged. 'Life isn't all work.'

He had fun. He visited friends and took part in a Sun Rise footrace and he helped Marta prepare for her dances. He loved to dance; his fencing master had told him it was the reason he was such a quick study. Because he didn't advertise his origins in the City, he never mentioned that Arnauts had swords, too.

Every day, the City seemed farther, home seemed sweeter, and the Studion seemed less important.

But his father wouldn't entirely let the matter of the sword go. The two of them sat in the house's main room, each holding a new calf on his lap while they spooned in milk.

'Did you even *try* to find the dead man's relatives?' Hagor asked. 'I imagine that if I was killed on the road, Matur would like to hear of it, and maybe have my things back. And my money.' He pointed at the initials. 'That's a coat of arms. A Byzas – probably a noble. X di B.'

'The man lived in Volta, which is in the middle of a civil war,' Aranthur said carefully. Or rather, he thought he said it carefully, but when he heard himself, he was disappointed to hear an adolescent whine. 'I *wanted* to be home for the Rising of the Sun, and to be honest, Patur, I was afraid to be on the roads.'

'I'm afraid that all they teach you at your school is that you are smarter than your parents,' Mira said, coming in softly. 'That is not the tone to take with your father.' And then, as she always did, she turned and took his side. 'But it's true, my love. Volta is another four days' travel – and even here we've seen refugees. Would you have him go there?'

Marta looked as if she'd like to chime in, just to be heard, but Hagor cut her off with a raised hand.

'Tell me why you even have a sword,' he said.

'Patur, you make it sound as if you'd have been happier if the soldiers had killed me,' Aranthur said.

His father looked him over carefully.

'No,' he said, after a moment. 'I'm damn glad you came out on top. But that doesn't change what I'm asking. Why do you even *have* a sword?'

Aranthur suppressed his anger. 'I bought it,' he said plainly.

'With what money?' Hagor asked.

'Money I make doing leather-work. I do some basic sewing for a leather-maker, and I do apprentice work for a purse-maker's shop, and sometimes for a bookbinder. He says . . .'

Aranthur slowed and came to a stop, because his father's face was, if not wreathed in smiles, at least less tense.

'You didn't say anything in your letters about work,' he said reprovingly.

Aranthur thought it through. Good oratory was all about *understanding* the points of view of other people. He took a deep breath.

'You were afraid I was stealing?' he asked.

Mira shook her head vehemently.

'Maybe not stealing – oh, Arry, dear. You know what happened to the Korontes boy. And your uncle Theo.'

'I know he's chaplain to one of the Vanaxsi – the army. Isn't he?' Aranthur looked at his mother. 'Uncle Theo?'

Hagor looked uncomfortable. 'Theo was a kind of soldier,' he said.

'He was a *bravo*. A villain!'

'Mira, you know that's not true.'

Hagor looked out of the small window and shook his head.

'Anyway, the Korontes boy was better in the end,' Mira said.

'He is now,' Hagor replied. 'But he came there by a hard road, and he gambled away all his parents' school money first.'

'The City is far, and very dangerous for folk like us,' Mira said. 'Please don't blame us if we worry.'

'So you bought a sword,' Hagor said. 'You know how to use it?'

Aranthur shrugged. 'I take lessons.'

He did not say *I killed someone with it.*

'Like a Byzas. A gentleman,' his father said. 'Well, I shouldn't be surprised – you always dreamt about it. With help from my damned brother. But, lad – doesn't your work cut into your studies?'

The truth was that it did. But Aranthur, who for the most part told the truth, had learnt in the city that there were *ways* of telling the truth.

'I have permission,' he said, which was true. 'Students are encouraged to get exercise. The richer students play games.'

There was, in fact, a City-wide craze for shuttlecock, a new game from somewhere far to the east, and everyone was playing it, including Aranthur himself. But he didn't mention that, either. Or that he could swim from the pier at the end of his street – a walk downhill for a stade – and do it for free.

'Wearing a sword is a statement that you are willing to fight,' Hagor said.

Aranthur took a breath for a poorly considered reply, but his father quickly raised his hand.

'I'm not saying you shouldn't,' he said carefully. 'Looks like it saved your life. Just wondering what it says about you, and where it'll lead.'

Aranthur tried not to sound surly. 'I think – I think I could be a good swordsman.'

Hagor smiled. 'That's what I'm afraid of, son. I can't think of anything more useless on a farm than a good swordsman.'

'A priest?' Aranthur asked. 'You want me to be a priest?'

'Never said so.' Hagor nodded. 'Stop pouring milk over that calf.'

They all laughed.

*

Later that night, his sister rolled over and kissed his cheek.

'I think it's wonderful,' she said.

He grinned, waiting for the tickle or the tease, but Marta shook her head in the darkness.

'No, I'm serious. You look grown up and civilised and you act it and you wear a sword. I wish I could go to the City. The boys here are all idiots.'

'The thing is . . .' Aranthur said. 'The thing is, Patur is right. Wearing a sword is . . . is a statement.' He shrugged. 'I like it, though.'

'Patur doesn't want us to grow up,' Marta said. 'But even I know he and Matur are occasionally right.'

The next day, Aranthur left the house on horseback, with his boyhood friend Stepan riding double behind. They had the ostensible mission of going to the upper pastures to make sure all the sheep were down. There had been snow, and the wolves had come in on Darknight.

Really, it was a chance to shoot his *cannone*. Stepan was entranced by it, and they rode out into the woods to the north. Aranthur knew where his uncle had his little hut – a hovel, really – and they went to it.

Aranthur found his uncle, sober, splitting wood. And the hovel was gone, replaced with a large cabin of new-cut pine.

'Uncle Theo,' he called. 'You remember Stepan?'

Theo was taller than his brother, with heavier muscles, and whorls of dark tattoos on his arms and hands, around his neck like a torq, and up one cheek. He wore his hair in the old way, half shaved, half very long.

He nodded carefully. 'Not very well,' he admitted. 'Stepan what?'

'Stepan Topazo, syr,' Stepan said.

Theo nodded. He picked up his axe.

'Matur know you are here, Arry?' he asked.

'No, syr,' Aranthur said.

Theo nodded. A woman's voice called from inside the cabin.

The cabin was much better than the hovel that had been before. There was a window of six carefully pressed panes of cow horn. The door had glass in it. Neat shutters covered the windows and there were curtains.

A child came to the door. He had dark brown skin and big, dark eyes.

'There's an Easterner kid in your house,' Stepan said.

'That's my son,' Theo said in a flat voice.

Aranthur, used to the City, was smiling.

'What's your name?' he asked the boy.

The child ran inside. A woman spoke sharply in Armean. Aranthur was still struggling with Armean, so he knew it instantly.

'Why'd you come?' Uncle Theo asked. He was sober, and surly.

Aranthur shrugged. 'I have a *cannone*. I thought you'd like to shoot it.'

For the first time, Uncle Theo smiled his warm smile.

'Damn,' he said. 'I wouldn't mind. But there's chores and chores . . .'

A little girl emerged from the house. She was more daring than her brother, and crossed the clearing.

Aranthur knelt down and offered her a hand, and very cautiously she accepted.

'I am Aranthur,' he said.

She made a little curtsey, the Eastern way.

'I am Aranthur,' he said in Armean.

Her face lit up.

Uncle Theo's face transformed.

'You speak Eastern?' he asked.

'Only a few words,' Aranthur admitted.

'Why do you speak it at all?' Stepan asked.

'I'm studying it at the Academy,' Aranthur said.

Stepan nodded. 'Makes sense, I reckon. Good way to talk to your hired men. Know what they say behind your back.'

Aranthur gave Stepan a glare, and he subsided.

But Uncle Theo gave Stepan a disgusted look and shrugged at Aranthur.

'Sorry, lad,' he said, the way he had as a younger man. 'But there's too much work. I have a family now.'

Aranthur hugged him anyway, and Uncle Theo surprised him by wrapping him in a strong embrace.

'But how do *you* speak Armean?' Aranthur asked.

Theo raised an eyebrow. 'I spent ten years killing 'em. I learned the language, eh? Where'd you get the horse?'

Aranthur glanced at Stepan, aware that, as soon as he told the story, everyone for three mountains would know it. Then he shrugged.

'I was coming home for First Sun . . .' he began.

A very handsome dark-haired woman came out, cautiously, and put a tin cup of water in Theo's hand. He shared it with Aranthur and Stepan. Aranthur finished his tale as the sun climbed higher and his friend fidgeted.

'You killed a soldier,' Theo said, and his lips twitched. Smile? Frown? The man had always been difficult to read.

'Yes,' Aranthur said.

Theo nodded. His eyes were very far away. He sipped more water.

'Best be running on, now, son.' He gave Aranthur another squeeze.

Aranthur remounted, trying to think why he was disappointed. As they rode away, Stepan spat.

'An Eastern family?' Stepan asked when they were mounted again. 'The Eagle priests won't like that.'

Aranthur didn't answer immediately. He'd learned silence at the Academy, too. Instead, he found them a place to shoot, although he was surprised to find that the woods in which he'd played with his sister now housed a whole row of huts with a little village of Armeans – refugees from the fighting in the East.

They played with the *canonne* all day, shooting rocks and trees until most of the balls were gone. It was in the process of searching the case for more balls that Stepan drew Aranthur's attention to the damage.

Someone had cut the bottom out of the holster case, neatly slicing the stitches with a very sharp knife. Almost no damage had been done, except that the bottom was gone.

'Bastards,' Stepan said. 'The world is full of bastards. Probably an Easterner.'

Aranthur looked at his friend. 'You know who Arnauts are, right?'

Stepan shrugged. 'We're the People of the Eagle,' he said proudly.

'We're a tribe of refugees. Of mongrels. All the remnants of a defeated Imperial Army – camp followers and soldiers and officers. They found these hills to hide in, and they allowed in *anyone* who would take the oath.' Aranthur smiled.

'That's not true,' Stepan said. 'Or, I mean . . . You make us sound like we were nobody. We were loyal to the old Emperors. We were rewarded for it!'

Aranthur shrugged. 'I think we just walked off and let the war fizzle out. And I think we occupied land no one wanted because it was all rocks.' He shrugged again. 'But I've touched some of the documents.

We weren't noble soldiers. We were a hunted remnant, and to some people, we still are. In the City, people think Arnauts are barbarians.'

Stepan shook his head. 'That's just stupid.'

And he could not be swayed.

It was the only cloud in an otherwise beautiful day. The two young men rode over the fells, shot the weapon, and justified their outing by climbing the ridge towards Korfa, the next major Arnaut village, nestled in the next valley to the east. There they found the Kelloi's strayed milk cow well up a hillside, miles from home and uneaten by the many wolves. They drove her, mooing piteously, back into the valley and to her owners' door.

That night, Aranthur cut a new leather circle from his father's small store of repair leather, trimmed it neatly, and punched the holes carefully; matching stitching on a circle was quite difficult.

When he was done, cutting the heavy linen cord with his neck knife, his father ruffled his hair.

'You've become quite a leather-worker,' he said.

Aranthur flushed. He'd double stitched everything to match the work on the scabbard, and because that's how leather-workers in the City did their work. It irked him that of all his accomplishments, the one that his *patur* praised was his leather-work.

But that night in the loft, listening to his sister snore, he realised that it was the accomplishment Hagor *understood*. And it occurred to him that his father's attitude towards the sword and the killing was all related to Theo, who had gone east as a sell-sword and come back a drunk. Except that lying there, thinking about it, Aranthur wondered what his uncle had actually done in the East. No one ever talked about it.

The last day passed too quickly, and Aranthur had to think about leaving – about another half-year in a tenement in the City, with the winter's deadly Black Wind blowing through the narrow glass-and-horn paned window, and the smell of three young men in his nostrils all the time, eating bad food cooked by uncaring merchants and writing until his cold fingers ached all the time. Walking through slums full of sullen refugees from the troubles out east.

All autumn he had missed his village, and when he was in it, he found it difficult to leave. His childhood Liote was much easier to speak than High Liote that the Byzas spoke, with its artificiality, or *Ellene*, the language of the ancients used for almost everything at the Academy. He hadn't realised how much he'd missed his mother's cooking. Or a clean bed. Even if it was a foot too short.

At the same time, he'd noticed things he hadn't wanted to notice. He heard his mother's broad upland accent – an accent for which he'd been ridiculed on arrival in the City, and which he'd worked hard to lose. He heard it in his sister and father, too, but Mira's was so obvious that she sounded like a comedian in the hippodrome imitating an upland Arnaut 'barbarian'. Two of his father's friends came and sat and discussed crop prices and the crisis in Volta, and the unsettled state of the kingdom of Atti across the straits. In the process all three of them betrayed a deep disgust for men who loved other men in their jokes and their gossip. In the City, it was not only acceptable but fashionable. The coupling of men with men and women with women – which on arrival had shocked Aranthur – now seemed so unimportant as to make their comments seem comic. Or boorish.

Fear that he was contracting such liaisons perhaps fuelled his mother's frenetic rush to pair him with a local girl. The process had been woven like a thread through every social occasion, whether Eagle Temple, dinners, or the Sun dance. His sister's best friend, Alfia Topaza, the eldest of the Topazoi children from the river's edge, whose parents jointly owned the most prosperous farm in the town – her property was presented as her foremost qualification – was the most prominent of Mira's choices.

Alfia was pretty – in a severe way – and Aranthur, who was at an age when most women seemed beautiful at least some of the time, wondered whether she might not make the most severe old woman in the village. He found her manners pleasant and her person very attractive – she had large, dark eyes and beautiful long black hair, and she could dance almost as well as his sister, so that to do the *haliardo* with her was to float in the air – but when she spoke, it was inevitably to belittle. If she ever had a nice thing to say about anyone, it was inevitably mixed with a favourable comment about her own family – or her own sweet self. She invariably used herself as an example of the best way of doing anything.

And yet she was very attractive.

So the last day was a day of mixed emotion. He found himself wishing to go and wishing to stay. He wanted to tell his mother that women loving women was really a thing of no matter. He wanted to tell Alfia that her critique of everyone else was merely a sign of her own fears. But he had learnt these truths from books and from observation, in just one year at the Academy, and life in the village, with all its complexity and traditions, made him question the learning of his books and masters. Or rather, it made him see that there were perhaps many truths.

He was currying his horse when his father came out to their small shed. It was dark inside, despite the bright sun that had already melted the snow, so that the olive trees stood proud and the fields looked ready for spring. He had lit the lanterns so that he had some light to work.

His father came in and touched the Lady shrine over the door. Uplanders had many old beliefs – the Lady and the Twelve were two that uplanders claimed they had received from the Fae People, the *Zanash* Ancient Folk who had lived in the hills at the dawn of time.

'How's your hayburner today?' Hagor called out.

'Still eating,' Aranthur confessed.

Rasce had done little but eat for nine days, and his sides had filled out and his coat gleamed.

'I'm guessing that animal hasn't had two days out of harness his whole life,' his father said. 'And still a pretty good horse. I wish he was going to be here when it's ploughing time.' He winked. 'And you too, of course.'

Aranthur considered. 'With a horse, I could be home for ploughing. Other boys go home.' He thought about it – and about all of his hesitations about the village.

'Would you, though?' his father asked. 'I get the sense you love it – there in the City. The sword. The clothes.'

Aranthur kept the curry comb going, realising this was likely to be a difficult conversation, and that he'd been currying while he spoke to Iralia – a woman who had been very much on his mind.

'I do and I don't, Patur.' He shrugged.

'Aye.' Hagor began to work on the mule. 'You'll be stopping at the Inn of Fosse on your way down to the City, eh?'

Aranthur looked up. 'I said I would. I owe for my other horse.'

'Other horse?'

Aranthur sighed inwardly. 'I received two horses as my share.'

'And a fancy fire weapon, and a dead man's clothes,' Hagor said. 'That carbine's worth as much as my mule – maybe as much as this farm. Men will kill you just to have it.' He coughed. 'Do men carry weapons in the city?'

'No,' Aranthur said. 'No, it is against the law. When I go to sword class, I carry my sword – sheathed – in a cloth.'

He didn't say that most criminals and many other people had weapons and in fact wore them – and that everyone wore a dagger – and that the alleys were full of casual violence, from dagger fights to armed robbery and outright assassination.

He didn't say that, because at the same time, a careful student could avoid ever seeing so much as a bleeding corpse by walking along the seaward edges of the city, where the rich lived, and staying out of certain neighbourhoods, and not joining the riots. Or just by using the canals and not the alleys.

His father sighed. 'You know, it's Theo.'

Aranthur didn't know. 'Uncle Theo?'

'He has a sword,' Hagor said. 'Bought one when we was boys. Went raiding with grandpatur.' He was silent a while. Then: 'He went east to fight for strangers. Some parts of him never came back.' He shrugged. 'Ever think what you will do, when you are done at the Academy?'

Aranthur managed a laugh. 'No. I mean—'

'It's not as if qualifying as a Magos will make you a better farmer,' Hagor said.

'It might,' Aranthur put in. 'I have learned . . .' He paused, realising that saying 'I see everything differently' was not going to make his father feel better.

That brought Lecne to mind, of a sudden – a boy who wanted to be a scholar, toiling in his father's inn.

'They do teach us things,' he said. 'Interesting things, about how people think, and what you can learn from them.'

'And how to cast spells and defy your parents,' Hagor said, but he winked.

Aranthur switched sides of his mount.

'Would you be a priest, lad?' Hagor asked.

Aranthur realised, with a shock, that he understood what his father was doing. He was trying to find a place for his son in his normal world of adulthood. Aranthur was more shocked at how easily he read his father's thoughts than by the revelation itself.

Aranthur smiled as he started on his horse's neck.

'I don't think the life of a priest is for me, Patur.' He paused. 'If I'm good enough, I might try to be a Magos. But it will be years before I reach a point where I'll know.'

Silence.

'My son, a Magos.'

Hagor whistled, and then Aranthur listened to the rapid sound of his father's brush starting work on the mud on the mule's legs.

'Ever wonder why the aristo chose you, lad?' he asked.

Aranthur realised he had never given it any thought.

'You do think you are smarter than most folks, don't ye?' he asked.

Aranthur counted in his head, thinking of answers.

'Yes,' he finally admitted.

His father laughed. 'Well,' he said, as if he was about to say something.

The mule – an old family retainer and a strong, capable animal – made quiet chirping sounds more suited to a bird than an equine. The horse – Soldier or Rasce, depending on Aranthur's mood – grunted in reply and let loose a long fart.

'That horse likes beans,' his father said.

'Soldier loves anything that counts as food,' Aranthur said.

'Don't tell your mother you want to be a Magos. In her eyes, you'll come home and marry and raise a family on a farm.'

'I may yet!' Aranthur said.

Hagor came around the shed and clapped him on the shoulder.

'You know what, son? I doubt it. I think it's even going to be difficult to hold your sister here. You're at an age when parents seem like fools. I know – it wasn't really so long ago for me.' He shook his head. 'I *always* wanted a sword, but it was Theo who went away and owned one. He fought in other men's battles, son. He was a sell-sword. We never tell anyone.'

'Why not?' Aranthur asked.

'Because we're Arnauts. And everyone thinks we're brigands and mercenaries anyway. I spent my youth as a farmer trying to convince Byzas merchants to trust me.' He shook his head. 'And yet we *are* Arnauts; *my* father told stories of the great raid, when they lifted six thousand head from the Byzas down in the valleys towards Lonika.' He smiled. 'Of course, we don't brag about that any more.' He laughed.

Cattle thieving had once been an Arnaut way of life. They sang songs about it, but they didn't mention it outside the valley.

But his father wasn't done.

'By the Rising of the Sun, I even prayed for a sword.' He made a face. 'And your mother's grandfather was a famous swordsman. At least, among the tribes in the hills.' He frowned and looked at his hands as if there was revelation here about how to raise a child. 'But those were different days. Anyway, what I want to say is, don't... Don't think we don't want good things for you. And your sword... It... reminds me of other times. Other... ways. Don't become a swordsman. And – don't think that the City is better than us. Please.'

'I don't,' Aranthur said.

Mostly.

Riding down the pass between the river and the deep, dark forest, he couldn't decide whether his announcement that he would return for ploughing was a craven surrender or a noble idea. It certainly made his mother and father happy. Even his sister seemed more animated.

He wondered to himself if going home made him younger. He had felt so much more... *manly* at the inn. His mother and sister, on the other hand...

He laughed at himself and watched the woods.

In youth, he and Marta had roamed the woods above the road, pretending to find signs of the *Haiarkayo* and the *Zanash*, just as on the high hillsides, they would delight in finding the ancient stone nests that once the Green Drakes had made, and pretending they found new eggs. They had pretended so hard that the games had become quite frightening.

Now he watched the woods with what might have been an unnecessary intensity, and all but fell off his horse when a stag leapt from the cover of the trees and bounded through the open ground, leaping felled trees and rocks, thrusting through the melting drifts of snow. He wondered if the *Haiarkayo* were still there. Or how many Easterners now lived in the woods, and what they were eating in the heart of winter.

One of the Masters had suggested that there were still *Haiarkayo*, in a lecture. That they were relatives of the Dhadhi. The idea seemed to take all their mystery away. And in Natural Philosophy they had discussed Eastern Drakes, the green monsters who could speak – and eat magik, or so his Master claimed.

But as neither dragons nor faery knights appeared in the stag's wake, he simply looked at the tracks and rode on with his heart hammering in his chest. He mocked himself as he checked the priming in his carbine.

He wasted a lot of time when he missed the side road that paralleled the main road. It had no tracks and fell down a steep slope – that much he remembered. But it took him too long to find it again and walking up the path with snow-melt running over – and through – his boots was deeply unpleasant. It left him wet to the knees and cold to the bone. At the top he mounted, and he and Rasce – a better team now – rode quickly. The ground under the melting snow was still frozen, and the sun had reduced the snow cover down here to a patchwork quilt. He alternated between trotting and walking as the sun went down, and was shocked – again – to see the trail widen into a proper road lined with stone houses and good wood cabins: the small town of Fosse that sat north of the inn, hidden by a low ridge. He was in the yard of the inn well before dark, and Lecne came out and wrapped him in an embrace.

'My pater's well – recovering every day. He's in the kitchen now and none can say him nay! Ha, I'll be a great poet!' Lecne laughed. 'An Imperial soldier came. Can you believe it? They weren't here when the attack happened, but we have to answer questions because some bandits died.'

Aranthur felt a touch of fear.

'What did you tell them?' he asked as they pushed into the kitchen.

'As little as possible,' Lecne said.

Aranthur passed into the kitchen, was embraced by Donna Cucina and Don Cucino as well, and the cook and one of the girls for good measure. The girl smiled at him – the same who had served him at breakfast the day after the fight.

He smiled back, reflecting how pleasant a smile was, and how different from a lecture on the failings of others.

'I'll bet you don't remember my name,' she said.

'Hasti,' he said.

Girls' names stuck in his head better than boys', and he knew why

– but the Studion also had games and strategies to help young people memorise details, because there were so many things a student had to remember.

'Oh, that's nice!' she said.

She had dark hair and a straight back and a face that was almost comically like a cat's. She was very pretty – in a very feline way. Aranthur was struck by how disturbed he must have been by the killing, that he had not really noted her prettiness, or her grace. She laughed, throwing back her head.

'Hasti!' Donna Cucina said. 'She's my sister's girl, and she thinks she's the Queen of the Spring.'

Her eyes stayed with his a fraction of a heartbeat more...

'It's almost as if Sun Rise never happened!' Lecne said. 'Master Sparthos is just back, and then you come in too. Perhaps the priest and the mysterious Despoina Iralia will come back too.'

'About that...' Aranthur cleared his throat nervously.

'Yes?' Donna Cucina asked.

'I'm wondering if anyone...' Aranthur shrugged. 'My *patur* asked if I had looked for the dead man. The man whose clothes and horse I have.' He looked around. 'So... I wondered if you have heard any news. From the west.'

Don Cucino shrugged. He glanced at the red line at the cuff of his shirt, where he'd had his hand cut off. He frowned.

'Those hell-sent bastards killed a lot of people before they came here,' he said.

'That close to Darknight?' Donna Cucina spat. 'They were more like demons than men. Possessed.'

Aranthur could tell that he'd dropped a shadow on the family, and he bowed and slipped away, but Lecne followed him out into the common room.

'Hey,' he said.

Aranthur stopped and slapped his back.

'Pater doesn't want to say it, but they found some bodies back down the road, when the snow melted after First Sun,' Lecne said. 'They died hard.' He shrugged. 'No one wants to talk about it. Loot is loot. Take your share – it was the inn that set the shares and no man or god can claim we were unfair. Right? And we've had customers from Volta. Six hundred houses burned. Someone started the fire with *magik*. It'll take them years to recover.'

'Right,' said Aranthur.

He had stopped, because the man in brown – Master Sparthos – was sitting at the same table that he'd occupied a fortnight earlier. He sat with two other men, and they were speaking with a quiet intensity that was a little troubling. The City had given Aranthur a taste of how men behaved on the edge of violence, and the recent incident was recalled all the more powerfully by the inn. Both of the new men wore swords – one a long sword with a complex hilt, and the other a mid-length sword with a plain cross-hilt.

Master Sparthos gave Aranthur a civil nod and went back to his guests.

'You still willing to give me a sword lesson?' Lecne asked.

Aranthur laughed. 'Do you have a sword?'

Lecne frowned. 'No,' he said. 'That is, we have an old one, but it's special.'

'Do you have a good stick?' Aranthur asked. 'Oak is good.'

'I have to do chores. I'll be back.'

Lecne bounded off. Aranthur went up to his room and changed into dry clothes. Then he went back downstairs to the common room carrying his book. He had scarcely taken it out at his parents' house for fear of their comments. He'd shown it to Marta, who had leafed through it, her mouth slightly open in astonishment. He'd formed an impression of a book full of terse comments and odd illustrations, including one of two people copulating which had made her giggle and him blush.

Now, however, he set himself to read it. An older woman poured him wine and he thanked her. Then he sat in the beautiful bay window and let the warm sun bring fire to the gold in the illumination, which was of a man being roasted over a fire by two hares. The illumination had nothing to do with the words on the page – or rather, it seemed to have nothing to do with them. But some scholar's instinct prompted him to stop and look at them from time to time, trying to look beyond the immediate. The words on the page were pious religious sentiments – the kind that could be purchased in brush calligraphy at stalls by the Great Temple of Winds in the Byzas quarter of Megara, for example:

91

The Sun is Great

or

Awe of the Sun is the beginning of wisdom

He looked up when the light changed. Master Sparthos was standing at his table.

'A pleasure to see you again, young man,' he said.

Aranthur rose and bowed as he had been taught to bow to a magister, with one hand all the way to the ground.

'Magister,' he said in reply.

Sparthos wrinkled his mouth, which seemed to be as close as the man came to a smile. With a civil nod, he passed outside.

He went back to reading, but the language – High Ellene – was not his best, and he had to puzzle out cases and tenses very different from Liote. And the simplicity of the text was at odds with the illuminations. Could the two hares roasting the man represent an inversion? If so, the author was a blasphemer.

Blasphemy was not so uncommon in the Academy, nor was outright atheism. Founded a thousand years before in the first flush of the Revolution to train young mages, the Studion had passed through a long period of monasticism. Even in the modern age a large proportion of the men, and even some of the women, remained initiates of one of the cults, or went out into the world as mendicants, with their *power* trained to enhance their faith. But at least two of the Magi dismissed the worship of the Sun as blatant superstition, and the most daring, the Practical Philosophy Magos, held that the juxtaposition of Light and Dark was a tool to force simplicity and superstition on the masses.

He was lost in contemplation of the simplicity – or complexity – when a serving girl cleared her throat.

He looked up into a severely beautiful face – the purest Liote looks: a long nose; black hair; stark eyebrows above deep black eyes. She wasn't looking at him, but at the book in his lap.

'You read Ellene?' he asked.

He asked with humour; the ancient language was only used by priests and scholars. He'd struggled with it for half a year, and the simple statements of *Consolations* were about all he could handle.

'Yes,' she said, with a sniff. 'Would you like something?' She looked down her nose at him. 'You are my brother's friend, aren't you?'

Aranthur saw that she had something of the Cucina nose and forehead.

'Where did you learn Ellene?' he asked.

She gave a little shrug.

Silence hung between them.

'I taught myself,' she said. 'Wine?'

'No, thank you. I am going to try and teach your brother a little fencing.'

He smiled to indicate that it wasn't her brother he was unsure of.

'And that's dangerous?'

'Wine won't improve me, I promise. You *taught yourself*?'

'Yes,' she said firmly. 'Want me to prove it? I can read any passage you indicate.'

'No, no,' he said. 'I believe you.'

'Is that *Consolations*?'

'Yes.'

Aranthur handed it to her, but she merely nodded and went to the table with the two friends of the sword master.

When Lecne appeared with a stout staff shod in iron, Aranthur picked up his book. After depositing it in his room (carefully tucked between his straw mattress and the ropes that bound the bed) he grabbed his sword and ran back down the stairs. The two young men cut through the kitchen without being stopped, to the inn's backyard, where horses were brought out from the barns.

If Aranthur had had the talent or training to draw, he would have sketched his friend on the spot, as the personification of *eager anticipation*.

He realised, facing his companion's ardour, that he had no idea what – or how – he was going to teach the other boy.

But after consideration and some uneasy silence, his brain began to work and he had some notions, and he shrugged.

'First, you can have my sword. I'll use the stick,' he said. 'Second, I feel it only fair to tell you that I've had less than half a year of lessons, and I'm not at all sure I know anything.'

He shrugged again, because there was an insistent temptation to play the great man – to start talking at length about the parts of the sword and the way to purchase one. That's how his own master had started, and it had been a very impressive, scholarly debut, including a display of his lineage, not as a man but as a swordsman – the name of his teacher, and all the teachers before him.

In an inn yard with a cold wind blowing, action seemed called for.

'Let's start with some simple cuts. There are many cuts, but we can keep it to six...' Aranthur began, and looked at his companion. 'No, let's start with how to hold the sword.'

He had just got his friend's hand comfortably around the grip, a little less like a man holding a claw hammer and a little more like a swordsman, when Hasti and the other girl, the one who'd *taught* herself Ellene, appeared on the kitchen's back steps in hose and doublets.

'My sister,' said Lecne. 'Nenia, can't I, please...?'

Nenia was a year or two older than her brother. If Hasti looked like a cat, she looked like an eagle, with a long, hooked nose that differed materially from any other nose in the family. She was striking rather than pretty. Her face dealt well with the family nose, and her eyebrows were dark and heavy above eyes of a surprising, almost indescribably dark colour. Given that she was in hose, it was easy to see that she carried a good deal of muscle and was as tall as Aranthur himself, a sharp contrast to Hasti's diminutive size.

'Cook is covering for us,' she said.

'Us?' Lecne asked.

Hasti laughed. 'We want to learn to use to the sword too.'

'Swords are for men,' Lecne said. 'Nenia, this is not fair.'

Aranthur cut in. 'In the City, there are girls as well as boys in my sword class.'

Hasti stuck out her tongue at Lecne.

'There was a nun here last week and she had a sword,' she said.

'You'll need sticks,' Aranthur said. 'I'm out of swords,' he added, hoping to lighten the mood.

A few minutes later, they all stood in a ragged line and he began to teach them the first exercise he could remember learning: a simple pair of cuts – high to low, first right to left and then left to right.

Hasti was hopeless, an endless series of giggles from beginning to end. Lecne laboured manfully, swishing the sword far too hard and ingloriously cutting the point into the dirt more than once, with a thousand embarrassed apologies.

Nenia, on the other hand, was a natural athlete. She mimicked Aranthur's pose so well that he laughed to detect his own flaw of stamping his front foot instead of gliding it.

Then he taught them some simple blocks, or *parades*, which in his lessons were called covers because, his master declaimed, it wasn't so important to block the opponent's sword as to cover the body. Aranthur found himself repeating this as if he'd made it up himself. He showed them the simple turn of the hand that best covered the centre of the body from the two basic stances he'd taught. He showed them a universal parry that covered all blows.

And then, when it was clear that everyone's wrists were tired, he showed them what he'd taught: two poses, the names of which he tried to teach; two covers; two cuts.

By then, Hasti had stopped giggling and even Nenia was tired. He bowed at the end of his summary.

Behind him, the sound of clapping.

To his mortification, he turned to find the Magister Sparthos leaning against the back wall of the inn. The man turned without a word and went inside.

'Men. I hate them, all arrogance and posturing.' Nenia smiled at Hasti, who smiled, in turn, at Aranthur.

'I'm cold, now that we're not moving,' she said. 'Let's have some cider.'

The four of them went into the kitchen, and Aranthur allowed the other three to soothe him. They'd clearly enjoyed the lesson and he found he'd enjoyed teaching it. But he shrugged as Hasti put a hot cup of cider by his hand and then sat by him, across the big kitchen table from Nenia and her brother.

'I'm sure I sounded like an arse,' he said.

Nenia shrugged. 'I liked it. I don't know much more than I did, but I have a sense of it now.' She raised her eyebrows. 'If you were staying, I'd have more lessons.'

'I don't really know enough to be teaching.'

Nenia leant over, as if scrutinising his face.

'Are you sure you're a man?' she asked. 'Men are overbearing, rude and boastful.'

Aranthur smiled and spread his hands – unconsciously imitating Magos Ulthese, the Memory Magos.

'Boasting is a way of saying you are weak,' he said.

'Bright Sun, there's a school that teaches that?' Nenia asked. 'Send my brother.'

Lecne demonstrated his prowess by feinting with his left hand to distract his sister and elbowing her sharply with his right.

'I think I'd be terrified,' Hasti said. It was odd that she said it provocatively, almost aggressively.

Nenia leant over the table.

'You only believe that because people tell you that women should be afraid,' she said. 'That's all crap.'

Hasti smiled, her head tilted and her eyes a little down, at Aranthur.

'Would you want a girl who was a better swordsman – swords*woman* – than you?'

All three of them looked at him.

'Be honest,' Hasti giggled.

Aranthur tugged at his short beard.

'Yes,' he said. 'I mean, unless I marry a fool, my wife is likely to do *something* better than me. Probably quite a few things.'

Nenia wasn't impressed. 'Men say that, but they mean unimportant things like raising babies.'

Aranthur knew that he had Hasti's attention, and his sense of what was right was warring with his desire to please her. Nenia did not seem like a girl who could be pleased at all – although she smiled more than she frowned.

'It's not likely to come up, is it?' Lecne asked. 'I mean, most women aren't strong enough to fight. They're too weak.'

'Really?' Nenia said, and glowered.

'We can't all be giants like you, Nenia,' Hasti purred.

Without another word, Nenia got up and left the table. The kitchen was almost as big as the common room, and it took her time to clear it. In that time, Aranthur could think of nothing to say. But the moment she was gone, he stood up.

Lecne frowned at Hasti.

'That was pretty mean,' he said.

Hasti hung her head.

'She's good at all the games,' she pouted.

Aranthur was fairly certain that the cat-faced girl had played the game exactly as she meant to. He almost admired her for it. Almost.

He rose. 'I'll go and find her,' he said.

Ignoring the protests of the other two, he passed into the common room, where Donna Cucina stood with her hands on her hips.

'What are you children doing?' she asked.

Aranthur flushed. 'Talking. I . . . er . . . taught. A little about swords.'

Donna Cucina raised one eyebrow.

'Why is my daughter crying?' she asked.

Aranthur shook his head. 'I don't know.'

He did know, but he thought that it wasn't his place to say.

'She's gone upstairs,' Donna Cucina said. 'And much as I like you, my lad, you are not following my daughter to an empty attic.' She smiled. 'I was young once, too.'

Aranthur was both amused and annoyed at how often older people had to insist that they had once been his age. He turned to go back to his companions when he saw Magister Sparthos beckon to him.

With some trepidation, he went across the floor. The man's two companions were gone.

'Sit,' he said.

With a bow, Aranthur sat.

The older man poured him some wine.

'Your lesson,' he said. 'Not bad.'

He drank.

Aranthur beamed. He drank too.

'I can see that charlatan Vladith's teaching in you.' He made a face, as if smelling something bad. 'Yet you *understood* the basics of the art. When you fought – here – you let your adversary take the scabbard off your sword. Brilliant.'

Aranthus flushed with praise. 'It's something we drill—' he began.

'So?' the old man said vehemently. 'You *did* it. With your life on the line, in a fight, you did it. Of course, as soon as your steel was clear you did almost everything wrong, but it didn't matter, did it? You had a drawn sword and you were determined to attack – you had the initiative.' He smiled, and his smile was colder than his frown. 'Of course your point control – your aim – was terrible, and you were merely fortunate in your blow, but what of it? All that can be trained.' He nodded. 'And you are strong as an ox and fast. You do a few things very well.'

Aranthur looked at the table. 'Thank you, Magister.'

He thought of all the wood he had cut over Sun Rise week.

'And you have the consolation of knowing that you've killed more men than *Master* Vladith.' The old man barked a laugh.

Aranthur was offended on his teacher's behalf.

It must have showed, because the old man shrugged.

'I can see you like him. He should treasure that. But he's a fake, boy. Oh, he's had instruction, but much of what he teaches is pomposity, complex dances executed very fast – eh?' He nodded. 'Would you care to see a really good piece of sword work?'

Aranthur didn't like his tone. But . . .

'Yes,' he said. It felt a little like agreeing to a loan shark's price. Which he had done, to his own consternation. Twice.

'Can you get up early?' the older man asked. 'At first light?'

Aranthur nodded again.

'Good. You saw the two men here? Both swordsmen. Mikal Sapu of Mitla – solid, conservative, flashes of brilliance. Kartez Da Silva is from Trantolo – far to the west, where oranges come from.' He leant over. 'Tomorrow they fight.'

'A duel?'

Aranthur realised that the swordsman was, if not drunk, at least tipsy.

'Yes. All perfectly legal – we're outside the City and I have the papers, signed by each.'

The magister leant back and drank off his wine, and then poured himself more.

'A duel,' Aranthur said.

In that moment, an image of the burst of blood when Don Cucino's hand had almost been severed came into his head, and he, in turn, emptied his wine cup.

His sense of the morality of the thing warred with his desire to see a bout of really good swordsmanship.

'I'll try.'

'Oh, do try,' the magister said, suddenly bored. He waved his hand, dismissing Aranthur.

He dined with the family in the kitchen, and the food was delicious – the sort of food that people ate in the City, but made with the best and freshest ingredients.

Donna Cucina took him aside after dinner.

'You said you think you'll come back this way at ploughing?' she asked.

He nodded. He'd talked a little – perhaps too much – about his family at dinner.

'I think you are a good boy. If you come, would you consider bringing me some things?'

She had a long list of rare spices.

Next to each was a price.

'You can write!' he said, and then felt like an arse.

But Donna Cucina smiled, the way women do when men are patronising.

'I run an inn, dear,' she said. 'Now look here. These are the prices I pay for them, to a tinker who I don't really like. Last year he sold me nutmeg that I think was solid wood, among other things. His cinnamon is not the best, and I need better.'

He was flattered, and a little appalled.

'The spice market is not so far from the Studion,' he said. 'But '

'We can send you with money.'

Aranthur wanted to do it. He liked these people. And it would give him more reason to go home for ploughing.

'I'll do the buying,' he said. 'You can repay me when I come back.'

She nodded. 'Very fair.'

She looked past him, where the kitchen girls and Nenia had cleared the table and then pushed it against the wall. A pair of Dhadhi – the wandering folk from the mountains of Atti and the islands east of Zhou, or so people said – had been fed, and now flourished their instruments: a mandolin and a pair of pipes. The Dhadhi were tall, often very beautiful, their faces narrow and their limbs elegant. They made fine dancers and musicians and swordspeople, too. Some said they lived an extraordinary time. Others said that was a myth. His mother and his Magi claimed they were related to the *Haiarkayo*.

'We'll dance in the common room, thank you very much,' Donna Cucina barked at her daughter. She looked up at Aranthur, who was a head taller than she, and laughed. 'The girls don't like dancing with customers,' she admitted. 'But it's good for business.'

They danced for hours. The two Dhadhi were excellent – far better than most of the street musicians in Megara – but their people were usually good musicians. The local farmers danced and some even

99

brought their wives and daughters. The youngest of the three swords-men – the dapper man from far-off Trantolo – danced, although it was clear he didn't know the local steps. The other two swordsmen kept to their table. It was odd to Aranthur to see the three sitting together and sharing wine, all the while knowing that two of them would fight in the morning. He assumed it was something great swordsmen did, and he felt a sort of religious awe.

The dances were the same as those of his own village – violent, fast, *haliardi* in which the best dancers competed to kick as high as they could, and the stately *Orta*, and the *Mati*, where two men danced with one lady who looked at them by turns while each tried to out-dance the other. The man who received the lady's nod got to lift her and turn her as high over his head as his strength allowed. Failure brought ribald comments and success only led to more nods. It was a pleasant sport, and Nenia and Hasti were very good at it. Nenia could kick as high as any man in the *haliardo*, but she was kind enough to leap – just to the music – when Aranthur's turn to lift her came. He managed to raise her high enough to get a burst of applause. When he set her down – with a proper whirl and a blessing for having a sister who insisted on practice – she smiled at him. There was something marvellous in her smile, her height, her presence, and the sweat on her neck and her obvious delight.

'You can dance!' she said.

But she stepped nimbly away before he could ask her to dance again, and danced with a local boy, a farmer's son.

Hasti replaced her. 'Well, sir? Am I not worth a dance?'

An older man might have replied with a quip, but Aranthur could only smile and beg her pardon, which she gave quickly enough.

'I wager I'll be easier to lift than Nenia.'

Aranthur danced the second *Mati* with the Westerner as his second man.

'Da Silva,' he said in an accent that seemed over-full of *s*'s.

The use of the surname might have been meant as an affront, but Aranthur didn't care. He was having a good time, and he preferred to assume the Westerner had a different custom.

'Timos,' Aranthur said.

He wished that he had a doublet on, like Da Silva, instead of a loose peasant shirt with some of his mother's tablet weaving at neck and wrists. But the man was older and clearly prosperous.

He smiled at Hasti. 'You are the beautiful one here.'

His diction was careful, but his intent obvious. He kissed her hand. She blushed. 'What fine manners.'

The dance began.

Aranthur was very careful of the Westerner, who seemed intent on cutting him off or stepping on his foot. And Aranthur, who was learning in the Studion to observe, already suspected that Hasti intended to choose his rival at the moment of the lift.

And so it proved. Da Silva moved before she nodded.

Aranthur was fairly sure he'd intended to barge into him, had he left his place. As it was, Da Silva was a beat late into the lift. Hasti had already bent her legs for her leap, and the results were not pretty. The Westerner had superb reflexes, however, and was strong enough to complete the movements. As he put Hasti back on the floor, he glared at Aranthur.

Aranthur would have liked to return that glare with the steady cool of a soldier, but he fell back a step, and his hands trembled. However, he was a veteran dancer. He came around and completed the figure well, skipping and changing step to the complicated beat of the *Mati* music. As he passed Hasti he saw that she would choose him for the second figure – which was only good manners in any village girl. But he was equally aware that the Westerner was intending to pick a fight. It was written on him.

So as the first notes of the second figure started, Aranthur spun – an allowable, if showy, alternative. He caught Hasti's hand and turned her under it so that when Da Silva moved, he bumped into the woman and not his adversary. These tricks were not so uncommon in village life, but of course the newcomer didn't know. Aranthur danced past him, sweeping Hasti along. When the beat came to raise her, he was exactly on the music and her leap was so high that he almost – almost – lost her over his head.

Aranthur raised her, turning, to place her in the correct direction for the rest of the figure. He put her down to the music – with the satisfaction that he'd lifted her all the way over his head, the way he could lift his sister. The two of them finished the figure with their kicks, and bowed as the music ended.

'You are tolerably clumsy, eh?' Da Silva said.

He chose to stand very close. He wore a small smile and seemed very much at ease.

Hasti laughed – probably the worst thing she might have done.

'You will learn our dances if you stay long enough, sir. But it was you who misstepped, not he.'

The Westerner ignored her as if she didn't exist.

'Do you always flinch when a man talks to you?' he asked, pushing closer. 'Apologise for your gross stumbling and beg my pardon.'

Aranthur knew where all this was going. He thought it all through – as best he could in the time it takes a young person to draw one breath and decide to capitulate. He needed none of this.

'No,' he said, as if his voice belonged to someone else. It shook, and it sounded high and scared. And yet he heard himself refuse to apologise.

Da Silva was surprised, and in the moment of his hesitation, Aranthur changed weight and pushed past him.

'You stand too close,' he muttered as he passed.

As well to be hanged for a lion as a lamb, he thought.

What made me say that?

He wasn't under a *compulsion*. It was his own bravado talking.

I'm a fool, he thought.

Right on time, Da Silva turned. His hand was raised to strike.

Master Sparthos glided between them and caught the Westerner's hand.

'You are making a mistake,' he said gently.

'This overgrown boy offended me,' Da Silva spat.

'You are wasting the very spirit that will make you the victor tomorrow,' the magister said.

'After I kill that idiot, I will kill this one. Boy!' he spat. 'You have offended me.'

'You intended to be offended,' Aranthur said to a silent room.

'I challenge you!' Da Silva spat.

The magister – he was in dark blue today – shook his head like a disapproving father.

'Must you?' he asked.

The Westerner pushed past him.

'I challenge you, peasant boy. Now run away and stop pretending to be a man, or fight me.'

The magister turned to Aranthur in the heavy silence.

'You have the choice of weapons, if you choose to fight.'

Aranthur's heart was beating very fast, and it was difficult to breathe. He saw Nenia looking at him – and Lecne – and he really didn't want to die.

'Magister,' he said, 'what would you do, in my place?'

The magister smiled. 'I would ask me to be your second. Then, it would be my duty to advise you.'

Da Silva shook his head and his face took on an odd look, like an actor's mask of anger.

'You? Sir? You would take this bumpkin's side?'

The magister shrugged. 'You are behaving badly, waving your vaunted prowess around a tavern full of yokels. For what? To bed this little kitten?' His smile was cruel, and Hasti flinched. 'I'm looking for something better in my swordsmen.'

Aranthur gave his best City bow.

'Magister, would you condescend to be my second in this matter?' He was proud of himself.

The magister nodded. 'Yes. Yes, I would.' He turned to the Westerner. 'You, too, will need a second.'

The Westerner shrugged. 'I'll take any of them.'

The magister looked around. 'You'd best find one, then.' He smiled his mirthless smile. 'I suspect that Master Apucu of Volta is your most likely candidate.' His eyes flicked to Aranthur. 'Except that you are already fighting him too.'

Da Silva sneered. 'I do not need a second.'

'If you kill this boy without one, you'll be arrested,' the magister said flatly.

Around them, people had begun to gather and talk. Duels were not so infrequent in the City, but at an inn ...

Lecne came and stood by Aranthur, and so did Nenia. Hasti had drifted away, and was standing with the farm boy who had been dancing with Nenia.

Aranthur found that his mind was running very fast – and his thinking was very clear. He was able to watch Hasti, and understand that she was flirting with her best friend's dance partner simply because that was her reaction to fear and discomfort. He noted the speed with which Nenia was breathing, and he smiled at her.

'You seem very calm,' she said.

He managed a smile. 'I am surprising myself.'

He felt very alive.

He turned to his adversary. 'I'd be your second. But I'm otherwise engaged.'

People around them laughed.

Kartez Da Silva turned to the magister. 'Tell this clod that he may no longer speak to me, as we are engaged to fight.'

The magister shook his head.

'Have your second tell him. Like your adversary, I am otherwise engaged.' He turned back to Aranthur. 'My first advice to you, young man: go to bed immediately – and alone.'

He smiled at Nenia, who flushed.

Aranthur opened his mouth to protest that he was nothing to her – that she barely had a civil word for him. But that seemed ungracious. So he merely bowed and took Lecne aside to arrange for a wake up and breakfast.

When he went back to the magister, the Westerner was gone.

'I assume we will fight in the morning?' he asked. 'I'm sorry, Magister, but I need to be back at classes.'

The magister laughed – genuine warmth.

'By the Sun, boy. You think you can beat him, and you are more concerned about classes?'

Aranthur sighed. 'I agree. Perhaps I will be dead.'

Just in that moment the reality of that statement struck him. His chest grew tight. He could envision it – his body lying in the slush in the yard, with that curious flatness of the dead.

'He wanted to fight you tonight,' the magister said. 'I forbade it. He can fight Apucu first, because that is what he is here to do. If he survives Apucu, and still wishes to fight, he can face you.'

Aranthur nodded. 'That seems unfair,' he said cautiously.

'You have some wonderful ideals, boy,' the magister said. 'Do you know why these two men have come here to fight?'

Aranthur shook his head.

The magister looked around. 'I am seeking a replacement,' he said quietly. 'There is no substitute for single combat in my profession.' He seemed amused by the whole situation.

Aranthur frowned. 'Magister, these men are fighting for your approval?'

'Nicely put,' the older man said. 'First light. You may as well have that rarest of advantages – that of seeing of your man in combat. My servant will knock at your door and I will arrange that you eat separately.' He smiled. 'I hope that you live. You are a remarkable young man, in your calm if nothing else. How will you fight him?'

Aranthur felt another jolt of fear as he heard the word 'fight'.

'Perhaps I should ask you that.'

The magister shrugged. 'I've not seen what you know. You are tall – you are strong – you have good co-ordination of your sinews. And you killed a man who fought by profession.' He looked around. 'I would say – do something you know and understand, and remember that your opponent is as afraid as you are yourself. Don't attempt to improvise, and try to banish your fear.'

Aranthur thought on that advice for a great deal of the night.

At some point he fell asleep – he must have, for he was awakened by a soft knock at the door.

'I'm awake,' he said.

'I brought you *chai*,' said a soft voice, and he opened the door to find Lecne and his sister with trays.

He took the *chai*, smiled at them both, and began to get dressed. He felt an odd pressure in his chest and his arms felt weak. Aside from those symptoms, which he thought were the direct effects of fear and lack of sleep, he felt ready for anything. He dressed carefully, in the clothes he'd avoided for days – a fine shirt, Drako's black hose, black shoes with soft soles. He pulled the heavy wool cote he had borrowed from Lecne over them all and drank his *chai*.

He almost forgot his sword, which made him smile at himself. Indeed, throughout his preparations, he had the oddest sense that someone was watching him. He was more aware than usual. He was so aware that he could see dust motes in the candlelight and hear the man snoring down the hall and think that he would, in many ways, give anything to be that man, snoring blissfully, and not about to die.

He met Nenia on the steps and she reached out and took his hand.

Her touch hit him like a *compulsion*, so that his eyes opened wider, but she meant nothing by it. Her hand was warm and very soft – and hard with ridges where work brought out calluses.

'I'm to take you to breakfast,' she said softly.

She was as tall as he, her face at eye level.

He wanted to say something to her. In his heightened awareness, he saw that she was slightly flushed, even if that was the candlelight in the hallway, and her eyes were very large.

'You must think me a fool,' he said.

She grinned. It was not a flirtatious smile or a cunning one, but a simple, open smile.

'I do, too. But I still hope you win. There, I was looking for a way to say that.'

'I'll do my best.'

She kept his hand and led him downstairs. He found the touch of her hand to be almost magikal – perhaps there was no *almost* about it. She released him at the kitchen door.

He ate two eggs, carefully coddled, and a piece of toast, and then it was time, the magister's blond servant beckoning from the doorway of the yard and the cold air like a malevolent thing. The Dark was still very close, even if Darknight was past, and as he rose to go out he felt the weakness in his limbs again. He thought that his knees might fail – and yet his head seemed to work perfectly well.

He took his sword and walked out into the yard, which was lit by eight torches – all pine cressets with pitch on them, so that the smell was beautiful, at least to a young man about to die.

He wondered if he was in love with Nenia. He could see her at an upper window, and he knew her comfort was the best gift she could give him. He wondered how he would feel – who he would be – if an hour later, he was still alive.

I'll still be a fool, he thought.

In the night, he had many times imagined how his father and mother would react. He'd had time to imagine Tiy Drako, or the priest, his mentor, or any of his Magi at school. And what each of them would say about his present predicament.

It had, in fact, occurred to him ten times or more that he could simply rise and go to the stable, saddle his horse and ride for the

City. He couldn't imagine that anyone would care, except perhaps the handful of witnesses at the inn.

And he himself.

He had come to the understanding, deep in the marches of the night, that he was not a fool for fighting.

He was a fool for wanting to fight. *He wanted to fight.*

His whole body was shaking with fear.

The sun cleared the distant horizon and the morning bells rang in the town up the ridge, and the two combatants drew their swords. One of his many fears was of doing the wrong thing, so Aranthur stood nervously watching them, unsure what to do with his sword, where to stand, what to watch. But as the red ball of the sun began to creep over the far eastern horizon, the magister told the combatants to stand to their guards, and both of them adopted postures that were familiar to Aranthur. The Voltain stood with his right leg forward and his sword hand, his right, covering his right leg, the sword point up, aimed at his adversary's throat.

The Westerner, Da Silva, stood with his left leg forward, his sword hand covering his left leg. Both men were tense, and Aranthur's heightened awareness caught their nerves. Both were tense where they ought to have been relaxed, and both swords trembled slightly.

The magister dropped his handkerchief in the muck, and the two men moved. But not towards each other. Instead, they circled. As their feet moved, their sword hands moved effortlessly to cover their legs – small hand movements to close the new lines created by each step. Several times in the first few moments their swords – the long one of the Westerner, the shorter sword of the Voltain – crossed with a dull *click* and then both men seemed to freeze for a fraction of a heartbeat, and nothing happened.

They circled for so long that the tension in Aranthur's chest began to ebb away, and then – in a moment – both men struck.

Aranthur, despite his heightened awareness, could not discern exactly what had happened. Both weapons seemed to miss; then both men raced their weapons – too late – to cover. The two swayed together, all elegance gone. Each released the pressure of that forceful cross and each swung a heavy blow on leaving the bind, and neither connected.

By the standards of a fencing *salle*, it looked fairly clumsy. Aranthur was skilled enough to suspect that actual combat reduced many of the elegant encounters of the art to this – two men hacking when each lost control of his opponent's blade.

'Halt,' the magister ordered, his voice like old images of the Sky God for whom Aranthur was named. 'You are both wounded. Will you continue?'

Now, in slightly brighter light, Aranthur could see blood on both men's forearms. They were fighting in shirts and hose, with no armour and no cotes.

'Yes,' they both said.

'Then carry on,' said the magister.

And then, in defiance of their first encounter, they were at it again, but this time with both fire and elegance. Da Silva attacked, two quick backhand blows from the shoulder. The Voltain caught the first in a fine cover and cut into the second, winning the cross and pushing his opponent, who fell back a step to avoid taking the blade across his face. Even as it was he was cut on the eyebrow, and he threw a powerful overhand blow to cover his escape. Somewhere deep in his fighting brain, Aranthur agreed that the heavy blow would compel the Voltain to make a big cover or parry, and they would again be at equilibrium.

But the Voltain's parry was a rising one, and he advanced, confident that he was about to make his kill. Da Silva also advanced, and so neither sword went where its owner intended, and they were breast to breast, hilts locked in front of their faces. Both men pushed.

The Westerner rolled his hand outside – the same movement from thumb up to thumb down that Aranthur practised endlessly – and his sword struck the Voltain master hard enough in the head to make a sound.

The man gave a choked scream and fell, his sword dropped, clutching his head with both hands as he sat in the muck of the yard. Blood poured out into the slush.

The magister went and looked at the Voltain. He nodded to his servant.

'Not mortal,' he said. 'Master Apucu, I have to declare your opponent the winner in this contest, and ask you to rise to your feet and go with my servant who will see to your wound. I assure you it did not penetrate the bone.'

He waved to Da Silva, who was stepping forward.

'Give him a moment.' he said.

'Bah.'

Da Silva stamped, and when slush sprayed over his hose, he cursed.

The Voltain did not lack courage. He got to his feet, wiped blood off his face, and bowed. He could barely keep his feet, but he then bowed to Aranthur.

'Your turn.'

He managed a shaky smile, and Aranthur bowed low in return.

He prayed that he might match the other man's performance. A head wound would bleed badly, but the skull was thick. Barring infection, the man would be healed easily enough . . .

Aranthur took a deep breath, as the Magi at the Studion told students facing tests to do – three deep breaths and begin his ritual trance. He didn't stay there, but the trance soothed him.

'Are you ready, young man?' the magister asked.

Aranthur drew his sword and then took his buckler off his belt.

'Bucklers?' Da Silva asked. 'What are we, savages?'

The magister neither smiled nor frowned. He shrugged instead.

'My principal has specified bucklers. Your second agreed.'

The local wheelwright, who'd probably never seen a duel in his life, nodded. He was shaking more than Aranthur.

Time passed while the magister sent a boy to fetch a buckler from his own baggage. Aranthur found that he was not really there, and that the cold and the fear had to some extent cancelled each other out, leaving him in a place a little distant from himself, like a man on a hill watching the smoke from the chimneys of his beloved village below him.

The sunrise foretold bad weather – a storm towards afternoon.

Perhaps I won't care.

Perhaps I will.

Some of his calm had come from having determined what he would do. He was half a head taller than Da Silva, and his own shoulders were broader. His sword was as long, and he suspected his arms were longer.

The man had two small wounds already– a cut on his forehead that kept bleeding, and a cut on his sword arm.

He is arrogant. And he has no idea how strong I am.

Eventually, the buckler appeared, and the Westerner, now obviously suffering from the cold, grasped it. Only then did Aranthur slip his cote off, and pull his shirt over his head, so that he was naked to the waist. The Magister of Physik had said that cloth carried more dirt into wounds than any other substance. He was a farm boy – he'd worked with no shirt every winter morning of his life until he went to the City.

'Ready,' he said.

'*Gardes*,' the magister said. He sounded bored.

Aranthur's *garde* was very different from his opponent's. He stood with his sword pointing almost straight behind him, and his buckler advanced as far forward as he could reach. Da Silva's sword was practically under his eye – which made him afraid all over again. But having a plan seemed a wonderful thing, and gave him hope. His sword was a long way from Da Silva – but he knew he was fast. And the Westerner could see neither his sword nor the arm that held it. He had no notion of the distance – the length of Aranthur's arm or the length of his sword.

That was his only advantage.

Without a buckler, the stance would have been suicidal. The first blow would almost certainly outrace any *garde* or cover that Aranthur could throw, and he'd be dead. But the buckler changed the options in every *garde*.

'Begin,' the magister said.

Da Silva wasted no time – probably due to the cold. He leapt forward as soon as the handkerchief dropped, his back right leg powering his left leg and torso forward – a feint to draw the buckler and a powerful thrust.

Aranthur's plan went out of the window in half an instant, but his buckler remained in place and his sword joined it, a crisp beat off the other blade. He didn't give back.

The Westerner turned his parried thrust into a cut with a wrist roll . . .

Aranthur covered the low attack to his leg by withdrawing the leg. His sword seemed to be fighting by itself. That is, he knew all these attacks and defences, but he wasn't *thinking* them. His sword, reacting to the leg-cut, was too slow, but the enemy weapon whistled past his leg, wrenched out of the way just in time. He counter-cut as he'd been taught, a backhand blow to Da Silva's temple that arose naturally from the failed parry.

His opponent leapt back.

He continued his cut all the way back to the *garde* in which he'd begun – his sword all the way outstretched behind him – mostly because that's how the drill he'd learnt worked. But finding that he'd put his sword there, and that withdrawing his leg had thrown his weight forward, he attacked without any more conscious thought than he had defended. He threw the heavy blow with which he'd intended to begin the fight – a simple, shoulder-level flat cut that came from behind his back and, powered by the whole weight of his hips and legs, snapped around like a scythe cutting wheat.

Da Silva snapped his parry, a turn of his sword hand, and immediately counter-hit with a thrust.

Aranthur felt the stinging pain and the cold of the sword, and then the other man fell to the ground clutching his neck, blood spurting into the snow and slush. Da Silva gave a garbled scream and his body arched with pain.

Aranthur felt the pain in his own neck, and the cold, and he went down on one knee. He was afraid to touch his neck. His vision tunnelled, and he could see the Westerner flopping in the muck.

Then there were hands in his armpits and a cold hand on his neck.

'It's nothing,' Lecne said. 'Blessed Sun!'

'Nothing?' he asked.

His heartbeat was calming. He had some control of himself. His vision returned. His gorge went down. He pushed himself to his feet, shaking off the hands on him. Blood was flowing down his naked torso.

Da Silva was losing blood at the rate of a dying deer in a winter hunt.

And the men in the yard were letting him die. Even the magister.

Aranthur focused. His earlier clarity was shredded, and he sought it again – that hyper-awareness.

'Hold him,' he shouted.

The sun was rising and he reached out to it for comfort and *power*.

'Stand away,' the magister said, misunderstanding. 'You are the winner, but he cannot defend—'

'Hold him,' Aranthur said, in something of his namesake's voice of *power*.

He struggled for his ritual – and once he found the peace of his words, he struggled the harder for his trance, and under his right hand, the man was dying. The dying soaked into him like blood, and he couldn't make it through the mud and blood to the calm place where magik lay. He tried image after image...

He sighed, opened his eyes, and was looking directly into the sun as it crested the distant eastern horizon, a perfect ball of red gold.

In a single exhalation, he had his trance and made his *working*. He didn't know how to knit muscle and bone. But he did know how to tell the skin and muscle to forbid the flow of blood, and he so ordered his opponent's body, and it obeyed.

He took a deep breath. It felt right. He opened his eyes, and then he was kneeling in the snow and blood, utterly spent.

Lecne helped him up, and he saw they were carrying the Westerner inside. The magister was standing with his hands on his hips.

Aranthur couldn't make himself smile. Or say anything witty.

The storm hit later that day, but the first Aranthur knew of it was waking in the same bed he'd awoken in three weeks before. Just for a moment he was at a loss – with no memory of the passage of time.

Lecne was sitting by the bed this time, sipping *chai* from a steaming cup. Outside the narrow window, snow fell as if there were mischievous Dhadhi sitting on the roof dumping the stuff from baskets.

'I want to come to the City and learn to be a swordsman,' Lecne said. 'But my mother and father refuse me.' He shrugged. 'Sun Rising, you were – something. I think even my sister is in love with you.'

Aranthur lay there for a long, long moment, and realised that he was alive. It was snowing outside, so the storm had come – the storm he thought he might not live to see.

'Oh,' he said, unable to find words to express it all. 'Oh, Lecne, I was a *fool*.' Then, rising on his elbow, he said, 'How's the Westerner – Da Silva?'

'Asleep,' Lecne said. 'And good riddance.'

An hour later, dressed and bandaged, Aranthur went down to the common room, where he found the Voltain playing dice with the magister.

Aranthur bowed.

'Happy to see you in health,' he said.

The Voltain laughed grimly. 'I've had worse from students. So I have to live to enjoy my defeat.' He nodded pleasantly. 'That's all right – I'm old enough to accept defeat.'

The magister rose and gave Aranthur a small bow.

'The victor,' he said, his usual mirthless smile coming to his lips.

Aranthur managed to laugh. In fact, it was quite spontaneous.

'I don't feel like a victor,' he allowed. 'What happened? He certainly hit me.' He touched the bandage at his throat.

The magister nodded. 'A finger's width more on target, and you'd have been dead before you struck the ground,' he said. 'As it was, he thrust past you and sliced your neck with his miss. And as he never actually troubled to parry your blow – hah! Had you cut for his neck and not his shoulder, I think you might have beheaded him. Even as it is, he may lose the arm.'

'But he's alive,' the Voltain said.

The magister sat back, putting his legs in front of the fire.

'I spent half a year putting this match together, and now I have nothing to show for it.' His eyes flicked from one to the other. 'But I have other competitors in mind.'

The Voltain nodded. 'I wonder if you are looking for teachers, Magister? Because I am out of a job in Volta. The small matter of a revolution.'

The magister nodded. 'I could find you a place, I expect.' He looked at Aranthur. 'I would take you as a student, if you were interested.'

Aranthur felt himself flush.

'I would be delighted,' he said. 'But I really must attend my studies.'

The magister's lips trembled, as if he was withholding a smile.

'I might find time to teach you anyway,' he said.

But Aranthur remembered the fear as well as the elation. And he thought *I'm not sure I ever want to do that again.* But he'd developed enough wisdom to avoid burning bridges.

'I'd be honoured,' he said with a bow.

Although the trip from the City to his home had taken him almost nine days and a sea voyage around Cape Athos and past the isle of Lenos, the ride back took only six. And everything about the trip was different. On the way out before Darknight, he'd worked passage on a small trader, a lugger with a lateen sail who moved along the edge of the main island, based on the port of Lonika. After days of working passage, he'd walked.

The route back was more expensive in every way. He rode the Nessan and led the bigger horse as a pack animal, and the two horses ate more than he did, rapidly biting deep into the money he'd kept. By the time he rode through the gates of Lonika, he knew he'd made a mistake in keeping them both; he lacked the baggage to pack, and the extra cost would defeat him.

On the other hand, entering Lonika was very different from leaving it. There were guards in old armour, the rust of the metal in their brigantines staining the cloth covering and fraying away in places so that they looked as if they had some armoured mange. But they were deeply respectful to a man in a doublet riding a fine horse. No one asked for a writ about his sword or even the conical case on his saddle bow. Rasce carried the clothing *malle*. When he left by the Megara Gate the next morning, the guards were just as respectful and just as negligent, although one mentioned, with a casual salute, that there were 'thieves and highwaymen' on the road.

'Arnaut bastards,' the guard said.

Aranthur took the advice seriously despite the insult. He rode carefully, watching the spruce-clad hills on either side. He was much lower than he had been on the Amynas River, and there was no snow here, unless you looked deep under the trees. The hills were high, and a dusting of snow showed on the highest trees. The landscape was beautiful; the rocky hills were stark above the trees all the way to the grey sky.

Aranthur kept his eyes down, on the trees either side of the ancient military road. In the Empire, most cargo went by ship; few places in the Great Archipelago were more than three days from the sea, at least in the south. So the military road was just wide enough for two wagons of the standard military weight to pass each other – stone sided, with a kerb stone all along the length, well maintained. The Empire had endless civil wars, but between fighting Atti and the Iron Circle and each other, the standing regiments maintained by the Emperor were used for road maintenance.

This road was well maintained. The verges were cut back the regulation twenty paces on either hand – a broad expanse of grass that allowed drovers to move herds of cattle along the roads, and feed them too.

At first it rained. The winter rain fell like misery, and Aranthur was wet through, and Ariadne was unhappy and skittish.

Aranthur saw other men on the road, and a few women. The women were farm wives returning from an early morning market, with empty baskets on their heads and voluminous straw capes that made them look like bundles of wet gold. The men were mostly farmers, although after the rain had stopped and the winter sun emerged, he passed a trio of soldiers in padded coats and tight breeches, using an instrument to measure something. If Aranthur had not been pressed for time, he might have stayed to watch them. Geometry interested him, and he suspected that they were making a map, a very new science from the East. At the Academy, they said the technique and the mathematics came from Zhou.

He passed more women. They were laughing, their straw cloaks rolled on their pack-baskets. One gave him a long look as he trotted by, and another whistled. Aranthur blushed.

He was still trying to imagine just how the tripod helped the soldiers take observations when he saw movement in the woods and a flash of metal. He immediately glanced back, but the soldiers were far out of sight, over a rise, the party of women well around the last curve.

He was alone on the road.

In turning, he gave contradictory orders to his horse. Ariadne wasn't used to such an inexperienced rider, although she was a joy to ride. When his weight shifted and he looked back, she turned, following his eyes. So, without intending, he turned a complete circle. Rasce, confused, followed them, but then tugged sharply at the leading rein, pulling free from Aranthur's hand as he put his hands down to hold on. Afraid of losing his seat, he leant forward.

By leaning forward, he told the little mare to *go faster.* Jolted by Ariadne's explosion of speed, he nonetheless leant over her neck. He *had* ridden before, but never such a well-trained horse.

She was at a gallop in ten strides, her neck stretched out, and Aranthur held on, his fingers in her mane as she raced along the road. He saw a pair of men on horses erupt from the tree line, and then they were behind him. It never occurred to him to draw his sword, or the *fusil.* It was all he could do to stay on Ariadne as she raced away, her steel-shod feet raising sparks on the road behind him. He looked back, his fear of the brigands greater than his fear of falling off. At least, he had to assume that they were brigands – they were big men on nags, with rusty weapons.

One was just putting a crossbow to his shoulder. Aranthur saw the man – saw his attention, his stillness, the gleaming tip of the bolt in the winter sun. But he didn't see it loosed, and it didn't hit him or Ariadne, and then he was flowing along the road like a ship in a good wind. The brigands were already slowing. There were only two of them. They shouted to each other, or so it appeared; they waved.

Rasce was right behind him, galloping heavily along the road without a lead rein, simply following the other horse. Aranthur's muscles began to relax. His fear was fading with every pace they left the outlaws behind. He sat back and Ariadne immediately slowed. In thirty more paces he had her reins taut, and he was able to pull her in, regain control, and slow her to an even walk.

She wasn't even breathing hard, despite her small size.

'You,' he said, 'are a fine horse.'

Ariadne snorted.

Rasce let rip a fart, as if to suggest that the same might not be true of the rider.

'I know,' Aranthur said. 'I have a lot to learn.'

He thought of the Select Militia. They served mounted and he had just received a lesson in humility; he wasn't as good a rider as he had thought. He whistled, looking back. The two men were riding for the trees.

Aranthur turned his mare and watched them.

The women, the farmers, the farm wives, and the soldiers. Aranthur included the last because they had had no weapons that he'd seen. All of them would come past here.

Didn't they deserve to be warned?

Aranthur cursed. It was an odd moment. He knew that if he turned and rode for the City, he was one sort of man; if he turned back, another sort. And yet, the odds were that the farmers were safe enough – three men with cudgels. The women might be at risk, but they might not come until night. The younger women had nothing to steal, but Aranthur was not naïve about what happened to women caught alone by bad men.

He might *die* if he went back.

On the other hand, he had a rifled *fusil* and a sword. He was probably better armed than the bandits.

If they were even bandits.

He tried to work out what else they might be, but the man had, without a doubt, loosed a bolt at him with deadly intent. That clinched it – and Aranthur was mature enough to admit that he was angry at being shot at. Vengeful, even. Which was stupid; he'd survived. But he wanted . . .

It was a little like the moment when he accepted the swordsman's challenge. He opened the top of the *fusil's* holster and took the weapon in his right hand. Then he put it back.

First things first. He dismounted and walked over to Rasce, who was quite calmly cropping grass, which seemed to be his sole interest in life. Aranthur hobbled him, which he accepted meekly enough. Then he took his sword off his baggage and strapped it to his saddle where it would ride, hilt up, under his left thigh. He had no idea whether he could draw it in combat, and when he had mounted, he tried.

More humility. Ariadne was patient, but the sword was very difficult to draw. It was straight, and long, and it took him some fiddling to find that he could only really draw it across his body, to the right. He could imagine the result of pricking his mount during the draw.

This all seemed insane. At least as insane as fighting a duellist in a duel.

Rasce ate more grass.

Aranthur pointed Ariadne at the edge of the woods, on the side from which the bandits had emerged, and let her pick her way across the soft grass of the verge. She was too sweet tempered to stop and crop grass, but she wanted to, and her eyes kept going to it. He gathered her a little to keep her eyes on the trees, and suddenly they were trotting.

He sat back and she walked. They were right at the edge of the big spruce trees now, and he turned her between the tall trees. The pine needles were deep, and the undergrowth mostly dead, and Ariadne had no trouble working her way along the slope.

It was hard to gauge how far he'd gone, but after a while, Aranthur drew his *fusil* and looked at the priming in the pan. He balanced the butt of the thing on his right thigh and watched the hillside like a bird of prey, his head turning back and forth, his heart hammering in his chest.

The mare was very quiet. It was surprisingly cold under the eaves of the wood, and the spruce needles were deep.

He came to a ravine that had been invisible from the road. He let Ariadne go up the ravine a few paces, but he was not a good enough rider to cross mounted, and he paused to reconsider the entire expedition. The idea of taking on the robbers, which out on the road had seemed wiser than trying to pass them again, now seemed very foolish indeed. It was cold and still in the woods.

Cold as the grave.

But even while his head whirled with doubts, he dismounted. Then, cautious as a deer in wolf country, he led Ariadne down a steep slope into the ravine. There was a tiny rill of water running at the base and he let her have a drink, his eyes glued to the opposite wall of the ravine. After what seemed to him a very long time, he pulled her up and walked to the best ramp up the far side, where the two of them scrambled up, making a lot of movement and noise.

Aranthur got to level ground to see the two bandits watching from no more than a dozen paces away.

'It's the boy with the horse,' said the man with the crossbow.

But he hadn't spanned it; it hung by its ring from his water-stained saddle, unloaded.

'Fucking *giving* himself to us,' said the other, drawing his sword.

'I want that horse,' Crossbow said.

Aranthur was dismounted, on the off side of his horse, holding her bridle. Every part of his plan was in ashes. He felt a fool – he should have seen them from the other side of the ravine.

'Don't get tricky, boy, and we won't fuck you up,' Crossbow said.

'Not more 'n a little,' said the other.

Aranthur raised the *fusil*. He chose Crossbow as the more dangerous man.

He pulled the trigger. The lock snapped – the shot crashed out instantly.

Crossbow's head snapped up, like a man loosening a crick in his neck, and the back of his head blew out, and he was lying on the spruce needles.

'Fuck me!' the other man said. 'You little cocksucker!'

But he was apparently paralysed, and simply sat on his horse, looking at his mate stretched on the ground.

The dead man's horse snorted, and backed up a few steps.

Aranthur turned the mare, watching the other man squint. He put a foot in a stirrup and mounted, his fear powering his leap so that he was secure in the saddle in a heartbeat. Ariadne turned a little, so that he was eye to eye with Squint, ten paces apart.

'Drop your sword,' Aranthur said, after a moment.

'Darkness blind you, you fucking...'

Then it all happened at once.

Squint put his long, barbed spurs to his nag.

Aranthur reached for the hilt of his sword.

Squint knew how to ride. His horse, whatever it lacked in grace, was well enough trained, and leapt forward like a warhorse. The man raised his sword over his head.

Aranthur drew. He drew straight up into an overhead *garde*. He didn't know a thing about fighting on horseback, but Ariadne was more forgiving, or just tired. She stood her ground against the bigger horse.

Squint cut.

Aranthur parried, although the other man's sword seemed to scrape down every inch of his long blade, the two sharp edges rubbing against each other with a wicked friction that screamed in the still air.

Ariadne turned, tracking her opponent, and Aranthur cut in time, but Squint had done all this before. He parried with the blade over his shoulder and crashed off into the dead underbrush towards the road.

Emboldened by his adversary's flight, Aranthur gave chase. Only when they burst out onto the verge, sixty paces apart, did it occur to him that the man might just be a scout or a lookout. When the fleeing man went straight across the verge, Aranthur followed him, but when he rode straight into the trees on the far side of the road, Aranthur's native caution finally overcame his boldness, and he reined in.

He was dismayed to see that his mare had a shallow cut on her neck. He'd cut her on the draw and she hadn't even reacted.

Then he sat on her back, the sword locked in his fist, and shook. It took him a few minutes to recover.

Very carefully, he replaced the sword in the scabbard.

He thought about it and then rode back to the dead man. Flies were already gathering, and thanks to the ravine, the site of the little battle was easy to find.

Battle? Murder?

Aranthur had an army of doubts, and he doubted them while he collected the *fusil* from where he'd dropped it. The lock was full of dirt, but the weapon appeared undamaged.

He went to have a look at the dead man, against his own will.

The dead man convinced him what he had to do.

*

An hour later, with the sun already dropping behind the nearest hills, he led the three soldiers into the woods and showed them the corpse.

The soldier in charge was an officer, a centark. He looked at the body for a moment.

'Sunrise,' he spat. 'I'm an engineer, not a watchman.'

He looked at the middle-aged woman who wore a sword at her hip, the only weapon the soldiers seemed to have.

She nodded. 'You have a *fusil*.'

'Yes.' Aranthur expected questions.

But she just nodded. 'What were you doing here?'

'I . . .' Aranthur felt a fool, and he felt fear, too. 'I passed you on the road, and the women . . . I was afraid these men would rob everyone. So I went back.'

'By yourself?' the woman said, her voice hinting that he should make some more admissions.

'Yes.'

The engineer shrugged. 'Fine. Are these the men we were warned about?'

The soldiers both shrugged.

'That crossbow has seen a lot of use,' the male soldier offered. 'One o' ours, I'll wager.'

He went and caught the horse, hobbled it with brutal efficiency, and took the weapon.

'Rack number, Imperial Armoury, Basilisk Regiment.' He tugged at the heavy cord. 'It works.'

'He tried to shoot me with it,' Aranthur said.

'Sunrise!' the centark said. 'Why didn't you say that before?'

The female soldier raised an eyebrow. 'You have a writ for a *gonne*?'

Aranthur produced his scholar's writ for his sword and then, when all three soldiers became more legalistic, the note scrawled in a very unscholarly hand by L. di. D.

The centark read it and shrugged.

'I know who he is,' he said. 'He don't make laws, though. Here's my ruling. Dekark, tell me if this sounds right. You help us dig the grave, we let you go. We have only your word that they attacked you, but then, they had weapons, and I saw you pass us today, and you're a Student. But son, do not, I beg you, ride around killing people with that toy. It's too fucking dangerous for a civilian, and frankly, you are not trained.'

The woman, addressed as dekark, nodded.

'I'm good with that. He's not harmless, is my read. Not a bad 'un, but not an angel. This the first man you've killed?'

The question surprised him. It disconcerted him. It was meant to – he understood that.

'Why?' he asked.

'Meaning you have. Cause you ain't puking yer guts out, and you seem pretty together.'

The male soldier tossed him a shovel.

'Bandits attacked an inn before Darknight,' Aranthur said.

All three soldiers suddenly became very focused.

'Where was this?' the centark asked.

Aranthur explained while he dug the grave. Darkness was falling, and the male soldier started a fire while the other two gathered wood. They brought up a mule from the road.

'I have another horse, hobbled. If we are camping here, may I fetch him?' Aranthur asked.

The centark shrugged. 'Take Nadia with you,' he said.

Aranthur nodded. 'Am I under . . . arrest?' he asked carefully.

'Not yet,' the dekark snapped.

The grave was finished before dinner was cooked: black beans and sausage. Aranthur picked out his sausage bits carefully and offered them to Nadia.

'You too proud for meat?' she said.

'We're told not to eat meat,' Aranthur said. 'Meat is the result of killing, and death . . .'

He paused, suddenly and painfully aware that he'd killed a man a few feet away.

The horses and the mule shuffled and snorted. The fire crackled.

'Seems to me like eatin' sausage would be the least o' yer worries,' the male soldier said. 'You sure don't dig like an aristo, though.'

'I'm a farm boy,' Aranthur said. 'My *patur* has a small farm up on the Amynas River.'

The soldiers all looked at him.

'Arnaut?' Nadia asked.

'Yes, ma'am.'

The centark sat back against a tree, using his pricker to pick his teeth.

'So you're an Arnaut. You have a fine *gonne* and a long sword and that high-priced nag *and* a pack horse. Have I got this right? And you saw bandits, saw them as a threat to society, and rode out to kill them. Right?'

Aranthur nodded. 'Yes, sir.'

'And you are a Student at the Academy,' he drawled.

'Yes, sir.'

Aranthur knew that being an Arnaut was not a path to good treatment, but the sudden chill in the air scared him.

'You're no more a fuckin' Student than I am an aristo,' the officer said. 'You stole the horse and the duds, and you're as much a bandit as that dead bastard.'

Aranthur didn't need a talisman to cast a simple *working*. He reached into the fire with his right hand and drew out a ball of flame so that it sat on his hand in the darkness. Conjuration, a little illusion. A *working* to protect his hand, a *working* to hold the heat of the flame, a conjuration of a little marsh gas to fuel it.

'Ah,' said Nadia.

'Fuck me!' The centark barked a laugh. 'All right, you're a Student.'

In the morning, the officer wrote a note on the back of the acolyte's note.

'Take this to the gate when you enter the City,' he said. 'They'll check your story, which saves me the trouble of repeating it. Don't try and take that *gonne* into the City without reporting it. We have ways of finding contraband weapons. *Ars Magika* ways. Understand?'

'And don't try to be the law,' Nadia said. 'Let us be the law.'

'Will you catch the other bandit?' Aranthur asked.

Nadia made a face. 'We're surveying to widen the road. Don't get any ideas.'

She did give him a chance to look at the instrument on the tripod. But the centark had already gone to fetch something, so he couldn't ask how the geometry worked.

He rode on.

*

In late afternoon on his sixth day from the inn, he rode up to the Lonika Gate of the great Wall of Megara. Historians said that Megara had been built by the very earliest men, in the Age of Bronze, thousands of years before. Certainly there were obelisks in the hippodrome that recorded events from the time of kings long forgotten, or featuring only in tribal poetry. There were whole rows of monuments decorated in lettering that was now indecipherable. One such row led to the Lonika Gate, which was sometimes called the Great Gate. It was itself a square fortress, almost a hundred feet high, the curtain walls loopholed for all kinds of torsion artillery and the more recent heavy *gonnes*, as well as having niches for statues – Sophia, of course, and a fine triangle, ten paces tall, hanging over the central gate, in black and white marble and shining gold, covered in angels, the symbol of the old Empire before the fall. The Great Gate had a garrison and doubled as the headquarters for almost all military affairs in the City, and the streets behind the gate were packed with lawyers and notaries and married quarters right up to the Square of the Pantheon, the military temple where all gods were worshipped.

Aranthur approached the gate with trepidation.

He dismounted, squatted a few times to ease his strained leg muscles, and reported to a dekark who sat just inside the barrier of the gate behind a desk, checking customs marks and wax seals on goods.

The man looked up, asked Aranthur's business, and sent him up the winding stairs of the north tower.

'Your horses'll be safe here, Student.' He smiled. The smile relaxed Aranthur considerably.

He went up the north tower and spoke to a succession of soldiers who were completely uninterested in his tale, until he was shunted into an office with a slim young man in a velvet coat. The man had fine boots, a long nose, and appeared to have no eyelashes.

'You have a letter of introduction?' the man said in an aristocratic drawl of educated Liote.

'Yes, milord.'

Aranthur bowed and handed over Drako's letter.

The officer sat down behind a table, put his boots up on it, and leant his folding stool back until it seemed to Aranthur as if it must collapse. He read one side, and then the other.

Aranthur watched him flip the piece of vellum over twice, and then a third time.

The stool went forward with a *clunk*. The man produced a wax tablet, the kind students used, and he proceeded to ask questions.

When had Aranthur left the Academy? What day exactly? What ship carried him? When had he passed the gate at Lonika? Who had passed him? And so on. The questions were polite, and very precise.

Aranthur didn't see any point in resisting, so he answered them all.

'Well, young man,' the officer said, although he didn't look five years older than Aranthur himself. 'You have had an interesting three weeks, can we agree on that?'

'Yes, milord.'

'Spare me the milord. I'm likely to be your Centark – Parsha Equus. Cup of wine?'

Aranthur thought about it. 'Yes,' he said. 'Please.'

The officer poured two cups of wine, gave Aranthur one, and sat.

'You are a Student,' he said. 'Technically a citizen of the City and a member of the Militia.'

'Yes, milord. Er, sir.'

Aranthur had learned these things on the day of his arrival.

'Are you willing to join the Selected Men?' the officer asked. 'Soon to be the Selected Men and Women, I'll note,' he said with a smile. 'That will be easy to shout on a battlefield.'

'Yes, I would.'

'You understand that means twenty days of drill a year, and some ceremonies,' the man said, with apparently no attention. He was reading over his notes on the wax tablet. Aranthur was fascinated to note that the man's marks in the wax were not in any language he spoke. Not even in a set of letters he knew.

'Yes,' Aranthur said.

The man raised an eyebrow.

'There's pay. The parades are pleasant enough. The fieldwork can be enjoyable or indescribably tedious. You have a horse and arms. I can offer you twenty silver crosses on the drum for joining. And you can keep your *gonne*, as long as you leave it here. You can keep a horse in the stables – it's far cheaper than keeping one in a tavern or a livery.'

Aranthur smiled. 'I have already agreed. But you make it sound better and better. Sir.'

The officer smiled his quirky, eyebrow-less smile.

'I do, don't I? The thing is, we're soldiers, even if we're hardly ever used. In a war, gods save us, we'd be a city cavalry regiment.' He looked up. Just for a moment, he looked like a different man – older, less kind. 'Dying on a Zhouian lance is one hell of a way to pay back the cheap fodder for your horse.'

Aranthur gulped. 'Zhouian?'

The officer smiled a lopsided grin.

'Silly thing to say. Bastards are too far away to fight. It just lights me up that people join to save money, or get away from their wives, or what have you.'

'Life is being a soldier,' Aranthur said, quoting an ancient philosopher.

'Good attitude,' the man said. 'Do you belong to one of the factions? You're an Arnaut – you can't be a Lion. Are you a Red? A White?'

Aranthur was vaguely aware, from a year at the Academy, that the Lions were conservative, the Whites were more open, the Reds were religious and the Blacks . . . There were blacks, he thought.

'I'm a Student,' he said.

The officer smiled. 'Excellent.' He stood up. 'Aranthur Timos. Raise your hand and swear.'

Half an hour later, Aranthur Timos had stabled Rasce in the military stables at the Great Gate and seen his *fusil* into the hands of an elderly armourer.

'Sunset's Children, soldier!' the old man spat. 'It's not clean!'

Aranthur was stricken with the memory of dropping the spent weapon into the holster after no more than pulling the dirt out of the lock.

'Just this once, I'll clean her for ye,' the old man said. 'Blessed Triangle, you've made a right mess of the lock. You know how to maintain this? It's a fine weapon. Look at the fuckin' rust. Brought up in a barn?'

'Yes, sir,' Aranthur said.

The old man's head turned and the eyes blazed at him.

'Don't call me sir. I'm an armourer. I fix things you lot break or damage. What's your name?'

He wrote Aranthur a ticket in a spidery hand – old Liote, as if the man was so old he dated from before the New Empire.

Aranthur had never entered from the landward side before, and he was lost almost as soon as he cleared the barracks and the Pantheon Square. There was a broad parade ground, called the Field of Rolan, for the old god of war from the Twelve, just north of the temple. He hadn't known there was such a broad, open field in the whole of the City, but on the far side there was a low wall with battlements, and another gate. Once he was through that, he was in a quarter of the City he'd never seen before. There were tenements, big buildings that towered over the muddy canals, seven storeys tall and packed with people. Their inhabitants stood around on the street, and there were open fires and street vendors, but Aranthur didn't like the looks he got with Ariadne and her fine saddle.

If the City was a thumb sticking out into the Great Sea, he had just entered from the hand, and he was now walking due east, towards the Academy atop the central ridge. The City had canals all around the edges, where hundreds of tiny islands had been joined to the peninsula ages before to make more land, but the Old Town was up on the ridge above and the Academy stood at the very crest. Otherwise, the rich favoured the canals and their fresh inundation of seawater every time the tide changed. The poor, aside from scholars, lived on the ridges. An aqueduct carrying the city's fresh water ran down the ridge from the Great Gate. The huge stone trestles carrying the Aqueduct ran from the distant mountains to the reservoir behind the Academy like the fin on a whale. There was supposed to be a wide boulevard under the arches, but the tidal waves of refugees from the fighting far to the east had turned the dry ground under the Aqueduct into a slum, a long ribbon of desperate humanity, and not a good place for an apparently well-to-do young man with a horse.

Despite their reputation, though, the Eastern refugees were in general quiet and well behaved. The beggars were aggressive, and the prostitutes were far too young. Aranthur had admitted to himself in his first year at the Academy that he avoided the 'Spine' under the Aqueduct because he didn't really like to see how bad it was there.

He was looking for a place to turn off the street and descend to a more savoury neighbourhood – some streets had steps or staircases unsuitable for a horse – when his eyes caught a young man with dirty hair and a long brown robe. The young man was kneeling with two beggars, and his eyes locked with Aranthur's.

He had a strong face, but he was very young, and his eyes were mild.

'Lost?' he asked, rising almost at Aranthur's feet from the filthy street. He smelt.

Aranthur took a step back. 'No, I know where I am.'

The young man nodded. 'Only, that horse will be a temptation to some of the young men, so please leave.'

Aranthur nodded.

'And if you came to buy sex, I will curse you,' the boy said.

'You're Byzas,' Aranthur said.

'You are Arnaut,' the young man said. 'What of it?'

'I don't buy sex,' Aranthur said, a little more archly than he intended.

The young man shrugged.

'Go with the god, then,' he said, raising a hand in blessing.

Then he squatted by two men sharing a hookah. He had something like a playing card in his hand, and they both looked at it, and then Aranthur was past them.

Aranthur turned and walked south along the First Canal. The way was narrow, and he had to walk his horse, but soon enough he emerged from the tenements. The water in the canal became seawater; the sidewalk, locally called a *fondemento*, along the canal widened and was made of stone, and he could ride again. He passed a row of palaces as opulent as the tenements had been poor and emerged onto the waterfront, the Fondemento Sudo, which ran all the way along the south shore of the City, pierced by a hundred canals and lined with ships. But as one of the City's main thoroughfares, it had bridges over all the canals. Aranthur walked and rode along through the afternoon, gawking openly at the huge round ships from distant islands and the plethora of smaller ships: single-masted coasters from Atti across the strait and from the Arnaut ports to the west; a low black galley from Masr; an enormous grain ship built of *vyrk* bark, from Magua or Ocvouych, far to the south; a trio of heavy merchant ships from Lydia, their sides painted a magnificent vermilion.

But where the Grand Canal crossed under the Fondemento Sudo, at the Pontos Magnos, was the largest ship he had ever seen – a four-masted round ship as big, it seemed to him, as the whole Academy. It was unloading straight onto the fondemento. And what it was unloading, from a giant crane powered by a hundred longshoremen, was a *monster*.

The thing screamed like a fiend from the Twelver hell. It was massive – ten times the size and weight of a horse, with massive hind legs covered in green scales and sabre teeth in a long narrow mouth. It hung from a pair of heavy straps around its midsection between its colossal legs, and it did not enjoy the process of being unloaded.

The engineer in charge of the crane was giving orders, carefully, to an army officer. A dozen men and women in the red coats of palace functionaries stood in various attitudes of excitement and boredom.

The monster hung suspended over the fondemento, swaying very gently back and forth on the huge crane.

The crane rotated and Aranthur couldn't decide where to look. The crane was the largest he'd ever seen. The monster was a drake, a near-mythical creature Aranthur knew had once lived in the Soiliote Hills; there were still stone nests on the highest peaks. Now the only drakes were in the East, or so people said.

Across the Grand Canal, Aranthur saw a coach, a rare sight in the City where the streets were too narrow. The coach itself was gilded, and had windows of glass.

He looked at the coach for a moment and then back to the drake. People around him discussed the monster and the good fortune it would bring the city. They began to crowd forward, trying to touch the magnificent thing.

A dozen soldiers armed only with staves were keeping the crowd back. Aranthur's mare gave him a better sightline than almost anyone else, and he sat and watched while Ariadne fidgeted and informed him of how little she liked crowds . . . and monsters. She'd begun to remind him of Nenia, because she was brave and calm, but now she was more like Kati, who had been much on his mind of late. To very little purpose . . .

The ship appeared to be from Atti. Or at least, many of the men on the dock were soldiers and sailors of Atti, in tall, conical red hats or turbans, bigger or smaller depending on taste and expense. The Academy was full of Attians, and although they drank no wine, at least in public, they were otherwise virtually identical to their cousins in Megara – light-haired, light-eyed, with pale skin that took a deep tan in summer. The saying went *Between Byzas and Atti there is only wine.* Attians did not drink wine.

But among the Attian soldiers was a man who had to be from Zhou, the fabulous kingdom of the East. He stood apart, in a short robe over heavy silk pantaloons and gaiters. He wore a long, curved sword unlike any of those from Atti or the Empire; his hair was tied back so tightly that it seemed to stretch his eyes. His khaftan was a lurid blue-green silk and his teeth were painted black.

The Zhouian soldier's eyes met Aranthur's twice. They were only twenty paces apart, and Aranthur was sitting up above the crowd. The second time, Aranthur smiled, and the Zhouian flashed a black-toothed smile in return. Behind him, ten paces away, the coach window opened and the Duke of Volta leant out, a look of anger on his face. He was watching the drake.

He made a motion.

The monster screamed. It was a long, angry sound. The man with the black teeth whirled and raised a hand, and a spray of crystal rose from it as if he'd thrown a glass of water in slow motion. The droplets, or crystals, caught the brilliant sunshine and Aranthur could feel the *power*, the raw *saar*, displayed.

Aranthur glanced back at the duke as the man slammed his window shut after throwing something into the street.

The crowd cheered as the monster's feet touched the ground, and they shuffled back, but the drake got his feet under him and stretched like an enormous cat. He tossed his head and gave a shrieking cry that terrified the crowd all over again. The drake looked pleased with himself.

But the handlers were not alarmed. Two women and a man in Zhouian trousers and short robes came forward with metal wands in their hands, and they laughed and clapped. The shortest woman fed something to the monster, putting her hand right in his mouth. He sat back and gave a series of very polite belches, and the crowd, calmed, laughed.

The drake rolled his neck and breathed fire. The monster was twice as tall as a warhorse, with lustrous green scales almost too green to be real, like a lurid dream. There was a jewelled collar on his neck and his talons, each as long as a man's hand, were gilded.

The Zhouian soldier came forward and spoke to the engineer, and then to one of the palace officers.

'That's the show, friends,' the palace herald bellowed. He was a big man with a thick beard, who wore the green tabard of the Heralds' Guild with a red border for the palace, and his voice was augmented with *power*. 'We don't want our new guest to panic on the docks. Please disperse. The Emperor will have open days to come and see this honoured guest in the Imperial Palace. Please disperse.'

Citizens in Megara didn't need to be told twice; the wooden staves hit hard, when the soldiers were ordered to use them. The crowd melted away. Because Ariadne hated crowds, Aranthur held her still until most of the people were gone, and then dismounted. She was trembling, her whole attention focused on the monster.

He fed her an apple, which she took daintily around her bit.

'Time to move on, son,' a soldier said.

'My horse is scared,' Aranthur said.

The soldier made a face. 'Smart horse. Move on.'

Ariadne relented at the sound of some calming words and the taste of the apple, and condescended to be led up the ramp to the first square, which was lined in taverns and stables. Richer students at the Academy kept their animals there.

Aranthur needed to check the prices of stable hire, but first he rode across the big bridge and down the *fondemento* to where the duke's coach had been. He dismounted, watching the Zhouians leading the drake away to the east towards the palace. The gangplank went back up into the ship and the great crane was being dismantled.

He walked Ariadne along the waterfront, looking at the edge of the street. He stooped and found what he sought – a dirty scrap of parchment with a hint of gold leaf on it.

It looked like a complex evocation chart, the sort of thing a relatively amateurish caster would use to cast a complicated *working*.

Aranthur folded it neatly and put it away in a saddlebag and went back to his self-appointed task of finding a stable. He spent half an hour determining that he could not afford ten nights stabling at any of them, and the social distinction of owning a horse in the City was brought home to him. His father resented the cost of keeping a 'hayburner' on a farm. In the City, the cost was exorbitant, more than a bed and dinner at the Inn of Fosse.

He had just emerged from the Sunne in Splendour, the best-known hostel on the square above the waterfront, when he saw the soldier from Zhou emerge from the Rat, across the square. Their eyes met.

Aranthur smiled again and the Zhouian crossed the square to him. It was only twenty paces across, with a bridge running across the Grand Canal to an even smaller square.

Aranthur could tell the young man was coming his way. He dismounted, and bowed holding his horse, the court bow that was taught to all new Academy students – the bow that the Courtesy Master said was never wrong.

The Zhouian stopped five paces away, put a hand on his sword hilt, and returned the bow, duplicating Aranthur's exactly. He never took his eyes off Aranthur, which gave the bow a different flavour.

'Aranthur Timos,' he said.

The other man was younger. His eyes were remarkable, both in shape and colour, and he looked very young, with smooth skin and delicate features, thin lips, and black teeth. He raised one thin black eyebrow but a very small fraction.

'Ah,' he said, as if considering the matter for the first time. 'A name, of course. My name, to be precise.' He smiled, as if at some private joke. 'You may call me Ansu.'

He offered his sword hand, somewhat hesitantly, to shake, and Aranthur took it. Both noblemen and farmers shook hands but it was not a City custom.

'Timos, I need a favour and I know no one here.'

Ansu bobbed, as if making a bow, but his face was frozen; it gave away none of the little cues that the Masters had taught Aranthur to look for in conversation.

'At your service,' Aranthur said. It was odd to be addressed by his surname, the way noblemen did.

'I need a place to stay. I . . .' The young man looked away. 'I don't have any money, and your people seem to require money.'

Aranthur nodded. 'All of the inns and taverns will require money,' he agreed. 'No matter how important you are.' He smiled to try to intimate that he was making light of the situation.

It was a little like the duel, and the bandits in the woods. He could walk away and disclaim any responsibility. He was, after all, a penniless student.

He shrugged. 'I am only a penniless student. However, I have a small room at the Academy, and I can no doubt find you a bed.'

'Ah, you are Student?' Ansu bowed. 'I hope to be a Student. I have some *power*. How hard would it be?'

Aranthur grinned. 'Not so hard. I saw you cast on the docks.'

Ansu's brow furrowed, almost theatrically.

'Yes. Someone in the crowd sought to arouse my guest-friend.' The Zhouian raised an eyebrow. 'Drakes, when angry, are . . . difficult to control.'

'What did you do?' Aranthur asked.

Ansu shrugged. 'I cut the emanation off from its source. What would you have done?'

Aranthur just smiled.

Cut off from the source. What a brilliant idea.

'Will you teach me that trick?' Aranthur asked. 'Is that Zhouian magik?'

Ansu laughed. 'I suppose it is. Of course, but it will only work against a very uneducated person.'

'You may be surprised.'

In fact, the greatest crisis awaiting him was that Kati had returned from her distant homeland to find that her penknife wasn't returned. However, the slim young man with the enormous sword seemed to delight her. Aranthur promised to run back down the stairs to her room and return the knife as soon as Syr Ansu was 'settled'.

'I am very sorry,' he said.

She raised an eyebrow. 'The beautiful boy is your friend?'

Aranthur was painfully aware that another young woman was shrugging into a gown behind her in the room.

'I just met him. He arrived with the drake,' he said, and left her in her doorway.

None of his three room-mates had returned. The room was just that: an attic room, with blankets hung to hide each of the three beds that stood in the gabled windows; a big work table set up under the fourth gable; a tiny flue going into the external chimney, and the small hearth. The room was large enough for four men who got along very well, but bitterly cold.

Aranthur got the brazier lit while Ansu looked out the window.

'Where are the servants?' he asked.

'There are no servants,' Aranthur said as he searched for the penknife.

Ansu nodded. 'Ah. It is cold. Do you have something I could wear?'

His Liote was perfect – too perfect. He had been thoroughly trained, but his enunciation was alien.

Aranthur fetched him one of Daud's robes. The man was a Byzas and his parents lived in the City. He was likely to be the last one back from holidays.

'I would also like to have sexual intercourse,' the young man said. 'Can you tell me where to find a woman to perform sex for me?'

Aranthur paused; his thoughts were full of warming his room, and finding a stable for his horse, and Kati's roommate and her naked, beautiful back, and the missing penknife.

'What?' he asked.

'I do not know the word. For a person who performs sex. For money. I want one.' He paused. 'I have been at sea for a long time.'

Aranthur smiled nervously. 'You have no money.'

'I will borrow it from you, I hope,' the young man said. 'Fear not! I would never cheat such a woman.'

Aranthur dropped into one of their reading chairs.

'Syr Ansu,' he said, using the Byzas honorific, 'we are forbidden to make use of prostitutes at the Academy, just as we are forbidden meat.'

'Prostitute!' Ansu said. 'That is the word! Or *Porne* in Ellene.' He struck his head, quite hard, with the palm of his hand – hard enough that his face flushed. 'No meat?'

'Meat is the product of death,' Aranthur said.

Ansu smiled knowingly. 'So is death. Have you killed?'

Aranthur felt as if the ground was dropping away beneath him – as if he was on Ariadne and she was galloping away and he could not control her.

He met the Zhouian soldier's eye. 'Yes.'

'I knew it,' the young man said. 'So. What is meat, then?' He smiled, and showed his black teeth. 'It is a rule. That is what you tell me.'

'Yes.'

The young man pursed his lips. 'So – I will go somewhere. Tell me where?'

'I don't know,' Aranthur admitted.

He could imagine the Aqueduct, and the ribbon of desperate

refugees. Some of them had been prostitutes. He was sure of it. He thought of the man in the brown robe, with his gentle eyes and harsh words.

'Bah, I am ungracious. I will wait until you want to go with me, and we can buy sex together.' He smiled.

Aranthur smiled back uncertainly.

'I need to stable my horse.'

'Ah,' Ansu said. 'I thank all of my ancestors that you were mounted, so that I knew you were noble, and a warrior. It is difficult for us to tell, among you . . .' He paused, and smiled. 'Among you Westerners.'

Aranthur rose. 'I am a warrior, of sorts. But I am only a farmer's son.'

Ansu bowed. 'Many of our greatest would say the same, and you speak like a gentleman.'

Aranthur surrendered. 'Of course. I'll be back.'

'Could we have food?' Ansu asked.

Aranthur took a deep breath.

'Of course,' he said.

On his way down he knocked at Kati's door and handed over her precious penknife.

She looked different. He couldn't exactly spot how, but she looked tired and worried.

'Is something wrong?' he asked.

'Everything is wrong at home. Everything. I may not even be able to stay here.' She looked into her room. 'I can't talk now.'

Aranthur was absurdly happy that she flashed a smile before she closed the door.

The next week passed in a torrent of crises. The horse went to a stable owned by the brother of Aranthur's sometime employer in the leather trade. Aranthur worked four shifts, finished a project for his fine arts class, layering gesso he'd made himself on an oak board, and took two fencing lessons from Vladith, his master. His room-mates stayed wherever they were, which complicated his life. Syr Ansu had moved in, and now sat in the best reading chair for most of each day, although on Fifth Day, Aranthur returned from the library to find Kati and both of her Eastern room-mates sitting cross-legged on his floor, playing *Kho* against Syr Ansu. He was leaning on one elbow, lying full length on the floor and smoking *bhang* from a pipe, which was strictly forbidden in the room – in any room.

Kati rose and kissed his cheek and introduced him to the other two women, who were both from Atti. Aranthur chose to ignore the smoke, and tried to hide his astonishment when the three women lit their own pipes.

'You said it was bad at home,' he said to Kati.

She shrugged; her features relaxed.

'There is war. Northerners, nomads. But perhaps something worse. My brothers have gone to fight and my mother wants me home.' She shrugged. 'Safi is not as it used to be. Everyone fears the nomads. And their masters, the Pure.'

'Pure what?' Aranthur asked.

She smiled. 'That is a good question,' she said languorously. 'But I am smoking *bhang* and I don't want to go there.'

Aranthur let it go.

The next day Daud appeared at mid-morning. He bowed to Syr Ansu and reclaimed his robe.

'Good job,' he said. 'Fast work.'

'Fast work how?' Aranthur asked quietly.

'Del went home and he's not coming back. We needed a fourth to make rent.' He looked at the Zhouian. 'Must he wear that sword all the time? He looks ridiculous. And the place stinks of stock. And *bhang*.'

Aranthur shrugged.

Daud shrugged. 'Fine, I don't really care.'

Aranthur captured the reading chair at midday and was deep in reading Kleitos, one of the most ancient philosophers, who, luckily for first year students, wrote in very simple, very clear Ellene. His *Words* were brief and sometimes pithy, sometimes deep, sometimes incomprehensible. '*War is the King and Father of All; some men he makes kings, and others, slaves,*' for instance, seemed obvious but dated from the Time of Troubles. '*All elements come to man from Fire,*' was another, and it was so odd that he went and searched up the verb to make sure he had it right. '*Time is a river, and no man can dip his foot in the same place twice,*' took Aranthur half the afternoon.

He looked up to realise that Syr Ansu was standing patiently by the reading chair.

'I didn't want to interrupt your reading,' Ansu said with a little bow. 'I need clean body linens and some clothes for court. I meet the Emperor tomorrow.'

'We wash our own clothes,' Aranthur said.

'Do we?' Ansu looked out of the window, his face blank. 'I do not. I wouldn't even know how.'

Aranthur eventually surrendered. He was washing his own clothes, and he added the Zhouian undergarments, which were at least simple. He washed them in the courtyard, in hot water, with one of Kati's room-mates, Atima. She giggled too much, but she was a good companion, and the time flew by, and he hung the washing on the line for both of them, being taller. Then he ambushed his silent room-mate, Arnaud, and asked him if he knew anyone who owned court dress.

Arnaud shrugged.

'Syr Mikal Kallinikos?' he suggested, and went back to reading.

Arnaud was a Westerner, from the barbarian islands west of Volta, but he was courteous and quiet and a good student.

Aranthur nodded and then went across the narrow street and knocked at the door of his richest acquaintance from first term.

Mikal Kallinikos had a whole suite of rooms to himself, and nonetheless was a good student whose purse was, within reason, at the service of his classmates. He was a conservative, and Aranthur had seen him in the red, gold and black colours of the Lions, the Academy club of old, conservative and sometimes violent aristocrats. The Lions tended to dislike 'foreigners' and above all Arnauts. Despite that, he and Aranthur had got along well enough to share an alchemical experiment in Practical Philosophy. He was known to be of an Imperial House.

'Timos!' he said, like the aristocrat he was.

'Syr Kallinikos,' Aranthur responded with a cautious bow. 'I have a problem. A friend who has an interview at court. Tomorrow. No clothes.'

'Who is he?' the nobleman asked.

'A soldier from Zhou.'

'Ah, now you interest me,' Kallinikos said. 'You know a man from Zhou?'

Aranthur nodded.

Fifteen minutes later, as the Academy clock rang the hour, Mikal Kallinikos was exchanging bows with Syr Ansu.

'Where did you find him?' Kallinikos asked.

'On the waterfront,' Aranthur said quietly.

'He's no soldier,' Kallinikos said. 'Ansu isn't even a name. It's a title.'

He turned to Syr Ansu and bowed deeply, and spoke in a fluid language with too many consonants.

驿外断桥边
寂寞开无主
已是黄昏独自愁
更著风和雨
无意苦争春
一任群芳妒
零落成泥碾作尘
只有香如故

Ansu smiled. 'Tolerable. And one of my favourite poems.'

He translated for Aranthur, in Byzas.

Near the broken bridge outside the fortress,
I go, lonely and disoriented.
It is dusk and I am alone and anxious,
especially when the wind and rain start to blow.
I do not mean to fight for Springtime,
I would rather be alone and envied by the crowd.
I will fall down, become earth, be crushed to dust.
My glory will be the same as before.

'It's better in Zhouian,' Kallinikos said with a smile. He turned and bowed very deeply to Ansu. 'Come to my rooms and I'll find you some court clothes. They won't be your – hmm – style, old chap. Or should I say, Highness. But I'll see you right.'

'The blessing of the hundred and forty-four be on your head,' Syr Ansu said with a deep bow. 'I have been worried about humiliation. I considered not going. But Tauri will miss me.'

Kallinikos, familiar with the court, looked at Aranthur.

'You are connected with the arrival of the drake?'

He winked at Arnaud, who sighed and went back to reading.

'I brought it across four seas,' the Zhouian said proudly. 'Tauri volunteered to come. To bring the drakes back here.'

'Tauri is the handler?' Kallinikos asked, opening a chest.

'Tauri is the drake.' Ansu smiled.

'A gift from your king?' Aranthur asked.

Why didn't I ask all these questions a week ago? he wondered.

'From my father,' the young man said. 'But the drakes, as you call them, are not slaves. He is a guest, not a gift.'

'For the Emperor?' Kallinikos asked.

'To save you from the barbarians,' Ansu said. 'The so-called Pure. They want to kill all the drakes. Don't you know?'

Aranthur nodded. 'I have heard of the Pure.'

Kallinikos turned his head, a little too suddenly.

'As have I,' he said.

That the Crown Prince of Zhou had been staying in their rooms for a week was a wonder, but it was quickly buried in the weeks of classes. Syr Ansu went to his interview in the palace and never returned. Kallinikos reported back midweek, by which time all of them were buried in schoolwork, that he was now living in a wing of the palace. A week later the young Zhouian was almost a memory, although Kati pretended to pine for him and blamed him that she was now a smoker. The only enduring effect of his stay, a month later, was that Kallinikos became a friend rather than an acquaintance. The two, who shared most of their classes, spent time dissecting a frog together in the nobleman's rooms. It was safer there, because dissection was technically against the law. They spent a good deal of time talking about philosophy and politics.

Kallinikos was tall and thin and had a long nose like most Byzas, with skin the colour of old oak, and coppery hair, but his widely spaced, deep brown eyes and long hair made him look like an emperor, and in fact dozens of emperors were in his family tree, although all from before the revolution.

Over the corpse of the frog, Aranthur was blunt.

'Why are you, a Lion, willing to dissect a frog with a lowly Arnaut?'

'Oh, the Lions,' Kallinikos said. 'Hand me the flint scalpel, there's a good chap. We need more towels. Chiraz!'

Chiraz, his all-round servant, appeared as if by magic.

'Towels, and two glasses of red wine.'

'Syr,' Chiraz said.

'I'm no longer a Lion,' Kallinikos said.

Aranthur was drawing the frog's intestines. He had wondered if this was the case, as Kallinikos hadn't worn his club's colours in a week.

'Oh?' he said.

Kallinikos was staring at the frog blood on his fine lace cuffs.

'Shit,' he muttered. Then he glanced at Aranthur. 'Listen, old boy. Things change. People change, even blue-bloods like meself. And I met a girl. A woman, rather.' He leant over. 'Aploun!' he said. 'You draw like a professional.'

Aranthur smiled. 'I practise.'

'Hah, we'll score in the top five, I guarantee it. Look at that! You even got the way the guts glisten.'

Aranthur sat back and stretched, and Chiraz appeared with two glasses of red wine.

'Have one yourself, Chiraz,' the aristocrat drawled.

'Of course, syr,' Chiraz said. He bowed and withdrew.

Kallinikos drank his off.

'I met this woman...' He looked at Aranthur. And shrugged. 'I promised her not to talk about her. But she's... Armean.' He shrugged, as if this explained everything. 'A noble,' he hurried to say. 'And a Magas. But she's taught me things...' He looked at Aranthur again. 'The Zhouian. You. And my Armean. Really, the Lions are so full of shit.' The last comment came out very quickly, angrily even. 'You believe things, and then one day you discover that... it's all horse shit.'

Aranthur had nothing to say, so he kept drawing.

'You are the first Arnaut I've ever been friends with,' Kallinikos admitted.

'I hear we make good, loyal friends,' Aranthur managed.

'More wine!' Kallinikos shouted.

Because of their new friendship, Kallinikos joined Aranthur at the *salle*, learning the sword. Master Vladith was always delighted to have more students, especially those who paid in advance, and he was openly pleased to have a member of the nobility. Kallinikos disliked being fawned upon, and made a wry face when he found his arms displayed over the door at the next lesson, but he was a good pupil, having danced and fenced as a boy.

Aranthur, for his part, had begun to lose his admiration for Master Vladith. He blamed Master Sparthos for the change. He observed his master's pettiness, his attention to details that seemed to have no bearing on the art, his insistence on the grandiose courtesy and elaborate terminology that often dominated his lessons.

It was not all clear sailing, being friends with Kallinikos. The aristo resented the Eastern refugees under the Aqueduct and spoke about them too often and too broadly for Aranthur's comfort. He felt that women needed to concentrate on having children and raising them, and he could be insensitive to anyone who didn't meet his own rather limited standards.

'Arnauts. A race of cattle thieves,' he spat, when an Arnaut soldier bumped him in the street. And on another occasion, he looked around the *salle* and referred to his fellow sword students as a society of felons.

And yet, despite his occasional bursts of petty intolerance and his instinctive leanings to the privilege to which he'd been born, he also had excellent, almost supernatural social skills. He was sensitive, even empathetic, about everyone he included in his acquaintance. He was intensely curious, and he was ultimately capable of changing his mind – about Easterners, about Arnauts, about geometry. It was this last quality that made him such a desirable companion. He would, sometimes, in the midst of a heated argument, smile suddenly and say 'Good point' or 'I hadn't thought that'. He was alone of all Aranthur's friends in this regard.

Vladith treated Kallinikos as the superior swordsman of the pair from his second lesson, and often paid him small, flattering compliments on his handling of the sword, the sort of accurate flattery that he never aimed at Aranthur.

All of that Aranthur could have tolerated, but a month into the new term, at the termination of a lesson, Vladith invited him to fence with heavy weapons – the long swords that were almost out of fashion but were still widely used for battle. Aranthur was aware that he was going to be demonstrated on – that Vladith was using him as a display of his own talents, probably to Mikal Kallinikos. There followed several painful minutes in which he was hit repeatedly by blows he didn't know: baffling feints and dodges he hadn't been taught. It was a little like dealing with his Practical Philosophy Magos, except that the blows hurt. Aranthur set his shoulders, took up his guard, and didn't complain.

But the next time his master started a series of feints, Aranthur raised his sword and thrust, using the *tempo* that his master was wasting by waving his sword tip in tiny feints.

His point went right over the master's hands and flexed against his neck guard.

A long breath later, his master's sword smashed into his helmet with so much vehemence that he was knocked to the floor. Despite the padding on the helmet, which was very like a cavalryman's closed helmet, but lighter, his head hurt.

'You should guard yourself,' Vladith said. 'That was really foolish.' The man turned to the other students. 'A typical idiot's error – choosing to throw his own blow instead of parrying mine.'

Aranthur had the habit of obedience. He submitted to another dozen attacks, and waited for Vladith to unbend, but the man was clearly angry. At the end he gave Aranthur a very small bow.

'Your ... *heritage* betrays you, those angry pokings and silly postures. Be very careful. You swing too hard and people will not cross blades with you. I suppose it's to be expected.'

Aranthur tried to breathe regularly.

Kallinikos frowned. 'But ...' he began.

The master turned, all oily good humour.

'I fear young Timos needs a dressing down,' he said, like one conspirator to another.

Kallinikos shook his head. 'He hit you. In your wasted *tempo*. While you played with his sword.'

Vladith drew himself up.

'Oh,' he said archly. 'In your years of fencing experience?'

Kallinikos shrugged. 'And dancing. A little harp. *Tempo* is *tempo*, Master. I think you are wrong, and should apologise.'

The three of them stood a moment.

'I *see*.' Vladith was clearly stung. 'In fact, I see a great deal.'

He turned on his heel and walked away.

Aranthur left the *salle* floor, stripped off the heavy arming coat and borrowed steel gauntlets and helmet, and touched his head, where he had a lump.

In the canal boat, headed home – one of the advantages of Syr

Kallinikos' friendship was his willingness to spend money on his friends
– he touched his scalp again.

'Thanks for standing up for me,' Aranthur said.

'You hit him, in case you were wondering, old boy.' Kallinikos raised
an eyebrow. 'Your sword fairly bent double.'

'Double hits are for fools,' Aranthur said.

'Humbug. You skewered him half an hour before he hit you.'
Kallinikos shrugged. 'He has some bad habits, our master. And there
aren't enough people to fight. Can we go elsewhere?' He looked around,
embarrassed. 'Why did you go to Vladith, anyway?'

'I saw a sign in a tavern,' Aranthur said.

'Hmm. Well, I don't think I'll go back. Nor should you.'

'I know another master,' Aranthur heard himself say.

Kallinikos had stood up for him, and he wanted to hug the man
for it.

In addition to practising his sword arts, Aranthur was working hard as
a student, and even his precious spare time was spent on his practices.
As soon as he had an afternoon, he spread the parchment he'd found
on the wall of his rooms, pinned it in place with tacks, and began to
practise the evocation and emanation. It was a very complicated piece
of work, and required the balancing of three forces. It directly involved,
in concrete magikal reality, the very principles that one of his classes
was discussing in vague terms. He revelled in being able to make the
conjuration and the emanation act together. It helped him understand
his Magikal Theory class, although the *working* itself was of no use to
him, since raising rage in someone's horse or dog was both illegal and
deeply unprincipled.

Arnaud, a more senior student, read the work through and shrugged.

'It's like a very wicked practical joke,' he said.

Another week passed. Aranthur successfully cast a *compulsion*, a
complex one, on the Philosophy Master's pet dog. Janos Sittar, the
Philosophy Master, gave him some astounding words of praise for
his work; Aranthur chose not to say that he had had some private
experience of *compulsion* and had learnt a great deal from a spell he'd
found in the street. He knew to develop a relationship with the target;

actually, Iralia had told him that, and for a moment he was distracted by thoughts of her.

As a result, at the test, he was the only student who spent time with the dog, and fed him, also following Iralia's advice. He thought of her often, but something was changing in his head, because suddenly he thought of every woman and girl who crossed his path. He had begun to feel strongly about Kati, for example, and to no purpose. She treated him with the same amused condescension with which she treated all men – like duelling partners

He tried to write Kati a love poem. It wasn't so much that it was terrible, as that he had nothing especial to say, which caused him some anxiety.

The next week, for a class, he cast his own horoscope and was shocked to see that he was under the sign of change – total, rapid change. He assumed he'd made errors, but his master smiled.

'Everyone your age lives under the sign of change,' he said kindly.

As if to prove it, his various infatuations seemed to stack up as the week went on, and he had no idea what to do about them except be miserable. He couldn't write poetry. He was too big and too poor and too much an Arnaut and not a Byzas to be attractive to anyone, and he suddenly found all women everywhere desirable.

He tried to work harder and do more fencing drills.

But a sudden attention to women was only one of the changes sweeping through his life that week. His success with the *compulsion* and his high marks on the winter writings had a strange result.

It was the Week of Books, when second years were assigned the book that they were to copy. Every student was assigned a book and would spend most of his next year or two, or sometimes more, copying that book and learning it thoroughly. Then the book became the student's possession and principal area of study.

When the masters assigned books, they were, in effect, telling students what they were going to study. It was a breathless moment, as students sometimes were assigned out of their preference. It was all too common for a student who wanted to learn magik in the Studion to find herself working in Practical Philosophy, Mathematiks, or Language in the wider, non-magikal Academy.

His room-mates did well enough. Daud was assigned *Compilations*, an early and fairly straightforward Liote grimoire. Arnaud, the Western barbarian, was assigned a book in Ellene: *Karmione*, a dialogue between a practical philosopher and a hermeticist that held some devious arcana. Arnaud was dumbfounded, and delighted, at the difficulty of the task. He had clearly made the grade, and he embraced both of his room-mates and bought them dinner.

Aranthur's name space was blank. No book had been assigned, and for an entire day, as he digested Arnaud's dinner, he worried about the blank next to his name.

Before the panic could destroy his concentration, though, a small star was inserted next to his name, and that the same star by Kati's name, far down the list, with an admonition to go to the Master of Arts.

Kati was renowned for her good marks, so he couldn't imagine that this was a poor result.

Facing the Master of Arts was something else again.

The Master of Arts was a woman. He'd never even seen her, but it was a first-year joke to call her Mistress of Impractical Arts. Altaria Benvenutu was one of the premier practitioners of the *Ars Magika* in all the archipelago, and Aranthur approached her office with trepidation.

There were a dozen students there. He knew none of them; all of them wore the full robes of third and fourth years, some with elaborate shawls and hoods. Practitioners tended to hide their faces, although Aranthur didn't know why; he assumed he'd be told when he reached such a dizzying height. No one had really explained why he shouldn't eat meat, either.

He hoped to see Kati, but either she hadn't been told yet or she had already been. Aranthur stood in an unfamiliar hall, hung with spectacular tapestries of women hunting arcane beasts, and strange, dreamlike men killing dolphins with swords underwater. He was in the hall for a quarter of an hour before he realised that the sea floor in the tapestry was a sea monster, its tentacles poised to take the men.

Behind the tapestries was a wall of dark wood panelling that seemed to stretch for stades. The Master of Arts had the only office on the enormous hall. Senior students came and went. A few wore swords; most wore long robes of black or deep blue. But one young woman wore a short doublet, like a soldier, and her head was bare, partially shaved in an elaborate and yet practical way, and she wore a light, straight sword. She smiled at him, and he smiled back, and she looked at him for a moment longer, as if recognising something.

'First year?' she asked.

Another student, as tall as a tree with skin dark as the night sky, smiled as he passed, as if just being a first year was a little funny.

'Second year,' Aranthur said. 'Ma'am.'

She flashed him a brilliant smile. 'I'll bet no one has told you that you must sign in with her secretary.'

He shot to his feet. 'No, ma'am.'

She nodded. 'Come. Someone did this for me. I'm Dahlia, by the way. Dahlia Tarkas.'

'Aranthur Timos,' he said.

She paused and looked back at him as if she knew the name.

'Ahh,' she said with a slight smile. 'So much the better.'

He followed her well-cut doublet to the door, and through it, where a middle-aged man in a notary's black cap sat, writing.

'Yes?' he asked.

'Aranthur Timos to see the master,' Dahlia said.

The notary glanced up. 'Eh?'

Aranthur leant forward. 'I am Aranthur Timos. My book assign-ment...'

The notary actually smiled. 'Ah, young sir. I will inform the master. I suspect she will see you very soon.' He nodded. 'Sit here, please.'

'There you go. Are you someone important?' Dahlia asked.

'Not that I know of,' Aranthur said.

She nodded. 'Interesting. Well, it was a pleasure, Aranthur Timos. When you go through the gate, come and find me, and we'll have a *quaveh* or something spicier.' She flashed him a broad smile. 'I live on the North Quad.'

North Quad meant she was rich enough to live in one of the residences with a fireplace and glass windows and fine oak panelling scarred by hundreds of years of student abuse. And the invitation was like having the sun shine on him. He bowed.

'Your servant, ma'am.'

She was almost out of the office before he managed to speak again.

'Do you fence?' he asked.

'Oh, yes,' she said. 'You?'

He nodded.

She looked at him for a moment longer.

'Good,' she said, and went out into the hall.

It was another quarter of an hour and three gowned students before a woman's voice said, 'Timos.'

He rose and entered.

The Master of Arts' study was as big as the room he shared with three men. There was a mullioned window behind her, as big as the sail of a small ship: a thousand panes of glass, each reflecting the light differently. Every other inch of all four walls was covered in books. Even the doors had shelves. Her writing table was the size of the feast table in a Great Hall, and on it were forty books and baskets of scrolls and pen cases, bottles of ink, and whole skins of vellum. The room smelt strongly of frankincense and myrrh. A skull sat on the table, atop a pile of black-bound books.

The Master of Arts was an elderly woman with a severe face and a bun. She wore ivory spectacles on a gold chain round her neck, and a long gown, cut to show her narrow waist. She had lace at her cuffs and neck, and a wristlet of blazing glory that had to be magiked.

He made his court bow, hand to the oak floor, knee touching the wood, eyes down.

'Hmm. Syr Aranthur.'

'I am not noble, Magistera.'

She favoured him with a slight smile. 'You are all equally noble to me, child. The purpose of the Revolution was never a nation of peasants, but a nation of aristocrats.'

Aranthur nodded. He'd heard the words before, but somehow, when the Master of Arts said them, they were *true.*

She picked up an ivory tablet, and flicked her thumb over it. Aranthur could feel the compilation of *workings*; the simple tablet was the most powerful artifact he'd ever seen. The *saar* seemed to radiate.

She glanced at him, flicked her thumb over the surface again, and looked at him.

'Ah. Yes. You're the boy with the marvellous *compulsion*. You have killed a man, I believe?' she asked, as if this was an everyday question.

'Yes, Magistera.'

'Don't make a habit of it – it might destroy your *power*. However, you did it for others so perhaps your *astra* will balance.' She sniffed, as if she doubted it.

146

He nodded as if he understood what she was talking about.

'Death masks spirit,' he said, quoting a lesson.

'Does it really? I've killed hundreds of sentient beings.' She smiled.

He had no idea what to say.

She nodded. 'We are assigning you a very difficult book. *Uhlmagest.*' She looked at him. 'It needs to be copied immediately, and we have chosen you.'

He was aghast. He had heard of it – a fantastically rare book. In a language he'd never heard spoken.

'It is . . .' He clamped his mouth shut on the word *impossible.*

'It is in Safiri. You will have to learn Safiri; perhaps even go there.' She pursed her lips. 'You score well on languages and you seem to have a great talent for complex *occultae*, especially *compulsions*. Also you know Katia ai Faryd. It is yours unless you refuse it.'

Aranthur's mind began to work. 'Refuse it?'

'Yes. Sunlight, young man, we don't execute students any more. You can refuse it, and we'll find you something else.' She looked at him.

He nodded. 'I think I must refuse.'

'Because?' she asked.

'Because my parents are farmers, Magistera. Because I can just possibly afford the materials to copy something like *Compilations* in Liote and I can't imagine what a Safiri dictionary will cost, even if there is such a thing.'

'A trip to the East?' he wanted to cry. Such an opportunity. A decade of adventure. And high magik. Not the playthings of the rich – the most serious and elegant old *workings*. A life spent in the *Aulos*.

She looked at him. And sniffed.

'You might imagine we know of your . . . lack of riches,' she said dryly.

She extended a hand – a surprisingly young hand for such an old face. On it burnt a single ring of amethyst or some dark purple stone, lit from within by a secret fire.

There before him was the codex itself, the size of a small table, as thick as an old door. The cover was leather over wood, worked in gold and gold leaf, and decorated in lapis blue – layers upon layers of complex patterns. The pages were entirely made of vellum; they shone as he opened it.

Every page was richly illuminated. The script ran in diagonals from right to left, sometimes only three lines of incomprehensibly foreign script. The first page to which he turned revealed a man in flowing robes fighting what appeared to be a hippogriff, with six diagonal lines of script, and then what had to be further notes extending to the page margins, all written in gold. Aranthur had never seen anything so incredibly, intensely beautiful in all his life. He flipped it to the back. He'd already worked out that the letters ran the opposite of Ellene, from right to left, and he found pages of carefully rendered glyphs. He looked up.

'That's "water",' he said. 'The true word. I just learned it in Signs and Sigils.'

The Master of Arts nodded. 'This part is not in Safiri,' she said slowly, as if revealing something she had not expected to say. 'The glyphs are Varestan.'

Aranthur nodded. 'The Dhadhian language.'

The Master of Arts raised her eyebrows and frowned at the same time, a remarkable facial expression.

'Not exactly. Varestan is the language most Dhadhi speak now. But it is also the root language of both Ellene and Safiri. We don't know enough about it. But there was a language spoken by the Dhadhi before that . . .' She smiled. 'Rendering these glyphs and learning what they control might be the most important part of the whole project. Listen, young man. People died to bring us this book, out of the wreck of the East. It might be the key to many things, and just the fact that it has been hidden from us and we have never seen a copy is revealing.'

Aranthur's hands shook as he turned the page.

'I am not worthy of this,' he said.

'I think otherwise.' She waved her hand at the desk. 'You will have all this to help you.'

Beside the glory of the grimoire – if something so magnificent could be called by so mundane a name – rested a scroll case with eight scrolls on Safian history; a heavy tome, brand new and blank, of laid paper, not vellum; and a beautiful pen case. Finally there was a worn, heavy book that proved, when opened, to be a lexicon of the Safiri language: hundreds of folios bound together, some clearly added later. He had never seen such a thing, because it had a gold and crystal object of great beauty attached to the cover.

'A reader,' he breathed.

'A very old reader. This is from the Imperial library. You may play with it to your heart's content if you accept. None of these items may leave this room, except the pen case, so you will get to know me very well.'

He was grinning. It was like the duel. He knew that to accept was to turn his back on his home and farm – to become something different, beyond his parents' imagining. By the time he finished copying the massive series of scrolls he would be a decade older. He might die working on it. But it was a great work.

"Thank you, I accept. Is the other student Kati, then?' he asked, overcoming his fear of her.

Then he realised that her thin-lipped smiles were not genuine, because a much brighter grin spread over her face.

'Excellent,' she said. 'I take on two students a year and I am already pleased with you. Come one hour after prayer, every day. I have no days off – neither do you. You may bring me *quaveh* – very hot. Try a different street seller every day and I'll tell you which one I like best. Some of them are from the East. You might even find one who speaks Safiri.'

'Yes, Magistera.'

She nodded and rose. 'I will see you in the morning. And yes, your partner will be Myr ai Faryd.'

He bowed and left her, and his knees were weak. But he managed to get to the notary, who rose and shook his hand.

'Congratulations,' he said. 'I like *quaveh* too.'

He wanted to go and find Kati, but that was out of the question, as he was due at work. Work paid his bills and for his horses – an extravagance that now seemed insane – and work was as important as the Academy and a great deal more important than fencing.

The leather shop was on the Square of the Mulberry Trees, the nicest portion of the not altogether savoury *keto* of the leather-workers, and served a fairly wealthy clientele seeking carefully crafted purses and belts – sometimes with very expensive accessories from the jeweller next door, who specialised in fancy buckles and paste diamonds, although he was also a fine gem cutter. On the north side of the shop was a wheelwright, and beside him a saddler, and both often ordered cut belts and straps for tack. The square was quite pretty, the buildings mostly of stone, but the stench of tanneries two streets away kept the property values low.

Ghazala, the elderly woman who owned the leather shop, always sniffed when she mentioned Ahzid Rachman, the gem-cutter.

'He fences stolen things,' she once said.

Bajolli Orla, the wheelwright, was, by contrast, a cheerful, open-faced woman with a hard-working partner. They mostly built heavy carts for the military. Ghazala took her *chai* with Bajolli, most days.

She and Manacher, her son, were master leather-workers, and they tended to take all the difficult projects, leaving a dozen piece work-ers like Aranthur to assemble pre-cut patterns: belt-purses for men, and day books and tablet binders; a great many belts and garters for hose; sometimes a week of simple cut straps for the saddler or the wheelwright. They also made items that required a wooden core – book covers, for example, and sword scabbards – but these were all custom work and Manacher tended to do them himself. The shop was small and cramped, a long, narrow building with a surprisingly pleasant garden in the back. It smelled of leather and dyes and beeswax, and Aranthur was happy there.

Aranthur came in, hung his Academy gown on a peg, tied on an apron, and spent seven hours cutting belts from carefully selected tanned hides. It was hard work, and doubly hard on his hands and concentration. Cutting straight lines was difficult enough, and more difficult when your thoughts wandered every minute or so into new pastures. Safiri. Kati. Dahlia. Kallinikos.

When his work was done, he had a meal of spiced rice and eggplant with the family. Manacher scratched his beard.

'I want to teach you to dye,' he said.

Dyeing was miserable work that left the practitioners with stained hands – or worse. Many dyes were poisonous.

Aranthur took another bite of rice. It was delicious, and the free food was one of the best parts of his job.

'We would pay you more,' Manacher said. 'And you would have more hours. You understand this work, Arry. You could have your own shop.' The Easterner shrugged and smiled. 'Listen, even if you never plan to be a leather-worker, it won't hurt you to move up and get your name on the guild list. I'd be happy to put you on now.'

Aranthur nodded. 'May I consider it?'

Ghazala smiled politely. 'Of course,' she said in a way that indicated that he had best not take too long.

It did occur to Aranthur that Ghazala was of Safiri extraction and he might be able to ask her about the language. And he liked her food.

After finishing his meal, he went out into the Square of Mulberry Trees. His mare was stabled here, and he spent an hour with her, curried her, saw to her stall, and paid for another week. He rode Ariadne out of the Nika Gate, headed north to the Temple Ridge, and enjoyed a gallop across the hard ground before trotting back through the gate, saluting the bored guards, and returning her to her stall for a last rub down.

More than anything he wanted to talk to Kati. He had a long walk home, along the spine of the isthmus, and thoughts of Safiri, about which he knew precisely nothing, and about the woman in the arming coat, who had been remarkably attractive, which became more thoughts about Kati. Would he spend a year copying next to her?

She was from the East. And of course she spoke Safiri?

And Dahlia was a swordswoman; it was written on her, and that made him think of Master Vladith, and Master Sparthos. He was under the Aqueduct, up on the 'Spine' or the ridge above the city, well along towards the Academy, when it occurred to him that he could probably find Master Sparthos' rooms by asking.

He paused, trying to figure out a route. Two men were selling *quaveh*, and he bought a tiny cup and drank it, and was thanked in Armean.

'Last time you had a horse,' said the young man in the brown robe. From the smell, he hadn't had it off since they had met.

'Last time I wasn't lost.' Aranthur thought the young man looked wistful. 'Do you need a cup of *quaveh*?'

The man in the brown robe nodded. 'I do. But I'm sworn to poverty...' He smiled. 'But not sworn to refuse hospitality,' he admitted.

Aranthur spent seven copper obols on *quaveh* for the men seated with the young priest, if he was indeed a priest. They all touched their foreheads, and the man in brown rose.

'Members of my order do not bow to anyone, or give or accept oaths,' he said. 'I am Radir Ulgul. I am a brother of the Browns, as you see.'

Aranthur had never heard of the Browns, but as an Arnaut he was used to seeing new things every day in the City where he was effectively as foreign as the Easterners. He nodded.

'Do I call you Brother?' he asked.

'It is not for me to define how you address me,' the young man said. 'My name is Ulgul, but I would be honoured to be your brother.'

Aranthur felt as if he'd fallen into a myth – one of the gods wandering the world, looking to see who was hospitable. Ulgul was a Northerner name: famous warriors, hired thugs and killers, and dangerous merchants.

'Well, brother, I am off to a sword lesson, I hope,' he said.

'A dangerous vanity.' Ulgul shrugged. 'But you bought me a *quaveh*, and so I'll spare you my lecture.' He smiled, and Aranthur couldn't help but like him.

He left, with the blessings of the *quaveh* merchant, and descended into the tenements below the Aqueduct and asked directions in three taverns. A pair of off-duty soldiers gave them, and he went back up, through the shanty town under the vast stone arches and went down past the tenements on the seaward side. He was surprisingly close to home: a fine neighbourhood with four-storey brick houses, colourfully stuccoed, in long connected rows with their own wooden walkways along the canal. This was where guild masters and bureaucrats lived, where middling aristocrats had their winter homes. Aranthur was out of place, but he had his student robes like a shield against the hard stares of the sell-swords who tended to provide the watch in such neighbourhoods. He crossed a pretty white marble bridge over the canal and found a tall pink building with a cherry wood door and a brass knocker in the shape of a cross-hilted sword.

It was a day for change; he'd seen it in his horoscope. He knocked.

There was no answer for some time, and then a girl, no more than seven or eight years old, answered, curtseyed, and then smiled.

'You're a Student,' she said. 'You don't really get my *best* curtsey.'

'No,' Aranthur grinned. 'I don't suppose I do. Is Master Sparthos at home?'

'Teaching a lesson,' the young girl said. 'I'll take you. Did you know that the world is as round as a cheese? And that it is round in every direction, like a ball? But of course you know that, you are a Student. What do you study? Is it wonderful? I want to go to the Academy and study fish. Or perhaps squid.'

The steep spiral stair did not stop the flow of her words, or even slow it.

'Are you the Demoiselle Sparthos?' Aranthur asked.

'Oh, la!' she said. 'I have never been called Demoiselle before. I suppose I am. *Patur?* This man called me Demoiselle.'

They had arrived on the third floor. The whole length of the house was open: all the interior walls had been removed, and the floor was sprung. Two young men were doing a drill. Mika Sula, the first duellist to fall at the Inn of Fosse, was standing very still with a long stave in his hands, watching them.

Master Sparthos frowned. 'Little pie, I have told you never to interrupt—'

He looked past his daughter at Aranthur, who met his eye while trying to imagine that the fearsome master swordsman had such a talkative daughter, or a daughter at all. Sparthos coughed.

The cough went on too long and left him with a look of distaste, as if illness was a form of failure. The swordsman pursed his lips.

'Timos,' he said. 'Had enough of Vladith?'

Aranthur didn't know what to say. 'I . . .' he began, and flushed.

The two students were doing a drill he knew: one would cut at the other's leading leg, who would remove his leg and make a counter-cut.

'I would like to become your student,' Aranthur found himself saying.

Sparthos raised an eyebrow. 'Of course you would. But I don't take just any ragamuffin who stumbles in, however good his manner with my daughter.'

Aranthur wanted to say that the master had in fact offered to teach him. But he shrugged inwardly.

'Yes, Magister,' he said.

'Good. The only possible answer. Take off your gown. Take a sword. Any from that rack.'

That rack held more swords than Aranthur had ever seen: all similar, straight double-edged swords with blades about the length of a man's arm, and simple cross-hilts and heavy pommels. They had sharp edges, covered in nicks, and rebated, round points.

Aranthur chose a heavy one with a broad *forte* and a heavy cross guard.

Sparthos took a sword, apparently at random. He was in an arming coat, quilted hose, and cloth shoes.

'*Garde,*' he said.

Aranthur had expected as much; his sword came up.

The swords were *sharp*.

Sparthos drove him around in a circle until he made a cut at the master's arm that slowed his attack. There followed a brief phrase, with a cut and a parry by each, and then Sparthos' sword was resting on his outstretched sword arm.

He didn't even feel the blow. He just froze.

'Adequate,' the master said. 'Try harder.'

Aranthur tried a deception in the centre line that deceived no one, and then a change of line, low to high, that got him a cut on his forearm – just a thread of a cut.

'Hmm,' Sparthos said. 'Show me something you think you do well.'

'Calligraphy?' Aranthur said.

Sparthos smiled. It was a thin smile, but it looked genuine.

'Eh,' he said, and attacked with a cut heavy enough that, had Aranthur missed his cover, he'd have lost a hand.

Aranthur set himself and made his own cut, a simple *reverso* from high to low. As soon as the blades crossed he launched forward, his left hand looking for Sparthos' sword wrist. Instead he found the elbow, but his cross remained intact and he drove the master's elbow up.

Sparthos allowed his arm to rise, pivoted his own blade on Aranthur's blade at the cross, and slid it along in a *glissade*. The round point came to rest against Aranthur's temple like a maiden's kiss, and was gone – Aranthur had finally mastered the man's sword arm with his own and had an arm lock.

He let go immediately.

Sparthos smiled. He gave a nod.

'That was very promising,' he said.

'Except you would have stabbed me in the head,' Aranthur said.

Sparthos shrugged. 'Perhaps, perhaps not. It is hard to know when we play with sharps and try not to hurt our students. The difference between a killing blow and a failed blow ... No one should be arrogant about such a thing.' He shrugged. 'Your arm strike was simple and you developed it well, though your set-up from the *reverso* blow was childish – you all but stopped the fight to inform me it was a feint. I played along because that's good teaching. You rewarded me by actually having an excellent second intention.' The man smiled. 'I will accept you as a student.'

'I have a friend . . .' Aranthur said.

'As good as you?' Sparthos asked.

'Syr Kallinikos,' Aranthur said, using the noble surname ruthlessly.

Sparthos sneered. 'Ah, a *Kallinikos*. Well, I do prefer *paying* customers. Splendid. Bring him and we will see.' He narrowed his eyes. 'His father is one of the Duke of Volta's friends, I believe. Still . . .'

Aranthur Timos all but skipped home.

He stopped at Kallinikos' rooms and found him with a crowd of aristocratic friends. Kallinikos waved at him, and introduced a freckled young woman as his sister, but the other young men looked down their noses. Aranthur heard 'Arnaut' and 'foreign' and knew he was not welcome. He wrote a note on a scrap of paper for Kallinikos' long-suffering butler, Chiraz, and went back into the street. He wished he was rich enough to take his friends out for wine, because he was wildly excited.

But his golden future turned into ruminations on the coming rent which he could not meet, because they were a student short in their rooms. All three of them had assumed that the Zhouian would join them and pay – eventually.

The pinch of poverty was especially tight because of the horses, which ate more than two students.

'I will have to sell them,' Aranthur said out loud.

He stopped at the gleam of bronze in the street, stooped and found a single bronze obol, the value of about half a fish pie. Fish pie was the students' staple food at the Academy. Aranthur had some pride, and he was only willing to force himself on Kallinikos once a week to get a larger dinner. Dinner at work was his usual method of quelling hunger, but he found that, like his sudden passion for women, he was suddenly hungry all the time.

He picked up the obol and turned for a walk and some food, going south along the canal as far as it went, threading his way through the tenement district on the north side of the Academy. The streets were narrow and the sun never really shone, and there were hundreds of rickety bridges and ropes above the little street, connecting families across the air above him. Here the tenements were ten storeys tall and he heard terrible tales of life in them: of people who were born and died without leaving their building's courtyard, because most of them were four-sided towers with a central yard almost as overshadowed and dark as the street. It was said that gangs ruled the towers, holding old people to ransom for street food, murdering pets, and kidnapping residents.

Aranthur walked along the street and saw little sign of such crime. There was graffiti on every building, much of it religious and the rest sexual: *Draxos is God* alongside *Fuck Everything* and *Bevan kisses like a fish*. And various signs and sigils, a few of them lit with *power*.

Almost anyone could access the *power*, since the Revolution. There were people who lacked the ability to concentrate, even with a talisman. Others lost the ability in old age, or with too much drinking. But in general, anyone could touch the source and cast, with a little instruction.

Midway up a tenement on the east side of the street, were the words *Follow the Master, Live in the Pure* in bold Liote, the letters three feet high, and neatly executed.

Aranthur kept moving quickly – more quickly now, because he was almost at the precinct wall of the Academy and he was too hungry to keep walking. But the smell of fish pie slowed him, and he turned his head to look.

There was a girl, maybe ten years old, with a scarf wound like an Atti turban, selling a delightful smelling pie.

'How much?' he asked.

'One obol,' she piped up. She was very young, her Liote heavily accented.

He gave her the obol and took the pie, and it was unusually delicious. Cardamom and something else. He chewed on a bit of cuttlefish. It didn't do to ask too closely what went into a fish pie – any more than a meat pie – and he ate it quickly, because he was ravenous, as he walked back across the Academy. He entered through the gate, which was only open to second years and seniors, because it led directly into the halls and the library, but Aranthur had never been one to obey every rule. He cut across the magnificent square, decorated with fifty marble statues, and Sophia in ivory and gold under a shimmering canopy of *power* that stood over her at all times and had since the Revolution.

He went down the steps on the far side of the square and along the high street to his door. At the Lady shrine in the foyer, he paused and said a prayer of thanks for the pie, and for the girl. She was obviously a refugee. She needed the Lady.

The pie got him up five flights of stairs, all the way to Kati's door. He paused, because he was suddenly afraid, and because his breath stank of fish, and other, foolish reasons, and then he knocked.

There was movement; his heart raced, and then the door opened and Kati's oval face appeared, the door only open as wide as her head.

'Yes?' she asked. 'Oh, Aranthur,' she said with an encouraging smile.

He sketched a little bow. 'Have you seen the Book list?'

She smiled. 'I have, too. Come in.' She smiled and backed away, opening her door. He followed her.

He was inside Kati's rooms. He would have smiled if he hadn't been so intimidated.

She smiled, her eyes bright. 'We will be together all year.'

He couldn't believe . . . she sounded as happy as he was himself.

'Are you all right?' she said, in a slightly different tone of voice.

He was not all right. A drop of something had just landed on his hand with a plop. He looked down.

It was blood.

Another drop of blood fell from the ceiling. The floors were only boards laid on the ceiling joists; the first drops of blood were followed by an evil trickle.

Kati choked a scream. She backed away, and suddenly had a knife in her hand.

'Those are *my* rooms,' Aranthur said, and he looked up.

Kati narrowed her eyes.

'Loan me your knife and I'll go up,' he said.

It was happening again – that thing that had made him fight a duel and attack the bandits.

Wordlessly, Kati handed over her knife. It was a good knife, an Eastern pattern-welded blade with a horn grip.

'Thanks,' he said.

He went to the door, but she kirtled her long robe through her belt, showing her legs to the knee, and took the iron poker from her fireplace. She had a fireplace. Only then did he note how much warmer her rooms were than his.

He was on the steps by then, and going up, and she was right behind him with the poker resting over her shoulder. The door to the sixth floor was still open, cold air rolling down the steps like an icy waterfall.

Arnaud was lying face down, a ragged gash along his throat, obviously dead. There was blood all over the floor. The pool had spread a long way and was congealing at the edges, fresh and scarlet in the middle. Aranthur's thoughts were frozen on the smell of the blood, the sight of it.

A tendril seemed to escape from the pool like water overflowing a dam. It ran over an uneven spot on the old wood of the floor and ran down towards the eaves.

Who the hell would kill Arnaud?

And is he still here?

Aranthur had Kati's knife. His sword was on its rack; he could see it beyond Arnaud. His own knife was ... somewhere. He'd left it somewhere.

A floorboard creaked. But he couldn't tell if he'd done it or Kati had. He knew a *working* that tested for *life*, for organic existence. But he didn't think he could muster the will to work it. And his talisman was hanging in the window.

Aranthur entered cautiously, and then moved to Daud's curtain, which was closed. He didn't want to open the curtain – he was deeply afraid of what he would find: an enemy; an assassin; Daud's dead body ...

He pulled the blanket back and the cubicle was empty. The bed was made; Daud's copy of the *Lexicon*, his most precious possession, was on the good wool blanket. No thief would have left either.

But his leather case was open, and all his clothes had been dumped on the bed.

All that in a glance. Aranthur whirled, and moved to his own cubicle, with Kati at his shoulder. He raised the knife and she flicked his curtain aside ...

Empty. His own bed was unmade, and he was vaguely ashamed that Kati saw how slovenly he was. But this was worse. It took him a moment to take in that his *malle*, the one from the inn, was upended. The ends had been slit open to get at the lining; all his possessions were on the floor, and looked like they had been stirred with a stick.

'Thieves,' he said, without intending to speak. 'Damn them to the icy hells.'

'Shh,' Kati cautioned.

He turned slowly, releasing his own curtain. The two of them went after the third set of hangings. Arnaud had well-sewn tapestry curtains worked with knights and goblins in a crude, Western way with wool yarn.

Aranthur scooped up his sword. He drew, and he motioned Kati back. She gave him a look – part exasperation, part admiration.

'Of course, you have a sword,' she said. 'Give me my knife.'

'You said *shhh*,' he whispered.

'There's no one here.'

He flicked at the tapestry and moved the curtains.

'No one,' Kati said. 'See?'

Aranthur didn't agree. He thought that there was a small man, or a woman, standing very still in the far corner of the hangings, hidden by a good *working* that he was penetrating because he knew what to look for.

'Wait . . .' he began, and the thing moved.

It wasn't a man and his senses screamed as it came at him, eyeless, with a fanged mouth, taloned hands, arms and no legs. His impression was of something *arcane, eldritch, terrible*, and then it was through the curtains, talons outstretched.

He cut. He didn't think, didn't measure, and the cut severed a reaching hand at the wrist. Just for a moment, the sword seemed to glow.

The arm deflated, and the monster struck with the other claw.

He sidestepped, stumbling, batting ineffectually with the blade . . .

Kati slammed her poker down on the thing's head. Its head crumpled as if she'd hit a bag of straw. It stopped moving; the severed hand bled smoke – black smoke – and something foul and oily dripped from the cut.

Then the empty arm grew a sword. It grew very quickly and cut at Aranthur, even though its head looked like a burst sack.

Aranthur made his cover, stepping to the left, tripping over Arnaud's body and almost losing his sword. He stumbled, wincing in revulsion at planting a foot in his dead friend's stomach, and almost falling as the black thing's sword crossed his blade. His blade bit deeply into the black blade as if it was made of horn. Aranthur's stumbling near run dragged at it. It didn't seem to have much mass.

Aranthur got his feet under him as his left shoulder slammed into the back wall of the room.

Kati hit it again.

It ignored her and came for him, sword first.

This time, he crossed the odd organic sword deliberately, from the inside, moving it to his own right. He rotated his hand, just as Master Vladith taught, and plunged his point into the thing's chest. At the same time, he put his left hand on its sword arm, as he had with Master Sparthos.

It was like grabbing ice.

Aranthur was too focused on the combat to worry about ice. He closed his left hand and shoved, spinning the thing, putting its talons farther from his face, keeping his blade through its chest. It was almost as light as air, and his shove collapsed it.

Kati slammed the poker into its head for a third time.

The taloned hand came up like lightning, but not to attack. It grabbed at its own mouth, a slash in the eyeless face, like a cut in a bag, and pulled. The head ripped open, and a black bird, like a songbird, but black and eyeless, crawled through the gaping mouth, beat its wings, and burst past Kati, who swatted at it with the fire iron.

She missed. It turned in the air like a starling and went up the chimney.

'Holy Sunrise!' Kati shrieked. Her fire iron slammed into the opening in the flue. 'Blessed Disa! Sunlight save us! Oh, fuck!' She teetered against the wall.

Aranthur was watching the small hole in the flue, more like a hooded opening than a fireplace.

'Get help, Kati,' he said. 'Get someone. Get...' His mind rushed through the possibilities. 'By the Eagle. Get us a Lightbringer.'

'Where do you think I'd find a Lightbringer?' she spat. 'On a street corner?'

She stumbled and he caught her, his sword still in his right hand.

'Oh gods, oh gods, oh *gods*!' panted Kati. She buried her head against his robe. Then she backed away. 'What the... What was that?'

Aranthur slumped. 'No idea. But the bird... The...' He was having trouble speaking, and the feeling of cold was spreading, not diminishing. 'Kati? Something is wrong.'

'Blessed Disa, save us!' Kati put a hand on his brow. 'Don't die, Aranthur Timos,' she said, as if scolding him, and then he heard her feet on the steps.

He put his back to a wall and watched the brazier. It was burning on the hearth, and the smoke was flowing into the hole in the chimney that served them as a fireplace. He couldn't cast, and he was losing consciousness. He set himself to fighting the latter, doing exercises in his head. His left hand was going an alarming red-brown colour, swelling rapidly and painfully.

He found that he was slumping against the wall, and he pushed himself upright. He thought he heard a stirring in the chimney. His vision was tunnelling. His left arm was unresponsive. He used the wall to get upright and made a butterfly cut in the direction of the brazier.

Right hand works.

He was slumping against the wall again. *But nothing else does.*

The floor began to vibrate. He was moving in and out of consciousness, having trouble holding on to the present reality. He awoke with a sense of falling and caught himself against the wall.

Master Kurvenos stood in the doorway, outlined in a purple-red light. He had a staff in his hand and looked fifty feet tall.

The tip of his staff rose and inscribed a Möbius strip in the air in blue light which flexed and began to travel, like the belt on a polishing wheel. It made a crackling sound. Sparks flew, and the black corpse on the floor began to smoke.

'Blessed Sophia protect us,' Kurvenos said.

He came into the room, and there were two men in armour behind him – heavy white armour, with big swords. The armoured men looked like faceless insects.

Aranthur could feel the *saar* in their armour. He'd never seen anything like them.

Their swords were four feet long, and their helmets were closed so that they appeared to be steel automata. One put his sword through the corpse – more sparks.

The other put his sword to Aranthur's throat.

The point was icy cold.

'He's clean,' said the armoured figure.

Aranthur was disarmed; he didn't resist. The armoured figure threw his sword across the room.

'It's gone,' Kurvenos said. 'It left through the chimney. All clear.'

The sword was lowered away from Aranthur, and he sank a little further down the wall.

The armoured figure sheathed his sword, took a baton from his belt, and spoke to it.

'All clear,' he said. 'There is a *Black Bird – a kotsyphas –* free in the City. Do you hear me?'

'*Black Bird,*' said the stick. 'We hear you.'

Aranthur slipped further to the floor.

'He's dying,' Kati said somewhere.

'Yes he is,' Master Kurvenos said. '*Sihr* poisoned.' He took the stick from one of the armoured men. 'Get me Magos Sittar, and be quick.'

Aranthur woke in a strange bed with strange blankets, and he had no idea how he'd come to be naked, or alone, or where he was. His heart pounded, and he tried to move, and he couldn't. He examined himself and found a *compulsion* – a heavy *compulsion* cast by an expert, a Magos or Magas – and the *working* was layered, complicated, and sat on him like a bright red skein of heavy yarn. He tried to follow it; he tried to imagine . . .

Kotsyphas. He thought the words and the memory flooded him. The fight. The terror.

He wasn't dead. At least, he didn't seem to be dead.

He awoke the second time to light. He lay in the chains of his *compulsion* and tried to look around, as much as the orbits of his eyes and his peripheral vision would let him. The ceiling above him was ancient, with a lofty ceiling supported by myriad fluted arches and beautiful beams. The beam ends had gilded roses carved into them.

'And you were supposed to bring me *quaveh* this morning,' a woman's voice said.

Mistress Altaria Benvenutu stood over him. She waved a hand and the *compulsion* was cancelled, its not inconsiderable *power* neatly collected by her waving hand and balled up, collected, and stored. She did it so casually . . .

'Take your time. Do not sit up suddenly,' she said.

He was in the Temple of Sophia, the chapel in the library, in the middle of the pentacle used for the most devout and advanced casting. It was a place that was strictly forbidden to first year Students.

'What . . . ?'

His mouth tasted like rotten fish and snoring and a lot of sandpaper.

She nodded. 'Your head will hurt for some time. Unfortunately, you have started the magikal equivalent of a riot and we need information.'

'How?' he began.

She leant over him. 'I'm sorry, Syr Timos, but I will ask all the questions, and you will answer them. What do you know about the spirit in your room?'

Aranthur was having trouble assembling complex thoughts.

'We found it when we went up the stairs.' He heard himself answering in great detail. His mouth was moving without his volition.

'Why did you go to Katia ai Faryd's room before you went to your own?'

'I look for any excuse to visit her,' he heard himself saying. 'I thought that since we were both to be your students, she would look on me more favourably . . .'

The Master of Arts laughed mirthlessly. 'Enough of that, please. She followed you up to your room?'

'Yes, with a poker, which proved as well, because—'

'Stop,' the Master of Arts said. 'As you see, he is innocent.'

A male voice, outside the range of his vision, said, 'Tell us who the master is.'

Except that the intonation suggested that it was *The Master*.

'Dariush!' the Master of Arts said.

Aranthur found himself compelled to answer.

'Everyone is a master but me,' he heard himself say pettishly. 'I make leather for a master leather-worker and I study with a Master of Arts and there are Sword Masters and ship's masters. I think my father is a master farmer, although I've never heard anyone accord him the title – someone must be a master farmer, don't you think?'

'Stop,' the voice said. 'Damn, damn. I thought we had one, alive.'

'The two children you are taking into this project are the very two targeted by the *kotsyphas*. I don't like it,' This was another voice, also a woman. 'I don't like that this happened at all. Nor that it might be related to what is coming out of the East.'

'I don't like laying *truth compulsions* on unco-operative sentients,' the Master of Arts said. 'Our likes and dislikes have nothing to do with it.'

Aranthur attempted to turn his head. The pain was blinding.

'But an attack? By sorcery? Inside the Academy?' the voice called Dariush asked.

'He can hear every word you say,' the Master of Arts responded. 'But I'll say this much: this was clearly done to send a message. Even if the two children had not interrupted the *kotsyphas*, the Western student was murdered for power and to leave a clear message.'

A hand was laid on his head. The Master of Arts said words in Ellene and he was gone.

The third time Aranthur woke he was in his own room. It took him time to realise where he was, because he was disoriented, and because he wasn't in his own bed. He was in Arnaud's bed.

Arnaud, who was dead. Murdered by a malign spirit, which was apparently called a *kotsyphas*.

He moved his head very gradually, and there was no pain. In fact, he felt wonderful – well rested and alert. His left hand was normal in colour and size. He sat up. Somewhere close by, someone was playing a tamboura.

Almost instantly, Kati appeared through the bed hangings. She flushed.

'I promised the Magistra I'd look after you,' she said. She set a steaming cup of *chai* by his head.

'You are blushing,' Aranthur whispered. His mouth felt as if it was full of resin.

Kati smiled. 'Where I come from, women do not spend time with men, alone.' She pushed him back. 'But you look harmless to me. Drink that. Does your head hurt?'

'Not at all. Oh, thanks, Kati.' He realised he was naked; paused.

'Good, because there is a man here to see you, who insisted that he could come in and showed me . . .' She paused. The tamboura poured out a storm of notes. 'I thought you were dead.' She kissed him on the forehead. 'I'm glad you are not.'

Aranthur smiled. 'Thanks!'

She stepped back.

The man behind her was Tiy Drako. He tucked the long neck of the instrument through his sash.

'Surprise,' the slim young man said. He flashed his brilliant smile at Kati. 'May I have him all to myself?'

Kati nodded. 'I have to be going anyway. Aranthur, you are commanded to speak to this man by the Magistra. You should return to her office again tomorrow.'

Aranthur nodded.

She leant over, took his hand, and kissed him again on the forehead. 'Get better,' she said. I . . . miss . . . you.'

She looked at Drako with apparent disapproval and he glared at her, as if they knew each other. She shrugged and withdrew. He heard her close the door.

'It's good to see you,' Aranthur said. It was, too. He was still puzzled at Kati's reaction. 'Do you know her?'

Drako winced. 'Just met her today. Listen, Timos, I have told you a pack of lies. Time to come clean, and all that. Very embarrassing.' He grinned like a guilty urchin.

Aranthur assembled information quickly, even when waking up.

'You are not really an acolyte,' he said.

Drako nodded. 'Although, of my many impersonations, that one was more . . . rewarding than most. No. I work for the Emperor.'

'The Emperor?' Aranthur asked. 'Not . . . the Watch? Or the Assembly?'

In fact, he realised that he had only the haziest idea of how the Emperor governed.

'Let's not go into details. I am here to answer a few things, get a promise from you, and tell you a story.' Drako shrugged, and sat back, and played a few notes of a stirring march. 'But I'll tell you this for nothing. The Assembly votes taxes. Only the Seventeen – the inner council of the aristos – has any power over the City or the Watch. And the army swears fealty only to the Emperor.'

'So you are with the army?'

'No,' Drako said with his actor's smile.

'What about Kati?' Aranthur asked, changing the subject. His head hurt.

'She got a different story. See, I'm going to be very honest with you.' Drako smiled.

Aranthur laughed. 'Really?' He thought of Drako as a mountebank. Like the tarot card – the evil jester. *Zanni, the trickster.*

'Hear me out.' Drako waved a hand. 'Ready?'

Aranthur sat back and sipped his *chai*. 'I'm ready.'

Drako sat on a stool, crossed his legs and clasped his hands over one knee.

'Here we go.' He looked out of the curtains for a moment. 'Actually, it is very difficult to know where to begin. Let's start simply. The man that the *routiers* killed, whose horse you are still riding, was a diplomat. I'll go a step further.' He paused for a long time. 'I simply hate telling the truth. It's almost painful.' He paused. 'He was an important man – possibly a double agent – and those bravos should never have been able to kill him. They must have taken him by surprise, in all the looting. I've checked up – our man was leaving Volta, probably trying to stay ahead of the rebellion there. And somehow, by sheer bad luck, he was trapped by a dozen drunken mercenaries and killed.'

'If you know who he was, I should give all his things to his family,' Aranthur said. 'I can't really afford to keep the horses anyway.'

Drako laughed. 'Well, we can discuss that. I don't think his mistress would care, and his wife is glad he's dead, and neither of them need a horse.' He shrugged. 'And to be straight with you, nothing I am telling you can go anywhere, even to Kati, even to your friends, and certainly not to the woman that our victim abandoned his family for.' He held up his hands. 'Please let me tell this my own way.'

Aranthur nodded. 'I get the feeling you're telling yourself as much as you're telling me.'

Drako fingered his short beard. 'You may be on to something there. Let's go on. This man was killed. The *routiers* took his three horses and baggage, and I freely confess I searched them all.'

Aranthur scratched his unshaven chin. 'You cut the bottom out of the *cannone's* case?'

Drako nodded. 'Yes. I was desperate. I still am. That man should have been carrying... something very incriminating. Supremely dangerous.' He looked serious, all his pretension drained for a moment. 'And deadly.'

'You are revealing very little,' Aranthur said. 'There was a man, whose name I'm not allowed to know, although I have his case, his coat of arms, and his initials, so I can probably find out. The mercenaries killed him. And I have his things.'

Drako nodded. 'Admirably put. Please do not go looking for his name. I'll tell it to you.'

There was a long pause, and Drako almost shuddered.

'He was Syr Xenia di Brusias. There, is that better?'

Aranthur shrugged.

'And anyway I have searched them all again, just so you know.' He sighed. 'It's possible he had already passed on his package. If so, then his treason is worse, and the damage he's done...' Drako frowned.

'Why are you here?' Aranthur was more annoyed than anything.

'Because the powers that were behind... *him*... just tried to kill you with sorcery in the midst of my city, and got past the wards of the Academy to do it,' Drako said. 'Because what was a matter for spies is becoming a matter for armies. Ever wonder where all the refugees are coming from, Timos?'

'Er...' Aranthur paused. 'The East?'

'Well, that's true enough. Ever wonder *why*?'

Aranthur frowned. 'No.'

'Because they are stupid foreigners and who cares why they move around?' Drako said bitterly.

Aranthur shook his head. 'No!' Then he slumped. 'Possibly. They just... *are.*'

Drako slouched back. 'There is a series of wars to the east. It is as if a curtain of war is moving towards us, and has been for years. Now the storm front is beginning to trouble the Sultan Beik across the water. Lightning just struck here, in this room.'

'What does that have to do with the man and whatever he carried?'

Drako tugged at his beard. 'I don't know. Or rather, I have no proof.'

He went to the window and brought back Aranthur's talisman of *kuria* crystal.

'Tell me what happened in the Revolution,' he said.

'Is this for my History exam?' Aranthur said.

'Humour me.'

Aranthur settled himself against his pillows.

'Well... The First Empire was founded on aristocratic principles, and the families that produced the best warlords, men who could both fight and use magik, were the aristocrats.'

'My ancestors, so watch yourself here,' Drako said. But he smiled.

Aranthur nodded. 'About a thousand years ago, the empire collapsed. Barbarians came – Souli and Alva and others, from the east and north. They took much of the farmland.' He smiled. 'Arnauts like myself.'

'Actually,' Drako said, 'my *patur* says that there were as many Arnauts in the Imperial army as attacking from the outside, and the Imperial generals were all Alva. But that's my dissertation, not yours.'

'Interesting. In the end an aristocrat from the City rallied the troops and made himself emperor. He conquered the barbarians, made peace with the other islands in the archipelago, and formed a very close alliance with the Sultan of Atti across the water.'

'The Diplomatic Revolution,' Drako said. 'Peace with Atti, the foundation of our prosperity.'

'My History Master says that the *Articles Against Practice* were more important than the Revolution itself.'

Drako smiled. 'What an idealist. How many priests died in the year after the articles?' he wondered aloud. 'We'll never tell. Go on.'

'Having established freedom of worship, the Founder set about eliminating the basis of aristocracy.'

'Not quite. The Founder wanted everyone to be an aristocrat.' Drako smiled. 'And the new emperor was as important as Tirase.'

'Everyone tells me that,' Aranthur said stubbornly. 'But Tirase repealed all the laws that required aristocratic birth to attend the Academy or perform magik or serve on a jury or as a Pennon in the army. He could just have left those laws in place and announced that everyone was an aristocrat.'

'Leaving aside that there was no Academy and every family trained its casters their own way, I accept what you say. I suspect it was pragmatism, but let's move on. Tirase re-established the empire based on more democratic principles. He created the Great Assembly and a system of elected representatives. He made it possible for everyone to use magik.'

'Yes. Everyone could use magik. And everyone could serve on juries and help choose the Councils, and so on.' Aranthur shrugged. 'It's not my favourite subject. The masters argue endlessly over details.'

Drako smiled. 'When you are a spy, you find that nothing matters more than details. Nonetheless, Tirase gave power to everyone. Political, military, and magikal.' He nodded. 'How did he do it?'

Aranthur scratched his stubble. 'The Academy.'

'That's true.' Drako paused. 'I hadn't actually thought that, until you said it. Of course, the Academy is the basis of the democratisation of *magik power*.' He whistled. 'And political power, too. Well, well, out of the mouths of babes. But aside from that obvious facet, which I had overlooked . . .'

'I assume you mean crystals, since mine is swaying in your hand. Anyone with a crystal – almost anyone – can focus *saar*. At least a little.'

'Enough to change the world, by lighting fires, purifying water, and arranging fertility,' Drako said. 'Ever consider what was the most amazing aspect of the Founder's Revolution?'

'I've been told repeatedly that it's amazing that the emperor would defy convention to raise the peasantry,' Aranthur said.

Drako smiled grimly. 'I don't find that amazing. Any leader who needs immediate allies against his lords will turn to the people. It's happened before. But this revolution swept the *world*.' He nodded. 'Hardly a drop of blood was spilt, and yet housewives in Zhou were lighting their own fires. Innkeepers had pure water. Farmers could dig wells to good water every time, fewer cows died, and women could decide when and how many babies they had.' He paused. 'Everywhere we've ever been on this great world, Tirase's reforms swept through.'

Aranthur nodded. 'Yes.'

'Now, if you train at the Academy, or at the Imperial Court in Zhou, you don't need a talisman to cast,' Drako continued. 'Right?'

'It's still easier,' Aranthur said.

'Right. How long have you been using crystal?' he asked quietly.

'Four years.'

Drako looked at the *kuria* crystal in his hand.

'And the price?' he asked.

'Goes up and up.' Aranthur stiffened. 'And?'

Drako stood and began to move restlessly.

'What if I told you that there were forces that never wanted *power* to be democratised?' he asked.

Aranthur sighed with young world-weariness.

'I'm surprised that it was ever democratised in the first place,' he said. 'Of course there must have been push-back.'

'This is *now*,' Drako said. 'Now. There are forces seeking to roll back the Founder's reforms. Because only the Pure should work *power*. The Impure should never touch it – they waste it. Like cattle in a fresh spring, they muddy it with their dung.' His voice took on an odd tone. '*Power* is only for humans. Only for men. All the other sentients should be eradicated. This is *our time*.'

'Drako?' Aranthur asked.

Drako sighed. 'I hate them.' He shrugged. 'Our dead man worked for them. That is, I thought he worked for me, but in the end he worked for them, and I was very close to catching him.' He raised his eyes. 'You asked Lightbringer Kurvenos if there were Darkbringers – men who actively work for the Darkness. Do you remember?'

'Oh, yes,' Aranthur said quietly.

'Well. The Pure and their Master do not think they work for the Dark.' He shrugged. 'But they do. They want to roll back a thousand years of progress and restore the world to slavery.'

Aranthur was shaken. 'Sunlight! But why?'

Drako shook his head. 'I have no idea. Up until now, it has all been about gaining control of the sources of the crystals in the East, and a ruthless programme to exterminate the Dhadhi, and kill off all the drakes, or so it appeared to us. We understood that the Pure wanted to control all the crystals, and they use that two ways – to control the market price, and to use the black market to fund their wars.'

'By the Sun!' Aranthur said. 'You are frightening me. And I have never heard any of this. It's like some traveller's tale told for a few coppers on a cold night at an inn. The Master. The Pure.' He frowned. One of the voices had asked him who The Master was. And the graffiti on the tenements... 'Kill the drakes?'

'Drakes are natural magik users. They can also consume *power*. Raw. They destroy it, when they choose, and the Pure hate them.' Drako sounded frustrated. 'Apparently. I have almost none of this first hand.'

Aranthur leant back, putting his head against the wall.

'No offence, Syr, but why should I believe you?'

Drako nodded. 'I really don't know anything. There are people – intelligent people – who say that the Pure are an invention of my faction at court, to seize wider powers.' He nodded. 'And I confess that up until the *kotsyphas* attacked my friend Aranthur, that seemed possible, *even to me*.' He nodded again. 'This is like hunting a snow hare in a snowy field, where the field is also studded with mirrors.'

Aranthur struggled with the whole idea.

'Does the Academy agree?'

Drako smiled. 'They do now. Everything I know I have passed to the Master of Arts and her council. And you. By chance or *tyche*, fortune, you were about to begin work on a grimoire from the Far East; in Safiri.'

'Yes,' Aranthur said, panicking at the word *were*.

'Don't worry, you still are. We need that book. We need people who speak Safiri. It is the Safiri kingdoms that are threatened now – if this whole story is true. And I think it is. The Safians are the front line – indeed, it is possible that the Safian heartland has already fallen.'

'By the Eagle, this is a mare's nest and no mistake,' Aranthur said. 'Why tell me?'

Drako smiled grimly. 'You were chosen to work on the Safiri. You were at the inn. You met the Prince of Zhou on the docks. Either you are at the very centre of a vast conspiracy – a possibility I have, in fact, investigated – or you have been tossed at my feet as an ally by Sophia herself.' Drako winked. 'I'm here to recruit you.'

'What's the Prince of Zhou have to do with it?' Aranthur asked.

'Join me and I'll tell you.'

'Join you and do what? With my minimal sword skills and my non-existent talent for Safiri and *power*, join you and we'll save the world?'

Drako thought about it for a moment.

'Yes,' he said. 'That's about it.'

'How do I know that you are telling the truth?' Aranthur asked. 'How do I know that you are even the side of Light?'

Drako smiled grimly. 'You never will. You know Tirase's statement about how principles are unprovable from experience? About hot iron?'

Aranthur nodded. It was like a school exam. But he did know the quote. When he'd been a boy, writing his first exams, coming to the attention of the village priest and the county noble, he'd learned Tirase's *Metaphysiks*.

'Yes,' he said, 'I know it.'

'Well,' Drako said. 'I can't prove we're cold iron. But we are.'

Aranthur stretched and yawned. 'Who were the men in armour?' he asked, ready to sleep again.

'Magdalenes,' Drako said. 'Members of a military order two thousand years old. Followers of an old goddess called Magdala. They fight sorcery.'

'They're on our side?' Aranthur asked.

Drako looked out of the window. 'Yes. No. Sometimes.'

Aranthur looked at him.

Drako shrugged. 'I'm not really good with truth. It's slippery.'

Aranthur lay back. 'Is the Duke of Volta on the other side?'

Drako stiffened. And then relaxed and turned with an oily smile.

'Oh, no,' he drawled. 'Why?'

Aranthur thought he was lying.

'Have you seen the drake that the Zhouians sent?'

Drako all but quivered. 'Yes, I've spoken to him.'

'Volta tried a *working* on the drake.'

Drako nodded. 'I'm sure you must have misinterpreted...' he began.

'I have his notes for the *working*, right there on the wall,' Aranthur said.

Drako tore the parchment off its pins.

'Damn,' he said.

Aranthur heard him pounding down six flights of stairs before he fell asleep.

The next morning, Aranthur dragged himself from his bed. His left hand still tingled, and his vision seemed... *odd*, in that he had unusual spots in front of his eyes – dark spots. Otherwise he felt capable. When he put on his gown, he discovered that it had a long tear from the hem almost to the waist. He couldn't find his sewing kit, and called out for Daud.

His room-mate appeared, fully gowned, and with a book bag on his shoulder.

'I'm moving out,' the young man blurted. 'Sorry, Aranthur. I can't stay here. Arnaud died. He *died*. Right there. Can't you feel it?'

Aranthur shrugged. 'Yes... Wait. The rent is due.'

Daud shrugged. 'Well, I put my money on a new room. Get one of your rich friends to pay.' He went through the door.

Aranthur began to look for his sewing kit, and found that all of Daud's kit was gone. The man had already moved out.

Aranthur found his own sewing kit in the wreckage of Syr X's leather case, sat on his own bed and sewed up the long rent in his gown. Then he ran down a flight of stairs, looking automatically at Kati's door.

It stood open, and there was a large man inside. Aranthur knew him; he owned the building and was showing the room to a trio of young men. The rooms were empty – not a stick of furniture, not a carpet left.

'Where is Myr ai Faryd?' he asked.

The landlord shrugged. 'She moved out. This morning. Her rent was paid.'

Aranthur fled for the street. He found a *quaveh* seller in the Founder's Square and carried two cups, piping hot, to the Master of Arts' study off the Great Hall. He noted that he received dozens, if not hundreds, of broad stares as he made his way through the crowded halls and narrower corridors.

The master's notary was busy copying a manuscript at incredible speed, but he stopped, wiped his nib, and rose to bow with great courtesy.

'That is very kind of you, Syr Timos,' he said. 'We were all sorry to hear of your troubles.'

Aranthur went through into the great office, where the Master of Arts sat on what might as well have been a throne of ivory, her slippered feet on an ivory stool with a silk velvet cushion.

'Magistera,' Aranthur said with a bow. He handed her the cup of *quaveh*.

She looked up at him and let the spectacles fall off the tip of her nose.

'Syr Aranthur,' she said. 'I hope that you have made a complete recovery?'

Aranthur nodded.

She rose and put a hand under his chin, and dragged him, like a child, to the light of her vast window. She looked into his eyes for so long that it seemed she was about to kiss him.

'Hmmf,' she said. 'That a second year student had to face a malign spirit *inside the precincts*. I offer you my apologies, Syr Aranthur. I have been told how this terrible thing happened, but it remains terrible that it happened at all.'

'Yes, Magistera,' Aranthur said. The whole idea of the Master of Arts apologising to him was more than he could take in easily.

'Well,' she said with a brittle smile, 'there are no certainties. We are trained to know that. You had a meeting yesterday?'

'Yes, Magistera.'

'Good. So you understand the relative urgency of your studies.'

'Not really, Magistera. Which is to say . . .' He paused. 'I understand that Safiri is important—'

'Yes.' The older woman sat in her throne again. 'Important immediately. A very important book. Work heals many wounds. Let us do some work.'

Aranthur looked down the table.

'Magistera, was not Kati . . . ?'

'Myr Katia ai Faryd is no longer at the Academy.' The Master of

Arts raised her eyes, and the weight of her gaze made Aranthur flinch. 'In less than a week, despite all the difficulties of communication, her parents called her home to Persepolis. In fact, every Safian family has removed their children from the academy, Syr Aranthur. Fifty-six students.' She looked down at her book. 'What does that say to you?'

'I, er, I wonder if...'

'I wonder too,' the Master of Arts said. 'I wonder if the Pure are already hard at work in Safi. Because by all reports, they forbid women to study *power*, on pain of death.' She glanced at him. 'Work, Syr Aranthur. It is possible that there is nothing in the whole of the Academy more important than your learning that book. I think you should get started.'

'Magistera, I don't know where to start. Why me? Surely there are scholars...'

He felt a sort of black despondency settle on him. Kati gone, Arnaud dead, Daud left, rent due.

'Yes,' the Master of Arts said. 'I have two good Safian scholars, neither of whom has much *talent*. Both will be available to you. I know some Safiri myself. You will *learn the book*. From it you will learn the basis of a different system of control and access to *saar* in a whole different way – a way that the Safians perfected before Tirase's reforms. I want a blank slate for this project, young man, and you are it. Now, please, get to work.'

'How?' he asked.

She smiled. 'The admission of ignorance is the beginning of wisdom. How do you think?'

Aranthur opened the first scroll. It was rolled on beautiful heavy bronze rollers, the vellum was so thin it was almost translucent, and the ink was *porphyria*, a strong purple red.

'Right to left,' the Master of Arts said. 'Let us begin with the first words.'

Six hours later, Aranthur walked along the third canal, his head awhirl with the sound and taste of an alien language, strange verb forms, a sentence structure that seemed inhuman.

'They say the Safians intermarried with the Dhadhi,' the Master of Arts had said. 'Perhaps that is why they are so beautiful.'

He bought a bowl of fish soup and ate it by the stall, using his folding spoon. Then he washed the bowl at the fountain like a good customer and returned it to the seller, a middle-aged woman with *zarca* scars on her face and the backs of her hands. She gave him a large smile and he went back to his room, where he sat looking at the spot where Arnaud's body had lain. Someone had cleaned up, but not very well; flies buzzed on the dried blood in the floorboards.

His things were still strewn over most of the room, which had seemed very small with four young men, and was now ominously large for one.

Aranthur sat for too long, so that the shadows began to form at the corners of the room. But a ray of the winter sun caught his talisman in the window of glass, and he sat up. He had two paradoxical ideas – that he should go for a ride, and that he should sell a horse. Perhaps both horses.

He put on his best doublet and hose, and went out. He had a single silver cross left, and half a dozen bronze obols; he'd missed a week of work and wasn't sure he was even employed. So he stopped first at the leather-working shop.

Myr Ghazala frowned when she saw him.

'A soldier came,' she said with some asperity. 'We were asked many questions about you.'

Manacher emerged from the back.

'Mama, they came back and apologised. What happened?' He gave Aranthur an odd look. 'You look like a noble. Where'd the clothes come from?' He glanced at Aranthur's long knife. 'You carry a dagger now?'

Aranthur had found his dagger, the belt wrapped around it, under his workbench in one of the Practical Philosophy classrooms.

'I was attacked,' he said.

Myr Ghazala put a hand on his shoulder.

'That is bad,' she said. 'Was it bad?'

He sat down, more suddenly than he had intended.

'Yes,' he said.

But he didn't want to tell them about it; he'd been told to keep the sorcery to himself. So the attacker became a mere man, with a knife, in his rooms – the story Drako had given him.

'That's terrible,' Ghazala said. 'Here, have a berry tart. You look pale. Get him some *chai*.'

Ghazala belonged to that subset of people who believe that food is the most sincere form of love.

Aranthur ate and drank and felt better.

Manacher smiled. 'The soldier worried us. Soldiers used to bother Rachman all the time, but we are not criminals.'

'I'm sorry,' he said. 'This is my first day . . . up.'

They asked no questions, with the sensitivity of people who have known some adversity.

'Can you work tomorrow?' Manacher asked.

'I have a new schedule now,' Aranthur admitted. 'I can only work in the afternoons.'

Mother and son exchanged a glance.

'That's fine,' Ghazala said. 'If you will work in dyeing, afternoon is best.'

Aranthur nodded agreement.

When he was clear of the food, he felt the weight of despondency settle on him again, but he took himself to the Nika Gate and rode out into the winter countryside. The gate was almost empty. The festivals were all done for a while, and there had been a thaw while he was unconscious. The world of ice and snow had become an endless vista of mud that almost convinced him to stay in. But after a hesitation, he rode out into the countryside, and Ariadne clearly enjoyed the exercise, galloping at the slightest weight change. It was as if she was determined to win him over. He had never loved her so well, and he rode for stades and stades in the mild air, his tattered old half-cloak fluttering behind him like a banner. With nothing to distract him, he thought too much about his life, and he didn't really like what he saw: Drako, Dahlia, and too much fighting. And no Kati.

Why had she left? Without a word?

He tried never to allow himself to wonder what in all the iron hells he was doing. But riding gave him far too much time to think, and his thoughts tumbled one over another, and he found that Ariadne was tiring because he was riding very fast.

As the sun went down, he rode back to the livery stable and used warm water and soap to clean her legs before drying her and brushing her. It was full darkness before he left the stable.

He was wary of going home along the spine of the city. The Eastern refugees looked more threatening than before, although he disliked that tendency in his thoughts; if Drako was right, they were as much victims as he was himself. But he made it back to his room untroubled. He disliked the darkness and he couldn't face the mess, so he curled up in Arnaud's warm bed, shut the curtains, and went to sleep. His dreams were dark and evil.

In the morning, he bought coffee from another seller, taking a different route to the Great Hall. This time he went all the way around to the reservoir side of the precinct, where a dozen Easterner women with magnificently polished bronze or copper pots competed to sell him *quaveh*. He bought three cups and was given a tray by a pretty, small woman with hands covered in marvellous tattoos. At least, her eyes were pretty; the rest of her was swathed in scarves.

Aranthur delivered *quaveh* to the notary, whose name was Edvin, a barbarian name, and to the Master of Arts, who waved him off after she had seized her cup.

'Visitors from the new government in Volta,' Edvin said. 'Sit with me and copy your work. She has Syr Eshtirhan coming from languages to work with you today.'

Aranthur sat at the notary's work table. The man was a legal professional, but he was, as Aranthur had already noticed, the fastest copyist that he had ever seen. His quill virtually flew along the parchment, and yet his characters were almost perfect, with little flourishes of penmanship that marked the truly elegant and educated scribe.

Edvin, who was over forty and thin as a rake, smiled over his pen.

'I was hired for my copying,' he said. 'I hardly ever do legal work here. But I can write out an entire copy of *Reflections* in a week.'

'Blessed Eagle,' Aranthur muttered. He had copied selections from *Reflections of an Emperor* for the whole of his first term. It was not a short work.

Edvin flexed his eyebrows. 'Sometimes I save first or second year scholars who fall behind.' His grin was wicked. 'For a price.'

Aranthur went back to his own work. The day before he'd written out the first four sentences of empty, flowery compliments in *Ulmaghest*, but he'd only written them on foolscap. Now, with time to kill, he copied the new letters over and over, seeking the fluidity of the Safiri scholar. He'd translated the table of contents. The Master of Arts had already directed him to three *occultae*, one of which was a simple shield. The compliments were just practice. Practice for practice.

'Here, let me have a go,' Edvin said.

'I can't afford you.'

Edvin laughed. 'Oh, I'm all bark and no bite. I like a pretty lad, I admit. You're a little big for my taste. Never you mind, my honey. You bring me *quaveh*. Let me have a look.'

Edvin's first attempt at the Safiri calligraphy was better than any of Aranthur's. Then he spent ten minutes talking Aranthur through just two symbols – showing how the pen must touch the paper, and what the strokes must be like.

Aranthur couldn't take it all in, but he got most of it, and he began to copy more fluidly.

'Not bad at all,' Edvin said. 'You *are* a good student.'

'I'm sure he is,' Dahlia said. She was standing in front of the two of them, hands on her hips. Today she wore a gown like other students. 'Where do you fence, Syr Timos?'

Aranthur blushed furiously and felt a fool for doing so.

'I ... um.'

He looked away from her, at Edvin, who laughed aloud at his confusion.

'I used to fence with Master Vladith,' he managed. 'Now, I ...'

'You left Vladith?' Myr Dahlia asked. 'Ah.'

'I will ... be fencing ... with Master Sparthos.'

He looked up at her, feeling ink-stained and immature.

'Sparthos!' she said. 'My, my.' She did a thing with her eyes that made Aranthur's heart jump. 'I'm to meet the Ambassador from Volta, Edvin, and take him to the Founder's Square and the Seniors' Mess, for lunch.'

'Right you are, Myr.' Edvin wrote out a message on a scrap he cut with his penknife and sealed it with his own ring. 'There you go.'

'My thanks, Edvin.'

She sparkled at Aranthur and might have said something, but the door to the Master of Arts' study opened and an elegant man appeared with the Master of Arts herself by his side. He bowed to Dahlia, who allowed her hand to be kissed with an air of detachment and took the visitor away.

Magistera Benvenutu peered over Aranthur's shoulder.

'Good work. Come, let us find Syr Eshtirhan.' She looked back at him. 'You should try being less serious,' she said with a smile.

Aranthur wondered what she meant.

The Safiri speaker proved to be a man of Atti, tall, fat, darkly bearded and full of good humour. He settled in the Master of Arts' capacious office and they worked straight through lunch – all on the verb *to be*. He corrected some of Aranthur's calligraphy and then went off to teach a class on Attian history. He was not yet a master, but only a senior student; Aranthur gathered he had been at the Academy for twenty years.

'I am, perhaps, too fond of smoking stock and drinking forbidden wine,' Eshtirhan said. 'But damn it all, there's more to life than verbs.'

This last sally coincided with Dahlia's return with the Voltain ambassadors. Eshtirhan eyed her like a connoisseur and she wrinkled her nose at him.

But then she kissed the other scholar on both cheeks, which told Aranthur that he didn't understand anything, and made him wonder again about being 'too serious'.

She looked at him. 'Care to fence this afternoon? Perhaps after evening prayer?' She leant over. 'Really, even in these decadent days, men are supposed to ask women these things, but a girl could grow old...'

She winked at Eshtirhan, who cackled.

'I have to work,' Aranthur said.

Dahlia raised an elegant eyebrow. 'Now that's not a line I've heard before,' she said, without apparent offence.

You should try being less serious.

Aranthur took a breath. 'I can be done by prayers,' he said, a little too suddenly.

As an Arnaut, Aranthur seldom attended the formal, incense-filled prayers to Sophia every morning and evening, preferring to visit a temple of the Eagle from time to time, or to visit one of the Lady shrines throughout the city. So he wasn't even sure why he'd said that...

She smiled. 'Good. Work? More work than this?' She shrugged. 'I am at Tercel's. I'll cover your fee – I assume you are poor.'

Somehow, that comment hurt.

'I can cover my own fee,' he said, stung.

'Oh, and doubtless buy a river of pearls. I'm sorry, Syr Timos, but I insist as your senior that I will pay your fee.'

She bowed like a soldier, and swept out of the room.

The magistera glanced after her.

'Sometimes I wish Dahlia didn't try *quite so hard* to be exceptional,' she said. 'And you, my dear Timos, need a sense of humour.'

A sense of humour? Aranthur, who was usually a calm young man, bridled. *You want me to fight evil and learn Safiri and get good grades and you think, perhaps, I need a sense of humour?*

It rankled all the way out of the Academy and across the squares and down the hill and over the spine to Ghazala's shop. He even framed the thought in Safiri: ؟مراد ىعبط خوش سح هب زاین نم ایآ. Then, while his dye was still wet, he lost himself thinking about what *humour* meant, as a word.

Ghazala shook her head. 'Hello?' she snapped.

'Do I need a sense of humour?' Aranthur asked.

'Yes,' Ghazala said. 'There is a woman?'

Aranthur flushed.

'Bah,' she said. 'Look here. This is how to dye blue. It is the most difficult.'

Aranthur was deep in Safiri even as Ghazala taught him to dye. They were working with indigo and *garza*, a liquid that smelled to Aranthur like a distilled alcohol that was apparently a trade secret. The best leathers were usually dyed in the hide, when it was tanned, but for very small jobs and repairs, in-shop dyeing was essential. It was messy and very smelly, and by the end of his second six-hour day, Aranthur's left hand was a mottled web of black and red and green.

He didn't really think about it until he arrived at the door of Master Tercel's School of Defence, which proved to be a tavern, brothel, inn, stable, *and* a fencing *salle* all under one roof. It was all comfortably shabby, but as soon as Aranthur pulled his scholar's gown over his head in the dressing room, he discovered that all of the other men were rich. Their sleeveless under-doublets were silk or superfine wool, their beautiful boots of pierced leather, with purses and belts to match. He was the only man with a scholar's gown; the rest of them had doublets finer than anything he possessed, a dazzle of colours carelessly tossed in corners.

Aranthur was the only man present who didn't have an under-doublet.

His hose were pointed to his braes, the short breeches that most Byzas wore to work, unlike the baggy trousers and smocks of the Arnauts. He wore the boots he'd found in the dead man's case. All the other men had slippers, purposely made for swordplay.

Aranthur had the humiliating feeling of being watched – and worse, commented on. There was a ripple of comment, and a snort of obvious derision.

Someone said *Arnaut* loud enough to carry.

He took a deep breath and considered leaving.

Instead, the same feeling that had pushed him up the stairs against the *kotsyphas* now pushed him out of the changing room and onto the tavern floor. Or pit.

The *salle* floor was surrounded by galleries, so that men and women could watch the bouts from either the ground level or the upper level, which was an extension of the upper level of the tavern. Out on the floor of the *salle*, two pairs were fighting. One was a pair of men boxing bare-handed; both had cuts on their faces. One of them was Tiy Drako.

The other pair were both women; one was Dahlia, and the other a slim woman Aranthur didn't know. They were using small swords – the light weapon that the gentry carried all the time, even at parties. The motions were incredibly rapid, compared to the more ponderous heavy swords that Master Vladith preferred. Both women had weapons with buttons on the points, and they circled, thrust, parried, discussed the finer points of their exchange, and went back to it.

Drako blocked a straight jab, seized his opponent's arm and threw him to the ground. Spectators burst into applause. Even the two women stopped fighting. Everyone clapped, and a woman threw a flower.

Drako tucked it behind his ear, blew a kiss and spotted Aranthur. He did a double take, and then, too smoothly, covered his surprise.

He came over. 'My dear fellow,' he said. 'What on earth are you doing here?'

'I invited him,' Dahlia said, leaving her bout.

Drako bowed. 'Your taste remains impeccable, Myr Tarkas.'

'I always think so, of course,' she said, with a tilt of her head and a raised eyebrow at Aranthur. 'You came! What dreadful thing has the Master of Arts done to your hand? Was that sorcery?'

Drako's look of well-bred insipidity was replaced with something like curiosity – perhaps even concern.

Aranthur was briefly tempted to lie. It was not that he was ashamed of working – he was far too much a product of the Revolution to be concerned about such a thing. And yet . . .

And yet . . .

'I am learning to dye leather,' he said.

'Of course you are,' Drako said. 'And damned creditable, too.' His tone was ironic. 'Isn't leather already dead?'

They had spectators, and many of them laughed.

Aranthur wasn't good at this sort of thing, and he shrugged.

'There's a lot to learn,' he said weakly.

But Dahlia rescued him.

'He's the Master of Arts' student this year,' she said to the spectators.

A few people clapped, in a way that indicated that they were not so impressed, but most people's faces expressed pleasure.

'Damme, I throw Folis on his fool head and you are all eyes for this fella,' Drako said.

His opponent, who was apparently Syr Folis, was rubbing his head.

'Damn your eyes, Drako,' he said. 'I thought we was boxing, an' all along you was wrestling!'

That led to a great deal of laughter, and the focus moved off Aranthur, who nonetheless feared he was flushed.

Dahlia looked at him coolly. 'Of *course* you don't own an under-doublet,' she said. 'Let's cross swords. What do you fancy?'

'I have really only practised with arming swords,' he said.

She smiled. 'Lovely.'

She was dressed like a man, in hose and an under-doublet that showed her figure was very unlike a man's, skintight to reveal billowing acres of snowy white man's shirt, black-worked at neck and cuff, long legs clad in knit hose that showed every muscle.

She went to a rack whose wealth of blades beggared even Master Sparthos' well-furnished rack and withdrew two arming swords. They were three feet long, had simple cross-hilts; the blades had square edges and the points were rebated.

Aranthur had never actually held such a weapon. Swords were expensive. A sword without edge or point took all the same smithing skills as a sharp sword, and thus, only the richest could afford to own both. At Vladith's, every man and woman brought their own swords, and mostly they had cut at straw or at bucklers.

He took the sword, rolled his wrist, and nodded. With a sword in his hand, he no longer saw her as beautiful; he simply looked at her muscles and where her weight was going. It was hard to describe, but the change was instant, and he was filled with purpose.

They bowed. Another bout had begun next to them – two showy men with heavy swords. Close to Aranthur, a red-haired woman wagered that fingers would be broken and people laughed. No one seemed to pay him any mind, so he and Dahlia circled after their salutes and no one commented.

He misjudged her distance and she slipped in and cut his sword arm. He didn't even cover; it was so fast he stood for a moment, unbelieving.

Drako laughed. 'Ah, Syr Timos, don't let her bully you. But she is fast as a cat, that one.'

Aranthur saluted again. Dahlia was grinning.

They circled. This time he saw her trying to close the distance, a sort of slow, lazy spiral. He cut back, stepping straight at her, and he threw a heavy blow from a high *garde*. She covered, and he rolled his wrist, forcing her to extend her *garde*. She backed and he followed, and suddenly she changed direction, seizing her own blade at the half-sword and going for his face with the point. His left hand took her right, and she punched with her left hand, snapping his head back and making him taste blood. He raised her right hand and threw her over his out-thrust foot with his superior weight and height.

Then, as any Arnaut would do, he knelt on her arms to make sure she couldn't strike again.

She licked her lips and laughed. 'Well, well,' she said.

Close by them, one of the swordsmen had just broken two fingers while swaggering swords, and the red-haired woman was collecting her winnings.

They both bowed and the third point started more quickly, as she came straight at him with a thrust and he parried. Her thrust was a deception, but he had made a circular parry. The two intentions defeated each other, and their blades ended up crossed, points down. She rotated her blade, down to up, slid her *forte* along his *foible* and put her point into his gut with a strong advance.

'Ouch,' he said.

She smiled. 'You don't know that one.'

'Not at all,' he said.

On the fourth exchange, he tried a flurry of very fast cuts – left, right, left, right. She parried three and tapped him on the shoulder before he could throw the fourth, a magnificent piece of control.

By then people were watching.

On the fifth exchange, he cut at her hard, again, from a high *garde*, correctly reading that she feared a heavy cut. But at the cross, he pushed her blade to his inside and grabbed it with his left hand, pulled hard, and found himself holding both swords.

She turned on her heel and mimed running away. People laughed.

'Nicely done,' Drako said. 'In oh so many ways.'

Seeing that Drako was speaking to him, a half a dozen other men and woman came over and introduced themselves. Drako told a very, very amended version of the events at the Inn of Fosse, where he claimed he'd had an assignation with a married woman. There were many knowing glances.

'Let's cross blades,' Drako said. 'She's already ruined your shirt.'

Dahlia blew Drako a kiss, and grinned.

'He's mine, not yours. And anyway, I think the tradition of the floor is that you face the winner, not the loser.'

Drako made an elaborate court bow that Aranthur couldn't have hoped to emulate.

'Your pardon, milady,' he said.

Aranthur understood he was to withdraw. Despite his good disarm, Dahlia had certainly scored more points. He stepped off the floor, where a tall man of his own age casually slipped a hand inside his shirt.

'Ah, excellent muscles,' he said with a winning smile. 'You're not pretty, but you are handsome.'

Aranthur writhed away, but not fast enough to avoid a casual pinch.

He flinched away from the hand. 'Excuse me?' he spat.

The tall man grinned. 'You are so fetching when you fight.'

He smiled at another tall man, this one very dark-skinned, with an elaborate velvet coat.

'Make him fight you,' whispered Velvet Coat. 'That will chill his ambitions.'

'Now that's unfair. I do not come out to fight. I come out to play,' pouted the tall man.

'We all come to play,' a woman said with a beautiful smile. 'But you have to fight first.'

She was older, perhaps forty. She had iron-grey hair in a queue like a military man's, and she was very fit. She looked familiar, but Aranthur didn't know many women who wore hose and baggy shirts like men, aside from Dahlia. She was, as Aranthur looked at her, the most attractive older woman he'd ever seen. She was ... dangerous.

Aranthur acted on his own whim.

'Would *you* care for a bout, ma'am?' he asked.

'Isn't she a little old for you, darling?' the tall man said. 'Ah, well. Be careful of the General. She'll eat you alive.'

Velvet Coat shook his head, as if in disapproval.

'And what did you have in mind for him?' asked the older woman. 'I would be charmed to cross blades with you, sir,' she said, turning back to Aranthur. 'Though perhaps you are unaware that . . .' She smiled. 'Never mind. Who brought you here?'

'I brought myself,' he said, with a little too much severity.

'Yes, yes, I was young once, too,' the woman said. 'Arming sword?'

'As you wish, ma'am.'

There was something about the way she held herself that led him to believe that she was a master, or at least an expert. And he knew her. He just couldn't place her.

'Arming sword.'

She fetched a short, straight blade very like the one he still held in his hand and they joined a line of couples. There were five pairs ahead of them.

'You are a Student?'

'Yes, ma'am,' he said.

Out on the floor, Drako and Dahlia had a surprisingly long engagement: blow, cover, counter, cover, riposte, parry, thrust. The two backed out of measure and there was a little applause; most conversations stilled.

Dahlia threw a low leg-cut on a long advance, to close the distance. Drako covered with a leg withdrawal and a point-low parry. Then Aranthur lost the action. The duellists were turning and Drako's back blocked what happened next. Then there was applause and Drako was saluting with a wicked grin on his face.

'What do you study?' she asked, pleasantly enough.

For the first time, it occurred to Aranthur that he ought to watch

185

what he said, contradicting his natural inclination to brag a little. The two warred within him. He shrugged.

'I hope to be in the Studion,' he said. 'I am in my second year.'

'Second year?' The woman smiled, and her smile was both flirtatious and somehow automatic, as if her attention was elsewhere. 'Ah, so very young.'

'And you, ma'am?'

'I do not love being called ma'am. Call me Alis.'

One of the pairs ahead of them left the line, having changed their minds; suddenly, they were next.

'You look familiar to me.' Alis smiled. 'Bah. We'll talk later. Fight well.'

Aranthur had the sense he was being toyed with, but he was focusing on his sword. She saluted without flourish, a mere twitch of her fingers, and settled into a high stance. Her legs were long, her torso short, and she seemed to be standing erect. Her shoes had heels, which made her even taller.

He saluted.

The moment his sword's point settled into a *garde*, she came at him. She cut at his head, and he covered. She cut from high to low, at his advanced leg, and he parried but she was so fast he couldn't withdraw his leg. When she went for a third attack, he didn't retreat and their swords crossed almost at the hilts as she thrust, but she was as fast as a tiger, and his attempt to take her blade came to nothing. He had it for a moment, but not enough to keep it. Still, he drove forward, attacking as she whipped the blade away and forcing her to make a hurried parry. He was too slow to force her blade off the parry and she cut at his bicep.

He made a high parry with his sword pointing almost straight in the air. He didn't have a thought in his head. He cut straight at her head and she made the same cover with which he'd started the phrase: a high *garde*.

She laughed. 'Very pretty,' she said. 'You must fence with Vladith.'

She thrust. He never met her blade all through an interminable double envelopment that ended with her sword bent almost double against his hip.

He was sweating hard. She didn't seem to have perspired at all.

He tried a hard blow from a high *garde*, the cut he'd planned to use in the duel at the Inn of Fosse. She covered it with a rolling action of her wrist that he didn't even know and her blade hit him hard enough in the head that he smelled blood.

He was woozy, and she hit him with an effortless cut to his left bicep that he missed altogether. He raised his hand. She stepped forward.

'I don't think I'm anything like an opponent for you,' he said.

'On the contrary,' she said, 'I like you very much, and I'll tell you why in two more hits. Come!'

He saluted, gritted his teeth and determined to see how long he could survive. He cut carefully at her wrist and hands, and otherwise parried and retreated. On their third engagement, she deceived his blade, moving her sword under his in a motion so small that it might have fitted inside a lady's ring, and put a light thrust into the back of his sword hand. People applauded.

'Oh, well struck,' he said, filled with admiration. A thrust to the hand was one of the most difficult targets.

Now the woman was flushed, almost red in the face, and her hair was plastered to her forehead.

Aranthur thought, after she'd scored seven times in a row, that in fact he was marginally faster. He didn't dare leave his blade in the middle, for fear she'd deceive him, which she did every time. But he didn't know how to counter her deception, so he took his blade away, and left it out behind him like a tail. No one was watching them. Everyone was watching two women fight with long swords.

They circled. Aranthur's sword pointed almost straight out behind him, invisible to his opponent. She changed *gardes* twice. He circled, keeping out of her range, which he now knew.

He could tell she was suddenly bored. Her stance became less alive, and she leant, and finally, she threw a cut, high to low, from the very edge of her distance.

He cut up, from low to high, into hers. He was stronger; his sword moved hers a fraction and his blade cut along her arm.

She paused, and then saluted, and then rubbed her arm.

'A little too hard, Syr Aranthur.'

He hastened to apologise.

She shrugged. 'No – no damage done.' She leant forward and kissed him on the lips; he flushed with surprise. 'That was fun. You owe me a drink, at least.'

They walked together to the bar, where two thick oak boards were laid across a pair of old casks.

'Dark ale,' Alis said.

'The same,' Aranthur said.

He didn't see Dahlia; Drako was talking to the tall man who'd pinched him.

A pair of dark ales cost him one silver cross and two bronze obols, wiping out his fortunes in an instant. He tried not to writhe.

Alis watched him with obvious amusement.

'Cheers,' she said, raising her chipped mug of ale.

He toasted her. 'To your deadly lunge.'

'My deadly lunge has nothing to do with it. You don't know how to deal with a feint.'

Aranthur nodded. 'I've only been fighting for half a year.'

She nodded. 'I gathered,' she answered.

He'd rather hoped she would add something about his natural talent.

'I enjoyed crossing blades with you because you get hit with good grace and you learn from experience,' she said, her face by his ear. 'Try not to lose those talents, and you'll be a good blade.'

She wasn't even looking at him. She was looking around.

'What do you do?' he asked.

'What?'

'What do you do?' he asked again. 'I told you I was a Student.'

She smiled. It was a wolfish smile. 'Oh, that.'

Dahlia appeared as if by magic and put a very warm hand on his shoulder.

'You are bleeding, and Drako says I ruined your shirt,' she said.

'I think the blood is my fault,' Alis said. 'He's a good sport.'

Aranthur saw the moment when the older woman's eyes locked with a richly dressed older man whose court clothes were out of place on the fighting floor. He could tell, immediately, that they were not friends.

Dahlia bowed. 'But, Majesty, I—'

Alis nodded. 'Of course. Excuse me.' She nodded to Aranthur and raised her cup. 'Save me a fight the next time you come.'

She walked off into the crowd, which was far denser than it had been when he arrived.

'Come,' Dahlia said with a tug at his shoulder. 'I'll clean that cut.'

She took his hand and pulled him through the crowd; they went up the steps to the balcony. Aranthur brushed past Drako, who gave him a smile. He was in an argument with the richly dressed man.

'I'm for hoping that it's not war,' said a short, wide man with a long beard. 'The Empire doesn't need—'

'Of course it's war. You and your precious mistress are simply afraid to face a real war. "The General" who never fights.'

'War?' Drako said. 'You're exaggerating, General Roaris—'

'War is the only thing that'll save farm prices,' a woman said.

'Masr's been arming for forty years...' said a tall man with a rich, red under-doublet of embroidered silk.

'Atti—'

'Masr is our natural enemy—

Drako shrugged, all his feral combativeness once again hidden under an air of foppish languor.

'If there's two words I can't imagine together,' he said, 'they are *natural* and *enemy.*'

'Oh, empty-headed Drako will now lecture us on philosophy,' said the man who seemed to want war with Masr.

'My dear,' Drako all but lisped. '*Natural* is whatever a fella is used to, and *enemy* is whatever a fella don't like, eh?'

Aranthur was going up the steps when he realised, in a cascade of discovery, that he knew the short, wide man with the long beard; he had been the guard at Lonika, when he was going home for First Sun. And the woman he'd just fenced with was the one who'd passed him through the gate.

General, someone had called her. *Majesty.*

Dahlia's hand tightened and she pulled him up the last of the steps. The crowd was even denser there, and a man slapped his back, and several men and women congratulated Dahlia. Up here were observers, people in magnificent clothes: silk and Eastern *pushmina* wool and brocade and velvet in every direction; a woman in shoes that must have taken a hundred hours to make; a man in boots with toes so pointy that he had gold chains from the points of his shoes up to his garters, which were embroidered with minute mottos. Another man was just removing his cloak in a swirl of fur. Aranthur, slick with sweat, pressed against a woman whose entire gown appeared to be lined in squirrel fur and covered in an Eastern brocade, high-necked and yet split so far down that Aranthur couldn't help but look back. She blinked.

'No, no, we need to get through,' Dahlia said, very loudly.

But they were hemmed in. The press was as close as a festival crowd at home. There were hundreds of people on the upper floors, trying to watch the fighting below, and they represented a level of wealth that Aranthur didn't even recognise. He had thought Syr Kallinikos wealthy, and he was, but right in front of him was a man wearing a dagger with a gold and ivory hilt worth more than his father's farm.

'You struck the General,' a male voice said.

Aranthur turned his head. He didn't know the man, who inclined his head in a very civil manner.

'Not many hit the General,' he said.

'Pah,' said his partner.

'A general who has never fought a battle,' the woman said dismissively.

Dahlia tugged him on. A woman with red hair smiled at him, a brilliant smile; she had a necklace of Zhouian pearls. She was stunning.

'I think I'm hurt,' she said. 'Don't you know me?'

Aranthur tried to bow, but the press of flesh and clothing held him up. He was caught up in a billow of *'Asseen* smoke from an unseen hookah, and his head swirled, and her perfume seemed to surround him, reach for him . . .

'Iralia!' he said. 'I owe you a—'

'Visit me!' she called.

She laughed, and the crowd moved.

'. . . the Emperor . . .' someone said, leaning close, as if to whisper in his ear.

Suddenly Dahlia's hand was gone and he was face to face with . . .

'Syr Ansu,' Aranthur said. It was the Zhouian prince.

The prince bowed, hand on heart – a very different bow from Aranthur's – and, as the first time, he bowed with his hand on his sword and his eyes on Aranthur the whole time. But then he broke into a grin that could not possibly be feigned.

'I missed you, damn it!' he said.

He was dressed in a scarlet silk doublet and matching hose that were a patchwork of expensive cloth, all perfectly cut and painstakingly stitched together like a crazy quilt of riches. He wore his long Zhouian sword in a sash, and held it close to him, the way a local aristocrat might have held a parasol in summer or a walking stick.

'I had no idea . . .' he began.

Aranthur felt his hand taken. A man tried to kiss Dahlia and she put an elbow into him and pulled. Aranthur had to glance back over his shoulder.

'I'll find you!' Ansu shouted.

Someone pinched Aranthur's backside and he jumped.

He stumbled after Dahlia. But in three more steps they were through the fringe of the press. A new fight was starting in the pit below them, and they were no longer the centre of attention.

Dahlia smiled at him. It was a smile full of a sort of promise.

'Well, well.' She looked back. 'I'm used to it. Did you get groped?'

'I did, too.' Aranthur smiled. 'I tried not to enjoy it.'

She gave him a lopsided smile. 'Was that Aranthur Timos making a joke?'

He shrugged. 'They're like . . .'

Dahlia rolled her eyes. 'They're like vultures, even the ones who are my friends. As if by touching us, they are part of the fighting.'

Aranthur leant forward, daring to put his face close to hers.

'It was good fighting,' he said.

She smiled. 'It does rather warm one up, though, doesn't it?'

Aranthur flushed. His heart beat as fast as it had fencing with the General, and he smiled and followed her. She walked along a narrow hall and out onto another balcony, this one overlooking another pit, which held no fighters, but only revellers. Nor was the crowd as well dressed – there were actual Students down there, and much less savoury types.

But Dahlia went up, not down. She went up a short flight of steps, along a hall with doors as close as soldiers on parade, and she pushed one open. There was a washbasin, and water, obviously hot, as steam rose off it. But it was winter in the City, and the water had cooled. She cast, casually, without a talisman, and the water boiled.

'Shirt off,' she said. 'Let's see it.'

Aranthur pulled his shirt over his head. He owned five, thanks to the dead man and his baggage, and he was somewhat ashamed to see how badly frayed this shirt was, now that he looked at it.

The General's thrust to his abdomen had punctured some skin and bled freely, and now that he was cooling, it hurt. Dahlia tossed him a cloth full of hot water and he washed off the blood. She lit a pair of candles in sconces with *power*, and then she carefully washed his various lacerations. When she was working on his back, he took courage and kissed her as she leant over him.

It was one of the bravest things he'd ever done, but he was inspired – he was capable of anything.

She kissed him enthusiastically, her tongue probing his mouth. Even in occasional encounters with the girls of home, Aranthur had never experienced a kiss like it.

And then she pulled off her own shirt. He reached for her, and she pushed him away.

'Later,' she said. 'Now do my back.'

She leant back against him, and he was as conscientious as lust could make him, working on her smooth brown skin. He got the blood off the long lacerations she had under her left arm.

'Damn Tiy Drako,' she said. 'He always hits me the same way.'

She turned, and put her lips on his, and there was a long interval of pleasure. And then a very exciting moment where they attacked each other's buttons and ties.

'Babies?' Aranthur mustered the discipline to ask, at a crucial moment.

She was above him, naked, backlit by candlelight.

She laughed. 'Tirase took care of that, silly. What do they teach you Arnauts?'

'Wake up,' Dahlia Tarkas said.

Aranthur looked up at her. She had two steaming mugs of *quaveh* and she was wearing his torn shirt.

'Wake up, lover. I assume you have to be at the Magistera's office this morning?'

He smiled. It was still dark outside; their room had a window. He took the *quaveh* gratefully, drank some, and then ran an exploratory hand up her bare leg under the shirt. She set her cup down carefully.

'Ah, that answers my *next* question,' she said softly.

Her body transfixed him, and he pulled the shirt off and gazed at her, all hard muscle and softness alternating. She grew bored of his gaze and turned him to more practical affections, and then she was looking out the window at the growing light.

'Come,' she said. 'Time to go.'

'My gown!' he said.

She winced. 'You left it downstairs? Damme. You may never see it again. And I should find you a shirt.' She kissed him. 'I am your first?' she asked, with a little hesitancy and a flip of her head.

'Yes,' he said.

'Well. How nice.' She leant over and kissed him.

His gown, it proved, was still in a ball in a corner of the changing room. It was undamaged and no more frowsy than it had been before, although Dahlia wrinkled her nose at it.

The two of them walked through the lightening streets. Dahlia wore a sword, and Aranthur was simply another Student in an old gown. She bought him a delicious pastry at a *quaveh* seller's, and they parted at the gate inside the precinct. He tried not to notice that she spent her money on him, and he could not have afforded even the pastry.

Aranthur was, in fact, early. He felt light-headed; it seemed like a year since he had been in the office, instead of a mere twelve hours. The dye-stains on his hands surprised him as being part of another experience entirely. But he sat and began practising his letters at the notary's desk, and when the Magistera arrived, she smiled at him.

'Now this is dedication,' she said.

She unlocked her office with a wave of her hand, and he followed her in and gave her the cup of *quaveh* he'd kept warm with spellcraft.

He went back to work. Twice she came and stood over him; the second time she laughed aloud. He was copying

آی ای نم نیاز هب سرح شوخ طبعی داره؟

And she followed it with her finger.

'The biter, bit,' she said.

He didn't like how the Safiri letters spaced, and once he angrily cut a whole page of precious paper out of his copybook and threw it away.

The Master of Arts took the page, uncreased it, and put it in a pile of scrap.

'Paper is too valuable to waste,' she said mildly. 'May I assume you got very little sleep last night?'

Aranthur considered lying, but there seemed no point.

'Yes, ma'am,' he admitted.

She shrugged. 'Well, I hope it was delightful. No more displays of temper, please.'

Aranthur copied until it was time to fetch food, working his way through the complex *occulta* of an arcane shield. Edvin gave him a silver cross, which saved him from penury, and he purchased food for the three of them. In the afternoon, Syr Eshtirhan came and worked with him on vocabulary, leaving him with a list of two hundred carefully copied out words to learn. As the next two days were a major Twelver religious holiday called the Feast of the Crafts, Aranthur accepted the brutal assignment with relative calm. He knew he was being pushed. He tried not to yawn.

The Magistera banished him to the outer office for the last hour, as she had private meetings. Edvin cheerfully helped Aranthur copy his word list, which saved him an hour. They were both copying away when Dahlia, dressed in her doublet, appeared at the door. She placed a messenger's tube on the notary's desk.

'It's not immediate,' she said with a grin.

Edvin leant back. 'I smell an excuse,' he said.

Outside in the central court, the great bell began to ring, *one, two, three, four.*

'Thy servitude is at an end,' Edvin said with a wink. 'Perhaps Myr Tarkas will protect you on the way home.'

Dahlia nodded, her smile both delightful and wicked.

Aranthur rose and put his writing materials together. For the first time he was taking his writing kit home. He wiped his nibs and put them in their slots, capped his ink bottle carefully, and gathered it all in a bag.

'I'm assuming you want to see me again,' Dahlia said.

Aranthur grinned. 'Oh, I suppose,' he said, and she swatted him.

'You might ask me, or ask me to dinner, or something. I'm doing all the work here.'

Aranthur followed her, tongue-tied. Then, after an internal conversation, he shrugged outwardly.

'I'm too poor to take you to dinner. And my rooms are . . .' She stopped under the Founder's statue and he shrugged. 'My rooms are in a terrible state and I went out last night instead of cleaning them.' He made a face. 'I have about forty hours of work to do in the next day, and right now, I'd happily follow you anywhere.'

She smiled. 'That was very well said,' she quipped. 'Why don't we clean your room, and then perhaps I'll buy *you* dinner.'

'I don't want you buying me things.' He said it before he thought it.

She tilted her head like a cat.

'But you have *no money.*'

He shrugged. 'I know where we can have Zhouian noodles in *hani* broth.'

She shrugged. 'Try me. I like a good noodle.'

Dinner was satisfactory.

'I've never been in one of these,' Dahlia admitted about the noodle shop. 'I pass them every day. How much were our noodles?'

'A few obols.'

Aranthur was uneasy speaking of money. He'd only had the change from lunch with which to buy this beautiful aristocrat dinner.

She shook her head. 'You bought the General a beer last night. What did that cost you?'

He thought, and then was bold.

'All my money,' he admitted.

She shook her head. 'Are all Arnauts this crazy and proud?'

'Yes,' he answered.

At the top of six flights of stairs, Dahlia was less sanguine. She looked at the dried blood, the flies, and the mess.

'Damn,' she said. 'You're not *that* good looking.'

She flashed him a smile and went in.

'I can do it,' he said.

'Good. I have servants to do this sort of thing.' She shrugged. 'No, I don't. I mean, my parents do . . .' She paused. 'I'm sure it will be a good experience. My father often tells me I need to learn what work is.'

Over the course of washing the floor, Aranthur learned a great deal about the lives of the lower nobility. The Tarkoi family was both ancient and poor; the combination was deadly, at least for Dahlia, trapping her in a social world she could not afford. And yet her idea of poverty was riches to him.

'I love that place,' she said, about the sword tavern. 'My principal entertainment. But I can't really afford to spend much time there.' She winked at him. 'You were an expensive treat.'

'You paid for the room,' he said.

'Yes, I like to be mistress of my own destiny. And I knew you couldn't pay.'

Somehow, that comment hurt, even through his haze of new affection.

When the blood was gone, Aranthur began on the wreckage of his leather case, and Dahlia shook her head.

'What in Darkness happened here?' she asked. 'Your room-mate was attacked and someone searched—'

There was a knock at the door.

Aranthur went and opened it, and Tiy Drako came in.

'Tarkas!' he said. 'I'm not at all surprised.'

'Drako!' She kissed him. 'I noted that you knew my lover.'

There was something . . . *artificial* about their words. Aranthur glanced back and forth, measuring them.

'One night, and he's your lover? Sunlight, you move fast, Timos.' He looked around. 'Damme, Timos, do you mean to say you have this sprig of the nobility washing your floors?'

'I will kill you. Dead. With a sword. If you use that phrase out in the world,' Dahlia said brightly.

'My lips are sealed,' Drako said. 'Dahlia, I'm sorry to say that I need a word alone with Timos on a private matter. Eh?'

'A boy thing?' she asked. 'His last lover is waiting outside the door?'

Aranthur said, 'I don't have a last lover.'

Drako barked a laugh. 'Never admit such a thing, my boy.'

'I'm damned if I'll be thrown out after washing the floor,' Dahlia said.

'Stay here and we'll go,' Drako said with a laugh. 'Five minutes,' he added.

He hauled Aranthur out of the door and down the steps.

'If I'd imagined that you were going to be friends with half of the aristocracy, I'd have concocted you a better story,' Drako said bitterly. 'The Prince of Zhou, no less. The General.' He shrugged. 'That's not why I'm here. Listen, Aranthur. You joined the Selected Men?'

'Yes.'

Drako nodded. 'Well, expect to be called to duty soon. Maybe three days, maybe a week.'

Aranthur stiffened. 'What?'

Drako shrugged. 'I have reason to believe that all the militia will be summoned for duty.' He smiled. 'Iralia says hello. You saw her last night?'

'She does?' Aranthur was confused. 'Oh,' he said. 'Yes.'

'Dahlia must have more *baraka* than I have credited her with, if you cannot remember seeing Iralia,' Drako said.

Aranthur tried to look worldly.

Drako snorted, and then shook his head.

'Do you know what goes on at that tavern, young Timos? People who fight... They go off and have sex, many of them.'

'Really?' Aranthur asked, imitating Dahlia's sarcasm.

'Yes, you are quick enough, for a country boy. Listen, be careful, that's all. They are my people, so to speak, and yet I find them...' He shrugged. 'The thing I really came to say is, please start wearing a sword. All the time. We're having a hard time tracing the people we're up against. And I will be uncommonly honest with you, old boy... That piece of parchment? Volta's. You were right. And it put the wind up all of us.'

Aranthur shrugged, almost uninterested in the politics of the City compared with the immanent magnificence of Dahlia.

'Listen to me. You have a writ. Use it.' He reached into his purse and handed over a folded square of parchment. 'A little contribution. Don't get all proud on me, my friend. Buy a small sword or something you can wear in the street. *Wear it.* Act like a bad arse. Understand me?' He paused. 'I saw you last night, with all those people... Do you even know what the sides are?'

'You are scaring me,' Aranthur said. 'No. I don't even know you are what you say you are.'

Drako flashed him the smile of the trickster, the mountebank.

'Good. Feel free to doubt me, as long as you doubt everyone else. Well – not Dahlia. I've known her since she was young and hit boys with sticks.'

Aranthur could imagine that. 'I have a sword...'

Drako glanced at the heavy sword hanging by the window.

'A collector's item from the First Empire. You need a nice sword that you can wear, not a killing machine like yon that you can't even draw in a crowd.'

Aranthur had never even thought of drawing a sword in a crowd.

'The Festival of Iron is coming – perfect day to buy a sword. When you are called for duty, *go!* No place safer for you. Understand?'

'I'm in over my head,' Aranthur said.

'You and me both. Kiss Dahlia for me.' He put a hand on Aranthur's shoulder. 'We have a password. Cold Iron.'

'You are mocking me,' Aranthur said.

'Not any more,' Drako said, and walked into the alley.

Aranthur was reluctant to take money from Drako. On the other hand, he could, and did, tell himself that he had rent due and no room-mates, and that was at least in part due to circumstances beyond his control. His conscience was elastic to the extent of a good dinner at the Sunne in Splendour tavern with Dahlia to celebrate the lines full of laundry in his yard and the clean floor and tidy spaces in his rooms, and his first successful casting of the Safiri shield spell from the *Ulmaghest*. It was one of the best, and most expensive dinners he'd ever had, but he fell in love with the Sunne in Splendour, not least because they treated him like a prince.

'You need to be rich,' Dahlia said. 'I think you might be good at spending money.'

She didn't ask him where his sudden wealth had come from.

The next day they studied, made love, studied more, fenced, and he still managed to find time to restitch all the linings on his travelling cases, which delighted Dahlia.

'You are so handy,' she said.

He tried not to hear that as an insult.

He had to try not to look at her, because she was wearing a mended (and clean) man's shirt that showed her muscles and her legs to their advantage.

'Make me something,' she said.

He nodded. 'Give me a few days,' he agreed.

Then they went out to the gates of the leather-worker's *keto*, where a priest of the Twelver's craft god Draxos gave an invocation and blessed shops. A cake was shared, an ancient ritual, and in the cake were *quaveh* beans. One of them fell to Aranthur, to his confusion, and he found himself an incense bearer in the religious procession. Dahlia taught him how to use the censer – Dahlia, of all people.

'My father is very pious,' she said. 'I've done this before. Trust me.'

She taught him to light the censer and swing it, and the priest nodded approvingly. They moved through the *keto* of the Kipkaks, an ancient neighbourhood that had once been owned by people from far north of the Sea of Moros. Now it was a mixed *keto* – Byzas and prosperous Attians and Armeans – and leather-work and tanning and associated industries were located along its filthy canal and cleaner upper streets. He and Dahlia processed with men and women in masks chanting prayers. There was a play about the death and rebirth of the Sun, and another play about the Lady. Another told how poor lame Draxos was thrown from the heavens by the Eagle and had to crawl to his workshop to make the Heart of the Gods, the jewel that earned him the Eagle's praise and his place among the Twelve. Every shop was blessed, including the one where Aranthur worked. Manacher embraced him.

'First Iron Day in the guild, and look, you're almost a priest already!' he said.

The next merchant on the street, Rachman, was staring at Aranthur as if he'd never seen an Arnaut before. His jewels were on flashy display for the guilds, but his shop looked dirty and his glass windows were dusty. He caught Aranthur's eye and smirked. Instead of responding to the censing, he ogled Dahlia. Aranthur lost the swing of his thurible and glared.

'Ignore him,' Manacher hissed. 'He's a crook. He sells stolen things and *ghat*. Maybe even *thuryx*.'

Manacher walked with them for ten streets. The three of them enjoyed ginger cake together after Aranthur passed the thurible to the next winner at the gates of the more prosperous Keto l'Aquilei. Aranthur was delighted by Dahlia's pleasure in the street scene, and her openness with Manacher. If she was an aristocrat, she didn't play one on the street. But her eyes were everywhere, and sometimes he found it difficult to gain her full attention.

'I may have a girl of my own,' Manacher admitted. 'And since my blessed mother thinks I'm with you . . .' He finished his *chai* and waved. 'I'm off.'

He and Aranthur embraced, and Manacher skipped off into the crowds.

'I like him,' Dahlia said.

'He is a very good man,' Aranthur agreed.

Even in saying this, he learned that he did, indeed, like Manacher. He'd never really thought about it before.

At the very end of the day, the two of them, a little tipsy from a dozen street parties, walked out of the *keto* and into the Festival of Crafts, the day of makers. All the guilds were in the streets, with floats and parades and stalls, and most of the skilled trades had shops open to sell the very best of their wares. It was accounted lucky to buy almost anything on the Day of Craft. The two of them roamed the city, eating fish pies and drinking cheap wine as darkness fell out at sea and rolled swiftly up the city.

About the ninth hour, they came to the street of sword smiths, and together they went from booth to shop. Arming swords were all the rage; they came in a dozen shapes with plain hilts, complex hilts, short blades, wide blades, narrow blades...

The street was full of revellers: dozens of young men and women, and older people, and families. Well down the street, almost three blocks from the fashionable Cutlers' Corner, they passed a blue door. It was open.

'Do you know who that is?' Dahlia asked.

Aranthur shook his head. 'I don't know anything.'

She laughed. 'You really don't know anything. That's Jate Palko. The greatest sword maker in the world.' She leant over and whispered, 'He's from Thule. Or beyond!'

The door was open. They stood, indecisive for a while and then, encouraged by the sounds within, they went through the gate and into the courtyard. There, dozens of apprentices drank at tables on the stone-flagged yard and there were three Dhadhi playing for dancing. Dahlia tipped the Dhadhi, and the tallest of them flipped back his hood so that his ears and eyes showed clearly, and bowed. Aranthur returned his bow.

They danced, with each other and with some of the apprentices. People wandered in; Aranthur went to the shop and played with a dozen swords left out, as was the custom on Iron Day.

A big man with a long beard came in, drinking hot mead.

'Yarl,' he said an old Northern expression.

Aranthur had a cup of hot wine, and he raised it. He saw movement in the yard behind him and he looked.

His heart slammed against the inside of his chest several times before full comprehension struck the rest of him.

There was Iralia. She looked like a goddess, in a white gown trimmed in fur and with jewels in her hair lit with *power*. Everyone in the yard was down on one knee, or at least clutching their companions in drunken panic.

The big man with the mead brushed past Aranthur and out into the yard. He bowed deeply, and then knelt by a man in a blue half-cloak. Then he rose into a warm embrace, and the two men pounded each other's backs.

Aranthur went out to Dahlia, disappointing an apprentice enormously by appearing.

She beamed at him. 'You know who that is?'

He nodded. 'I assume that's Master Palko himself.'

Dahlia shook her head. 'You are the most pig-headed . . .' She paused. 'No, you are not. That's the *Emperor*. With Master Palko. I have heard they are close, but to see it . . .'

Aranthur was watching Iralia, who looked as if she burnt with a magnificent inner fire – like the thurible of bronze he'd lit in the parade. Her eyes sparkled; her body all but glowed, at least where her skin showed at throat and hands.

'I suppose that's his current lover. Some Western courtesan,' Dahlia said.

'Her name is Iralia.' Aranthur was looking at her, willing her to turn her head.

'You know her?' Dahlia asked, incredulous.

Iralia turned her head. Her gaze passed over the two of them and swept on to the Dhadhi and then suddenly came back to them. Her smile, as permanent as a tattoo, suddenly focused on Aranthur. She let go of the Emperor's arm and swept forward.

'Aranthur!' she said. 'I was just speaking of you!'

Aranthur was like a moth caught in a volcano. This was not the woman of the Inn of Fosse. This was a force of nature – a sun whose beams were focused just on him.

'Uh . . .' he managed. 'Um . . .'

She nodded. 'You are at the Academy?' she asked, her voice rich with pleasure.

He felt her release the *compulsion* she was using – a light one, and some of it tied to her jewels. She had emeralds around her neck – a dozen or fifteen of them, big enough to matter.

'Yes,' he heard himself say. 'Yes, I'm working to enter the Studion.'

'And who is this?' Iralia asked, extending a hand to Dahlia.

Aranthur had an odd thought, as the two women were almost the same age – Iralia perhaps a year older, and yet she seemed much older still. And far more beautiful, so that Dahlia, who he found captivating beyond his wildest dreams of women, seemed drab and plain.

'My . . . lover. Dahlia Tarkas.' He had never used the fashionable word, *lover*, in public.

'Oh my,' Iralia said. 'At Fosse I rather thought you didn't know what a lover was.' She smiled to take away the sting. 'Tarkos? From Nika?'

Dahlia was not happy. 'Yes,' she snapped.

The man in the blue half-cloak took Iralia by the elbow.

'A friend of yours, my dear?' he asked.

He was, close up, a very ordinary man: perhaps sixty or sixty-five, with cold blue eyes and a strong face; middling height. All his clothes and leather were the very best that could be imagined, although nothing was ostentatious – plain wool with very discreet embroidery, superb, rich leather with very little metal.

Aranthur gave his best bow, and Dahlia executed the amazing complex court reverence that he had seen at the fencing tavern.

'Yes,' Iralia drawled. 'Aranthur and I saved a tavern full of people together. I have told you the story,' she said, turning her head and flashing her smile at the Emperor. 'This is the young man . . .' she said carefully.

The *Emperor*. Aranthur didn't even know what he thought of the Emperor. It was fashionable at the Academy to view the Imperial House as a relic of the past, a holdover from the world before the Revolution. And yet, Tirase had himself saved the Imperial family, and Giorgios, the imperial *legatus* who had saved Tirase from execution and engineered much of the military part of the Revolution, had insisted on their continuation and direct participation in the politics of the City. And the outlaw, Rowan, but that was another story entirely.

So Aranthur looked at the man with unhidden curiosity. The Emperor surprised him with a quick smile, and then he kissed Aranthur on both cheeks, the way two apprentices might greet each other. Then he smiled at Iralia.

'Was this the night the former Duke of Volta threw you out of his carriage?' he asked.

'This very young man picked me up and carried me into the inn,' Iralia said.

The Emperor smiled. Aranthur had a moment to wonder if this was, indeed, the right way to be introduced to the richest man in the world, but the smile appeared genuine.

'Well, well,' he said. 'You didn't say that he was a giant, nor a handsome giant, when you spoke of him. What is your name, Syr?'

Aranthur didn't even know how to address an emperor.

'My lord—' he began.

'Imperial Highness,' Iralia said with a shrug. 'Or just Syr. He is incognito.'

The Emperor nodded.

'Syr...' Aranthur tried.

It sounded terrible, with the reality of the Imperial person standing two feet away. Say what you would, as a Student who was against the Imperial power, but the man himself had incredible dignity *and* a sense of humour.

Aranthur bowed his best bow, again. 'I am Aranthur Timos.'

The man made a face. 'Timos. Splendid name. People of the Eagle, eh?'

'Yes, syr.' Aranthur bowed again.

'Enough of that,' the Emperor said. 'Do you work for Master Palko?'

'Oh, no, syr. I am a Student...'

Suddenly the Emperor was looking at him and seemed a different man. Focused, and perhaps even a little dangerous.

'Timos,' he said, 'do you by any chance have one of my books? And a little gold reader, an artifact of the First Empire?' He glanced at Iralia. 'This is that Timos?'

'I do' Aranthur said, breathing faster.

'Yes,' Iralia said, with catlike satisfaction.

'Well,' the Emperor said.

Master Palko had joined them with a woman – an older woman who had to be his partner. She made a deep curtsey. The Emperor nodded to her and smiled, but his eyes went back to Aranthur's.

'See that you take good care of that reader, lad. It's older than the Empire. Do you know what being Emperor means, lad?'

Aranthur flinched. 'No, Majesty. Syr.'

The older man nodded a few times, his eyes on Iralia.

'It means living with a lot of treasures and riches that belong to your nation. Your job is to hand over as many as you received, when you die. So don't lose my reader.' He bowed to Dahlia. 'And happy Craftday to you, Myr Tarkas.'

Dahlia put her hand on her heart. 'Syr.'

The Emperor put a hand on her head, the way a man would put a hand on his daughter's head – a very familiar action. She smiled.

The Emperor turned away with Master Palko and his lady. Iralia looked back over her shoulder.

'Come and see me,' she said to Aranthur. 'At the palace. I'm in when I don't go riding.'

She walked away, her eyes aglitter.

Dahlia tugged his arm, hard.

'*You* know the *Emperor*,' she said.

Aranthur paused, thinking of all the things he was not at liberty to say.

'You know him too.'

'I am the eldest daughter of one of the oldest Houses in the land. I have been introduced at court. I could wear the blue feather in my hair, if I chose to have enough hair to do such things.' She shrugged. 'I've known him since I was a baby.'

Aranthur shrugged. 'I know Iralia,' he said, vaguely.

He was in a pleasant sort of shock. It wasn't altogether pleasant, because he had the idea that he had the reader and the job reading Safiri because of her. It wasn't anything he'd done. It was good old-fashioned nepotism.

'The Emperor's paramour. You *know* her?' Dahlia looked at Iralia and back at Aranthur. And shook her head. 'You know *her*?' she asked again. 'Beastroot! I thought you was a virgin.'

He frowned. 'You are my first lover—'

'I don't care! Virginity is a fancy word for inexperience. She might have taught you better, but then, you ain't bad.'

She smiled to show she meant no harm, but he bridled when she didn't believe him.

'I never . . .' he began.

'Save it for the cheap seats,' Dahlia said.

Soon enough, they moved on, going down the street of cutlers and smiths, Aranthur fighting an inclination to spoil the evening by showing his anger. But he fought it off. Dahlia's presumptions were annoying, but they reflected her life and class.

Aranthur was feeling a little drunk by then, and Dahlia was still stewing over Iralia. He wasn't sure what to make of that, or what to say, so he went back to looking at swords. In a candle-lit booth that smelled of incense, he found a blade he loved: straight, not too short, with a finger ring for defence and a straight cross-hilt which appealed to his Arnaut nature.

The owner of the stall was an old man with a tonsure of white hair around the bald head, contrasted by a very elegant moustache and beard.

'Swordsman?' he asked.

Aranthur shrugged. 'I hope so.'

Dahlia played with the blade and said 'Like'. She grinned at the balding man, who smiled back.

'It is a good blade. The hilt is plain – I can rehilt it in something fancier—'

'No, I want it to use,' Aranthur said. 'How much?'

The older man raised an eyebrow, looked behind him at the lit window of his shop, and gave the smallest shrug Aranthur had ever seen.

'In truth, young syr, I would like ten golden sequins. I could tell you thirty, and you could tell me five, and we could spend what is left of the night on it, but I have not made a sale all evening and my wife would like to go and dance. I made this sword for a client who never came and picked it up – I've already been paid half. Ten sequins. My only offer.' He winked at Dahlia. 'I'm trying a whole new technique in sales.'

'Do it!' she said. 'I can loan you . . . two . . .' She frowned. 'Three, if I pretend I can't pay my rent. And don't eat.' She gave a shrug herself. 'It's perfect. For you. Heavy, and balanced, and a little Arnaut and a little City.'

Aranthur had drunk wine and danced, and Iralia, who had briefly been between them, had vanished with the appearance of the blade. He felt at peace with the world. He opened Drako's tiny leather bag and shook the contents into his hand. Sequins were not much bigger than the size of the end of his last finger, not much thicker than paper, but pure gold. Whatever the Emperor's shortcomings – and the man was very unpopular at the Academy – his coins were solid gold.

There were fifteen sequins. He counted out ten, his hands shaking a little. It was different from taking a dead man's money, somehow.

'I am Leone Techne,' the old man said. 'I didn't make a scabbard.'

'I am a leather-worker,' Aranthur said. 'I can make a scabbard, but not the metal parts.'

The cutler frowned. 'Come back in a day or two. Leave the sword – I'll make you some scabbard fittings.' He nodded. 'That's fair, eh?'

They spat on their hands and shook.

Aranthur handed over the money, and then he and Dahlia went off into the City in search of other adventures. They danced and sang and listened to music, drank and ate until dawn.

Aranthur thought it was the best day and night of his life. But Dahlia was a little distant, even when they made love.

The next morning, the second day of the festival, Aranthur woke early, copied his letters and wrote out his verbs. He cast his shield several times, both from inside himself, the true Safian way, and from his *kuria*. Dahlia slept. He went out and got her *quaveh*, which he paid for from his own – that is, Drako's – money.

He went back up all six flights of stairs, passing what had been Kati's room and remarking on the relative silence of the new occupants. He'd never seen the door open.

Dahlia was awake, standing by the glass window, washing from a basin. Aranthur thought her incredibly beautiful, but he had a clear memory of finding her dull beside Iralia. This suggested to him that she had cast a *compulsion*, either directly on him, or a very powerful general *compulsion*. Perhaps she had made an artifact with the emeralds.

He frowned.

Dahlia turned. 'Like what you see? Too skinny?'

He handed over the *quaveh*. 'My love for you is such that you are worth twelve flights of stairs.'

'Damn.' She drank her *quaveh* with relish. 'I want to *do* something.'

Arathur laughed. He nuzzled her neck and put his hands over her breasts.

'I want to do something too . . .' he began.

She shook him away. 'No, something . . . fun.' She met his eye. 'I didn't mean that.'

Aranthur rubbed his jaw. 'Ouch.'

She raised an eyebrow. 'I don't know much about you,' she said suddenly. 'You know the Emperor and his mistress. And Tiy Drako.'

'I don't know the Emperor.'

'You do now,' she said.

'I only met Iralia once. We were *not* lovers.'

Dahlia looked out the window. 'But she's spoken to the Emperor about you.'

Aranthur began to be annoyed. 'This is a little too much like being interrogated by the Watch,' he said. He lacked the experience with naked women to be able to talk well to one.

She nodded, pursing her lips. 'We were better off fencing. I want to go out. Do you have any nice clothes?'

'I have a good black doublet. Here.' He took it off its peg.

'Right, I thought I'd seen that. Very nice. Almost fashionable – a little too Voltain. Let's go and watch the opera,' she said.

'What's opera?' he asked.

The curtains parted for the second act.

The *viola organista* began to sing under the stage, and Aranthur looked around. He was in the pit, with Dahlia tucked in by him. Tall as she was, he was a head taller and much broader, and the press of people in the pit was oppressive. The tip of someone's scabbard was pressing into Aranthur's ankle, and he wasn't even sure which of three men was the culprit.

And then the first actress began to sing. Aranthur was almost positive she was Niobe, the title role; he knew the myth well enough, and she certainly seemed arrogant enough to be Niobe. But the whole work was in Ellene, and while he was a student and he used the language every day, it was crushingly difficult to make out the words when sung rapidly.

The *viola organista* played, and almost beneath his feet, a dozen gitterns and ouds played faster, and Niobe, if it was she, launched into an aria.

The music was incredible. Aranthur forgot that he was sweating, forgot that Dahlia was annoyed, forgot there was a scabbard pressing into his instep. There was nothing but his ears and the music, and when the aria ended he wanted to beg the artist to continue.

The second act came to an end with the Twelve gathering like Dark

Furies to punish a single human woman for her *hybris*. The writer, whoever she was, captured the heart of the myth: that however guilty Niobe might be, and however awful a mother, the gods were about to slay all her children as punishment for...

Nothing. The twelve of them, draped in dark grey instead of the traditional white, sang together. Their sound filled the theatre, and yet the music sounded pompous and smug.

The crescendo was limited, the roar of triumph *almost* false. The audience was asked to question the gods.

Aranthur slammed his hands together hard enough to make them hurt, despite the press. He found that his foot was asleep, and almost fell.

Dahlia looked up at him. 'You like it?'

Aranthur's heart was full, and he felt as if he was on a drug.

'The music...'

Dahlia shook her head and shouted something that was lost. People began pushing past them, fighting for the doors to get chilled wine before the third act.

'I can go,' Aranthur said.

Dahlia shook her head. 'I was going to let you leave,' she quipped, rolling her eyes. 'But you are enjoying it.' She slipped in front of him as the press grew less. 'We can go closer. I know two of the actors, and the lyricist is my cousin.'

'Lyricist?' he asked, feeling foolish. He seemed to feel foolish all the time, with Dahlia.

The press became merely a crowd, and then was almost thinned out.

'Look, it's your friend and the Emperor,' Dahlia said, pointing.

Above them was the Imperial box, a massive confection of gold leaf and ribbons that appeared to be suspended from the ceiling above all the boxes. But it was behind them, and Dahlia was right. Aranthur could see the Emperor, waving down at his subjects, and Iralia, whose eyes seemed to reach for his.

He looked away. At Dahlia.

'Does she have a *compulsion* on her all the time?' he asked.

'That's what it looks like to me. I don't like her. Damn it. Women have to do everything the hard way, and then some little flounce like her wanders up, spreads her legs, and takes everything. I hate it.'

She avoided saying 'I hate her.'

His head was working well; he was organising the things he was learning, and assigning causes to effects.

'And then she uses a powerful spell – Aploun's dick, she must be a first-rate Magas, and she uses her *work* to power her . . . her *appeal*. It demeans women.' She looked at him.

He shrugged. 'I like her.'

Dahlia looked away. 'You would.'

Niobe's children died at the hands of Aploun and Potnia – a shower of very well-executed magik arrows slew them – and they died singing, a convention which Aranthur loved. The special effects were startling, and somewhere offstage a theatrical Magos was casting in perfect time to the performance. Aploun and Potnia danced a sinister and dark ballet of bloodlust and lost innocence that suggested everything from incest to malevolence in the very gods themselves.

It was magnificent, and a little horrifying for a farm boy from Soulis. Granted that tales of the Twelve, like the tale of Niobe and her children, were myths told as frightening stories, it was still somehow blasphemous.

In the end the gods gathered and sang a magnificent chorus of their earlier song of godly triumph. It was loud, and strident, like military music. Was it intentionally bellicose? Did the author imagine that people were at war with the gods?

'Come on!' Dahlia said, grabbing his hand.

She pulled him forward as the crowd began to head for the exits. It was a little like the night in the fencing tavern relived, as they pressed through the crowd. Several men turned to take offence at their passage and then paused to leer at Dahlia, who had dressed for the occasion in traditional Byzas finery, with her hair piled atop her head in a rope of pearls that she assured Aranthur were fake. Her gown was a simple midnight-blue silk kirtle, but slit well up the leg and cut low enough to require a very straight back to carry it off.

A wide man with gold earrings moved to block her.

'In a hurry, darling?' he said.

'Yes,' she said.

He pushed towards her, his bulk forcing them back into the crowd.

'Maybe I want to get to know you better.'

Aranthur pushed forward. He was, if anything, bigger, if not wider.

'We're in a hurry,' he said.

'Not speaking to you, cock, so fuck off,' the man with gold earrings said.

Another man in a jewelled beret laughed.

Dahlia shrugged. 'I don't know you.'

'I'm—'

'Nor do I want to, so get out of my way.'

Earrings grew red in the face.

Dahlia moved to push him, and he slapped her.

Aranthur caught his arm, twisted, and dropped the big man on the floor.

'Let him go,' Dahlia hissed. 'He's from the Iron Circle. Fucking barbarians think they own women.'

Earrings was getting up, helped by his friends.

'Do you have the *baraka* to meet me?' Dahlia asked. 'First light, the Field of Rolan, behind the Temple. Any weapon you fancy.'

'Fight a bitch?' Earrings asked. 'I'll fight the farm boy here. Is he your pimp?'

'You're drunk,' Dahlia said. 'Fight me, or I'll tell everyone that you are a coward.'

'Men don't fight women,' Earrings said.

'You should go home,' Dahlia said. 'But first, tell me your name, so I can tell everyone who you are.'

Jewelled Beret leant over and whispered.

'Fine. You're dead. First light,' Earrings said. 'Then maybe I'll fuck your corpse.'

'I suppose that passes for a witty exchange, in the North?' Dahlia said. 'After I kill you, I will not make any attempts on your corpse. Although I suspect your member will work as well, or ill, after death as before, eh?'

Earrings turned so red that Aranthur, who was full of the spirit of combat and ready to fight, wondered if the man might explode.

'Dead. You are fucking dead!'

Dahlia just walked past. Aranthur avoided the man's spittle, and managed a little bow. Then he followed Dahlia's regal progress up the steps to the stage, where she was immediately embraced by one of Niobe's children. Closer up, the make-up was broad and over-coloured, and all of the performers looked a little like monsters. The face paint had a particular smell...

Aranthur continued to watch the little knot of Northerners.

'Forget them,' Dahlia snapped. 'They came in drunk, and they wanted trouble. Volta pays them to do it.'

Aranthur felt as if he'd entered a dark world he didn't understand. 'Why?' he asked.

Dahlia shrugged. 'Because the Emperor supports the opera,' she said, as if it was obvious.

She introduced a wave of actors – two of Niobe's children and a tiny blond imp who turned out to have been one of the angels in the ballet.

'Anyone you want to meet?' Dahlia asked. 'I know them all. My sister is a principal dancer, although not tonight. My cousin writes the lines.'

Aranthur was a little starstruck. 'I...' He shrugged, still full of the daemon of combat, and a little light-headed. 'The Magos?'

Dahlia led him backstage, where he met Potnia herself, revealed as a middle-aged woman with the most amazingly muscled legs he had ever seen. He bowed deeply, and she grinned.

'Dahlia, who is the handsome giant?'

'Magistera Oroma, this is Aranthur Timos...'

'An Arnaut,' the dancer said. But she smiled.

'Your dancing is amazing,' Aranthur managed.

Even without her mask and make-up, the woman projected an aura not unlike that cast by Iralia, if less... sexual.

'Do you dance, young giant?' Oroma asked.

Aranthur grinned. 'I love to dance. But our dances are nothing like yours.'

'Dance is dance,' Oroma said. 'Look at Dahlia fight with a sword, and you see the same muscles her sister uses to dance.'

She turned as a man in a mask approached. The man, an elegant fop in wine-coloured velvet covered in pearls, bowed low over her hand, performed a pirouette, and produced a rose from the air.

Oroma laughed and took the rose. 'The most beautiful clown.'

The man lowered his mask, and Aranthur was looking at the dark-skinned man who'd been at the fencing tavern.

'Darling,' the man said. 'Suddenly you are everywhere.'

Dahlia rolled her eyes. 'Hands off, Harlequin.'

The dark-skinned man bowed low. 'Your very devoted slave, Columbina.'

Magistera Oroma leant up for an unmistakably amorous kiss with 'Harlequin'. Aranthur followed Dahlia further into the backstage darkness, to where a young man was shrugging into his doublet and having trouble with it.

'Oh,' Dahlia said. 'I expected Bouboulis.'

The man turned and Aranthur laughed, because the young man fighting his doublet was his friend Mikal Kallinikos.

Kallinikos raised his eyebrows. 'Caught,' he said.

'You were the magiker?' Aranthur asked after a warm embrace.

Kallinikos was back to playing with his laces.

'Yes and no,' he said enigmatically. 'Magistera Bouboulis is sick. They had no one else. I can run the simpler effects and a . . . highly placed personage . . . did the rest.'

'The effects were perfect,' Oroma said as she passed. 'You can work with us any time.'

Kallinikos shrugged and turned back.

'This is Myr Dahlia Tarkas . . .'

'I know,' Kallinikos said, with a civil kiss on each cheek.

Dahlia turned and shook her head. 'Somehow you really seem to know everyone.'

Aranthur shrugged.

Dahlia looked aback at Kallinikos. 'Are you on my marriage list?'

Kallinikos nodded. 'Sadly, I am.'

They both laughed.

'Are you being *paid*?' Dahlia asked.

'I am, too,' Kallinikos said, as if it was a guilty secret. 'I'll call myself Kalagathos, Theatrical Thaumaturge.'

'Try and remember us little people when you make it.' Dahlia pulled on Aranthur and he followed her.

'What's wrong with being paid?' Aranthur asked.

'It's sort of forbidden for aristocrats. We have estates, supposedly, and should not engage in commerce.' She shrugged. 'Mostly, we just fight among ourselves.'

Aranthur looked back at Kallinikos. 'What does that mean?'

Dahlia smiled. 'Aristocrats inhabit a whole world of factions and alliances – marriage, lovers, creditors and debtors, old vendettas and insults that must be avenged, all tinged with City politics and Imperial policy. Surely you know the Lions and the Whites?'

Aranthur frowned. 'Yes,' he said automatically, and then he grinned. 'Not enough. Tell me. I mean, I know the Lions from the Academy. No friends of my kind.'

Dahlia shrugged. 'Hard to know where to begin.' She rolled her eyes. 'Fifty years ago, one of the Cerchi had an illicit affair with a Thanatos boy who was actually on her marriage list. Then she ditched him for a better marriage with one of the Ultroi – who, by the way, are cousins of the Kallinikoi and an Imperial House—'

'You're making this up,' Aranthur said.

'I'm not. When she ditched him, she was deemed to have insulted his House. There was already political trouble – this was back when the guilds were first allowing nobles to join. Anyway, more than a thousand people died. The Whites are the faction that backed her, and the Cerchi and the Brusias – modernists. The Lions were – and still are – the old families, like the Kallinikoi. They claim to be loyal to the Emperor and the constitution, but really they are only loyal to their own power. Like my family, of course, except that I think they're all fools. My mother was always against the Lions, even though she's a Roaris. My father's brother is ... Bah, never mind. And there's Blacks and the pious Reds and I think Greens ... Those are old racing factions from chariot-racing days in the hippodrome. Once there were Blues, but they were all executed. That was a long time ago.'

'Roaris?' Aranthur asked, although he was alarmed by the name *Brusias*. He made himself smile. 'All still fighting over a marriage gone wrong?'

'It's not funny, farm boy! The Roarii are another old family. Verit Roaris is the acknowledged head of the Lions – he's also Tribane's rival to be the *Capitan* of all the Imperial armies. I have three Roaris boys on my marriage list.' She frowned. 'No. I know it sounds foolish, but the fighting is always over what matters to them – money and power. The causes may seem petty, but the power is genuine.'

'And what is a marriage list?' Aranthur asked, a little too sharply.

'Oh,' Dahlia laughed, her rich voice rippling in the darkness. 'We all have them. Twenty-four approved matches, based on House business and alliances. Kallinikos isn't bad. He used to be very conservative indeed, but he's coming around. I like seeing that he wants to work

and not be a drone. He used to belong to one of the Academy clubs…
The nasty ones for the old boys – the Lions. He's left it. Come. I'm
fighting that disgusting prat in the morning, and I want to make love
first.'

'There's a party,' Kallinikos shouted from the darkness. 'Come on,
Aranthur!'

'But there's a party…' Dahlia said. 'I might be dead tomorrow.
Party or love?'

Aranthur thought of his desire to be a *daesia*.

'How about both?' he offered.

Dahlia was dressed like a man, in a doublet and hose. Aranthur wore
an Arnaut fustanella and dark blue turban out of a perverse urge to
annoy the Northerners, and carried his own long sword. Kallinikos and
Dahlia's sister Rose came along, as did Oroma's lover, whom they all
called Harlequin. They were armed, because no one trusted the men
of the Iron Ring not to cheat.

Dahlia chose Aranthur as her second. He was aware that he probably
was not the best blade, and that perhaps she chose him to flatter him.

'Don't die,' she said. 'Drako would kill me.'

That was another unfathomable comment, although even half-drunk,
Aranthur had noticed how much time Drako, the life of the party, had
spent in an apparent argument with Dahlia. Aranthur had spent most
of the party being surprised at how easily the Byzas aristos accepted
him. Rose, the dancer, called him by the familiar 'di' before the singing started. He'd danced with Kallinikos' sister Elena, and Mikal had
repeated, drunkenly, the faction talk that Dahlia had given him.

'Everything is gods-damned factions,' the young man said bitterly.
'Maybe it is time to finish what Tirase started. Disestablish the nobility.'

'From the Lions to the Whites,' Dahlia said, slapping him lightly.

Kallinikos drank off a cup of wine. 'Maybe. Maybe it's time for me
to say what I think.' He shrugged. 'Except that my father would have
me killed.'

'You're drunk,' she said. 'He might cut off your money.'

'You don't know him,' Kallinikos muttered.

It had, altogether, been a very interesting party.

The square was not empty as they crossed towards the Temple and
the cloister behind, which was apparently where the gentry fought

their duels. There were farm carts rolling noisily through the Great Gate, dozens of huge wains filled with produce, and little knots of Easterner refugees. A pair of prostitutes, drinking from a glass bottle and obviously hoping to see a duel, giggled and followed them. A dozen soldiers were asleep on the ground for whatever reason.

'Here they come.' Dahlia was sober, but all of them had been awake all night.

Aranthur was just drunk enough to be unafraid. Neither excited nor scared.

'Which of you is the second?' Aranthur addressed the seven men in dark cloaks. They wore black leather masks.

'They're going to charge us,' Rose said. 'Fucking morons.'

Harlequin, still in his outrageous velvet doublet, shook his head.

'Don't do it, boys,' he said. 'More than two on two is against the law, and the law . . .'

All seven Westerners dropped their cloaks and drew. They had an assortment of weapons   three small swords, two arming swords, and two long swords.

'Make it quick,' Earrings said in his odd Liote. 'Kill them all.'

Three of the Westerners drew puffers. One pointed his at Aranthur, and even as he raised his shield, Harlequin snapped his fingers and the puffer exploded, pulverising a hand. The Westerner dropped to his knees as the acrid reek of *saar* wafted past Aranthur and clashed with the rotten egg smell of the puffer.

Aranthur had the oddest feeling that the tall black man was protecting him. He got his shield up anyway, his first such casting under pressure. The edges of the little red shield seemed to waver.

The second man fired, but his ball exploded against Aranthur's little ruby shield. The other pulled his trigger. The shot hit Dahlia's sister and she went down with an ugly whimper.

Aranthur didn't wait for his friends. He ran at the man who'd shot Rose. He wore a black mask, and he had a heavy arming sword with a complex hilt.

Aranthur swung at him from his last stride, anger powering his heavy overhead stroke. The man made a classic overhead parry, and used his pistol barrel to clear his sword.

Aranthur took a stinging blow to his left arm. He was two steps ahead of his friends, and alone against three men. He made a wide swing, right to left, across all three blades, and his strength and his heavy blade kept him alive. One man actually stepped back. The pistoleer hacked at him and Aranthur responded without thought – a cover, a rotation of his wrist – and he won the bind. His point scraped across the other man's face and eye, even as the other man's blade snapped. He screamed and stumbled back and Aranthur hit him again, a wrist cut to the crown of his head that dropped him, dead or wounded.

Aranthur turned, a simple pivot. Harlequin had his sword through one Westerner's body. As Aranthur watched, he turned like a dancer, whipping the blade free and pinking another man in the hand – luck or extreme skill. He whirled again, and his left hand seemed to pulse with violet light, and the man who had stepped back was choking on something that smelt like expensive perfume.

Dahlia was standing over her sister, her sword moving in precise arcs. She was facing Earrings, who was cutting at her with heavy blows from a long sword.

Mikal Kallinikos was backing from his man, making simple parries.

The choking man facing Harlequin dropped his sword, reached into his sash and produced a long puffer. As he raised it, Aranthur's sword cut into his neck.

Kallinikos' opponent looked around and took a hit in the bicep from Kallinikos. He dropped his sword and ran.

'Mine!' Dahlia shouted. 'Don't you touch him!'

Earrings cut at her, and cut again. And again. But Rose was not dead. She was crawling away, to where Harlequin simply picked her up and began to carry her away, casting as he walked.

Dahlia now had room, and she used it, backing, darting, and retreating again.

Kallinikos was as white as a sheet, but he cleaned his blade on a downed adversary and then turned.

'Drop your weapon. Don't be a fool!' he called. 'These people need a doctor.'

Dahlia backed, and Earrings cut at her again; his three-step combo – cut, cut . . .

Dahlia's sword went right through his right forearm in her stop-thrust, almost to the hilt with the force of his own arm. Then she reached in and took the heavy sword from his hands, whirled it around her head, and her blow decapitated him.

'Potnia!' Kallinikos said, and threw up.

Harlequin laughed his deep laugh. He managed a deep bow, even with Rose's body in his arms.

They spent some hours – some very uncomfortable hours – with the City Watch. The presence of four aristocrats both helped and hindered them. The corroboration of both prostitutes that the Westerners had puffers and used them, as well as the evidence of the Watch magiker, saved them from worse. The Watch's medico cleaned the wound in Aranthur's left bicep.

'Get an Imoter to knit the muscle or you'll never have full use of the arm,' he said. 'And while I'm giving advice ... Don't get mixed up with this faction shit, kid. People like you and me – we aren't shit to they aristos.'

Aranthur started. 'This wasn't faction! They tried to kill us!'

The City Watch officer shrugged. 'Sure, whatever you say,' he opined. 'Looked like a bunch of Lions going for some White aristos to me, but what do I know?' He smiled grimly. 'When you have a belly full of steel, don't say I didn't try to warn you. Now get to an Imoter.'

Imoters had once been priests of Imotep, the God of Healing, but now they were usually magikers with a specialty in medicine.

'Aploun!' Aranthur cursed to Dahlia. 'All my word lists are due tomorrow.'

'Aploun,' Dahlia said. 'We're alive. Don't be such a prig.'

Aranthur helped Kallinikos home. The aristocrat was silent and withdrawn.

'What's wrong?' Aranthur asked.

Kallinikos gave him a bitter smile. 'Have you ever done something you really regret?'

Aranthur shrugged.

Kallinikos shook his head. 'Never mind.' He shrugged. 'I'm having a fight with my father.'

'Can I help?'

Mikal shrugged. 'No way I can think of. I just don't believe things I used to believe. That makes everything ... complicated.'

Aranthur thought of his father and mother as he walked home, and nodded in sympathy.

*

Whatever crisis Drako expected did not materialise. Over the next weeks, Aranthur worked on his Safiri, attended a lecture series on moral philosophy with Dahlia, went to work and did dyeing, and started a belt-purse for Dahlia with Ghazala's support. The furniture for his new sword took the cutler almost two weeks to make – not just a day or two – but when it was finished, it was beautiful, polished like a mirror on a water wheel. Aranthur took the sword and the various pieces to his employers, and negotiated for a scabbard and belts. He worked on Dahlia's belt-purse, his own sword belt and scabbard, and a purse for himself, all while doing his own work, his Academy work, and his sword work. He tried not to think about the men he'd killed.

Mikal Kallinikos was now very much his friend, as if the early morning fight had taken them over some divide or other, and Aranthur took Kallinikos to Master Sparthos. Sparthos was courteous to the young aristocrat. He sent Aranthur to train with Mikal Sapu, the young duellist from Volta who had lost the first fight at the Inn of Fosse. He taught Aranthur a rule, a little like a dance, very different from the way Master Vladith taught. The 'first rule' had sixteen postures or stances, but they were merely stopping points between actions – cuts, slashes, thrusts, parries. He spent two hours on Aranthur alone, which cost half a sequin. After that, as often as Aranthur could attend, he was in a class with a dozen other men and women, learning other rules (it proved there were forty-seven), or unpacking one into the details of weight change, or action – drills to force the student to imagine what facing an opponent would be like. There was a great deal of memorisation. Aranthur thanked the Eagle that Vladith and Sparthos at least used all the same terms, most of them in Ellene, for *gardes*, postures, and attacks.

Sometimes Kallinikos joined the class, and sometimes he took a private lesson with Sparthos. There were various weapons: the long sword, the arming sword, even the master's weapon, the five-foot long *montante*. The last was one that no one ever actually carried – Masters used them when judging duels, or when marching in city processions. Aranthur was astounded at the speed of the huge weapon, and its elegance, and the strength it took to wield it.

The master stopped him one day. 'You were born to wield this,' he said simply.

Aranthur flushed with pleasure. 'Thank you, Master.'

'Thank *you*. You brought me an excellent student – talented enough, and willing to pay.' He raised an eyebrow. 'Starving wastrels like you do not keep my child in school.'

Aranthur was aware that he did not pay what Kallinikos paid. So he bowed, and hurried off to find Dahlia, who spent as much time in his rooms as in her own. She seemed busy all the time and yet never seemed to do any work related to school or her *Ars*. Sometimes her sister joined them for fish soup, or took them out for *polpo*, the city's famous octopus dish. She had been healed within an hour of the duel.

'Harlequin is a great man,' she said with a shrug.

'Did he heal you himself?' Dahlia asked.

'Who is he?' Aranthur asked.

'He's a Magos, and a great one. From Masr, or so people say. In fact, no one knows anything about him.' Rose smiled. 'He took me to Kurvenos, the Lightbringer. Some people say he's a Lightbringer himself.'

'Aploun! As my lover likes to say all of a sudden. *Kurvenos?* Harlequin knows Kurvenos? You are living in a fabulous tale, sister.' Dahlia laughed. 'And Lightbringers don't fight duels. They are forbidden to kill.'

'Oroma is his lover. She must know more.' Rose made a face. 'But Kurvenos knows you, sister. Why do you pretend not to know him?'

Dahlia was clearly disconcerted, and Aranthur thought she behaved exactly like someone caught in a lie.

'I didn't say I didn't know him,' she said gaily.

Rose looked quizzical and then relented. 'Well – maybe Oroma will know, anyway.'

Dahlia shrugged. 'Timos is my lover, and I really don't know much about him.'

She said such things too often, along with occasional anti-Arnaut comments and vague references to the shortcomings of her social inferiors – very much like Kallinikos, but without his sense of humour. It wasn't that Aranthur thought that she meant any of them; but the casual comments irked, nonetheless.

She leant back. 'For example, have you changed fencing masters?'

'Yes, I'm studying with Master Sparthos now.'

Dahlia rolled her eyes. 'My provincial farm boy knows the Emperor and his mistress and Tiy Drako and now he's fencing with Sparthos.'

Aranthur shrugged. 'I met them all the same day, almost the same hour, in a tavern.'

Rose leant back. 'Interesting.'

Weeks passed. Aranthur discovered that he and Kallinikos had won a First in Anatomy. They celebrated with a dinner at the Sunne in Splendour, and Kallinikos brought his lady friend, who was mysterious, beautiful, and Armean.

Dahlia rolled her eyes, and after dinner, snuggled close, she said, 'That woman is someone's wife. Kallinikos had better watch out.'

'How do you know?' Aranthur was more interested in Dahlia's neck and shoulders . . .

She shrugged, kissed him, and then wriggled.

'I don't *know*. But she was evasive about . . . *everything*.'

'Not about her life out East,' Aranthur said.

Dahlia licked his chin like a cat. 'Yes, now we know why Kallinikos is suddenly a White.'

They moved on to other things.

The next morning, Sparthos taught him in person, or rather he took the larger class which was not, strictly speaking, on swordplay.

The master was waiting for them on the third floor, and Mikal Sapu put on an arming coat and joined the class as a student. The master taught all of them, carefully, how to fall. Then he began to discuss non-lethal techniques, demonstrating plays from covers and parries and crosses that could be used to strike with a pommel or break an arm or dislocate a shoulder.

He smiled his thin-lipped smile and coughed into a handkerchief, and then he nodded.

'In war, perhaps, you will always want to kill your enemy. In a fight that is desperate – against footpads, perhaps – you may have to kill.' The master's eyes seemed to bore into Aranthur's and he wondered how much the master knew. 'It is important to know that you can kill, evenly, ruthlessly, without pause to wrestle your conscience, because the world is full of people who will kill you while you prevaricate.' He coughed again. The class was silent, waiting.

'But more often, you will face a genteel fool of good family, or a case of mistaken adultery, or a spouse seeking revenge. In all of these cases, my friends, you will prefer to break an arm. If you kill a noble in a fight, the very least you can expect is the full attention of the law, as young Timos has recently experienced. Even in a licensed duel with contracts and the agreement of both parties, lawyers and notaries will find a way to sue you for unlawful death. So consider what you intend before you draw, and then, like any other tactic or doctrine, pursue your chosen end carefully and ruthlessly. I recommend the broken arm or the dislocated shoulder.'

After class some of the students ridiculed the notion of non-lethal results. There was a good deal of posturing, followed by a heated debate about the Duke of Volta, who was making a fuss at court. Aranthur was surprised by how many of the young men supported Volta, including Kallinikos, although he was more guarded in his comments than the other gentles. And several young men were adamantly *against* the duke. Rude words and shoving followed, and only the entrance of Master Sparthos calmed them.

He looked around. 'If any of you wish to fight a legal duel,' he said with a sneer, 'I can get you one.'

Silence followed.

'Well then, behave.'

Aranthur was now attuned enough to understand the factions – but that was the first time he realised that his *salle* was infected with Imperial and Voltain sides. Nor did the sides actually line up with his understanding of the Whites, who seemed to be democrats, or the Blacks, who appeared to be liberal oligarchs, or the Lions, who seemed to love power.

Aranthur didn't really want to care. None of it was as interesting as sword fighting, Dahlia, or studying Safiri. Since Dahlia was unavailable, he went home and worked on his Safiri. He had other subjects, but he was neglecting them for Dahlia. However, he couldn't seem to talk to her without one of them offending the other, and that wasn't good.

He did receive an official summons to military drill, delivered by an Imperial Messenger and making him a sort of five-hour wonder in the Academy. It proved that there were dozens of men and women in the Academy who were also summoned, and the whole crisis turned out to be nothing more than a day-long drill session. They were summoned to the stable at the Great Gate.

They curried their horses and then laid out their tack. Then they laid out all their weapons, and various officers came around and looked at things. They were in the old Imperial Stables, a huge building as big as a palace, where Rasce was stabled with two thousand other horses. It smelled beautiful, of horse and hay, and summer.

Rasce was glad to see him. He curried the gelding a second time, until the big brute shone. A month or more in a good stable with oats had made the big horse bigger, and he'd filled out.

'You need to do some work,' Aranthur muttered to Rasce.

Then there was another inspection, this time a set of three deeply tanned officers, two men and a woman, who went over the weapons again, and paid minute attention to the horses.

'How many of you own a second horse?' the woman asked.

Aranthur thought it ironic that he, the poorest student he could see, raised his hand. The other militia who raised their hands were obviously aristocrats.

The woman came over and looked at him.

'Hmm,' she said, and they walked off.

The woman at the stall next to his was in her thirties. She grinned.

'Now you are in for it,' she said. 'It's as if you volunteered. Never volunteer.'

She held out a hand and they shook. She owned a stationery shop on a canal very close to Sparthos' house. They had a brief conversation about paper, and the man from the stall on the other side joined in. He made ink from squid, and he was looking for buyers.

'With *kuria* crystals so dear,' he said, 'sepia is cheaper.'

He explained that most black ink was made from substances that were burned, like bone, in very hot ovens, and that the rise in crystal prices made fire more expensive everywhere.

Then they were standing stiffly with their horses for another inspection. This time, their feed bags were inspected, and canteens. Aranthur had neither.

'You've had months,' a dekark spat. 'Didn't occur to you to buy 'em? What the fuck do you think the bounty is for? Wine?'

Trooper Timos shrugged. 'I never received the bounty. And no one ever told me what to buy.'

'We'll see,' the dekark said.

He went away and returned with a clerk. There was a great deal of muttering, and then the dekark shook his head.

'Timos, your status is signed by a centark of City Cavalry – a regular officer.' He shrugged. 'I guess he didn't finish the job, so instead of chewing on you, I'll apologise. I've sent for him to validate you. If that goes well, we'll get you your bounty. But, truth to tell, right now you are not even a member of the Select and if you are unlucky, some bastard will now charge you for feeding your horse.' He smiled. 'On the other hand, I note you know how to curry and your kit is in fine shape. You have another horse?'

'Yes, syr.'

'Hmm. Right, here's the centark.'

The dekark gave a salute, touching his heart with his closed right fist, and Centark Equus returned the motion. He was dressed in a scarlet jacket like a short khaftan and breeches with thigh-high soft boots and a fur hat, with an elaborately braided half-cloak slung rakishly across his shoulders, lined in fur. Aranthur had never seen a cloak he wanted so much.

'Damme.' Equus smiled. 'I remember you, lad. Seems as if I dicked the dog, what? Never completed your enlistment.'

'I took the oath,' Aranthur said.

'So you did. Good point. He took the oath,' the Centark said to the clerk.

The clerk rolled his eyes. 'What possible reason—' he began.

Equus peeled back the fur-lined collar of his half-cloak and flashed something.

'Understand me?' he asked sharply, his suave drawl gone.

The clerk stood rigid. 'Apologies.'

'None required – needs of the service an' all, what? Besides, it's all me. I forgot to do the paperwork. Bad show.' He winked at Aranthur. 'All sorted now?'

'He needs to receive a bounty,' the dekark said. 'Also, syr, since you are standing here and you asked for a tally of all the Select who have two horses, this man has two horses.'

'Perfect. I'll take him.' Equus smiled. 'Good duty. Timos, am I right?'

'Yes, syr.'

'Did I see you on a watch list? You dropped some Westerner in a duel?' He winked. 'Dangerous Arnaut boy. We watch you like a hawk, eh? And I've seen you crossing blades with some sprig at Master Tercel's School of Defence? A little flash of Cold Iron?'

Aranthur flushed. 'Yes, syr.' He all but froze.

'Good blade, are you?'

Aranthur didn't know what to say. 'I . . . am learning.'

Equus nodded. 'Terrible place. Too many people. Drinks too expensive.'

He turned, as if this made sense, and walked off, his gold spurs jingling.

'Well, well. Timos . . . Is that right? Arnaut?' the dekark asked.

'Yes, syr.'

The dekark nodded. 'I have a new trooper who knows the senior centark of the Imperial Nomadi – I'll have to watch my arse. Are you a troublemaker, Timos?'

'Not at all, syr.'

The dekark grinned. 'Too bad. I like a fuckin' struggle. Good. Your tack is excellent. Here's a chit for your bounty – you'll get it when you draw your pay.'

The dekark went off to deal with some other crisis.

Aranthur spent the rest of the day learning to stand at attention and walk about like a soldier. It was all less alien than he had feared, and at the pay table he drew twenty-one silver crosses, roughly what he made in five weeks of leather-work. He went with his new friend, the paper merchant, and met with her husband, who sent him to a cousin, where the next day he bought a forage bag, two net bags, a haversack, a canteen, and some other equipment for eight silver crosses. Then, when his classes were done, he walked across the city to the Stables with Dahlia and hung all his gear in his stall as was required by regulations. He had them with him; he asked her to read them aloud while he arranged his kit.

She laughed. 'You take everything so seriously.'

That was too true to dispute.

'Care to take a ride with me?' he asked.

She nodded. 'I like to ride.'

She mounted in front of him, and he took Rasce for a ride outside the Lonika Gate with Dahlia riding double. The road was like a tidal pool of mud and they were late coming home.

'I enjoyed that,' she said. 'I could rent a horse . . .' She shook her head. 'You are supposedly a penniless Arnaut. I had to buy our first dinner. But you have a horse.'

And you know Ty Drako better than you admit, Aranthur thought.

In fact, those weeks were an endless whirl of activity. There were moments of happiness, like drinking wine at the Sunne in Splendour when Dahlia got a first in *Polemageia* or battle magik. Aranthur had never been more proud to be with Dahlia, and they took Kallinikos and his Armean partner Salla, a beautiful woman with red-blonde hair and slanted eyes like a cat's. She was very well-read, and spoke Safiri, and Aranthur was surprised to find that she knew of the grimoire he was translating.

Salla patted his hand. Aranthur thought that she was a good deal older – perhaps as old as thirty-five.

'Do you work in Safiri?' Aranthur asked.

'Not well,' Salla admitted. 'I tried. My husband does.' She frowned, and Kallinikos flushed.

Later, Salla took them all to a tavern with gambling. She and Dahlia were laughing together. They rode home in a pair of gondolas. Aranthur had never been able to afford one. The gondolier made broad comments on the utility and comfort of his 'private cabin'.

'Never *ever* make love in a gondola. The fucking gondoliers will mock you first and blackmail you later,' Dahlia said.

The next day, after fencing, Kallinikos was ebullient.

'I love her,' he said. 'She is changing my life. Her husband...' He looked around. 'Not here.'

'That woman needs friends,' Dahlia said later, in the privacy of Aranthur's cold room. 'Not boyfriends.'

She gave him a look he couldn't interpret, but he knew she was angry.

It was a good time, a pleasant time. He got to know Kallinikos better; he and Dahlia began to find other things to do together; and he tried to enjoy it while he did a great deal of work. His Safiri began to make noticeable progress; his sword work began to feel fluid and easy. His arm-trap became natural – he could play it against senior students. He found that he could practise all of his *montante* rules with the heavy blade he'd purchased almost a year before, and he entertained his neighbours by whirling it around the courtyard where they all hung their laundry.

Somehow he got a First in Practical Philosophy, largely because

Dahlia sat up with him and read his notes aloud, as well as her own room-mate's notes from the same class, which were much better organised – and because Kallinikos had laid out the money for all the dead animals they needed to do careful dissection, and his drawings, he had to admit, had played a role.

'If you are so poor,' Dahlia said one night, 'why not sell that sword?' She pointed a bare arm at the heavy sword he'd purchased in the Night Market, what seemed like a lifetime before. 'You can't wear it on the street.'

'I use it to practise my *montante*.'

'It's very old.' She rolled off his bed, and walked over to the sword and took it down. 'It makes me feel old just holding it in my hand.'

Aranthur just lay there, watching her with the sword.

People began to know his name. Dahlia never seemed to have work of her own. She was available whenever he was, which seemed odd, as sometimes Aranthur wondered if she even liked him. Her lovemaking was enthusiastic, but she was distant, virtually uninterested in conversation. When they walked together, she didn't look at him; her attention was elsewhere. And he had the vaguest suspicion that she'd searched his room, which was probably insane of him, but he'd found her standing there . . .

As the term began to wind down and the sun began to climb the sky and the ground began to soften and everything smelt of mud, Aranthur's whirl became a maelstrom. He'd fully translated his second full spell from the Safiri grimoire; it was not a high-*power working*, but it was very complicated – much more advanced then the simple shield. Now he was working directly with the Master of Arts, which was very frustrating, as she would be interrupted constantly, leaving him to efface himself.

He had two more drill days, which effectively sabotaged any attempt he made to hoard a little time.

After the second drill day, when he forgot to tell Dahlia that he could not meet her for even a fish pie, she came to his room. He was asleep in his reading chair and she slammed the door.

'No one stands me up,' she spat.

'I'm sorry.' He really was tired, but he tended to wake up badly, and his 'I'm sorry' sounded petulant.

'There's mud on your shoes. You went riding?'

'Yes. Ariadne needed exercise.'

Dahlia shrugged. 'I understand. You are a compendium of duties and obligations, not a person. Your swordplay comes before me. Your horse comes before me.'

Aranthur could have said many things, but what he chose to say was, 'Yes.'

She nodded. 'Well. That was refreshingly honest.'

She turned and walked down the stairs.

Dahlia stopped speaking to him, much less sharing his room or his bed. The issue between them was time; he understood her position, but he didn't see a solution. He was embarrassed to discover that when she left him, he had time to study and he got a great deal more sleep.

He spent more time on his Safiri, and on the spell.

He couldn't imagine that he was *really* going to ride home for ploughing, which was only a few weeks away. But, paradoxically, he'd asked Kallinikos, who was studying weather-related magiks in addition to his theatrical effects – or perhaps to cover his interests with his father – to tell him when the Arnaut hills would be ready for ploughing. He knew what a difference a horse would make.

Finally, a week before ploughing time as delineated by Kallinikos, he attempted to visit Dahlia in her rooms. She was out, and her room-mate looked embarrassed.

'I don't think you should come back,' she said. 'Dahlia doesn't like men who persist.'

Aranthur had to accept he'd been supplanted.

He felt bitter, and he thought dark thoughts as he strode across the precinct. One of the main paths into the central Academy square had tape across it and a huge pit was open, down to darkly gleaming water that smelled terrible. Workmen were doing something filthy, and he had to walk up the spine of the city to get to his home. He was wearing his new blade, which seemed like very little consolation for losing Dahlia. In his bitterness, he had to admit that he'd been a complete fool; he hadn't even reassured her in his mad rush to *do everything*. In fact, his assertion that he preferred his horse and his swordplay seemed infantile now, and maybe even wicked, and his enjoyment of additional sleep told him he had no idea how to live. He was angry – angry at himself, angry at the world, at the stupid situation that Arnaud's murder had put him in.

Anger made him blind, and he was not paying attention to the world around him until a man bumped into him, hard. He grabbed at his purse but the man was not a thief. He half spun, well up on the ridge and hence in one of the Eastern refugee districts.

There were even more refugees than before, and they were living worse than ever. Aranthur tried to pass through unmolested by beggars, but his sword didn't dissuade anyone, and the younger children were like leeches. The area under the Aqueduct was worse then the slum tenements north of the Academy, now. The tents crowded on each other trying to stay out of the rain, and the smell of urine was everywhere, and the people . . .

There were girls offering him sex, and they were younger than his sister. There were men crouching against the stone supports, their faces averted, their hands out. Their abjectness warred with their pride, and somehow he felt for them more than any of the others. There were older women washing, a long line of them at a leak in the Aqueduct. There was an infinity of dogs – wild dogs, angry dogs, and the worst of all, sad dogs who only wanted a human friend.

He hated it. He hated that he wanted to run away and pretend it all didn't exist.

He wasn't brave enough to give money to a girl and tell her not to prostitute herself – what did he know? He wanted to take a dog home. To save . . . something.

He thought of the Easterners on the roads and in the woods by his father's farm.

'Don't tell me you are lost,' said a soft voice.

Aranthur opened his eyes and saw the Brown Robe, Ulgul, standing with his hands in the sleeves of his robe. He had two very black eyes, as if he'd been on the losing side of a fight.

Ulgul stepped up close, the reek of his unwashed hair and body stronger than the smell of urine and smoke.

'I see your horror,' he said.

'This . . .' Aranthur waved a hand weakly at the two child prostitutes standing against one of the pillars, smoking stock. 'It's not this,' he corrected. 'It's all of them. They deserve . . . better.'

Ulgul made a face. 'They are dying out west. One of our sisters is working there, in the mountains.'

'Sisters?' Aranthur asked.

'Our order. The Order of Aploun. We were founded to bring music and dance to the poor, but we are being tested with armies of poor; multitudes. We are not prepared.'

'And yet you *do* something,' Aranthur said.

'And you care for these Easterners,' Ulgul said, as if that was remarkable.

Aranthur shrugged. But conscience got the better of him.

'Yes,' he admitted.

'You are a scholar, are you not?' Ulgul was tired; his northern accent was heavier than usual.

'I am,' Aranthur agreed.

The Brown Robe nodded. And smiled enigmatically.

'I can take you where you could help, maybe.'

Aranthur wanted to say 'no'. But rather like the duel at the tavern, before he could find the 'no' inside him, he had agreed.

Ulgul took him by the hand as if he was a child and walked across the opposite buttress. The two young girls frowned and moved away, raising their hands as if to prevent the priest of Aploun from speaking. Before they made it to the next pillar of the Aqueduct, they were intercepted by a man with a scimitar. The three gesticulated. The girls pointed at Ulgul.

'Do you speak any Safiri?' Ulgul asked.

Aranthur became suddenly conscious that the Brown Robe seemed to know a lot about him.

'See that man?' Ulgul pointed at a huddle of rags. 'A famous musician. A powerful swordsman. A warrior. Now he is an addict. He won't talk to me. Perhaps—'

'Didn't we already have a conversation?'

The newcomer's accent was lighter than the Northerner's, but there nonetheless, and he wore a scimitar and the flowing trousers and tight doublet of Atti. He had on a fine felt fez, and his hands were on his hips, and his face wore a broad smile that didn't reach his eyes.

'Ah, Famuz.' Ulgul nodded as if he'd forgotten to introduce an old friend.

'I thought that you understood me, priest. We don't want you here. None of my people worship your Twelve.' He stood very close to Ulgul.

'You mean, I make your child prostitutes remember that they once had lives?'

'You think that my people gave you a beating, priest? Listen – those were kisses. Who is this?' he asked, pointing at Aranthur.

'A man – he's lost. No better than you.'

Famuz turned. 'You are lost, young sir? For a small fee, one of my boys will take you home safely. If you have one of my boys with you, no one will accost you, I promise.'

Aranthur was trying to work it out. A crime boss . . . certainly. But beating a priest of Aploun was not a good practice for a City criminal. On the other hand, Ulgul was distancing himself – he'd already taken two steps away.

Aranthur was a big man with a sword at his side.

'I don't think I need an escort,' he said, as pleasantly as he could manage.

Famuz shook his head. 'That's where you are wrong, sir. These streets can be very dangerous, and it is bad for my people if anything happens to a foreigner.'

Aranthur smiled. 'Foreigner?'

'I don't think you understand,' Famuz said, the smile vanishing. 'Pay me a couple of silver crosses, and you will be perfectly safe.'

'Or?'

Aranthur was looking at the Easterners, trying to see if any of them was one of the criminal's thugs or bodyguards.

'Or something unpleasant might happen,' Famuz said.

'Like . . .' Aranthur smiled his uncle's smile. 'Like I put my sword in your guts and make you dance?'

He was pretending to be something he wasn't, but he knew the language from his uncle.

Ulgul was gone, vanished like a man with magikal powers.

Famuz glanced behind him.

'No one here to help you,' Aranthur said. 'For a couple of silver crosses, I'd protect you from me,' he added.

It was enjoyable. He understood the lure of the tough talk and the bravado. It was entertaining to watch the bastard flinch.

'You're fucked,' Famuz snapped, and walked away.

Aranthur stood his ground for a moment longer, and then walked a little too briskly around the Aqueduct's supporting tier towards the safety of the steps and the City.

But just around the next pillar, at the entrance of the narrow alley that led down to his home, as he walked quickly, he passed a man crouched against the huge stone buttress. His long sword, which he wasn't used to wearing, slapped the man as he turned.

'Whoa!' the man spat. 'Eat my dirt, citizen.' The beggar sounded almost casual.

'I'm so sorry.' Aranthur said.

'Sure.' The man's words were very slightly accented, and slurred. He smiled – a genuine smile. 'Nice sword. You a sword guy? I was a sword guy, once.'

Aranthur understood then that the man was a *thuryx* addict. He could see it in the man's eyes – the slightly red centres – and the hands . . .

But what stopped Aranthur dead was that the man had said the last sentence in *Safiri*.

He turned. He'd actually walked on three rapid steps before the words penetrated. He wasn't used to spoken Safiri.

'How's your Liote?' he said.

'Fine,' the man said. 'Amazing. I'm sure I can get a job as an ambassador, or maybe someone's secretary.'

Aranthur walked back. He was instantly surrounded by beggars and dogs. But the crouching man pushed himself to his feet. He stank – urine and other smells: an unwashed body; a lot of mud with its own cargo of smells.

One of the beggars threw a stone. The unwashed addict *caught* the stone, mimed throwing it, and the whole pack of children screamed and ran. A young girl was knocked flat, and she screamed. Dogs barked.

Aranthur knew he'd already decided. He was getting more used to these moments, when his inner mind made decisions that he hadn't examined at all.

'Let me buy you a meal,' he said.

'You could just give me a couple of coins and I'd buy my own,' the unwashed man said. 'You can feel all holy and you don't have to smell me.'

'I need someone to practise Safiri with. I'm willing to save your life in exchange.'

'Madar ghahbe! مادر قهبه,' the man said, in Safiri. Aranthur assumed he was swearing. Then in fluent, accented Liote, 'I don't want to be saved, you pompous fuck. Bugger off. Buy one of the girls and pretend you make her feel good, you pervert. May your beard fall out and your balls wither.'

Aranthur backed away from the flow of invective and the dirty man burst into tears.

Aranthur shrugged at his own lack of indecision. He knew exactly what he was going to do.

'Let's start with a fish pie,' he said.

'If you're serious,' the dirty man said, 'I hate fish. I'd take *labou*. I never feel hungry, but I wanted *labou* yesterday.'

'What's *labou*?'

The man's face seemed to shrink. 'Don't know,' he admitted. 'Don't know the word.'

He stumbled to his feet and lurched. Aranthur took his arm and got a face full of his breath and his odour. He steeled himself and supported the man's weight.

'Fuck, I don't want *labou*.' The man frowned. 'Let me go.'

'Let's find some *labou*,' Aranthur said in very stilted and probably incorrect Safiri.

The addict laughed. 'Who's teaching you, boy? You sound like a fucking priest.' He laughed. 'An Armean priest speaking Safiri?'

But despite his foul smell and his swearing, Aranthur got him along the line of the Aqueduct as far as the Pinnacle, the second highest point in the city. The highest point was the Academy and its central fortress; the other high points were the Temple of Wisdom and the Palace. But the Pinnacle was the high point of the Aqueduct, and from there, water could run *down* into every home. There was a broad reservoir high in the air, supported on glorious stone arches with hundreds of flying buttresses and abutments, and under the elevated reservoir was the *agora*, a marketplace of everything. Stolen goods went there, and thieves and prostitutes and tax collectors and soldiers, but also refugees and the poor. And everyone else. A local proverb said that a person could go a month without sex, but no one could go a day without visiting the Pinnacle.

Aranthur, in fact, seldom went. But tonight, he had a mission. He half-dragged, half-carried his new Safiri teacher along, alert for Famuz or another thug as he walked across the mud and gravel under the Aqueduct until he entered the torchlit *agora*. There were scantily clad women, tougher than iron nails, doing acrobatics on stilts, with swords. There was a troop of Keltain mercenaries, with iron ring shirts and gold foil braided in their hair – no one of them less then six feet tall, and every one of them in a coat of maille that swept to the ground. They were armed, and watching the crowd warily. One looked at Aranthur, looked at his companion, and then at his sword.

Then he walked on, uninterested.

Aranthur asked the first soup seller if she knew what *labou* was. She didn't. Nor did the next soup seller, nor a wine seller. The dirty man had lost interest.

'I'll never get my fucking corner back,' he whined.

Aranthur grew bolder. 'Labou?' he asked four or five times.

Finally, a *chai*-girl frowned.

'I'll take you,' she said, hoisting her little *chai* set in its basket and putting the sash around her waist. 'For a silver cross.'

'She'd fuck you for a silver cross,' Dirty Man said. 'Does my beard look so short, honey? She doesn't know where to find *labou*.'

She spat on the ground. 'Is there a beard under all that dirt?' she shot back. But she didn't walk away.

'Two bronze obols,' Aranthur said.

'Nah, she won't fuck for that,' Dirty Man said. 'And it's too much for directions.'

'Pay first,' she said. 'You should make better friends.'

'He should, right enough,' Dirty Man said.

Aranthur was a country boy, but he'd been almost a year in the City. He took one obol from his waist sash without showing his purse.

She shrugged, almost as if she was pleased by his caution, and walked off. She took them all the way across the *agora*, to the north side, closest to the Academy.

'There,' she said, pointing as if she was wisdom personified in the statue. '*Labou*. It's a Safiri thing.'

The *labou* seller was an old man with a cart. On the cart was a small brazier that burned charcoal, and on the grill sat a lidded copper pot.

Aranthur was in a daring mood.

'Two, please,' he said. He turned to their guide. 'Want some?'

She laughed. 'You're not so bad. Yes. Anyone want to buy some *chai*?'

'Three,' Aranthur showed his fingers to the old *labou* seller. 'And we'll all have *chai*.'

The old man had a magnificent beard and a gold earring and was otherwise dressed in the traditional clothes of the East, with a long robe over sandalled feet. He smiled.

'Beets.' Aranthur laughed. '*Labou* must mean beet.'

The *chai* seller wolfed hers down.

'Damn,' she said in Liote.

Then she rattled off what was clearly a blessing, making with her fingers the sign of Themis the Huntress, one of the Twelve – deer antlers.

The *labou* seller bowed to her, and she nodded to Aranthur.

'You owe me an obol,' she said. 'And three more for the *chai*.'

'Now you say that sheep are goats, and black is white,' Dirty Man said. 'His purse is not as deep as yours.'

The young woman turned as red as the beet she'd just eaten. She launched at Dirty Man, a stream of rapid Armean that Aranthur, who had just one year of that language, couldn't follow.

Dirty Man smiled.

Aranthur stepped between them and opened his purse, only to find that he had no obols, only silver.

She dropped a deep curtsey. 'Now all the blessings of the Twelve and all their saints be on your head, prince of *chai*-drinkers,' she said. 'And if your beneficence extends so far, my lord, please pay three obols for the old man.' She smiled – a very pretty smile. 'He only speaks Safiri and Rafiq. And no, he can't make change.'

There followed an annoying time while a street seller was found to break a silver cross. He took an obol for his trouble, and Aranthur paid his debts – six silver obols to get an addict a beet and some over-boiled *chai*.

But the man had eaten the whole thing.

'Want another?' he asked.

'I want to die,' the man said. 'Fuck.'

The beet seller spoke in Safiri, very fast. Suddenly Dirty Man shot to his full height. He spoke in Safiri, very clearly.

He said, 'Father, I do not steal. I swear on my father's head.'

Aranthur patterned his pronunciation of Safiri on that one sentence for weeks thereafter.

The old man handed Dirty Man another beet, and he ate it slowly, as if savouring it.

The *chai* seller had a small crowd by that time, and she served them all until she was out of water to make *chai*.

'You brought me luck,' she said. 'And you're clean and pretty enough. If you have another silver cross, I'll go home with you.'

Aranthur made himself smile. 'I'm taking the dirty one home.'

She laughed. 'Oh, my mistake.' She walked off, giggling.

Aranthur was sorry, in a way. He wondered if the girl spoke enough Safiri... At another remove, he wondered later how she managed to be so cheerful with her lot in life, which looked cruel and hard to him.

But he'd survived the Pinnacle, and the addict was all his.

Aranthur woke in the morning to find his guest, filthy, and naked, standing in front of the glass window, holding Aranthur's precious razor. He didn't take in what he was seeing, and then he did – the man was getting up the courage to cut his throat. Aranthur thought so, at least; he had spread an old coverlet on the floor, and he had neither hot water nor soap nor a strop.

'Please do not,' Aranthur said, in Safiri.

'Oh, fuck!' The man threw the razor at the wall. 'I was close. Go back to sleep. I'll get this done...'

'I'll have to clean it up,' Aranthur said. 'And my friend Arnaud died right about there, a month or two ago. The blood gets into the floorboards. It dries on the wall. It stinks, and the flies come. And by the way, that's my razor, and I don't have another.'

He got up and fetched the razor, which he wiped on Arnaud's spare coverlet and placed on the window sill.

'Did you sleep?'

'No!' the man shouted.

The new tenants downstairs began to slam sticks into the floor. The sun was just rising.

Aranthur was just considering his incaution in bringing this man home. He stank, and he needed to wash, and Aranthur had to go to school and to work and Dahlia...

Dahlia was more of an ache than a reality.

He thought of the man before him and what he'd said to the beet seller.

'What's your name?' he asked. In Safiri.

'Sasan,' the man answered. 'See? Wasn't that easy?' He nodded. 'Why do you speak Safiri at all? You're Arnaut.'

Aranthur raised an eyebrow. 'Even a Safian refugee can speak ill of the Arnauts.'

The Safian shrugged. 'Whatever. Why Safiri?'

'I study it in school.'

'Huh,' the man said.

'Sasan, I want you to give me your word, as a man who does not steal, that you will not kill yourself and will not wreck my rooms or steal while I am gone.' He nodded.

Sasan laughed. 'Once, that oath would mean something to me. Now?' He shrugged. 'The only god I worship is *thuryx*. Got any?'

'No,' Aranthur said.

'Then I won't be here when you come back.'

Aranthur thought for a moment. It was time, as his people liked to say, to trust the Eagle.

'That's as may be,' he said. 'Promise you will not steal, or wreck my room. Or kill yourself.'

'Because that would make a mess,' the refugee said.

'Exactly.'

The thin man smiled. 'Well, you made me laugh.'

Aranthur ran down the stairs and across the street to where Kallinikos lived, and begged the loan of Chiraz, his excellent butler.

'I need a companion for my . . . *friend*,' he said.

Chiraz bowed. 'I am often called on for such roles.'

Kallinikos laughed aloud. 'He's hoping she's beautiful.'

'He is a Safian and a *thuryx* addict and I'm afraid he'll injure himself.' Aranthur bowed to Chiraz.

Chiraz gave a very small smile. 'Ah. I had rather hoped for Myr Tarkas.'

But the butler's face took on a more human aspect. He packed a small leather case and left.

'His brother was a *thuryx* addict,' Kallinikos said. 'You came to the right house.'

Aranthur nodded. 'I thought you'd said that,' he admitted with a sigh of relief.

The two men walked to the Academy together.

'You look better,' Aranthur said, finally.

It was true; his friend looked cheerful and almost relaxed.

'I've made a decision.' Kallinikos smiled. 'You may have to loan me money and a butler eventually, but I'm ... Let's say I'm changing direction.'

'Loan *you* money?' Aranthur asked.

'We'll see. Congratulations on your First in Advanced, by the way. I did rather well myself.' He laughed bitterly. 'If all else were as usual, my father would be ridiculously proud.'

'I got a first in Advanced Enhancement?' Aranthur asked.

'Don't get all proud. I got one too,' Kallinikos laughed.

Aranthur had a long day. He worked on translation and on his new *occulta*, his spell, which he was almost ready to deploy. As soon as the Master of Arts released him, he went and worked on leather. Then, as the light was fading, he took his mare for a ride north of the City on the high ground. After currying her, he went and drilled under Syr Sapu until his wrist and arm were almost stiff from fatigue – arming sword and *montante*.

He was about to leave when he saw Kallinikos.

'Nothing to worry about,' the young noble said. 'Chiraz has your man in hand.'

He bowed, making light of it, but he looked pale, and agitated. He opened his mouth; Aranthur was sure he was trying to say something important.

'Are you all right?' Aranthur asked.

Kallinikos clasped his hand. 'After class.'

Sapu invited him to a bout and he accepted. The Voltain excused himself to see to another student first, and Aranthur sat down with a dozen young men and a couple of older women. The women had just been fighting, and each had wounded the other lightly, and they were laughing together. The Master was talking to them, clearly well pleased.

'It's daft, letting women fight,' a man behind Aranthur said. 'They're no good at it, and they waste the Master's time.'

'They only come to pick up men,' said another.

'The same might be said of you, Djinar,' another young man quipped.

Everyone laughed, except Djinar, whose face grew red.

'When the duke goes back to his own, he'll change things,' Djinar said, a little too loudly. The young man was wearing the full, resplendent red and gold and black of the Lions. 'What are you looking at, syr?' he asked Aranthur.

Aranthur smiled. 'I'm not sure.'

He was proud of the answer; it was steady, and someone laughed, anyway.

Sapu came back. 'Are you ready, Timos?'

Aranthur rose and bowed.

The other young man nodded to Sapu.

'Sapu, you are from Volta. Won't the duke's restoration go a long way to—'

'I'm no friend of your duke, Syr Djinar,' Sapu said curtly. 'Excuse me.'

He led Aranthur out onto the floor and they saluted. Aranthur used the new, elaborate salute that was a symbol of the school, and then settled into a *garde* – his new favourite – with his left leg forward and his light sword held point down, covering the leg.

They were using bated sharps, and Sapu thrust immediately. Aranthur covered, a rising parry, and tried for Sapu's hand, but the Voltain was far too fast, too canny, and his sword was already back. Aranthur played for it, following it. Sapu deceived him and planted his blunt tip *hard* on Aranthur's sword arm bicep.

'Ouch,' Aranthur said, saluting.

Several young men jeered.

'Go fight with women,' Djinar called.

'Ignore them,' Sapu said. 'But that was foolish.'

Aranthur vowed to be more cautious, and the second time the blades did not cross, as both fighters kept their blades off the centre line and circled. To Aranthur's mortification, Sapu circled, deceived him on distance and slashed his wrist with a fast cut that Aranthur failed to parry – a simple attack.

The young men jeered again.

The sharp blade had cut Aranthur's glove but not his wrist, so exact was the Voltain's control.

'You are thinking too much,' Sapu said.

Aranthur tried not to think, although the cost of the ruined glove would irk him all week. He threw feints, and circled, and when Sapu pressed he backed. He kept his parries small and simple.

He risked a heavy cut, rising from a low *garde* that forced Sapu to make a fully developed parry. The blades bit into each other. Sapu had not backed with his parry, and both men went for holds. The blades crossed and locked. Each men had the other's sword arm, and Aranthur allowed himself to be pulled forward a step, rotated his hips and threw Sapu to the floor. The Voltain rolled, coming to his feet fluidly, his sword still in his hand. He thrust, and Aranthur parried from the middle to the outside and countered with a light cut to Sapu's upper arm . . .

And hit.

He immediately stepped back into *garde*. There was a faint red line on Sapu's bicep.

The little crowd of young men was silent.

Sapu smiled. 'Hah, I deserved that. So proud of rolling out of your throw!' He wiped a practised thumb along the cut, licked the blood, and flicked his blade in a salute. 'Where was that nice counter-cut all the other times?'

'I don't know!' Aranthur was flushed with excitement.

He was eager to go, to get home, but Sapu kept him after class, drilling him on a particular way of delivering a neat counter-parry – a circular motion that required perfect timing.

'This sets you up for that counter-cut,' Sapu said. 'Learn the two together and you will have a powerful strike.'

'I understand,' Aranthur said.

'The timing is different for every opponent. Never try this on a novice. Their movements are so clumsy and so are their perceptions . . . All your finesse will be wasted.'

'I *am* a novice,' Aranthur joked, rubbing his forearm where Sapu had hit it so easily.

'Mmm,' Master Sparthos came by. He'd been working with Syr Kallinikos, and Aranthur hadn't seen him stop to watch. 'Is he ready to test?'

Sapu nodded. 'Barely. But yes.'

Sparthos nodded. 'Right now?'

'Yes, Master,' Sapu said formally.

Sparthos nodded. 'Good.' He smiled a very thin smile at Aranthur. 'Three weeks, Draxday, you will be tested on your knowledge of the arming sword.'

'He's really better with *montante*,' Sapu said.

Sparthos smiled. 'I know. Arming sword. Three weeks.'

Aranthur was tempted to shout that he had other things to do, thousands of them, but something told him that would be a mistake.

'Yes, Master,' he said.

The day still wasn't over. Kallinikos waited for him in the changing room.

'I need a favour,' the young man said. His body language suggested it was more *you owe me.*

Aranthur shrugged. 'At your service.'

Kallinikos played with his laces for a moment. 'I have been challenged,' he said.

Aranthur paused. 'What?'

'To a duel. A legal duel.' Kallinikos looked desperate, but resolved, now that Aranthur looked closely. 'Maybe not so legal,' he went on.

Duelling was a very carefully regulated matter in the City.

'Someone challenged you?' Aranthur asked.

Kallinikos had recovered his composure.

'Sure.' He shrugged. 'It is a private matter. I need a second. Would you be my second?'

Aranthur considered it for a moment. 'Fighting?'

'Probably,' Kallinikos said.

Aranthur didn't bother to think. 'Of course.'

His rich, aristocratic acquaintance suddenly grinned and embraced him.

'Damn,' he said. 'I needed to hear that.'

'When?' Aranthur asked.

'Tomorrow, Square of the Water Clock, sunrise.' Kallinikos was shaking. 'Damme, I'm sorry. I feel ... like a coward.'

Aranthur shook his head. 'Don't. When I fought my duel ...'

He paused, because his friend was looking at him as if he'd just said *when I had two heads.*

'You fought a duel? Not the brawl we were in at the Temple?'

'What?' Syr Sapu said, pushing through the bead curtain. 'You are fighting?'

Kallinikos looked away. 'I wasn't going to let the Master know.'

Sapu nodded. 'Nor will he know from me, but he always knows. And as a professional, I'm forbidden to duel any but my own kind. But I can still show you something. You want to wound your man or kill him?'

'Kill him,' Kallinikos said.

Sapu raised an eyebrow. 'You know the implications? I speak not of morality but strictly legally.'

'Yes,' Kallinkos said. 'I'm afraid I have little choice.'

Sapu frowned. 'Very well.' He winked at Aranthur. 'For you, I have no worries. You will likely have a foot of reach and muscles. Strike hard repeatedly until your opponent is terrified.'

'And throw him,' Aranthur said.

'Exactly! Damme, you do pay attention, Timos. Go home. I'll take care of Syr Kallinikos.' He winked, and took the other man by the arm. 'Come. One hour, and I'll make you a killer.'

Aranthur arrived home having not thought at all about his guest for an hour, at least until he got most of the way up the steps. Then he heard a creak from the floor, imagined for a moment it might be Dahlia, and then remembered. He pushed the door open as a rush of musical notes came to greet him.

Tiy Drako stood at the darkened window. He had his tamboura in his hands, and his head was bent over the instrument. He was playing a form of music that the Arnauts called 'Betika'.

Sasan sat in the reading chair. He was clean and shaven. He was terribly thin – too thin, like a wraith or a corpse. Clothes made it worse; he'd been better off naked. But he had an instrument across his lap – an oud. And he was playing softly, the heavier notes of the oud balancing the rapid flow of the tamboura.

Aranthur was exhausted and he had to fight in the morning.

'Do you two know each other?' he asked, pettishly.

Drako frowned. 'No,' he said. 'But I brought him an oud.'

'No,' Sasan said. 'It is very odd to be so clean, don't you think? How long will it take me to build up a good layer of filth?' He smiled. 'No one will give a clean addict an obol.' He ran his fingers through his beard. 'On the other hand, my beard is longer. Is there some lesson there?'

'I've been here long enough to learn that he speaks Safiri,' Drako said. 'Aranthur, you really are some sort of miracle worker. Or Dama Tyche follows you around like a strumpet following a customer who hasn't paid.'

'You two sat here for an hour and didn't talk?' Aranthur asked.

The butler, Chiraz, emerged from behind what had been Daud's curtain.

'They have been perfectly polite, and Syr Sasan needed music. I took the liberty of sending Syr Drako for an instrument.' He bowed.

'Thanks so much!' Aranthur said.

Chiraz bowed, the perfect servant. 'I am always at your service, Syr Timos.' He raised an eyebrow. 'I assume that my master is home?'

'Just home, Chiraz. He's in a bit of a mood.'

The butler walked off down the steps with his usual dignity.

'You played for an hour?' Aranthur asked Drako.

'Yes.'

Aranthur blew air out of his cheeks in exasperation.

'Really, I need to go to bed.'

'I'm here for Dahlia,' Drako said. 'This isn't about the other business. Well . . . a little bit that. This is personal.'

Aranthur rolled his eyes. 'I thought . . . Never mind.' He paused.

'Just pretend I'm not here,' Sasan said. 'I'd like a beet, please.'

'She . . . misses you, and she won't admit it,' Drako said.

Aranthur shook his head. 'She can say so herself.'

'I doubt it,' said Sasan. 'No one ever can.'

The other two men looked at him.

He shrugged. 'Fuck, whatever. But people don't say they are sorry and they don't admit they are wrong. Except in romances and songs. And in love? Pfft.'

Drako nodded. 'This is true,' he admitted.

Aranthur wondered why they were ganging up on him.

'My message is delivered. She doesn't even know I'm here – but I'm tired of her pining and hanging around.' Drako shrugged. 'Also, I need some of your time in the next few days.'

'I have no time,' Aranthur said. But as he said it, he considered that the sword he owned and the rent on his room had been paid by this man. 'Very well, I will make time.'

'Good.' Drako looked at Sasan. 'You *really* speak Safiri?'

'Like a native,' the man said bitterly.

'When were you last there?' Drako asked.

'When the Disciples sacked my village and killed my wife and my father,' Sasan said. 'When was that exactly?' He blinked. 'I've been working hard to kill that knowledge off, so fuck yourself.'

'I need to go to bed,' Aranthur said into the silence.

'No,' Drako said.

'I'm fighting a duel in the morning.'

Sasan turned and looked at him. It was a completely different look from any other he'd seen from the man, except when he drew himself up and spoke to the beet seller.

'I forbid it,' Drako said.

Aranthur sighed. 'I've promised. And who are you to forbid me, anyway?'

'And I thought I was crazy,' Sasan said.

Drako folded his arms. 'You know what, Timos? There's a lot going on out there in the City. And the world. Your new friend here is the very flotsam of a tidal wave sweeping the archipelago, and you want to go fight a duel. Over what? A girl?'

Aranthur shrugged. 'No idea.'

Drako rolled his eyes. 'Sunlight, and my father thinks *I'm* an idiot. You are going to fight, and possibly die, and you don't even know why?'

Aranthur smiled. 'I agree that put that way, it does sound stupid. But I'm doing it for a friend. He asked me. I owe him.'

Sasan smiled. 'I like this. It sounds like home.'

It was the second real smile the man had made, and it made him look younger.

Drako narrowed his eyes. 'Fine. If you live, come and see me.'

He was very angry, and he slammed the door on his way out.

Aranthur found that he didn't care. He lay down, and tried to go to sleep, but it was a long time coming. He was working through Safiri verbs in the historical past tense when sleep finally overtook his fears and threw him down.

In the morning, Sasan was again with Chiraz, both of them playing ouds, and Aranthur was standing in the Square of the Water Clock in his best doublet and hose over his best shirt. He doubted everything, including his clothes. Clothes he'd won in a duel. He had spent a quarter of an hour trying to decide which sword to wear. Now he felt like a fake; he was pretending to be a gentleman, an aristocrat, a duellist. In fact, he was an Arnaut Student and he assumed everyone could tell. He was tempted to run home and put on baggy trousers and a vest like his uncle used to wear.

He was beginning to feel even more like a fool because he was waiting alone, with a sword, by a canal in a beautiful neighbourhood. He expected to be arrested. A man kept watching him from a doorway, and Aranthur spat in the canal and cursed quietly in Safiri, which had become his language of cursing.

A young woman in a beautiful short silk gown came by with her shoes on her shoulder. She crossed the street to avoid him.

Aranthur shook his head and considered walking home, or at least retreating two canals to a neighbourhood more in keeping with his doublet. He turned away from the water, and there was Kallinikos hurrying along the canal with a small sword on his shoulder, like a farmer with an axe.

'I'm late,' he said.

Aranthur shook his head. 'No, we're both early.' His hands were shaking. He bit his lip.

Kallinikos said, 'I have a letter for my family. I just want to know... Fuck it. Thanks, Timos. You came through for me when my so-called friends walked. You really are a gentleman, unlike some. I have learned a lot from you.' He frowned. 'Even Chiraz likes you.'

Aranthur looked across the canal, where a man in dark clothing was addressing three big men.

'Why exactly are we doing this?'

'Remember Salla? Her husband. That's him...' Kallinikos pointed. 'The worst of it is that my father tried to patch it up. This is so fucking complicated, and I want out. But I want Salla. He hates her anyway.'

'He's an aristo?' Aranthur asked.

'Yes. Country house, but an old one, like mine. He's a nasty piece of work, too.' Kallinikos shrugged. 'And I did sleep with his wife. I like her. Fuck him. If I kill him, maybe she'll marry me.'

Aranthur blushed. 'Aploun. Sunrise,' he said.

Anything else he might have said was banished by the arrival of the much older man and his three large companions.

'Uh-oh,' Kallinikos said.

'Kill them,' the old man said. He pointed. 'Both of them.' His words were very clear across the canal. Aranthur saw him motion with a short stick.

He was *casting*.

The three began to come forward.

'We could run,' Kallinikos said. His voice squeaked. But the man himself stood his ground.

Aranthur's heart beat like a drum. 'I'm here if you are,' he said.

The dark old man was still casting. Aranthur caught a phrase; it sounded like Armean. An Eastern incantation.

'Does everyone cheat in duels?' he asked.

Kallinikos was white as a sheet but he managed a smile.

'Damn,' he said. 'Why didn't we think of that?'

The three bravos began to move faster – not to run, but to move in extraordinary, quick ways, like badly managed marionettes.

Kallinikos reached out and touched Aranthur's left hand with his own.

'You are a prince,' he said.

The three bravos had long, narrow swords with cup hilts – a Western style beloved of criminal enforcers and street bravos.

Aranthur looked the three over as he had been taught. Master Sparthos advocated caution and a long, careful summing up of the opponent, but odds of two to one militated against that. And two of the bravos went for Aranthur. They were faster than wolves.

He drew. He was wearing his new arming sword and it was comfortable in his hand, but much, much shorter than the weapons the bravos had.

'Aploun,' he said again. He wasn't sure whether it was an invocation or a curse.

His two opponents were competent, but shorter than he. Both hesitated to cross blades first despite their rapid, jerky advance.

Aranthur named them, in his head, Doublet and Big Nose. Doublet was slightly closer and when Aranthur shifted a step to his right, the man stepped left, unwittingly placing his own back to the canal. The motion was as quick as the blink of a tiger, but Aranthur committed instantly. He stepped forward, crossing Doublet's sword with a crisp tap, and then immediately charging him, collapsing his *garde* into his chest. Aranthur had a moment of surprise as his tactic worked so easily. Then he had the man's sword arm, which he broke before throwing the man into the canal with his hip and turning, the man's incredibly rapid counter-punch to his jaw just starting to throb.

Kallinikos was down on one knee with a sword through the meat of his thigh. He'd dropped his sword.

Aranthur pivoted on the balls of his feet and charged.

Kallinikos' opponent, despite his supernatural speed, was hampered by his sword being stuck in Kallinikos' thigh. Big Nose was eager to cross swords with Aranthur. The result was a collision as all three men tried to enter the same space. The bravo's sword came out of Kallinikos as the young man screamed, but it was far too slow. Aranthur took the man's sword hand in his left, dashed his hilt in the man's face, and attempted to throw him to the ground with blood pouring out of his mouth.

Using his preternatural speed, the other man turned into the throw and leapt back, still on his feet – an incredible physical act. He cut at Aranthur despite the blood streaming from his nose and mouth.

Aranthur's parry had more luck than skill to it; the man's incredible cut went into his sword with a clang.

Aranthur, even in the very heart of the fight, wondered at the speed of the men and what kind of *occulta* might have *enhanced* them. He whirled, but Big Nose stepped back and threw his sword like a thunder-bolt of Coryn the Thunderer.

Aranthur cut it out of the air. He didn't catch it all – it was too fast – and the hilt rotated and slammed into his hip, staggering him.

Bloody Face came at him a beat after the thrown sword, striking like a snake with his long sword from a long measure. Aranthur hammered the sword's point to the ground with a clumsy, off-balance parry. But the man's point caught between two cobbles, and quick as he was, he couldn't free it before Aranthur stepped on it, trapping it under his sole.

Big Nose was already running.

Bloody Face dropped his sword and reached for his dagger. Aranthur cut without thinking, and fingers fell. The man screamed. He backed as fast as a spider and then looked with horror at his right hand and screamed again.

'Daaamn,' Kallinikos said through gritted teeth.

The old man was still standing on the far side of the canal. He raised a hand.

Aranthur looked at the rapidly forming puddle of blood under his friend. He knew...

He knew some *occultae*, recently learnt to help him understand the Safiri spells. He had his talisman around his neck and he knelt by Kallinikos. He had done well in practical philosophy, and he knew, academically, how to combine his *occultae* with his practical knowledge.

'I'm—'

'Shut up and let me concentrate.'

Aranthur tried to clear his mind and nothing much happened except that more blood flowed out. A surprising amount of blood. From the colour, an artery was cut.

There was a loud *bang*.

Puffer, Aranthur thought.

He wasn't hit; neither was Kallinikos.

I should raise a shield, he thought too late.

The man across the canal drew something from his belt.

Aranthur took a deep breath and *dropped into himself. It was not his best trance, but it was sufficient to look for the signs of the occulta he wanted and unravel it like a string. And tie it to the world's wind... There.*

But something was contesting with him, fighting to promote the blood loss, to keep the little vessel pumping his friend's blood. He could feel it. Malign, careful, a heavy weight.

Aranthur was a big man. He was used to getting his way in contests, and in his mind, he was a farmer – stubborn. Solid. *He pushed.*

It was as if the world came into focus. He almost felt as if there was a tangible click.

He breathed.

Opened his eyes. The Master of Arts told him that closing his eyes was a bad habit. He believed her, but this time...

Kallinikos was watching him like a drowning man watching a raft. The man across the canal was casting again, and *now* he raised a small red shield, the first casting from the Safian grimoire. To his left, a dozen armoured men appeared – City Watch with a magistrate.

Their assailant began hurrying away, clutching his chest as if having trouble breathing. Aranthur was tempted to follow him. But Kallinikos was not saved. He was merely not bleeding to death.

'We need a doctor,' Aranthur said.

The Watch found them an Imoter who worked hard to save Kallinikos. Kallinikos refused to name their attacker and claimed that they had been set on by footpads. Aranthur had no chance to talk to his friend at first, and no one wanted to talk to him, anyway.

Aranthur spent the night in the prison of the Great Gate, mostly because he was an Arnaut, and all of the Watch assumed he was a criminal of some sort, until an embarassed jailor released him to Centark Equus. The centark was not amused.

'Fucking civilians,' he muttered. The officer was a little drunk. 'I could be in the arms of a beautiful woman right now,' he lamented. 'Why did they arrest you?'

Aranthur tried to explain.

Equus shook his head. 'Timos, do me a favour? Next time, get killed, or run away. Don't call me!'

'I didn't!' Aranthur insisted.

Equus shrugged. 'Someone did. Bah. I can't go back to her rooms, so I might as well... Hmm. *Quaveh* or wine?'

Aranthur shared an early morning cup of *quaveh* with his officer, thanked him profusely for his release, and walked home.

He wasn't even sure he'd succeeded in saving Kallinikos until an hour later, when he looked in and found Chiraz tending to the young man. His healthy brown skin was the colour of ash, and he could not speak. But Chiraz insisted that he would recover.

And then Aranthur went to class. After class he went to work. At work, he kept reliving the fight. He'd been lucky, but it had all... *worked.* Instead of riding, he stopped at the *salle* and waited for Syr Sapu. He told the story, and Sapu shook his head.

'You have the luck of the very goddess of fortune,' Sapu said. 'But... I should tell the Master. He always wants to know when a student uses his skills. For real.' He put out a hand. 'Everyone cheats in duels, Aranthur. Don't be naïve again.'

Aranthur bowed. 'I promised to be silent.'

'As did I,' Sapu said.

Inside the *salle*, Djinar was lecturing on Voltain politics. He didn't look up, and Aranthur didn't stop to listen. He went through, did his drills, and went home.

Sasan was gone.

Aranthur feared the worst. He ate, drank some bad wine, and went across the street to find Kallinikos. His butler met him at the door.

'Master is in a bad way,' Chiraz said.

'But my friend...'

'He is well. See to Master.'

Chiraz bowed, and Aranthur hurried in to the bedroom. Kallinikos lay propped on pillows, looking very near death

'He killed her,' Kallinikos said.

'What?'

'He killed her. Her maidservant is in hiding – my father smuggled her out of the city. He came back from the fight and killed her with a puffer.' Kallinikos' face was pinched. His cheeks burned. 'Thanks, Timos. You stood by me. Saved my life. I will fucking avenge her. And defy my father.'

Aranthur shook his head. 'Do you know he killed her?'

'Oh, yes. The maid described it all. He's insane. And he threatened my father with a House war if I was not *punished*.' He lay back suddenly. 'Is it my imagination, or did he put a magik on those bravos?'

'Not your imagination.'

Aranthur thought of the *occulta* and how much it had resembled the complex *enhancement* he was learning from the Safiri grimoire.

'You may have to testify. In a Court of Honour.' Kallinikos shook his head. 'I'm very sorry, Timos. I have been a bad friend.' He shook his head. 'He is a... business partner... of my father's. It's all twisted up.' He shook his head. 'You are well clear of it.'

Aranthur took his hand and shook it.

'Never say so. In a few years we'll laugh about this.' He made a face. 'House war? In the City?'

Kallinikos shrugged. 'There are two hundred Houses. Mine is one of the Ten, the Imperial Houses. But what matters is the web of alliances that bind us together or separate us – marriages, divorces, bastard children, unpaid debts, loves, hates, politics. It's all very...' He turned away. '*Personal*,' he said distinctly. 'Aristocrats think that they are so important that they don't need an ideology to dress up greed or rage. They just do what suits them.'

'Like Arnaut farmers, then. It'll pass, Mikal. You will see. Ten days wonder, and then something else...'

Kallinikos frowned. 'I doubt it. I loved her. Not a student fling. You had to know her.'

Aranthur nodded.

'He's insane,' Kallinikos said.

Aranthur almost forgot the *thuryx* addict, but Chiraz stopped him on the way out.

'Your friend, Syr Drako,' he said. 'He took Syr Sasan.'

Aranthur put a hand to his forehead. 'Of course he did,' he said bitterly.

Another week passed, and Aranthur successfully summoned the wind of magik and powered the Safiri *occulta*. In the very act of writing it on himself, he was sure that this was a much more powerful version of the same spell that he had seen cast on the three bravos. Or perhaps, cast across three men, it was weaker.

The Master of Arts squeezed his arm. 'I'm off to cross the straits. I won't be here for two weeks. The ground is hard. I suggest you go home for ploughing, and come back ready to work.' She paused. 'You cannot go on at this rate, my young friend. You fought two duels, eh? Let me be clear – you are now forbidden to fight. That is my word. You are forbidden to risk yourself in any way.' She smiled gently. 'You are an investment, Syr Timos. You do not belong to yourself. Am I making myself clear?'

'Yes, my lady.' He was suddenly angry. He couldn't explain the anger, but it was there, and he blurted, 'Why am I even here?'

'You are my choice to learn Safiri. And you continue to justify that choice. But all this swordplay must end.'

'Your choice?' he asked. 'Or the Emperor's choice?'

She looked at him as if he was a dying rodent brought into her study by the cat.

'What?'

Aranthur hadn't even known he harboured so much resentment, but out it came.

'Wasn't I chosen by the Emperor?' he asked.

'No,' the Master of Arts said. 'That's the strangest thing I've ever heard. If the Emperor had ordered me to take you, we'd have one of those ugly confrontations that the Academy has with the Imperium.' She looked at him. 'Why?'

Aranthur deflated. 'Oh.'

She raised an eyebrow. 'Best tell me, young man.'

He shrugged. 'I know Mistress Iralia.'

The Master of Arts threw back her head and laughed.

'And you thought...' She smiled. 'Well, she has certainly mentioned you. And the Emperor knows your name. Now, I need to ask you to stop working. You look bad, and you are sometimes inattentive. Nonetheless, your work is excellent.' She looked at him. 'You like to fight. You enjoy the violence.'

Aranthur didn't know what to say.

'Perhaps I can channel that,' she said. 'Why have you ceased seeing my Dahlia?'

'I...' he began. His mouth opened and shut.

'I'm sure she said something dramatic and overblown. Or perhaps you ignored her?' Her eyes bored holes in Aranthur's mind. 'You should try seeing her.'

Aranthur looked away.

'Youth is wasted on the young,' she said.

'May I ask you a question?' Aranthur said.

'Anything,' the Master of Arts replied.

'Is there anyone else in the City who knows the spells in this grimoire?'

She looked at him for a moment. 'I can't imagine so. If there was, you'd be training with them.'

Aranthur bowed. But in his head, he was thinking, *The crazy husband used my spell. My Safiri spell. I saw his gestures and heard Armean. Similar, but not the same. Weaker, maybe. But the same.*

He didn't know where to go with that.

'I know you don't want to hear about my duel,' Aranthur said. 'But the man we were supposed to fight... He used a variation of this *occulta*. And then he tried to make my friend bleed out... I can't tell you why, but I feel that it was another Safiri spell. Or Armean. It's a hunch,' he said, as she frowned.

'There cannot be another registered Magos in this city who knows these *workings*,' she said. 'If there was, as I said, you'd be working with him. Or her.' She frowned. 'Get me his name.'

'I will,' Aranthur said.

*

Aranthur had a feeling of repeating his own life; he was repeating the week before First Sun. He went to the spice market, which was one of his favourite places in the City; a huge building constructed to support commerce, where five hundred merchants, local and foreign, sold everything from rare spices and Zhouian silk to local grain and even speculations in coin values. He enjoyed the smell and the taste. There was so much cinnamon in the building that he felt as if he was breathing the stuff; cinnamon and mace, pepper and *quaveh* beans; candies coated in saffron, and barrels of nutmegs. He bought the whole list of spices for Donna Cucina. Then he hurried back out of the merchants' quarter to write his mathematics examination with both eyes half-open and left with the impression that he'd done very poorly. He went and checked on Kallinikos, who was propped up in bed and surrounded by admirers in fine clothes.

Aranthur might have slunk out, but Kallinikos called out 'Timos!' and the other young men and women made way.

'Ah, the other hero of the hour,' a short man said. He had perfect teeth and white-blond hair and a magnificent doublet in red and blue wool trimmed in fur. 'And you are?'

'He's Timos,' Kallinikos said, as if Aranthur was an aristocrat.

'Arnaut?' The short blond was trying to look down his nose, only Aranthur was a whole head taller.

'Yes,' Aranthur said. 'And you, sir?' He meant to be annoying, and he succeeded. The man backed up a step.

'I am Siran, of the City.'

He wore the colours of the Lions, the Academy club for the most conservative and snobbish aristocrats. Aranthur had reason to remember them.

Kallinikos laughed. 'Come and see me tomorrow, Timos. The company will be better.'

'I say.' Siran frowned, clearly insulted. 'I am honouring you, my friend. We want you back among us!'

Kallinikos ignored the man. 'Where are you bound, Aranthur?'

Aranthur bowed. 'I'm away to help my *patur* with ploughing.'

Kallinikos nodded. Their relationship was altered; Aranthur could have said, 'I'm going home to kill my *patur*,' and Kallinikos would have nodded the same way.

'Well,' the aristocrat said. 'I'll likely be out of bed again when you return. Visit me.'

Aranthur took his hand, left to left as swordsmen did.

'I'm glad to see you better. And the other matter?'

Kallinikos gave a small shrug. He was changed; Aranthur could see that more than his body was wounded.

'The husband is still threatening war. Hence, my House allies.' Softly, he said, 'Who want me to go back to being a Lion.'

'Be careful,' Aranthur said. 'Would it be plebeian of me to ask our enemy's name?'

'Tangar Uthmanos,' Kallinikos said.

'Uthmanos,' Aranthur repeated to himself. 'Very well. Be careful while I'm gone.'

'This, from you?' Kallinikos lay back. 'You too, take care. The Uthmanoi make bad enemies.'

Aranthur bowed, and withdrew.

'Going west?' Siran said. 'A good many of us may ride out that way soon.' He smiled a smile he probably meant to be dangerous.

'Really?'

Aranthur thought of recommending Lecne's inn, then decided he didn't like the man, so he stayed quiet.

He bowed again and left, feeling fairly pleased with himself. He sat up late and, instead of writing out a religious text for his sister, he wrote a poem for Dahlia. He liked it. He had things to say, and he said them.

He copied the poem out fair, on a scrap of vellum he cut to size with his eating knife. Then he put the poem in her finished belt-purse and dropped it at her rooms. Again, he felt pleased with himself.

'I may yet make a *daesia*,' he said to the air, and sketched a bow to nothing. 'I write poetry, and I fight duels. All I need to learn to do is sleep late.'

His last call was on Drako, who lived in a veritable palace, a house five storeys tall that towered over the Great Canal, with coats of arms set in the marble facade under dozens of arches supported by twining pillars of coloured stone. Over the loggia was a mosaic of the Lady, set in tiny tiles of gold-infused stone, and the place was called 'Casa d'Oro,' the house of gold.

Aranthur had never visited before, and in the end he climbed the slick steps of the loggia with the same feeling he might have had throwing himself into battle, but Drako was not at home. The steward, when summoned, consulted a list, smiled, and bowed.

'You are on milord's list,' he said. 'Syr Drako is at *this* location.'

He copied out directions, and Aranthur found his friend sitting behind a writing table in a building very like a fortified keep at the end of the canal.

'Port master's office,' Drako said after an exchange of bows. 'I rent a table here.' He smiled. 'You ain't dead.'

'No,' Aranthur said.

Drako leant back and put his expensively booted feet up on his writing table.

'Good for you. Stop duelling, Timos. You'll get killed. You were lucky – your friend Kallinikos was sleeping with someone's wife. Someone powerful. None of my business, except that his bravos would have killed you both. The man's an *advocato*. A man of law. He has power and money, and his House is old, rich, and touchy.' Drako shrugged. 'And people say he's a fucking warlock, an old-style magiker. All I'm saying is, know what the fuck you get into. You make me feel old.'

Aranthur winced. 'I . . . Listen. The Master of Arts wants the man's name. He was using . . . an Eastern *occulta*.'

Drako steepled his fingers. 'So? He's married to an Armean. She's a Magas.'

'Not any more. Kallinikos says he killed her.'

Drako looked at him for twenty heartbeats.

'Which Kallinikos?' he asked in his smooth, mountebank voice.

'Mikal. My friend.' Aranthur leant forward.

'How do you even *know* Mikal . . .' Drako shook his head. 'Uthmanos . . .' he said aloud and wrote the name down on a wax tablet. Then he tossed a tiny bag on the writing table. 'Change of subject. Going home for ploughing?'

Aranthur nodded.

'I admit, I already knew.' Drako was looking out to sea. He had a magnificent window, and it was a brilliant early spring day. 'Keep your eyes open. That's all I ask. There's something happening which I do not understand. No, that's a foolish statement. I don't really understand much of anything, and included in my shopping list of lack of understanding is this: a lot of armour has recently been purchased, and it isn't going east, as we thought it would, to face the Disciples and the

Pure in Safi and Armea and Atti. In fact, we allowed the contract to go through City armourers because we thought that the armour was going to our friends in Armea.'

Aranthur summoned up his mental map. Armea was on the same island as Atti, but farther east. With Safi to the north and Masr to the south.

'Yes,' he said. 'I get that.'

'Then it disappeared. And now it's in Lonika, or even further west. You understand, this is Cold Iron business. The armour is not ours – there's no law allowing us to seize it. Makes no sense to send armour west when Volta makes the best armour in the world. So we're watching it. Something has been rotten in Lonika all year.' He shrugged. 'Never mind. It's probably nothing, so in the meantime I get to pay you to go home for ploughing, which is a very gentle form of corruption. I hear you met the Emperor.'

'Yes,' Aranthur agreed.

'What did you think?'

'I liked him. He's with Iralia!' Aranthur said. 'He's so old!'

'You are a dear. He's just fifty. She's not yet thirty. Both at the height of their powers.'

'Iralia should have someone younger.'

'Iralia is a courtesan, and if she plays her beads right, she'll be the grey empress. Sunlight, he may even marry her – he's besotted enough. But it's all political. The Duke of Volta hates her, and the Emperor has had enough of the duke, and so . . .' Drako spread his hands. 'Go home, keep your eyes open, and give me a written report about the roads on your return.'

Aranthur rose, took the little suede bag, and bowed.

'Your servant, syr,' he said.

Drako smiled. 'I wish I was going to that inn . . . Where is it?'

'Fosse?' Aranthur asked.

Drako smiled. 'Pretty girls, good stock, good wine.' He uncrossed his legs. 'Damme, why am I sending you? I could go myself.' He sighed.

Aranthur waited, because Drako was clearly not done.

'Yes?'

Drako looked at him. 'I hate telling people things. Knowledge is power. But you keep being a nexus.' He scratched at his short, fashionable beard. 'How's Dahlia?'

'I don't know. I wrote her a poem.' Aranthur smiled self-consciously.

'Good. She loves a good poem.' Drako's sarcasm was thick enough to spread on toast.

'Her room-mate told me not to come back.'

Aranthur hated the whine in his voice, but he was hurt.

Drako looked away. 'Like that, is it. Sorry, then. If she's moved on.' He shook his head. 'But now that she's left you, I want you to be even more careful.'

Aranthur wondered what he meant.

'And where is Sasan?'

'Safe, and drying out,' Drako said.

'I'd like to see him.'

'Listen, Timos. I hate coincidences.' He paused. 'Dahlia left you and then you met this Sasan . . . You know Mikal Kallinikos . . . No, never mind. Not today. Go home.'

Aranthur thought of asking questions, but Drako was too enigmatic and it would all take too long. He determined to try Dahlia again when he returned.

Aranthur was still pondering the complexities of Dahlia and Drako and Sasan and Iralia when he packed. He interrupted his reverie on the people he knew to hang his City sword on the wall and take the old blade. He'd built a new scabbard for it, and he wore it differently now. It was meant to be worn by a man on a horse, and he wore it that way.

The sword felt good tapping against his shins. It seemed to comfort him as he moved Ariadne to the military stables and mounted Rasce for the long ride home. It was almost like a companion as he rode along, watching the woods, and more than once he was tempted to talk to it, which seemed fairly odd. After a long, damp, cold day he met other travellers and he rode for two days with some religious players, all the way to the gate at Lonika. They performed the standard religious plays, and not the modern versions with dance and special effects that the opera did. He saw them perform their *Niobe* and he thought of Dahlia. But their *Niobe* was the traditional one, with Niobe herself as a scheming villainess and the gods regretful, careful of human dignity.

He stayed the night with them and drank too much wine. Then he rode on into the west, passing a long convoy of heavy wagons that surprised him, and noting, as the sun dried the ground, that there were military road crews almost everywhere. At Lonika, there were armed soldiers at the gates. Aranthur was unsurprised to see the tall woman in armour, although she was mounted on a superb black horse this time. She was chatting with the same short man; the two seemed inseparable.

On second glance he realised she was Alis – the General, the majesty – and that her mount sported an ebony horn two feet long and fluted like the best Iron Circle armours: a black unicorn. The magikal beast gave off an aura of power that he could feel like the heat of the sun on a warm day. Aranthur had never seen a magikal beast before, except the green drake on the docks. He couldn't help but stare.

Aranthur wondered if a bout of swordplay in a tavern counted as an introduction. Since meeting her, he had learned that she was an Imperial general, or *vanax*. Her name was Alis Tribane. She was part of the Emperor's family.

He looked at her for long enough that she felt his regard and turned her head. She smiled, touched her monster's sides with her heels and trotted to Aranthur, who was waiting to pass the gate.

'You have come up in the world,' she said.

Rasce was flinching away from the dark unicorn.

'My lady.' He grinned to show he meant no offence. 'But you might say the same. Last time you were a gate guard.'

She threw back her head and laughed. 'Damme, the biter is bit!' She leant forward. 'You're friends with Syr Drako.'

He nodded. 'Yes, milady.'

She nodded 'Another time, Syr Timos, it would be my delight to have you to dinner.' She smiled a businesslike smile. 'But at the moment I am very much engaged.'

'I didn't mean to intrude!' Aranthur said. 'My apologies...'

She laughed. 'You're not intruding, young man. I'm just busy. Have a good trip home. Eagle Valley?'

'Yes, ma'am.'

'Alis,' she said. 'Or General Tribane.'

Mounted and on dry roads, it only took another day to reach the Inn at Fosse. Aranthur was sure of his welcome, and he rode into the yard and was almost instantly in Lecne's arms. Within an hour he was giving a sword lesson; that night he was invited to dine in the kitchen with the family. Hasti flirted with him, somewhat automatically, and

Nenia was herself, with a cautious smile. Don Cucino had regained control of his hand; Donna Cucina was delighted by her spices. It was a triumphant dinner.

'You have become quite the gentleman,' Nenia said to him as they cleared the table.

Aranthur didn't think of a reply until he was lying in bed that night in Lecne's room.

He was still thinking of her words, with their implied compliment and unstated concern, when he was walking along in the deep loam behind Rasce. His gelding looked back from time to time, over the plough handles, as if to say *I'm a warhorse, not a plough horse.*

Home was different. Everything was different, and it was difficult to describe just how. The house seemed smaller, although suddenly it had a fine porch of new wood with lovely curling dragons' heads at the eaves, an Arnaut custom. Inside it seemed stuffy and close, despite a new oak chair with a padded back and arms, bought off the back of a wagon. It was obviously loot from some rich house in Volta during the *Stasis* or civil strife wherein the duke was overthrown.

There were new workers on his father's farm, white-skinned men from the east whose families now had shacks along the western edge of town. Hagor had three families, and there were dozens more on the other Arnaut farms in the valley. Mira had a Armean servant girl.

Aranthur ploughed all day for three days, sometimes with his father taking a turn. The wiry foreign men helped, but they didn't have the size to handle the deep plough. Aranthur did, and he enjoyed the work. It was simple, and it tired him. He learned the Armean names – Sali, and Souti, and Dras. Dras was silent and Souli had a bad scar on his face that wept pus, and which he didn't bother to keep clean.

Sali was the only one with a sense of humour, although all three men would smile if they thought he wanted them to. They would also flinch if he moved quickly. Their women were never to be seen, and their children were dirty, even by liberal Arnaut standards.

They were all Sun worshippers, and they prayed, loudly, to the rising sun and again to the setting. Aranthur scandalised Hagor by kneeling and joining them.

'Is the Eagle too simple for you, lad?' his father asked.

Aranthur shrugged. He was avoiding having a fight with Hagor. There was nothing particular about which he felt the need to fight.

'Is that *another* sword?' Hagor asked later.

'Yes.' Aranthur didn't mean to be sullen, but it certainly sounded sullen.

'You own two swords now.'

'Patur, I own two horses, I'm in the militia, and I'm an Imperial Student.'

Aranthur was trying to tell his father that he had status, but it sounded petulant.

'Far too good to be a farmer,' Hagor said wearily.

'I love ploughing,' Aranthur said, looking for some middle ground.

His father looked him in the eye.

'Eagle grant you always love ploughing,' he said. 'You cut a straight furrow.'

'I'm an apprentice in the Leather-workers' Guild,' he said at dinner, and showed his craft ring.

Hagor nodded. 'Will you keep at it?'

Aranthur nodded. 'I expect I'll be a journeyman by First Sun. I was an incense bearer for the Iron Day festival.'

He smiled around at his family, who fairly glowed with pride now he was telling them about things they could understand. Studying Safiri with the Master of Arts and working an ancient and complex and possibly lost *occulta* – such a thing would only frighten his mother. Fighting a duel for a friend over his affair with a married woman . . . not so good. But leather-working was good. Their town had a leather-worker.

'I was never an incense bearer,' Hagor said, approvingly. 'How were you chosen?'

Aranthur told the story of the *quaveh* bean.

'Pure luck,' Marta laughed.

'Will of the gods,' Aranthur countered.

Then they were poking each other, and the room didn't seem so small or close.

The next day, they went to the Topazoi farm to share dinner. Alfia had grown, and Aranthur had to consider her in a different light. Her severity was still there, but she was taller, her shoulders broader, her breasts fuller. When she stood on her tiptoes to fetch a crock of marmalade for her mother, Aranthur was shocked at her beauty.

He was also a little shocked at how differently he saw her. She was working to attract him, and she was worried, a little unsure of her powers. When, while clearing pewter plates, they were together in the winter kitchen, he smiled down at her.

'You are suddenly very beautiful, Alfia,' he said, and she flushed.

'I...' she said. 'I don't compare to city girls, I'm sure.'

She stood still and licked her lips, and Aranthur thought that if he was in the City, he would probably kiss her. Here, if he did, he'd be married to her in a matter of days. It was still tempting.

It was like fighting. He put his mouth over hers without further hesitation. He never made a decision, and she responded after a long second.

As they parted she licked his lips with her tongue.

And stepped back as her mother came into the kitchen suddenly and laughed.

'What on earth are you two doing alone in the kitchen?' she said. 'When I was a girl...'

She winked at Aranthur, and fetched the pudding in its cloth, leaving her thought unspoken and ambiguous.

But when the pudding was done and some tarragon brandy drunk, the women cleared the pudding plates and put out the little glasses men used for *raki*. Then they vanished, leaving Aranthur and his father, and old Hari – Topazo Primo – and his two sons Marco and Stepan, Aranthur's boyhood friend.

The *raki* went around.

'Alfia says Aranthur here was an incense bearer in the City,' Marco said. Aranthur nodded. 'Do you intend to be a priest, then, Arry?'

Aranthur fingered his beard. 'I don't think so.'

'How'd you come to be the incense bearer, then?' Stepan asked.

What he really meant was *Are you coming back?* Aranthur could almost hear him ask the question. He wondered if Hari already knew that he'd kissed Alfia.

To amuse them he told the story again, leaving out Dahlia. But when he was done, all of them wanted to know how Iron Day was different in the City and he told them, with a little embellishment, because he was a good storyteller. And he described Master Palko's house and yard, and the festivities, and the Emperor.

'You met the Emperor?' Hagor asked.

There was a hush.

'You're a liar,' Stepan said, in just the tone he'd used at the age of ten.

'No, it's true,' Aranthur said with a laugh. 'And what is rarer, he knew me. Knew of me. Knew I was Arnaut, and knew what book I was studying at the Studion.'

He smiled at his father, expecting praise, and instead Hagor looked worried.

Aranthur was keeping a lot from them: Dahlia, Iralia, the roles of women in the city. He was pretending to speak with their accent, and he was annoyed when they doubted him.

'Were you wearing your sword?' Stepan asked.

'No.'

'Did you bow?' Hagor asked.

'Yes, Patur,' Aranthur said. 'My best bow.'

His father shrugged. 'I'm not much for bowing.' He made a face. 'Did you ever find out what happened to the poor man from Volta? I mean, who he was? The one whose horse you have?'

Aranthur nodded. 'Yes. A friend of mine knew something about him. He had no family.'

'A man with all that wealth had no family?' Hagor exclaimed.

Aranthur was rankled, but he let it pass. 'You can spend the money now.'

'Already have,' his father said. 'On the house, and on our new hands.'

'Easterners.' Old Hari shrugged. 'Not much as workers. And they steal anything you leave out.'

'And godless,' Marco chimed in. 'All that fool pagan caterwauling at the sun, and not a prayer for the real gods.'

'Armeans,' Aranthur said quietly.

'What's that?' asked Hari.

'They are not Easterners,' Aranthur said. 'They are Armeans, from the old kingdoms just east of Atti. Bordered on their east side by Safi and on the south by Masr.'

'Pah, they're all Easterners to me,' Marco said. 'Work 'em hard and watch 'em like the Eagle, right, lads?' He raised an eyebrow at

Aranthur's father. 'Your brother's got one to kindle, eh? But then, he's always been ... odd.'

'They are thrifty, and they work hard,' Hagor said carefully. 'I haven't seen any stealing.'

'You will. The young ones are like wild cattle – vicious.' Marco showed the heavy-bladed knife at his hip. 'I'm ready if they want trouble.'

'There's folk in the valley say they will kill us and take our farms if'n we let them,' Stepan said. But he said it experimentally, looking for a reaction.

Aranthur's father wrinkled his nose. 'Not the way I see them, lad. For my money, they have had all the trouble they ever need, and now they just want to live.' He turned to Aranthur. 'Many Easterners in the City, son?'

'Yes, Patur.' Aranthur thought of Sasan, of the *chai* girl, of all the refugees.

'And they do all the crime, eh?' old Hari asked.

Aranthur thought. 'Not really. Though they are very poor.'

'Why don't they go back where they belong?' Marco asked.

'Then we'd have no workers,' Stepan said.

'We worked these farms on our own before,' Marco said.

Aranthur shrugged. 'We came here as refugees, didn't we, Patur?'

Hagor raised an eyebrow. The eyebrow told Aranthur that his father wasn't impressed – that he appreciated Aranthur's argument but this was not the time or place to express it. All that in the twitch of an older man's bushy eyebrow.

'We weren't refugees,' Hari said. 'Our folk were soldiers, and we took what we *won*.'

'Not the way I heard it,' Aranthur said.

He smiled when he said it, because Mira said *you catch more flies with honey than with vinegar*.

'And what did you hear, in your precious City? That farmers as dumb as dung and stupid as cattle?' Marco frowned.

Aranthur had, in fact, heard such foolish talk in the city. He shrugged. 'I'd say the evidence suggests—'

'What kind o' priest talk is that?' asked Marco. 'Say what you mean.'

Aranthur shook his head. 'I *am* saying what I mean. The evidence is unclear.'

'Our folk have stories going back two thousand years,' Marco said. 'I know 'em. Best you know 'em too. Seems to me the Academy is filling your head with nonsense.'

'Our stories are mostly myth,' Aranthur said. 'Most of it is dung, as you say.'

There was a long silence.

'Really?' Marco said.

'Yes,' Aranthur said. 'Most of the Arnauts were soldiers for the Old Empire, or so I understand. We carried Eagles as our standards, and that's why we were People of the Eagle.' He looked around. 'When our side lost, we took refuge in these hills, because we could defend them.'

'Horse shit,' Marco said. 'We *led* the fucking revolution.'

'Show me some evidence of that?' Aranthur said.

'Everyone round here knows,' Marco insisted.

'Everyone around here knows how to take Armeans and make them servants and slaves,' Aranthur spat. 'Everyone knows how to blame them for being victims. There's a *war* in the East, and these people are in no way at fault, and you blame them. They are poor because *everything* has been taken from them.'

He got up and walked out.

Behind him, he saw old Hari bar the door and say 'Oh no you don't,' to Marco.

Aranthur walked across the mud of the yard and then turned and began walking home, his feet plunging deep in the cold earth. It reminded him of the first night he met Iralia.

In the morning, at home, breakfast was silent.

'You are growing away from us,' his father said, when ploughing was done.

Aranthur frowned. 'It feels as if I am the same and you are growing away from me.'

Hagor nodded, staring at the ground. 'They are not fools. I don't like their . . . righteousness. But this is our land, and we've worked hard to make this, and we're not of a mind to lose it.'

'Lose it? To Sali? To Souti?'

'To an endless flood of people from other islands and other archipelagos. You haven't been here. There's folk living in the deep woods. They ain't nice folk. There's robbers on the roads.'

'Two men tried to rob me last winter,' Aranthur said. 'An Arnaut and a Byzas.'

'What'd you do – use your sword?' Hagor asked, with a smile that suggested that they'd bested his poor son.

'I killed one,' Aranthur said. 'The other got away.'

'You killed . . .' His father looked at him. 'You scare me, son. You sound like my brother.'

Aranthur sighed. 'I may work in the City this summer.'

'You'll put your matur in her grave, you know that,' Hagor said, only half joking.

Aranthur shook his head. 'Whatever I do,' he admitted wearily.

Nonetheless, when he rode away, he had three new shirts in his saddle-bag, and a hide of beautiful leather, fine-grained and supple, for some project or other, and a vast array of potted vegetables and other delicacies. He'd eaten meat almost every day while home, and it upset his stomach – not the least of the afflictions of home.

He trotted down his father's farm lane, waving at Marta all the way. They were all standing on the new porch. Souti was stacking firewood behind them. Sali was working in the eastern fields; Aranthur gave him a wave and received one in return.

He turned into the road, which was thick with spring mud, and he guided Rasce along the grassy verge where the ground was drier and less work for a horse. As he came to the bridge, he saw a woman walking; as he came up, he was surprised to see Alfia. She raised her head, saw him, and gave him a dazzling smile.

'Marco is an idiot,' she said, by way of greeting. 'But I have to assume our wedding is off. Are you going to Korfa?'

Korfa was the next major Arnaut village, three long leagues away and over the ridge.

'I'm bound for Fosse and the City.' Aranthur considered. 'I can go to Korfa,' he said agreeably. 'If you'd like a ride?'

'You speak like a gentleman. My matur praised you to the skies, but I'm not sure I'm allowed to ride your horse.'

As 'ride your horse' was an Arnaut expression for sex, her cheeks suddenly burned. But then she winked.

Aranthur laughed. 'Well, I'll dismount, then, and we'll walk a ways together.'

In fact, they talked very easily. He felt as if Alfia had become another person; gone was the severe and self-praising young harridan, replaced by ... a woman. He kept peeping at her over the horse's neck, surprised each time by her loveliness. Interested that she gave no sign of a passionate kiss in the kitchen.

She asked him to retell the story of the evening's argument and he did. She laughed.

'So much fuss over the Easterners,' she said. 'Does your uncle really live with one?'

'Yes,' Aranthur said.

'Do you really speak Armean?'

'Yes, a little,' he admitted. 'I'm working on Safiri.'

She nodded. 'I'd like to know how. Teach me to say hello, and goodbye, so I sound like less of an arse. Your sister and I take food to them, sometimes.' She pointed into the woods below the main pass. 'There are villages all through the woods. You know that?'

'Stepan and I found a couple of them,' he admitted.

The time passed very pleasantly.

But she refused to be drawn on her own views, and kept asking him things, so that he found himself telling her about the Master of Arts and the Emperor, and finally about his duel in the inn yard.

They were at the top of the ridge, with the Valley of the Eagle behind them and Korfa laid out below them like a painting: red tile roofs and a beautiful quilt of fields; young barley, newly turned earth, winter grass.

'We are alone on the road,' Alfia said. 'Are you leaving, Aranthur?'

He looked out over the valley. 'Maybe.'

She nodded. Her dark hair blew in the stiff breeze.

'You know,' she said, 'I'm the richest girl in the Valley.' She made a face. 'I'd trade it to be you. I want to go and swing a sword at my enemies and cast magiks. Instead, I get to sit and wait to see which mud-booted Faroi or Bastoi or Timoi comes and wins my hand.'

Aranthur didn't know what to say.

'Sometimes I daydream that you marry me,' she said carefully. 'And take me away to the city.' She looked back at him. And shrugged. 'But that's not going to happen, is it? It is in my matur's head, and your matur's.'

Aranthur said nothing.

'So part of me wants you to go and never come back, so I can imagine your adventures.' She shrugged. 'I think a lot of nonsense. My matur tells me so all the time.'

Aranthur reached out a hand and put it on her shoulder, and in a moment they were kissing, on the mountain above the pass. Sheep's bells tinkled on the slope above them.

She pushed him away. 'Oh, dear. That'll be enough of that.'

She smiled, and her face was flushed, and she was beautiful. And she turned, and walked, straight-backed, down the road to Korfa. Three steps, she walked.

He took a step after her, without considering...

Alfia turned into his arms, and again her mouth was under his.

Rasce cropped grass.

Later, they lay together, naked, in a patch of sweet-smelling thyme. Alfia stared at the sky above her. She was laughing, or weeping.

Aranthur knew he'd done something that he could not change. Without thinking.

She wasn't weeping. She was laughing.

'If we've made a baby...' she said. And stretched. She leant over. 'You've done that before.'

'Yes,' he admitted.

She licked the tip of his nose. 'Pray with me,' she said.

They knelt, naked, and prayed to Aphres the Lover.

'My horse is going to leave us. Or someone will come,' Aranthur said after the second time.

Alfia was still watching the sky.

'I know. I never want this to end.'

And then, like a practical Arnaut girl, she rose, went to the Bektash, the saint's spring, and washed in the freezing water. And dressed.

Aranthur did the same, a little embarrassed at the rapid passing from intimacy to reserve.

But then she licked his nose and danced away.

'No more kissing,' she said. 'Or I'll never be able to walk away.' She picked up her basket. And stopped. 'If we made a baby...' she said carefully.

'I'll marry you,' Aranthur said.

She nodded. 'But that's not what you want.' She shrugged. 'Never happened.'

266

He smiled. 'Two hours ago, I'd have said no,' he admitted. 'Now, I admit that a farm in the Valley seems...'

'We'd never get any work done,' she quipped. 'I'll write to you.' She shook her head. 'Pray Aphres I don't kindle. Go be a Magos, Aranthur. Someone from here should escape.'

She walked away down the hill and didn't look back.

Aranthur stood on the high ridge for a long time. And then he took a deep breath and let it out, and led Rasce across country, into the old woods north of the road. It was instantly colder, like riding downhill into winter. Under the trees there was still snow, whereas up on the ridge the thyme was soft and sweet...

He walked carefully, and Rasce, as an old campaigner, was quiet. They descended from the ridge and plunged into the tall spruce, and soon enough they struck one of the better trails. Aranthur knew the woods well enough, and he enjoyed the adventure. But he was thinking of Alfia, and he was afraid of what he'd done.

An hour later, he found the first of the little bark shelters. No smoke came from the mud chimney, and no one responded to his calls.

The smell told him what he would find inside, and indeed outside, as wolves had already been at the dead baby. The father and mother were dead, too, and their corpses were horrifying. He didn't grasp what was terrible about them, because he averted his gaze and backed out of the blanket-door.

Aranthur stood in the rotting snow under the eaves of the spruce trees and tried to breathe.

He found two more little bark houses. In one, all the inhabitants had been killed with a sharp knife. He had no idea whether it was murder or suicide. But none of them had any food, and all of them had dead children. In the other, no wolves had been at the bodies. Again, the corpses had that awful look; this time he looked longer. It was as if they had no bones. They were swollen, but somehow... soft.

In the fourth little hut he searched, he noted that the man – the dead man – had a *kuria* crystal clutched in his swollen, boneless hand.

After the fifth, he stopped looking in the huts. He retched, mounted his horse, and rode away.

*

It was after dark when he rode into the yard at the inn. He unsaddled Rasce and put him in the stable and gave him extra grain.

In the morning, he was careful and polite with Nenia and Lecne. He said very little.

Lecne demanded a sword lesson.

Aranthur set his mouth and provided it. Hasti didn't come, but Nenia did, and he was thorough, and worked them until they were tired, cutting and parrying at each other with sticks.

Finally, over dinner, he found himself telling Don Cucino about the dead Armeans in the woods.

'Sunset!' spat Cucino. 'Why didn't they say something?'

'Proud,' Donna Cucina said. 'Proud and cold. It was a hard winter.'

They summoned the priest of the Lady and the doctor and a few other citizens of Fosse, and Aranthur testified to what he had seen.

'Mayhap there are some alive,' the doctor said. 'We'll find them. We should have looked weeks ago.'

He glared at the priest, but the priest shrugged.

'We had our own starving folk this winter.' He glanced at the priest, who was praying.

At dinner he told them all about the City while Donna Cucina praised his care in buying spices again. He told again of meeting the Emperor.

Donna Cucina rose when he was done.

'We have some news too, don't we?' she asked, looking at Nenia. Hasti looked away.

Nenia flushed. Aranthur found her as beautiful as Alfia – much the same straight-nosed, high-eyebrowed beauty.

What's wrong with me? he wondered.

'I'm to go to the Academy,' she said. 'I was recommended by the vanaxia commanding the troops on the road.' She spoke with quiet happiness.

'She translated all the Ellene on the old stones for them,' Donna Cucina said.

'That's splendid!' Aranthur said. 'Wonderful! When do you start?'

'In the autumn. I can't wait.' She blushed. 'I plan to catch up with you.'

'You can learn Safiri,' he said happily. 'I could use the help.'

'Safiri?' she asked. 'An Easterner tongue, yes? That would be a challenge. A different alphabet and everything?' She whistled. 'I've been playing with Armean whenever the Easterners come for grain. And Attian. What does Safiri sound like?'

Aranthur repeated Sasan's phrase about stealing, using his intonation.

Nenia got a faraway look in her eyes. 'A little like Armean, then.'

Aranthur shrugged. 'If you say so.'

'Armean is difficult,' she said again. 'And they all speak it . . . differently. It's a fiendish language. So . . .'

Aranthur glanced at her parents. 'Watch out,' he said. 'The Academy will never let her leave.'

'And I'll just stay here and run an inn,' Lecne said. 'You two can have all the adventures, and I'll . . .' He paused. 'Rot!' he spat.

'Lec,' his sister said, but Lecne had risen, a dark flush on his face, and he slammed the kitchen door.

Aranthur followed him out into the biting spring air.

Lecne was leaning against the back wall of the stable. He had a stock cheroot burning in his hand, and he was looking out over the vineyards that ran west from the inn on the Volta road.

'I want to have a life too,' he said, as Aranthur came round the stable's corner.

'Innkeeper of a fortified inn on the Empire's trunk road?' Aranthur leant back against the rough stone. 'Really doesn't sound so bad.'

Lecne laughed. 'I agree. Until you show up with your posh accent and your sword. And now my sister, to rub my nose in my provincial backwardness for the rest of my life.'

Aranthur took a draw at the stock. He didn't smoke often, but he would sometimes have a pipe at home. This was good stock, as good as his patur's.

'Your mother doesn't like stock.'

'My mater is against everything.' He shrugged. 'She doesn't want Nenia to go to the Academy. She wants her home with babies. She said so, just that way.'

They stood looking out into the darkness.

'My matur is trying to get me to marry the local rich girl,' Aranthur said, in the patois of home. 'I walked with her today. She was . . . different. Grown up. She, too, wants adventures.' He shook his head. The stock took his head in unaccustomed directions. 'Home is different. Full of refugees and greed. No, I don't mean that. Sunlight, Lecne, the dead kids shook the hell out of me yesterday. And I suddenly thought that I could have a good life, at home.'

Lecne nodded. 'Sounds bad,' he agreed. 'This girl is as pretty as Nenia?'

Aranthur shook his head. 'Yes. No. Fuck off.'

They both laughed.

Lecne shook his head. 'I hate that there's people dying in the woods. We'll go tomorrow and find 'em.'

'Yes. Yes, there's good folk here.'

Lecne was looking out over the vineyards again.

'There's horsemen moving out on the road,' he said suddenly.

He ran for the inn. Aranthur lingered for a moment, listening. He could hear the clink of horse tack and the rattle of men's harness – armour. It was a sizeable body of horse.

He followed Lecne.

Inside the inn, they were closing the gate to the yard and then the heavy inn door, studded with huge iron nails. Aranthur threw his back into it, and then helped Nenia with the shutters. The inn had dozens of heavy oak shutters, each weighing about as much as a child, loopholed for crossbows.

'Why are they moving at night?' Nenia asked Aranthur.

'I don't know,' he said. 'Sometimes soldiers practise marching – maybe they practise at night?'

'It's too much like the night Pater was hurt,' Nenia said.

With the shutters barred, the inn was like a fortress, and all the sound was muffled. There were only half a dozen patrons, all local men and women who finished their food and left through the kitchen door for their homes in the village on the ridge behind the road.

'I want to see what's happening,' Nenia said, as the wheelwright slipped out of the kitchen door, the last drinker.

'So do I.'

Aranthur followed her into the dark yard. She knew her own ground, and he almost lost her when she went into the dark stables. He followed her movement, stubbed his toe on a stall and then saw light when she opened a postern door in the north side of the stable. He followed her out into a shock of spring jasmine that grew right against the door. The smell was remarkable. Nenia grabbed his hand and pulled, and he emerged into the spring night.

Then she dropped into a drainage ditch that ran along the edge of the newly ploughed and manured field to the north of the inn, and ran along a path so narrow he couldn't see it. He followed more carefully, watching the evil-smelling water to his left, and then followed her up the bank. She stood under a leafless tree.

'That's how Lecne and I slip out of the house,' she said very quietly, in his ear.

Aranthur, still full of stock smoke, was moved to think that her hair smelled beautiful, and that he'd already kissed another woman, and that the night was very still.

There were men talking on the road. A horse neighed, and another, and then there were hoofbeats.

'Let's go closer,' Nenia said.

Aranthur was unsure, but she was off, and he was following her, wondering if he knew anything about human nature. She had seemed so cautious at First Sun; now she was bolder than he.

They moved along the road in the scrub – ground too uneven and rocky to be farmed. Then, barely breathing, they climbed the scree towards the road.

They were almost *among* a troop of cavalry. There were hundreds of them, in half armour. Horses were grazing in the field opposite, and some men had started a fire.

They were speaking the western form of Liote, the language of the Iron Ring, the twelve cities at the other end of the Empire. It wasn't entirely unlike Arnaut, and Aranthur listened, acutely aware of the warmth of Nenia next to him.

'Volta,' she said. 'They are from Volta.'

Aranthur knew she was correct as soon as she spoke.

He tried to think. Volta was invading the Empire? But Volta was technically part of the Empire. With the fall of their duke, everyone said they were restored to stability and that they only wanted to make money, anyway.

He had no idea how many armed people he was looking at. Hundreds? How much did hundreds of mounted, armoured warriors cost?

'What are they saying?' he whispered.

She said nothing. After what seemed like a long time, she tapped his shoulder and they slipped back into the rocky ground and then all the way back to the inn.

'They were talking about attacking,' she said, her voice high.

Aranthur tried to think his way through it. Armed men in large bodies were not bandits. There were not that many bandits in the whole of the Empire. People talked about mercenaries, but the only mercenaries he ever saw were the men who guarded shops in the City.

'They seemed rich, to me,' Aranthur said. 'Good horses, expensive armour. Aristocrats.'

Nenia was leading him through the stable.

'Aristocrats from Volta?' she asked.

Aranthur tried to make it all go together. He had certainly heard men at the sword school talk about Volta – about the duke, who some of the sword students seemed to think was a great leader . . .

Armour.

Drako.

'I'm going to ride east,' he said suddenly.

'They'll stop you,' Nenia said.

'No, I can go up onto the ridge and take back roads for a few hours. Time could matter.'

'Take Lecne. He knows every path around here.'

In five minutes it was done. He pushed his clothes into his travelling *malle* and Lecne saddled horses. Donna Cucina was still wringing her hands.

Aranthur bowed to Don Cucino.

'Syr,' he said, 'I have a duty. It is not something I can explain, but more than your inn may be at threat.'

Don Cucino made the blessing of the Eagle, and then the same for his son, and Nenia, instead of shaking hands, brushed his lips with hers.

'Bring my brother back,' she whispered.

And then they were away, riding north. His lips burned from Nenia's kiss, and he thought *I'm an idiot.*

They rode for two hours, until the sickle moon was up, riding along farm tracks between looming hedges, and then right across muddy vineyard tracks. A dozen times one of them had to dismount to open or close a gate, but they were both country boys and despite the haste, they were careful to close what had been closed or leave open what had been left open.

'Where are we going?' Lecne added, as if he'd been holding his breath for the whole time.

'Lonika,' Aranthur said.

They paused to give the horses a rest where they rejoined the main road. They alternated trotting and galloping along the road until the sun was rising in the east behind them, staining the sky salmon pink. There were normal folk on the roads, farmers and farm wives, and a tinker with a cart, and little knots of Easterners, their heads down, their belongings on their shoulders.

'Poor bastards,' Lecne said. 'And now we aren't searching the woods.'

Aranthur watched the trees. He was excited, and tired, and when he closed his eyes, he could see the dead children. He felt odd, and he could still taste the stock he'd smoked.

He loosened the sword in the scabbard at his side, and they gave the horses a little food and rode on.

They came to the Volta Gate of Lonika just before the bells rang for midday prayers.

'Now what?' Lecne asked.

Aranthur rode straight up to the soldiers at the gate.

'I have to speak to General Tribane,' he said.

The dekark was summoned. He glanced at the two men, took in the mud and the sword and the tack, and frowned.

'Who are you, any road?' he asked.

'Timos, City Cavalry,' Aranthur said, as he'd been taught. 'I have a report on something west of here, and I know the General.'

The dekark was an older man, a professional more familiar with road construction than with fighting. He nodded.

'Come with me.'

The two of them followed the dekark into the town and then to the central square opposite the Temple of the Twelve. There, at a big writing table in the main hall of the town's palazzo, sat General Tribane, writing furiously.

She looked up. 'Timos,' she said, not very pleasantly. 'I'm working.'

'My lady,' he said. 'General.'

He realised he wasn't sure how to proceed. He glanced at Lecne and the dekark.

'There's a big company of armoured horse on the Volta road, out

273

by Fosse, or they were there at midnight,' he said. 'I think they were Voltain.'

'Why?' she asked sharply. 'What?'

'They sounded like Westerners.'

She shot to her feet. '*Bucceleri*, on me, right now.' She looked at Aranthur. 'Who's this?'

'My guide and friend, Lecne Cucino of the Inn at Fosse.' Aranthur nodded and Lecne made an excellent bow.

General Tribane nodded. 'Good. You saw these men yourself?'

'Yes, General,' Aranthur said.

Out in the yard of the palazzo, a few dozen men and women in full armour were checking their girths. A few were already mounted, and a short woman was squinting down the barrel of a puffer. She thrust it into the saddle holster and shouted something, and the rest of them began to mount.

There was a lot of blasphemy.

'Get these two fresh horses,' she said. 'Timos, are you City militia?'

He nodded. 'Yes, General. Selected Cavalry.'

She nodded. 'Good, I own you, then. You are now on active duty and subject to orders. Do you understand?'

Aranthur's heart gave a lurch. 'I'm a Student, ma'am . . . That is, Alis.'

'Now, I'm ma'am. Or General. Jennie? We ready to ride?'

The woman who'd been first to mount snapped a salute.

'All present.'

'Get new mounts,' General Tribane ordered, and turned aside.

Behind her, two young men had laid out a whole suit of armour – black, with red leather lining that showed at the edges.

She was wearing it minutes later when she emerged, mounted on her tall black unicorn. Rasce was in a stall and curried; Aranthur was just about holding himself upright on a big cavalry charger a hand taller than Rasce.

The General looked directly at Aranthur, so he approached her with Lecne beside him.

'You two with me,' she said.

'They have a lot more cavalry than you do,' Lecne said.

The General smiled. 'They have a lot more people on horses. I have all the cavalry. Right, boys and girls?'

The short man was right behind the General, with a banner on a lance. The banner was a black rose on a gold ground.

'That's right,' he growled.

And they were off.

Aranthur thought that he and Lecne had made good time riding for Lonika, but the General's cavalry rode like Eastern nomads. Every trooper had two horses, and they rode fast, paused to change, and rode again. Aranthur could just barely manage to stay in the saddle, and Lecne began to groan before they passed Adriano.

There was no conversation at a canter or a gallop, and they were alone with their fears and their fatigue. The tinkers and farmers and refugees scattered off the road as soon as they heard horses' hooves. Aranthur watched them as he rode by in the bright sunlight. Towards evening, as they entered the hills, the road was empty. There was smoke on the horizon.

'Rest,' the General ordered, reining in. 'Ten minutes.'

She dismounted, walked to the ditch, and spat. A trooper brought her a canteen of water and she cast a complex *occulta* that took Aranthur by surprise. He hadn't known she was a mage, much less that she had so much training, rare among fighters.

She shook her head and ate a sausage.

'Don't talk to her,' the female officer, Jennie, said from behind Aranthur. 'You're Timos? City cavalry?'

'Yes, ma'am,' he said.

She handed him a sausage. 'Myr Jeninas, Buccaleria Primos. Like being a centark, but with a fancier title.'

She smiled. She had the most deeply tanned face Aranthur had ever seen.

The very short man stumped over.

'You are the proverbial bad penny,' he grunted. 'You keep turning up.'

He took a chunk of sausage from Jeninas, munched, then held out a slightly greasy hand as big as a rich man's plate.

'Drek Coryn Ringkoat,' he said.

Hearing the three names, Aranthur's face broke into an unfeigned grin.

'You are a *Jhugj*?' he asked.

The short man shrugged. 'I am. At least half. The short half, I reckon.' His deep blue eyes seemed to bore into Aranthur's. 'General likes you.'

His face was amazingly immobile. He gave nothing away.

'That's ... good?' Aranthur said.

'Maybe so, maybe no.' Ringkoat shrugged.

'Boots and saddles,' Jeninas called. 'Check your priming.'

'Want to be useful?' Ringkoat asked.

'Yes.' Aranthur glanced at Lence, who nodded.

'Give me a hand up. I have the tallest horse for the shortest legs.'

Ringkoat nodded to Aranthur. Aranthur reached down and made a step with his hands. The *Jhugj* was incredibly heavy, and despite his strength, he almost gasped, but the man stepped up and got his leg over the high-backed saddle.

He looked down. 'Stay close, where I can see you two.'

He put the black rose banner into a leather cup on his stirrup, drew a long puffer from his saddle holster and opened the hammer to peer at the priming.

Aranthur mounted. Lecne got on his own horse, a smaller gelding.

'I don't have a weapon,' Lecne said.

'Good,' Ringkoat said. 'Fighting ain't for amateurs. Don't die, is all.'

He turned his horse and walked to where the Primos was waiting, and the other cavalry began to form on them. A dozen were already gone; Aranthur had noticed them riding up the ridges on either side of the road.

The General was on her big black monster, as still as a statue.

'Syr Timos,' she said. 'Something tells me you know more than you are saying.'

Aranthur nodded. Her comment helped him decide; he hadn't known what to say, and now he did.

'I only had one long look,' he said. 'But most of the horsemen had new armour.'

Her head turned a fraction, and her eyes seemed to kindle.

'In the dark, you saw their new armour?'

'Yes. And I heard it. New straps. New leather.'

'And you knew to look for new armour,' she said.

He was silent, aware that her whole troop of cavalry was watching him.

'Ma'am, is it enough if I say I'm friends with Tiy Drako?' he asked. 'Sometimes I work with . . . *cold iron.*'

She nodded sharply. 'Yes indeed. Music to my ears, in fact. Right. No trumpet. No one acts until I say, or do. Understand?'

There was a loud murmur.

'Let's go,' she said.

The compact column set off west along the Volta road, towards Fosse, a few miles away.

The shadows were long. It was a spring evening, with a red sun setting in splendour and mayflies rising from the stream that came down out of the Arnaut hills. The road west appeared to run through the dark green, temple-tall spruces and on into the setting sun like a path to adventure.

There were still hundreds of cavalrymen there. They had spread across the fields, and some had picketed their horses while others stood about. In the middle distance, smoke rose from the chimneys of the inn, and off to the north, more smoke from the chimneys of the village.

The General's troop rode swiftly along the road, scattering a handful of mounted men who had probably been intended as guards. Off to the left of the road, on the apron of a farm gate, stood a huge coach with eight horses, surrounded by men in full armour.

The General's troop rode straight for the coach. There was no resistance, although all over the fields to the north men stood, and some gathered the reins of their horses.

Aranthur and Lecne stayed by the banner, as they'd been told.

The armoured men by the coach had time to mount, and form two crisp lines facing the road. They were in full white armour, magnificent armour full of Gothic curlicues and elaborate, baroque metalwork, and they wore long, pointed sallets on articulated bevoirs that hid their faces.

The General's troop rode right up to them. It was not as Aranthur had imagined. Myr Jeninas' horse was breast to breast with one of the armoured men, and Ringkoat with another. Aranthur was pushed aside, and so was Lecne. He could tell that this was something the General's people practised; their formation was so dense that a spear would not have fitted between man or horse.

'Pennon Malconti,' the General said.

'General,' said a heavy voice from within the helmet.

'You are taken in arms within the borders of the Empire,' the General said. 'You and all your people are under arrest. Stand down. Dismount, and stand by your horses.'

'We outnumber you by many,' the deep voice said.

The General shrugged. 'You will die first, Malconti.'

'I require instructions,' Malconti said in his hollow voice.

'You mean your precious duke didn't tell you what would happen if you were caught?' the General said. 'Ask him. He's in the coach, no doubt.'

Malconti backed his horse out of the line, which closed. Two walls of horseflesh and steel faced each other, and they were not silent. The horses had begun pressing and nipping, and Aranthur's heart raced.

'What's happening?' Lecne asked.

'Don't ask me,' Aranthur said, but when the Duke of Volta emerged from the coach, he understood some of it.

The duke was beautifully dressed, as he had been the day the drake had been unloaded on the docks. He seemed unimpressed and un-hurried as he came down out of his coach. Malconti dismounted and offered his horse. The duke shrugged and walked forward as if oblivious to a hundred armoured warriors on the edge of violence.

'General,' he drawled, 'I had hoped that the Emperor might help me, but his whore has poisoned his mind against me, so I took matters into my own hands.' He smiled. 'If you will just turn a blind eye, in a few hours I will be Duke of Volta again.'

'I arrest you in the name of the Emperor,' the General said loudly and clearly.

'I am blood-immune to your laws,' the duke said.

The General nodded. 'Of course you are. But a court can decide that, or the Emperor. Perhaps you will find you are not immune. Any road, my lord, no one else here is, so we'll take your men and leave you to reconquer Volta alone.'

The duke looked around. 'No. We will fight.'

The General raised her voice. Aranthur felt the moment at which she augmented her voice with an *occulta*.

'All of you will dismount and stand by your horses. If you raise or touch a weapon, it's assault on an Imperial officer. If you use that weapon, you are a rebel. Whatever you think you are doing, you are at arms inside the Empire, and that cannot be tolerated.'

Men were looking at each other.

The duke said nothing. He just watched, a slight smile on his face. Then he turned to Malconti.

'You have until the count of three,' the General said.

'You know what to do,' the duke said.

'One,' the General said.

Malconti looked at the duke, and then at the General, his helmeted head turning like a hawk's.

'Two,' the General said in her augmented voice.

Men were dismounting all over the fields. But none of the men in the baroque armour had moved.

'Dismount,' Malconti called.

Like automata, the whole troop of elaborately armoured men each swung a leg over their saddles and slid to the ground.

'Really?' the duke asked. 'For what I pay you?'

Aranthur was close enough to hear Malconti's response, but the armoured man said nothing.

'Your *condotta* is voided.' the duke said. 'You have wasted a great deal of my time.'

Malconti said nothing.

The duke walked back to his coach, and the door slammed shut behind him.

Aranthur watched as the hundreds of men were gradually rounded up by the General's black armoured cavalrymen. No resistance was offered, although there were some jibes, and some outright anger when Myr Jeninas began to take the captured horses and corral them separately from their owners.

The General sat silent, watching, her banner fluttering over her head.

Aranthur approached for orders. She gave him a thin-lipped smile.

'Don't get involved,' she said. 'You and your friend have done enough, and I'll see to it that the Emperor remembers you, but I'm already worried all these bastards will remember you too. Don't get involved.'

'We're already involved,' Lecne said. He smiled; his head was up, and he looked like a hero from a romance. 'I think we'd like to help.'

The General seemed to see him for the first time. She nodded.

'My thanks,' she said. 'And the Emperor's. Help the Primos with the horses.'

Aranthur followed his friend.

'Bold,' he said.

'I like her,' Lecne said.

'Hard not to like her,' Aranthur said.

They worked past the fall of darkness, picketing and then feeding five hundred horses. The work went on and on, and troopers came and went, and at one point, deep kettles of beef with broth and greens were brought. Aranthur ate only the broth and greens. He was aware that the broth had meat in it, and he prayed, but he needed food. He was bone weary.

The two of them slept curled in their cloaks and woke to a grey day, with fog over the farm fields. Their cloaks were wet through and there was no possibility of further sleep. In the darkness, the General had decreed that the prisoners be released, and now, two by two, they came and fetched their horses. The men – and they were all men, every one of them – were subdued, but not hostile. Their armour had rusted in the night. Every one of them came forward, in two long lines. Those who were wearing their own armour were allowed to keep it. Those wearing munition armour – armour apparently stolen or illegally purchased by the duke – had to take it off and hand it over to the Primos to receive their horses.

Aranthur brought horses from the picket lines to one of the dekarks, a bow-legged man called Erp. He stood in the mist, already fully encased in his black armour, took the horses from Aranthur's fist with a nod, and waited for the Primos to finish with each prisoner. Then he handed over the horses silently. It was all very quiet.

When they were about half done, Lecne, who was working the other line, must have said something. Erp laughed a single, sharp bark like a dog.

'Listen up, boys,' he said quietly. 'You want to take the fight out of a man? Give him no sleep, a little rain, and no food. These ain't farm folk. These are rich boys.' He gave a smile that was very like a frown. 'We don't want a fight. Right?'

The Primos nodded. 'Fightin' is for fools,' she said.

She rubbed her neck, the most human gesture Aranthur had seen from any of the soldiers for hours. They were deliberately behaving inhumanly, and he understood that they were weaving a glamour, a suggestion of invulnerability. The black armour and the silence served the same purpose as Iralia's hair.

Aranthur was just pondering on glamours and other spells of influence when he saw a face he knew. Two faces he knew. They were close to each other, and both looked different – drier, and less defeated.

He knew them both from Master Sparthos' school. One was Syr Siran, and by him was Djinar, who was rooting in a pair of saddlebags on his shoulder.

Erp stood motionless while the Primos spoke to the two young men, and Aranthur brought up their horses, a bay and a black.

'You the lad who cooked breakfast?' Erp asked Djinar.

Djinar nodded. 'I'm not a city boy. I know how to make a fire.'

'What are you doing with this lot?' Erp asked.

Djinar shrugged. 'I thought we were going to change the world. It needs some changing.'

'Really?'

Erp's face closed. He'd clearly had enough talk. He took Djinar's horse, and Djinar turned to take the reins and saw Aranthur.

'Well,' he said. 'The man who only fights with women.'

'You know this one?' Erp asked.

'I do,' Aranthur said.

'Anything I should know?' Erp asked.

Aranthur thought for a moment. 'No.'

Djinar took his horse. 'Sparthos should be more careful who he allows in his *salle*. It's a place for gentlemen. Not bravos and government spies.'

Aranthur nodded. 'At your service.'

'*You* say that to *me*?' Djinar asked. 'Do you even know what those words mean?'

Aranthur shrugged. 'I believe so.'

His heart was hammering, but he kept his tone low and his words slow, with a massive investment of will that had more to do with his training at the Studion than in the *salle*.

'You are challenging me to a duel?' Djinar asked.

Erp put a black-armoured hand on the rebel's shoulder. He wasn't gentle.

'That's all very nice, but you have no sword, and you are a rebel, a criminal, and right now, if you don't take your horse and ride for home, I'll revoke your bond and forfeit you.'

'So he hides behind your skirts.' Djinar didn't seem a bit afraid.

Erp dropped him, a simple leg sweep. He rotated the younger man's arm behind his back and Djinar grunted.

'Stupid,' Erp said. 'Go home. Last chance.'

'Later,' Djinar said to Aranthur. 'You are dead. I will tell everyone in the City that you were with these hired killers, against true men.'

Erp spat. But Djinar mounted easily and turned his horse. He pointed to Aranthur.

'Look what I found, Siran,' he said.

Later, when all the rebels had dispersed and only the captured mercenaries were left, the whole group moved to the inn. The tone changed, as well, and Aranthur found the soldiers almost festive. Equally, it was clear to him that the soldiers and the mercenaries knew each other well enough to trade insults without heat, and even to chat.

Malconti finally took off his helmet. He was a handsome man, younger than Aranthur had expected, with a narrow black moustache and a curled black beard and earring. His eyes were bright; his face was more a poet's than a killer's.

Erp nodded. 'We've shared a campfire or two,' he said. 'Malconti is one of the best. General likes him.'

'Are they lovers?' Aranthur asked, because it seemed like a proper question.

Erp turned his head, and his blank stare rested for a moment on Aranthur.

'We don't ever talk about the General and her lovers,' he said. 'In fact, I only say this to you because today at least, ye're family.' There was no smile, and no warmth.

'Understood,' Aranthur said.

Erp nodded. 'You're a quick lad. Ever think of being a soldier?'

Aranthur shook his head. 'No. That is, yes.' They both laughed.

Aranthur noted that the General was riding with Lecne and Malconti, and both of them were leaning in to talk to his friend.

'Well, I am in the militia, so I suppose I'm a soldier,' he laughed.

Erp laughed too. 'Not so much,' he said gruffly. 'But I take yer point.'

At the inn, the mercenaries were settled in the barn and Aranthur returned to being a part of Lecne's extended family. There were hugs and stories, and then the General had to have the whole situation in the woods explained.

'Lady Sophia protect us,' she proclaimed. 'That won't wait.'

Everyone was silent while Aranthur explained what he had seen – it seemed like weeks before.

'Can you take us there?' the General asked.

She looked at the sun. It was after midday on a grey day.

Aranthur was tired, but he forced a smile.

'Yes, ma'am.'

The General looked around. She had her bannerman and her primos close to hand.

'Can we get this done today?' she asked the air.

Myr Jeninas nodded. 'Yes, ma'am.'

Malconti had been sitting in the inn's big window with a cup of wine. He stretched.

'If we work for nothing, will you hold it in our favour?' he asked.

'Parole, and your word in addition,' the General said.

'Of course,' Malconti said with a bow.

The General stepped closer to the mercenary pennon.

'Then I'd throw in my thanks, as well.'

Malconti gave a very slight smile. 'Well, that has some worth.' He took both of the General's hands and crossed them over his heart. 'My word is given.'

The General nodded. 'Primos?'

'Noted,' Myr Jeninas said.

An hour later, mounted again in the wet, they were riding through open woods of old tall trees that ran off into the Arnaut hills to the north. Aranthur knew the road well enough, although he'd only ridden it once, and he took them to the dozen bark hovels full of dead people.

He'd ridden out with Lecne, who could not stop talking about how admirable the General was. But when they entered the little circle of hovels, he was summoned forward to the General. She dismounted, entered a hut, emerged, and looked into a second one.

'Fucking Darkness,' she said.

Most of the soldiers made the sign of the Lady, but some made the sign of the Sun or the Eagle, and one made a horned sign.

The General looked at Aranthur. 'I am sorry I doubted you. There's more of these?'

'Yes, ma'am.'

She shook her head. 'Darkness Falling, how has this happened?'

'The Empire is falling apart,' Malconti said.

'You, keep your mouth shut,' the General spat.

'You know it as well as I,' Malconti said. 'Nothing is as it was. *Nothing.*'

But the black-haired mercenary looked as discomfited by the dead children as the General.

'All right. We'll form skirmish lines. The woods are open enough. Twenty paces between each pair. Spread out, listen for bugle calls.' She pointed with a short stick. 'Primos, take first troop north and west. I'll take second troop north and east. Malconti, take your people south due west towards Volta.'

'I'll need a guide,' Malconti said.

'Take this one,' the General said, pointing to Aranthur. 'I'll keep the other one.'

She smiled at Lecne, and Aranthur had a pang of something – it wasn't jealousy, but it was like jealousy. His friend was about to become one of the General's lovers – he could see it.

Malconti flashed a toothy grin.

'I get the pretty one? You are too kind.' Then his smile changed and he glanced at Aranthur. 'You know the ground?'

Aranthur was hesitant. 'I've been through these woods once. I know the valley over there pretty well.'

Malconti nodded. 'That's good enough.'

The mercenaries formed a long line, two deep. The distance between pairs was great enough that a loud-voiced man had to fuss, riding up and down until he was satisfied.

'March!' sang out Malconti. The mercenaries moved forward.

It took two miserable hours. There were black flies in the woods, little midges that bit men and horses right under their armour, or anywhere that cloth met skin. The long skirmish line passed across terrible terrain: a marsh full of old dead trees; over a stream swollen with mountain snow melt; through open woods; back to bog and marsh. The line extended and contracted, and the men searched every pile of reeds. They worked hard.

Aranthur followed the pennon, and was silent. No one spoke to him, and when the mercenaries spoke among themselves they tended to use the Western tongue, the one Nenia knew: Langarde, the bardic language of the Western Isles. But they were fast – fast enough that when there was still light in the sky, they came to the edge of the ridge where the ridge road met the road into the Valley of the Eagle. Aranthur was so tired by then that he was almost asleep in his saddle. They'd found forty Easterners alive; the refugees went into tents provided by the mercenaries. A pair of Imoters were looking them over while the cooks prepared food.

'What's over there?' Malconti asked.

He wasn't pointing up the road, which led, eventually, to Aranthur's home, but across it, towards Volta.

'I don't know, syr,' Aranthur said.

Malconti glanced at him. 'Smell the smoke?'

'Yes.'

Malconti's voice was surprisingly light; he seemed far too much like a philosopher or a playwright to be a soldier.

'They put out the fire when they saw us.' Malconti said something in Langarde. His people began to move, fast.

'Stay by me, boy,' he said, and suddenly they were cantering through underbrush, and then they burst into a clearing.

Malconti had his sword in his hand. Aranthur had drawn his own without thinking.

But there was no resistance, only two old men, thin as scarecrows, and two women with children huddled in their arms.

Malconti reined in as soldiers entered the clearing from every direction. It was very well done; even Aranthur, veteran only of militia training, knew how neatly the mercenaries had surrounded the clearing and entered it. On horseback. In near total silence.

Aranthur could smell the *occulta*. It was a more sophisticated version of one he cast himself.

Malconti smiled. 'Do you know how to use that thing, boy? Or do you just wave it about?'

Embarrassed, Aranthur put his sword in the scabbard.

'Talk to them,' Malconti said. 'Men in armour aren't anyone's friends.'

The children were weeping. Aranthur dismounted, unsure what to say, and he approached the two old men cautiously, as if they were wild animals.

'Good day,' he tried, in Armean.

'The sele of the day of the Sun upon you,' said the one with teeth. His Armean was odd, and sing-song.

'We are here to help you,' Aranthur said.

The man didn't even twitch. 'Of course,' he said heavily. 'We are very hungry,' he admitted.

'Are there others?' Aranthur asked.

'Alive?' the old man asked, as if it was not an important question.

'Yes, alive.'

'Perhaps,' the old man said.

A day later, Aranthur couldn't remember how long they had been riding through the woods. Two days later, he was no longer thinking in terms of fatigue. His borrowed horse was so tired that Aranthur was often walking beside him to rest his back.

There were hundreds – or possibly even thousands – of Easterners in the dark, damp, cold, fly-ridden woods. Many were alive. And every little camp had a rumour of another, farther west, or north. Aranthur's Armean was the most sought-after commodity after fresh horses and food. He scarcely knew five hundred words, but his vocabulary was expanded with every encounter.

How many?

Where?

Alive?

How many days ago?

He fell asleep in the saddle, and he got lost multiple times, moving from one patrol to another, one cluster of wretched hovels to another, sometimes with Erp, once with Malconti. The dark-haired man was silent, and moved so fast that Aranthur had trouble keeping up with him. Erp was better company and taught Aranthur a little about packing his gear and moving quickly. The second night, Erp shared his blankets in a dry shelter made of bark, with a fire outside. Aranthur slept without waking once and woke to a clear day and a cup of hot soup before riding out again on a barely refreshed and very wet horse.

'I'll get you some hot mash,' he promised.

He did, too, in the early afternoon, when he rode into the mercenaries' camp south of the main road, sixty stades and more from the inn.

'You the boy that speaks Eastern?' said a big man with bright red hair and tattoos all over his face.

'Yes, syr,' Aranthur said. 'Can I get something hot for my horse?'

'*Ja*,' the man said with a nod. 'The pennon wants to see you.'

Aranthur found Malconti, in armour, drinking hot cider with two Easterners, a man and a very old woman. He already had a translator, and he listened to three full sentences before he realised it was Nenia in man's clothing. In the City, women wore whatever they wanted, but in the country it was rare to see a girl dressed in breeches, unless it was for hard chores.

Malconti glanced at Aranthur. 'Timos,' he said with a nod. 'Syr Nenos has come to give you a rest.'

It was the most pleasant that the mercenary pennon had been to him.

'I didn't know that you knew any Armean.' Nenia was blushing furiously.

'Not much. More now.'

'You know your way back to Alis?' Malconti asked.

Aranthur nodded.

'These have to be the last people,' Malconti said. 'We're in Volta and Cursini would love to claim this as an act of war. He'll ram a spear up my arse if he catches me, so I'm not eager to linger, am I, darlings?'

Nenia looked at the mercenary, her face bright red. 'Cursini?'

'My rival. He overthrew my former paymaster and took Volta for his own.' Malconti shrugged, despite the weight of his elaborate shoulder defences. 'I am now an out of work sell-sword. Anyway, Syr Timos, I am out of men and out of food, and these two assure me there are no refugees west of here. Right, Syr Nenos?'

Nenia nodded.

'So I will be shepherding these good people east, towards...' Malconti made a face. 'Towards what, I wonder?' He winked at a slim man in armour who rolled his eyes. Malconti frowned. 'Get me some orders from the General, there's a dear. Some of them have some sort of disease. I need... support. I'd rather we didn't just massacre these poor creatures, although I will understand if Tribane chooses to go that way. Saves everyone time. And money.'

Aranthur lost the ability to speak for a moment. Especially as it was clear as a crystal talisman to him that the pennon meant exactly what he said.

'Although,' the pennon continued thoughtfully, 'I owe them, rather. Without them, Tribane might be considering ridding the world of me. Funny how the worm turns, what?' His eyes met Aranthur's.

They were black, and featureless. As if there was nothing behind them.

'Go and get me orders,' Malconti said.

Aranthur rode north, found the General, reported, and rode back at sunset with a tube and written orders.

He found Malconti and his gendarmes camped where the old Imperial Road crossed the Alder, about thirty stades from the Inn of Fosse, safely back on Imperial soil.

Malconti read the orders. Aranthur didn't know what was in them and was afraid of what they might say, and afraid of what he might see.

The sell-sword tapped the rolled parchment on his chin.

'Interesting. Stop looking so worried. No one is going to be massacred tonight.' He nodded. 'Well ridden. You are a good courier. If you ever lack employment, I'll take you.'

Aranthur had to smile. 'Thanks, milord.'

'Milord?' Malconti shook his head. 'No one loves a sell-sword enough to ennoble him.'

He smiled again. It was the first time the man had relaxed at all, or shown any humanity. Aranthur wondered if he, too, had dreaded the orders he might have received.

'May I ask a . . . professional question?' Aranthur asked.

'If you have to ask, my dear, you probably shouldn't.' One of his grooms handed him a silver cup of wine, which he drank off and handed back for a refill. 'Wine for my courier.' He shrugged. 'But I'm feeling good. Alis has offered me a short contract and some money. I may yet emerge from this shithole.'

Aranthur hesitated.

'Ask,' Malconti snapped.

'Why . . .' Aranthur now felt foolish. And stupid. 'Why did you . . . order your men to dismount?'

Malconti nodded. He took his wine cup, and this time he sipped it instead of emptying it.

'What a good question. You won't like the answer.'

Aranthur didn't move.

'It was the only action with a possible positive outcome for me. And my people.' Malconti shrugged. 'Not the best outcome for the duke. But for me and mine, the only possible avenue.'

Aranthur nodded.

A cup of wine was held out to him. He took it, and the sell-sword raised an eyebrow.

'If I killed Alis, who I rather like, the Emperor would hunt me to death. Maybe assassins, maybe sorcery. And even killing Alis and all her people wouldn't change the duke's outcome. Except that now, in the aftermath, I wonder if he didn't *want* the confrontation.' He looked at Aranthur and smiled. 'Tell Alis what I'm telling you, boy. Because it occurs to me that he tried to cast a subjugation on me when I went to fetch him.' He drank some wine. 'But why?'

Aranthur bowed. 'I will tell her.'

Malconti nodded. 'Get along to your boyfriend, then. I rather fancied him myself, but he made his views plain.' Malconti handed his silver cup to a groom. 'Refill his cup,' he said. 'I was young once.'

He walked off into his tent, leaving Aranthur alone with a brimful cup of good wine. He still needed to groom his horse, and he had to wonder who his boyfriend was. But he managed to find a place on the last picket line, and he started work, and one of Malconti's grooms brought an armload of fodder. Another servant came up behind the groom . . .

'I need to leave these people,' Nenia said.

Aranthur had been thinking of her, and her appearance was like a conjuration. He grinned.

'Thank the Lady you are here,' she said. 'I heard your voice and then I couldn't find you.'

He realised that she was working very hard to keep her face together. He wrapped his arms around her as he would have with his sister and she burrowed against him.

Aranthur's borrowed cavalry charger butted him with his nose, repeatedly.

'I need to feed my horse,' he said awkwardly.

'I'll bet you tell that to all the girls. Thanks, I'm all better. And Lady, they're a hard lot.' She took a deep breath. 'And these people are dying on their feet, and the sell-swords don't care.' She looked down. 'They really *do not care*. If the General had ordered them all killed . . .' She shuddered. 'Is the City like this?'

Aranthur thought a little before he answered.

'No. I mean, it is not like the Valley of the Eagle, either. But it's not all violence and greed.'

'Where is my brother?'

'With the General,' Aranthur answered.

'He doesn't speak any Armean at all.'

'The General herself speaks some Zhouian, some Armean . . . maybe even a little Safiri.' Aranthur smiled.

'Safiri!' Nenia said. 'Oh, just the name is exotic.'

'I'm studying Safiri,' Aranthur said again, aware that he was trying to impress her.

She looked at him under her brows. 'You?'

'I'm not a complete fool.'

She smiled. 'I know that, silly. I'm just wondering . . . The General asked me if I spoke Safiri. Does she know you do?'

'No,' Aranthur sighed.

'If Lecne doesn't speak any Armean, why is she keeping him?'

Aranthur was running out of little chores to do on his horse. He'd got the feed bag on, picked the hooves clean, and given him a rub down.

'No idea,' he said.

Nenia laughed. 'Well, I do.'

'Why did you ask me, then?'

She rolled her eyes and turned away.

'Reasons. Tell me about the City. I can't wait.'

After a while they were still standing. The ground was soaking wet and cold, and anything like a blanket was on a cold Easterner.

'Do you have a tent?' she asked.

He made a face, but it was getting dark. 'No.'

'We'll be cold,' she said.

'Malconti thinks you are my boyfriend. He sent you wine.'

She drank half the cup.

He nodded. 'We can make a shelter, the way the soldiers did.'

'I think the pennon thought I'd spend the night with him,' Nenia said, quite calmly.

Aranthur was too tired for shock. 'But?'

'Well, I was flattered but not available. He was quite apologetic.' She smiled. 'I wonder what rules guide a person who can massacre innocents but doesn't rape his friends?'

She sighed, her face closed. She was trying to be amusing, but she was struggling with too many little horrors.

She looked up. 'Of course, that's when he called you back, too.'

'Not my type,' Aranthur managed, a sally he was later quite proud of.

She giggled, more like Hasti than like his memory of Nenia.

The two of them borrowed a sharp hatchet and cut poles. To Aranthur's surprise, the red-haired man with tattoos and two other big men in arming coats and rusty voiders came and helped them build a shelter, even to helping peel huge sheets of *vyrk* bark. Aranthur used his saddle and Nenia's to make pillows. He wasn't thinking about much of anything until she came into the shelter and pressed against him in the small space.

Suddenly he was very aware of her.

'I have some bedding,' she said. 'Alder. Out.'

He backed out and she laid spring alder in bunches. Outside the little shelter it was already full dark, and there was firelight from a dozen big fires.

'Can you borrow a lantern?' she asked.

Aranthur leant in and made a light, a simple but very powerful *occulta.*

He set it on the ridge pole, and it shone out of both ends of the little shelter, making the whole bark lodge a lamp.

She laughed. But she finished laying the alder, and Aranthur used the light to savage a couple of young pines outside the lodge and threw them atop the alder for a soft layer. The pine was wet, and cold.

It smelled magnificent, though.

Aranthur considered among his very limited repertoire of spells and tried a very warm breeze. He blew it out of his mouth, to aid the evocation, and the warm breeze blew over the newly cut bedding, drying it rapidly.

Nenia nodded. 'Good. You do that all night, and I'll be warm as toast.'

'Need the axe back, mate,' said Red-hair.

Aranthur had it in his hand. He passed it to the big man, who grinned.

'Magelight?' he asked. 'Can ye make me one, lad?'

Aranthur reached into his creation, which was far too bright, and took a little of it, and attached it to a stick.

'Here you go, syr.'

The man looked at the stick from several angles.

'Amazin',' he said, and wandered off into the night.

Aranthur could hear him playing with the stick and showing it to other men.

He stood outside the shelter for a little while. The rain had started again.

He bent down and went in.

'You're wet,' Nenia said. 'I'm dry. Hardly the act of a gentleman.'

Aranthur took off his wet cloak and considered attempting to dry it with magik, but he was too tired. He wasn't even sure he could attempt it without a focus, and his talisman was hundreds of stades to the east. He took off his sword, and wrapped it in his spare shirt to keep it dry.

He lay down. The bedding was soft.

'Yech,' Nenia proclaimed, touching the wet wool, but then it warmed a little. He threw half over her.

'My mother will be asking me where I spent tonight,' she said.

'Ahh,' Aranthur said. 'We could put my sword between us. They do it in the old Byzas romances.'

'No thanks,' Nenia said. 'I'll just tell her I slept with the pennon, of course. I expected you to be warmer.'

Aranthur began to laugh. She put her head on his shoulder and wriggled up against him and relaxed.

'With my eyes closed, I can see them,' she said suddenly. 'Lady's Blessing, there were so many. And some died, Aranthur. One woman just fell to the ground while we were . . .'

He gave her shoulders a squeeze. His own mind was a whirl, and he wanted to say something, but his head was closing down.

'Malconti says some of them have a disease,' she said.

'I saw the dead,' Aranthur said.

His voice sounded strange, and the words escaped him, as if he hadn't decided to speak. When he let his eyes close, there they were

– the dead, like stuffed human pillows, like bundles of flesh, curiously boneless. Aranthur was a farm boy. He'd seen death. They looked *wrong*.

'How can this happen?' Nenia asked.

Aranthur's mind was turning like a wagon wheel and he felt as if he was drunk. He'd used too much *power* on the light and warmth *workings* and now he was almost without volition, turning, turning . . .

'Oh, Draxos.'

He rolled to his knees, leant out into the rain and was violently sick. After only a moment, Nenia came and held his long, dark hair out of his face.

'Are you sick?' she asked anxiously.

'I overspent my *power*.' He was trembling all over.

'Come on,' she said. 'I promise not to attack your virtue.'

Aranthur wasn't sure, even with a mouth that tasted of bile, that he wanted that promise.

He listened to her breathing as she fell asleep. He wondered if he was supposed to have made love to her, replayed various moments, and didn't see a sign of it. Nothing woos a girl like throwing up, he thought bitterly. And she was so different from the woman with whom he'd danced at the inn. He hadn't known she was so brave.

His thoughts tumbled together; he tried not to think of her warmth, her body pressed close to him. How many days since he had made love to Alfia?

I am an idiot, he thought. *Am I in love with any woman who will have me?*

He listened to her breathing and thought of her until all his thoughts calmed from a tumble like an avalanche to a slow passage like a stream. Then he gave a minute shrug and went to sleep.

He dreamt of using a sword that burned like white fire. He was surrounded by the bloated refugees, but when he touched them with the sword, they were cured.

He awoke to find that Nenia was virtually on top of him. His head was clear. He lay, wishing she'd move, and then he fell asleep again.

The whole series of events came to be called the Duke's Rebellion, at least by liberal Whites who disliked the duke. In the weeks thereafter, Aranthur heard every part of it debated by Byzas and Arnaut alike, as if some of the action was open to question. There were men and women at his *salle* who denied that there had been a rebellion, and claimed that the Emperor surrounded himself with Whites who hated the duke and made up such events to blacken his name.

Aranthur ignored them, mostly because time passed too quickly. There were too many things to do, and he was late for everything, always. The very few days he had spent at Fosse had been more like a month, and the rest were just a blur.

And yet, the weeks after the rebellion were *not* uneventful. They were merely uneventful in comparison to the daily stress of living outdoors. One of the first people he met at the Academy, the day after he returned to the city, was Dahlia. She bowed coldly and passed him in a hallway.

He returned her bow. Hesitantly, he said, 'Did you receive my gift?'

She looked down her nose at him. 'What was it for? Payment for services rendered?' she asked, and walked off.

He let her go.

Aranthur was having trouble sleeping. His attention wandered easily to the Easterners in the woods; to the dead in their odd postures which seemed somehow menacing; to Nenia, Alfia, Dahlia. But he pulled himself together long enough to get to work, to practise Safiri, to practise his swordplay and his exercises. He moved briskly through streets suddenly filled with men and women wearing swords and House colours – tabards, armbands, belts, hair ornaments. The rich Lower Town was full of people posturing, and there were fights. He did his best to avoid them.

He performed the whole of his Safiri *occulta* for the Master of Arts and she kissed his forehead.

She held him at arm's length. 'You overspent,' she said.

'Yes, Magistera,' he said.

'It's a terrible thing to do. You can lose your *power* altogether.' She looked into his eyes a while longer. 'Or become stronger. Was it terrible? I've read reports.'

He bowed. 'I never really understood what was happening,' he admitted.

'How like real life,' she said with a smile. 'I can explain, if you like. The Duke of Volta planned a military coup to retake his duchy.'

'That much I guessed.' He felt better for hearing it.

She nodded. 'Our mutual friend can explain better, really, but something went wrong. I will guess that his supposed allies within the

294

Iron Ring failed to materialise. So there he was with a very small army and no supplies in Imperial territory. He has a great deal of support here, among the old aristocrats—'

'I got that,' Aranthur said, with a little of his new humour.

'Yes. But five hundred horse, no matter how well-born, were not going to be a match for Cursini and his Steelbacks, much less the Militia of Volta, who hate him. Technically he was a rebel in arms.' She shrugged. 'Tribane didn't even arrest him. All very careful, all under the rose.' She shrugged.

'None of that is what . . .' Aranthur paused, trying to find words. 'None of that troubled me.'

She leant forward. 'What troubled you, then? The refugees?'

'Has anyone told you about the disease?' he asked hesitantly. He described the bodies. 'And Nenia – that is, Myr Nenia Cucina, who will be a student here in a term – she said that they had stopped using . . .' He looked out of the great window, trying to piece together things he'd seen. 'They didn't use talismans. Or didn't have them. Many of them couldn't, or wouldn't, start fires. Or heat water. So they starved.'

'The power that is rising in the East,' the Magas said carefully, 'seeks to hold all the *kuria* crystal for itself.' She shrugged. 'We all know the price has risen. Do you have a good one?'

'Yes, Magistera.'

She nodded. 'Perhaps the Easterners couldn't afford any. I have heard mutterings from the countryside – villages sending priests to beg crystals from the Temple.' She rubbed her hands together. 'I will look into this, Aranthur. I have troubles of my own – there's a move to unseat me.' She sighed and looked out of her window. 'I have ceased listening to reports about refugees dying because there's little I can do. But apparently I missed something vital.' She reached out and made the sign of Sophia on his forehead. 'But you have done very well. If anything, your overuse of your *power* stretched you a little. I will tell you an uncomfortable truth. We send you Students out into the world to do research, yes, but also simply to stretch you, so that you are ready to confront the paradox that is the use of the higher powers.' She raised an eyebrow at the word *higher* as if she was unsure she meant the word and looked out of her window a moment. 'I understand that you are acquainted with the Prince of Zhou?'

Aranthur nodded.

'He is my next visitor. He seeks admission to the Studion. What do you think?'

'Oh, yes!' Aranthur said, almost without thinking. 'That is, I liked him.'

She smiled. 'Excellent. What will you do if I give you the rest of the day?'

'Swordplay,' he said. Then he paused, almost stricken. 'Blessed Rolan! I have a message from Malconti for the General and I have never delivered it.'

She sighed. 'Go see Myr Tribane. She is in the City – probably at the Crystal Palace. Do you have court clothes?'

'No.' He rubbed his beard. Weeks of living with soldiers had given him a rich, full beard like his father's. Courtiers were generally clean shaven.

She shook her head. 'Couldn't you confine yourself to smoking stock or political dissent? Go, and don't die.'

He bowed deeply. Somehow, in an hour's conversation, she had lanced the boil of his disquiet. He felt better than he had since he'd seen the first dead Easterners.

Dahlia was another source of discomfort. He had enough empathy to see that, from her point of view, he'd used her badly. He felt guilty, in fact; too swept away in his own concerns, which must, to her, seem petty. Like work.

He collected his sword from the corner behind Edvin's desk. The man was writing at his usual incredible rate.

'How's your copying?' he asked.

'I haven't copied a word in two weeks,' Aranthur admitted. 'She gave me the day.'

Edvin raised his eyes. 'I've missed the *quaveh*. And you. And there's a rumour that you met Malconti, the world's most fascinating man. So be early tomorrow.'

'Yes, syr.'

Aranthur turned to leave and there was Syr Ansu, in Megaran clothing. The young Zhouian bowed, his hand on his sword hilt.

'I am afraid I owe you money and have not troubled to repay my debt,' he said.

Aranthur returned the bow, keeping his eyes on the Zhouian as he'd learned in their week together.

'It is nothing,' he said.

'Ah, I know better now, Syr Timos. I am very sorry.'

Aranthur grinned. 'If you are accepted, you can come and live with me. No one else will, apparently.'

Ansu nodded. 'You mean, I should give up half a wing in the Crystal Palace for a curtained bed on the sixth floor of an ancient brothel? Eh?' His impassive face developed a very slight smile. 'I cannot refuse such a hospitable offer.' Suddenly he flashed his real grin. 'Besides, I'm sick to death of the palace.' He bowed, and leant close. 'I really am sorry.'

'I told the Magistera she should accept you.' Aranthur paused. 'Do you know Myr Tribane?'

Ansu laughed and showed his black teeth.

'We've been lovers,' he said. 'And we're on good terms.'

'I need to see her.'

'Nothing easier. Where can I find you in an hour?'

'The *salle* of Master Sparthios.' Aranthur picked up his sword, winked at Edvin, and headed for the *salle*. 'I'm testing.'

'Oh,' Ansu said, suddenly eager. 'May I watch?'

Three hours later he found himself standing opposite Mikal Sapu in the *salle*, sharp sword in hand, as he was required to demonstrate the nine *gardes* and nine attacks of the arming sword as if teaching a student. He demonstrated the first and the second Rules, the long, dance-like sequences that Master Sparthos used to teach postures and simple responses. The audience was small, but there were a dozen people there, including Ansu and Tiy Drako.

'What is *tempo*?' Sparthos snapped out, as if giving orders to an army.

Aranthur took two breaths, a trick that the Master of Arts had taught him.

'*Tempo* is time, Master,' he said. 'The time an action takes, whether mine or an opponent's, whether the turn of my hand, or a step...' He looked at the two impassive teachers, hoping to see if he'd said enough. He took another deep breath. 'And sometimes in a passage of arms there is a *tempo*, like music or dance, and that *tempo* can be manipulated.'

Sparthos nodded. 'Acceptable. Tell me of *mesura*.'

Aranthur took two more breaths. Sapu had drilled him on *mesura* – it was a core concept in the master's teaching.

'*Mesura* is the distance between the opponents,' Aranthur said. 'But there are different measures, dependent on the length of my arm and my blade, my opponent's arm and her blade, length of stride, and angle.'

The master leant back. 'What is *out of measure?*'

'The distance at which neither I nor my opponent can strike.'

'Which is faster? A long sword or a short sword?' Sapu asked.

'A short sword turns faster, but . . .' Aranthur gazed at a very faint crack in the plaster of the wall above the master's head. 'But it seems to me that a long sword, by closing measure, is faster in a thrust.'

'Interesting.' The master had a slight smile. 'Djinar says you acted as a government informer. Is this true?'

Aranthur's heart slammed against his chest like a hammer on an anvil.

'I am a soldier in the militia,' he said.

The master made a noise like a cough.

'You did better on *tempo* and *mesura*. That's a simple answer to a difficult question.'

Aranthur took two breaths. 'Master, I did what I thought was best, for the people . . .' He paused. 'For people I love.'

'Dangerous,' the master said. 'You took a side. So did Djinar. You certainly chose wisely, but he will challenge you. Will you fight him?'

Aranthur's heart was going fast enough to endanger his breathing.

'Yes,' he said.

'Interesting. Good. Show me a little of this poise that Sapu speaks of.'

The master waved his baton. A servant opened the doors of the *salle* and a dozen more people came in to watch. Aranthur didn't look at them. He was trying not to see them.

Aranthur considered how similar the Master of Arts and the Sword Master were in many ways. They unbalanced him. They also restored his balance.

He took a *garde*.

Sapu came forward one step, and then, without pause from the end of the step, he attacked with a single, deceptive thrust. The point of his weapon tapped gently against Aranthur's blade, crossing to the right, scraping down at the speed of thought. Then, faster than an observer could see, Sapu turned his wrist. His point transcribed half a circle as small as a young girl's ring and his sword blade changed sides of Aranthur's blade.

Aranthur over-parried, using far too much force against the deception, sweeping his own blade in a half-circle to the left. His cover defeated the deception and when Sapu attempted to reverse his blade Aranthur stepped back out of range.

Aranthur immediately came forward with a head cut, drew the expected high parry, and whirled his own blade through a half-circle much larger than Sapu's against his outstretched leg.

The leg vanished, pulled back by Sapu as he counter-cut to the head, which Aranthur parried. Having expected that counter, a standard school counter, he tried turning Sapu's blade. His timing was just *barely* off; the blades locked a little too long, sharp edge to sharp edge. Instead of taking Sapu's blade and winding it for a cut to the inside of the instructor's thigh, he found himself almost hilt to hilt with Sapu.

He grabbed the other man's sword wrist just as Sapu took his. Both men went for a throw, and there was a sharp struggle. Aranthur was stronger, and taller, but Sapu knew tricks. Both men attempted to put knees in each other's groins...

'Halt!' roared Sparthos. 'You look like men in a bar fight, not a *salle*.'

There was a spatter of applause, and some boos.

'Silence,' said the master.

Sapu was grinning, which Aranthur took as a good sign.

They saluted. Aranthur was covered in sweat; Sapu gleamed.

Sapu took up a middle *garde*. Aranthur left his blade behind him on the right side, the so-called *Long Tail*.

Sapu smiled. 'Aha.'

Someone laughed.

Aranthur ignored him, and circled. Sapu tried to close the measure, and Aranthur didn't let him. Aranthur sought to keep the measure even...

Then, in one small step to the left, he closed the measure and struck, a gliding step with a rising cut from his low *garde*. Sapu had to make a heavy parry, because the blow was hard.

Aranthur had had a plan, but it vanished as *nothing* happened as he expected. He reached with his left hand as he turned his blade...

Sapu stepped forward, turning his own blade off the heavy crossing. Suddenly the two men were very close. Sapu lifted his blade, a small cut from the outside. Aranthur crossed it, and as his hand was forward and his body aligned, he slammed his left hand into Sapu's sword elbow, lifting it. But Sapu was lithe and fast and canny. As soon as he felt the pressure he was moving back, his balance stable, and he even managed a defensive thrust, *imbrocatto*, to cover his retreat. Aranthur covered it.

Both men stepped back and saluted.

Aranthur stepped forward as he formed his *garde*. Sapu struck like a serpent, closing the distance and cutting Aranthur lightly on the inside of his sword wrist.

Most of the onlookers laughed.

'Madar ghahbe! ردام هبهق,' spat Aranthur, cursing in Safiri. But he made himself bow and salute.

'You need to learn not to fall for that,' Sapu said. 'You come forward, not yet in *garde*, not yet prepared. You do it often, especially after a difficult passage.'

'Well said,' the master nodded. 'Nonetheless, the first two phrases were played well, were they not?'

Aranthur flushed.

Sapu smiled. He saluted. 'You really almost had me with the wrist grab. Any idea what you should have done?'

'I should have pulled, so you were off balance and couldn't retreat.' Aranthur sounded whiney, even to himself.

Sapu bowed. 'I fear that with your size and speed you will soon be my teacher, and I hope we will remain friends. Of course, you will have to stop offering me a wrist cut.'

Sparthos got up out of his chair and produced a yellow silk garter from his purse.

'I took the liberty of expecting you to pass,' he said. 'You are shaping well.'

Aranthur bowed.

There was some applause.

'It seems to me you merely cheapen the value of your garters,' Djinar said.

Aranthur hadn't noticed him; perhaps he'd been sitting with the observers all along.

'Let us see, Syr Djinar,' Sparthos said, and his voice was flat, emotionless. 'Why don't you pick up a weapon and engage him? We'll see which of you is better.'

Djinar narrowed his eyes. 'I plan a meeting that is a little more... permanent... for your *scholar*.' He turned to the other students. 'He's a government informer. A toady. A spy.'

Sparthos raised both eyebrows and turned to Aranthur.

'Is this true?' he asked in mock ignorance.

'You lie,' Aranthur said.

The words emerged without his volition. Or rather, the moment they were uttered, Aranthur knew he'd been manipulated to this moment by the master.

Djinar was, for once, taken aback.

'You say I lie?' he asked.

Aranthur nodded. 'Yes. You lie. You are a liar.'

Djinar nodded his head a fraction. 'We will need a licence, Master.'

'A licence I happen to have,' the master said.

There was an excited rustle among the observers.

Aranthur turned to Sapu. 'Will you be my second?'

Sapu nodded. 'If you promise not to succumb to a wrist cut.'

His warm smile did more to calm Aranthur than all his training.

He walked across the *salle* floor and spoke to Djinar's friend, Srinan. They bowed to each other.

A servant served wine.

Sapu came back. 'Very civilised. First blood. I'll wager he means to kill you, but that's his problem. My advice, as your second? Engage, land a scratch and walk away. His father owns more land than all the temples in the City. His second's the richest boy in the *salle*, and there will be trouble otherwise.' He nodded at Srinan. 'Understand me?' he asked quietly. 'You've fought before. So has he.' Sapu raised an eyebrow. 'How many men have you killed?'

Aranthur winced. 'Three? Or four.'

Sapu shrugged. 'You should stop, before it becomes a habit. You are getting... hard.'

'I understand.'

Aranthur took a deep breath and exhaled slowly. The Master of Arts had forbidden him to fight...

'Good,' Sapu said. 'Do you want one of the *salle* duelling blades, or your own?'

'I'll use my own,' Aranthur said, painfully aware that it had rust from hanging on the wall in an unheated garret and there were untouched nicks in the blade. Nonetheless, it was clean enough.

He went to his scabbard, hanging on the wall, and drew. He walked back across the floor. Djinar was already armed and waiting, stripped to his shirt. Aranthur was naked from the waist up as *salle* rules demanded.

Srinan stood on one side, and Sapu on the other. The little crowd was perfectly silent. Master Sparthos nodded.

'My friends,' he said softly. 'As this is a legal duel between willing adversaries, I do not need or tell you that this is a sober occasion. I will stop the fight if I hear a word or sound from you.'

He turned. 'Salute,' he said.

'No,' Djinar said. 'He is not my peer, and I do not need to salute him.'

Aranthur saluted, nonetheless.

'How childish,' Sparthos said, his lip curling in a sneer.

'Perhaps the master should declare a bias and remove himself,' Djinar said.

Sparthos bowed with exact correctness and went to the gallery, where he sat.

The two seconds looked at each other.

Sapu bowed. 'Since your principal is so *very* concerned, I cede you the right to give the word to commence.'

Srinan's face was frozen. 'Very well. Commence.'

Whether by mistake or on purpose, Srinan omitted to invite the duellists to take their *gardes*. Djinar had been standing in a casual pose, legs together, weight on his back foot. Suddenly, explosively, he leapt forward and exploded into a lunge. Aranthur wasn't quite caught by surprise. He had Sapu's last attack very much on his mind, and he had already taken up a *garde* – sword low, left leg forward.

Djinar's lunge contained within it a deception, but Aranthur's low *garde* and simple, sweeping parry enveloped the deceptive thrust. Like many opponents, Djinar had underestimated the strength of Aranthur's wrist. His rising parry with the back of the blade lifted Djinar's thrust. He sidestepped with a counter-cut, a small wrist roll, to cover his *garde* change, turned . . .

Sapu stepped between them. 'That will do,' he said. 'Take your man, syr.'

Aranthur couldn't see anything through Sapu. In retrospect, he had felt some resistance to his tip cut. He couldn't see Djinar, but there was a great deal of blood on the straw matting of the floor.

Suddenly, Djinar fell, arterial blood spurting from the inside of his wrist.

He didn't look angry, or formidable.

'I can help him,' Aranthur said.

Srinan bowed stiffly. 'I would appreciate your . . . support,' he admitted.

Aranthur knelt in the blood, and Srinan took his hand. Aranthur provided *power* and Srinan, a much more advanced student, drew some, and worked.

The blood stopped spurting.

Srinan stood. 'My thanks,' he said, and that was all.

Sapu led Aranthur away to the dressing room, and provided him with a cup of wine. It was a heavy red, and it looked a little like blood. Aranthur stood there for a moment with a terrible version of the corpses in the woods floating before his eyes. He put his head down because he thought he might vomit. Then he shook his head.

'I don't think I'm made to be a duellist,' he said.

'On the contrary,' Sapu said. 'You didn't even know you hit him?'

'No.'

Sapu nodded. 'Drink it. Do you have a friend here to walk you home?'

Aranthur nodded. 'The Zhouian, Ansu, is my friend.'

Sapu shook his head. 'What a little bundle of surprises you are. Prince Ansu has just put down a purse of silver to be a student here.'

Aranthur left with Ansu. Srinan and Djinar were long gone.

'You were very good. You strike like a serpent. I liked it.' Ansu was grinning. 'I am excited to try this Byzas way of the sword.'

'Different from your own?' Aranthur asked.

Ansu shrugged. 'Swords are swords and bodies are bodies. But you thrust and we cut – that is a difference. Have you been to the palace before?'

Aranthur nodded. 'The first week of First Year, they take you for a tour. The Greeting Hall and the Hall of the Gods.'

Ansu smiled. 'Imagine; I will be a First Year in a few months. They will take me on a tour of the palace.' He laughed. 'Myr Tribane has her own apartments.' He put a warm hand on Aranthur's shoulder. 'Are you all right?'

Aranthur shook his head. 'I need a moment. And everyone will know. The Master of Arts will have me eviscerated. She ordered me not to fight.'

Ansu shrugged. 'Bah. How can we not fight? We are people of the sword.'

Aranthur finished the wine, drank two cups of water, and found his heart rate slowing.

Aranthur was as dazed by Master Sparthos' praise, delivered at the doorway of the *salle*, as by the events of the duel.

'Food,' Ansu insisted.

They walked out into the late afternoon and ate noodles.

'Now the palace,' Ansu said. 'Listen, I must tell you something.'

Aranthur was still in a daze; he found it difficult to do more than shrug.

Ansu looked embarrassed. 'My name is not, strictly speaking, Ansu. Ansu is more of a title... It's my royal name. Listen – Zhou is as complicated a place as Megara, perhaps moreso. My name is pronounced 靖江安肃王; I suppose I am Jingjiang Ansu Wang to you, although Wang is also a sort of title...'

Aranthur nodded. 'I'm not sure I can even say that as you do.'

'My sister would call me "Zhu Jingfu",' the prince said. 'If she wasn't muttering dark obscenities or using sweet nothings like *blockhead*.' He shrugged, as if at a happy memory. 'I miss them. You are all so... alien.'

'Barbaric?' Aranthur asked.

Ansu raised an eyebrow. 'Perhaps a little. Don't hate me for my superior civilisation.'

Aranthur smiled. 'I'm an Arnaut. Everyone thinks they are more civilised than me.'

They walked a few more steps, and Aranthur waved at a leather-worker he knew; they were only a few blocks up from the Square of the Mulberry Trees.

'So... if I may be so bold, what would you like me to call you?'

'If I do not seem overweeningly arrogant,' Ansu said, 'I'd like you to call me "Ansu" or "Prince Ansu" in public. But as we have lived together and shared a fight, I think I will allow you to call me "Zhu Jingfu" in private.'

Aranthur turned and bowed, exactly as the prince had done at their first meeting.

'You honour me,' he said.

'Yes, I do,' the prince replied. 'Don't let it go to your head. Now let's go and face the General.'

Even an hour after the duel, and with his belly full, Aranthur was not paying the attention he might have as they moved down the thumb of the city towards the palace. As they drew closer, his breath was taken.

The Crystal Palace was the dominant structure in the Imperial Precinct, which itself had a wall and seven gates. The wall was entirely white marble; it had forty towers, each of white marble, roofed in tall copper spires that had been carefully gilded, so that they appeared as spikes of gold in the sunlight. Inside the wall were a dozen temples, four formal gardens, a sports field, a magnificent amphitheatre said to date from before the First Empire, a red marble barracks block for the Guard, and another of green and pink marble for the palace servants and officers. But at the very tip of the peninsula stood the palace itself: a behemoth of glass and gold and veins of white stone to support the structure, and a waterfall of white stone buttresses and arches outside; a garden of curving stone shapes supporting eight naves; and a central cupola that soared twenty storeys above the highest building in the city and appeared as if ready to take flight – a vast dome of glass, and atop it a needle of gold and glass, itself the size of a yacht.

The light inside the naves was a haze of gold – the light in the dome was unearthly. The whole was the work of Renardas, the greatest of the Flamabard architects and stonemasons; it was less than two hundred years old. One of Aranthur's professors referred to it as the 'pinnacle of Byzas culture' and another called it a 'remarkable piece of vulgarity'.

Ansu stopped at the Barracks Gate to the Imperial Precinct and pointed.

'I admire it every time I see it,' he said. 'It is not quite my style – I could show you things in my home that please me more ... but it is ... breathtaking, nonetheless.'

Aranthur, who saw it every day, looked at it for the first time. That is, really looked.

'It is . . .' He shook his head.

'Yes,' Ansu agreed. 'Come. The General doesn't choose to live in the palace. She's in the military hall, and it is being rebuilt. You Byzas are always tinkering . . . In Zhou, when we build well, then we leave it alone.'

Indeed, the pink and red marble structure was covered in scaffolding. Two man-powered cranes were lifting the weather-worn statues that crowned the roofline and placing them, face down, one at a time, the operators calling out a rhythm as sweating soldiers pushed at the capstan bars. In the courtyard there was a line of covered statues, as well as a dozen small trees, their root balls wrapped in burlap, waiting to be planted. Two imperial guardsmen stood at the main door.

'They're going to drop it,' one said.

'Kerkos' swelling member,' said the other. 'Five crosses that they get it to the ground.'

'Done,' said the first. 'Halt. Whoever you are.'

Aranthur halted.

Ansu just pushed past. 'I'm Prince Ansu!'

'I don't care if you are the fucking Emperor,' one of the gamblers snapped.

Aranthur stood there.

The statue swayed and then righted and the base touched the ground.

'Dammit!' one gambler complained. 'State your business.'

'You know who I am,' Ansu said.

Aranthur could see that the Prince of Zhou was not used to obeying like an Arnaut.

I'd just be killed, he thought, with his hand well away from his sword hilt.

'I have a message for the General,' Aranthur said.

'Let's see it,' the loser of the wager said.

'It's a personal message,' Aranthur answered. 'Verbal. I was with her in the west.'

'Of course you were,' Winner replied. He rolled his eyes. 'Prince An—' He began.

'He's with me,' Ansu snapped.

The guards didn't move. They hadn't drawn their weapons, but they had blocked Ansu from passing the inner door.

'Rules are rules,' Loser said.

'You know me!' Ansu said again, frustrated.

Winner shrugged. 'No offence to either of you gentles, but there's shit happening out there in the city, and we've orders to take care, so some care we are a-taking.'

Ansu let out a long sigh.

Loser tapped a bell with a wand of ebony that Aranthur could see was *potent*. There was no sound, but there was a distinct emanation of *power*.

Ansu was restless. 'This is a waste of time,' he said, and he began to walk back and forth. 'I feel humiliated.'

Aranthur had a lifetime of toll checks and anti-Arnaut suspicions and this seemed perfectly normal to him.

'I'm sure we'll be fine,' he said, with a reassuring look at the guards.

'Why do these men not trust me? They have seen me for months. It is absurd.' Ansu pulled at his moustache.

Drek Coryn Ringkoat appeared from the closed door.

'Well, well,' he said. 'Look what the cat dragged in.'

'What is that to mean?' demanded Prince Ansu.

The *Jhugj* laughed. 'Whatever I want it to mean. Only the General was just speaking of this young scapegrace.'

'I have a message for the General,' Aranthur asserted.

'The Arnaut is on the green list,' Ringkoat said casually.

'Damn,' said the guardsman who had lost the wager. 'Damn. By the sword of Enyalios.' He took out a tablet and read down the marks in the wax. 'Timos?'

'Yes, sir,' Aranthur said.

The guardsman bowed. 'My apologies, Syr Timos. If you'd ha' said you were on the list . . .'

'And me?' Ansu asked.

'I don't think the General wants to see you just now,' Ringkoat said.

The *Jhugj* and the Zhouian glared at each other.

'I'll be quick,' Aranthur said.

'I just want to see you get out alive,' Ansu said. 'Since we're to be room-mates.'

Aranthur followed Ringkoat down a long hall and then up two

307

flights of marble stairs. The sound of the cranes outside provided a counterpoint to the rhythmic sound of stone hammers shaping stone in the courtyard.

They climbed to the topmost level and walked across a beautiful garden laid out on the roof, surrounded by stone patios. At the east end of the building was a two-storey tower.

'The General likes her privacy and she isn't much for court,' Ringkoat said.

Two palace servants opened the magnificent bronze doors to the tower. One took Aranthur's sword.

'There have been threats since the confrontation with a certain duke,' the *Jhugj* said. 'We're taking precautions. Wait here. She'll see you, I expect.'

Aranthur was handed a glass of excellent white wine, which he drank too fast.

'Aranthur Timos,' General Tribane said. 'The man who just keeps turning up.' Despite her words, she smiled. 'May I help you?'

'Majesty, I didn't see you when the Pennon Malconti was ordered north.' He bowed, a little nervously. 'Malconti assumed I would see you and left me with a verbal message, which I . . .' He couldn't see how to lie about it. 'Which I forgot.'

'Old messages are worse than old eggs,' Ringkoat said sourly.

'Tell me anyway,' said the General. She was dressed in a long blue gown and pearls; there was something disconcerting about seeing her dressed as a woman.

'Malconti said he thought that the Duke of Volta had *wanted* the confrontation, and he accused the duke of trying a *compulsion* to make the pennon attack.'

'Wine,' the General said. 'When did he tell you this?'

The night I was too tired to make love to Nenia.

'The last night I was encamped with the pennon.'

Aranthur found that he had more wine. He drank it. The General's scent reached him – it was sharp, and had a little lemon in it, and it was like a drug. As soon as he smelled it, he inhaled more.

Lust went through him like a sword blade through a pumpkin.

The General watched him with concern.

'Damn,' she muttered. 'Timos, that scent is not for you – I have other plans for the evening.'

Aranthur was not sure he had ever seen a woman as attractive as the General; her authority was dizzying and her poise and athleticism stirring. He moved a little closer to her without conscious thought, and inhaled again.

She rose with a sigh. 'Thanks for coming here. Damned perfume. Who needs it, anyway? Ringkoat, take him out and give him something nice...'

She slipped through a curtain, leaving Aranthur in a state of ecstatic arousal.

Ringkoat looked at him with something like pity.

'Come with me,' he said.

Prince Ansu had either not waited for him, or not been allowed to linger. Aranthur hoped the latter was true, but he walked home alone, and carefully. He went home to an empty room that seemed full of ghosts. His belly was full of wine, and he didn't want to be alone, and he was there with the dead, like Arnaud and the creature that had attacked him, and the ghosts of the living, like Dahlia and the increasingly difficult image of Nenia, who was entangled with the rebellion and the woods... and Alfia...

Finally he sat at the window and read *Consolations* for quite some time. It helped.

He needed food, and he considered buying an Easterner girl, because... Because he didn't want to be alone, and it was too crowded in the room. He wanted to talk to someone. Reading didn't shut off his mind, although it helped. He put on a good doublet and went to visit Kallinikos, but the man's rooms were locked, and no one was there, not even a servant. He did note that his friend's window was ajar, and he called out. There was no answer except from the pretty Western Isles woman in the next house, who looked out. She was in his Arcana class; he waved.

'I haven't seen him,' she called.

'I am an idiot,' he said aloud.

He felt vaguely guilty just for his various imaginings.

He went out, bought a fish pie, and went home without buying either a body, a measure of stock or a flagon of wine. He lay in bed, thinking of the dead Easterners. His dark thoughts were interspersed with flashes of erotic imagination; Tribane's perfume was still with him. And then he surprised himself by going to sleep.

The next morning he awoke on time to his summoning spell, and his head was clear. He dressed carelessly, in robes and old breeches, and he didn't put his hair in a queue as Dahlia had taught him, and he didn't wear a doublet or his sword. He was the first customer for a new *quaveh* seller in the Founder's Square and he had, for once, brought his own cups on his own tray. He arrived triumphantly to present Edvin with *quaveh* while the notary was still sharpening quills.

'My, you *are* early,' Edvin said. 'Let's work on our Safiri calligraphy, shall we?'

They spent two hours, writing until Aranthur's wrist and fingers were cramped and aching in a way that swordsmanship never tired him, and until Aranthur had said everything he remembered about Malconti, who was clearly Edvin's hero.

'The pen is more tiring than the sword,' he said.

'Make that up yourself, did you?' Edvin asked. He reeked of a scent – something exotic: patchouli or spikenard. Nothing as eloquent as the General's scent, though.

Aranthur was trying to breathe through his mouth. But he laughed.

The Master of Arts came in, her elegant scholar's gown floating behind her. Her face was more severe than usual.

'Your *quaveh* is hot,' Aranthur said, proudly.

He'd kept it hot with a Safiri incantation, a far more efficient *working* than the one he'd used to dry the alders for Nenia, powered from his own essence in the Safiri way.

'You fought a licensed duel last night after I specifically asked you not to risk yourself,' she snapped. 'You are dismissed.'

She turned on Edvin. 'You stink. Wash.'

She swept into her office.

Aranthur sat in the ashes of his future.

'Ignore her,' Edvin said. 'I mean, you're an idiot if you actually disobeyed her, but she'll forgive you. I need to wash. Is it bad?'

Aranthur's heart began to beat again. 'Yes,' he said weakly.

'I had the most delightful evening.' Edvin got up from behind his desk. 'Not a Malconti, but very . . . exciting.' He raised both eyebrows expressively and grinned.

'Where is this hot *quaveh*?' demanded the Master from inside her office.

Edvin winked.

Aranthur took two deep breaths, summoned his courage, and walked in carrying his covered cup. He placed it by her.

She looked at him over steepled hands. 'You anger me.'

'Magistera.'

'Explain yourself.'

He was smart enough not to shrug. 'I . . .' he began. 'He challenged me. He was one of the rebels and he claimed I was a spy. I gave him the lie.'

'It is all over the Precinct. He's a Da Rosa,' she added. 'So close to the gods? Yes?'

Aranthur had never heard the joke, so he shook his head.

'The Da Rosas, so close to the gods, so far from the Imperial throne . . . No, eh?' She shrugged. 'Never mind. I believe I ordered you not to fight any more duels,' she continued with more asperity.

Aranthur met her eyes. She was angry. 'I did not understand it was an order. And I didn't kill him.'

'You could have *been* killed. Are you an idiot?' She shook her head. 'I want you to talk to Tiy Drako. Very well, you are not dismissed. I was angry with you and everyone else in this bureaucratic hell of a city.' She looked out the window. 'Listen, Timos. I may lose my position here. There is a great deal of nasty politics going around right now, and you have managed, in four weeks, to fall afoul of the Uthmanoi and now the Da Rosas, both prominent Lion families. Out in the streets, we're edging towards a House war. There have been at least two further sorcerous attempts on the Precinct wards while the Duke of Volta is trying to bring me down and change the government. Someone tried to *kill the General*. Please, do not make my life any more complicated. Let's work.'

Kill the General. Hence all the unexpected security.

He worked. He worked on the grimoire for hours, and then he went out of the Precinct and cut straps – mindless work that he did well – with Manacher. Manacher was in a very good mood indeed, as the business was thriving. He was full of the gossip of the court and the Temple and the various legal battles of the city.

At some point, Aranthur had a chance to interject.

'Isn't Manacher a Safiri name?'

Manacher nodded, clearly pleased. 'My grandfather was a Safian. My mother still knows a few words, I think.'

'I am studying Safiri at the Academy,' Aranthur said.

'Why?' Manacher asked, without much interest. 'I mean, I assume everyone there speaks it quite well.' He laughed and laughed, convinced he was a wit.

Aranthur was too tired to go to the *salle*. He was poor, and the next day was a militia drill day, and he would be paid. He went home, passing a surprising number of young women and young men wearing daggers and House colours. He wondered if it was a festival he'd forgotten. His hands were still stained red and green from the leather dyes he'd used at the end of the day. He was so tired that he had to rest before climbing all six flights of stairs, where he found Tiy Drako sitting in the window.

'You again,' Aranthur said.

'I sent you on a mission and you didn't report back at the end,' Drako said.

Aranthur felt like a fool, a feeling that was becoming quite common for him.

'I'm sorry,' he said. 'I—'

'You saved me and the General a great deal of work, discovered hundreds of Easterners living in the woods, revealed what may have been a nasty plot preying on the Empire, and then went back to class. Then you skewered a very powerful man's son in a duel. Have I missed anything?'

Aranthur sighed and settled into the second-best chair, which creaked.

'It's my fault,' Drako said. 'I have never explained anything to you because for the longest time you were a suspect in my mystery of mysteries. Even now...' He shrugged. 'Never mind. I need your help, immediately, and then we'll talk. I've lost your Safian. He wandered off. Where did you find him?'

'In the *agora* next to the Night Market,' Aranthur said.

'Help me find him again. He's a gold mine of useful information, when he's sober.' Drako made a face. 'Through him I have been able to question other Safian refugees. I need him. By the way, wear a good doublet to your drill day tomorrow.'

'You are as enigmatic as the Master of Arts.' Aranthur pulled his student gown over his head without touching the buttons and then threw on his mud-stained doublet and his sword belt. 'Ready.'

'The duel with Djinar Da Rosa was foolish,' Drako said on the stairs.

'So everyone tells me. You know he was one of the rebels.'

Drako paused. 'Was he? You're sure?' He glanced at Aranthur. 'And your friend Kallinikos? Was he one of the rebels?'

Arantur stopped. 'No,' he snapped.

Drako shrugged. 'A year ago he might have been.'

Aranthur kept going down the stairs. As they climbed the stone steps above the canal, he said, 'The duel was because of the rebellion.'

'Of course.' Drako paused. 'It was still stupid.'

'Really? Better in the *salle* than in a back alley with his bravos.'

'That may still happen,' Drako said. 'We're being followed.'

'How do you know?'

It was late evening; the sky was just barely pink somewhere off to the west over Volta and the Iron Circle. The narrow streets seemed to be full of people, most of them armed.

'I really need to spend some time on you. How did it go with Dahlia?' he asked.

'Badly,' Aranthur said. 'I wrote her a poem and made her a belt-purse. She ... suggested I was treating her as a whore.'

'Darkness Falling!' Drako cursed. 'I had forgotten how exciting youth is. She *asked* me ... Never mind.' The aristocrat passed Aranthur, moving quickly, and turned to cross the canal on a very narrow bridge. 'Listen, you know that aristocrats are ... forbidden ...' He shrugged and looked back. 'This is going to sound asinine. Forbidden to *fornicate* with other aristocrats. Casually, if you take my meaning. We can only *marry* each other. It prevents unwanted alliances and babies.'

Aranthur walked along, mulling this over.

'So you ... What?' he asked, suddenly angry and confused.

'Don't look back. So, the way you spot people following you is more a lifestyle than a technique,' he said. Their shoes made the wooden slats of the bridge sound hollowly beneath them, like a bass drum in a *taverna* act. 'But the simplest principle is this: look for people to appear multiple times, in areas well spread apart, so that it can't be logically explained. Then assume they are following you.'

Drako was a little breathless because he was moving fast. Now he turned along the richer side of the canal, led Aranthur through an alley so narrow that they could touch the walls on either side, and which smelt of cat urine, and they emerged into one of the smaller temple squares: the Lady of the Law. There stood the Lady, with offerings around her feet – some to her as the Lady and some as Sophia.

'Dahlia...' Drako began, and then he paused. 'Later. Now we go to the temple.'

The two of them went in through the open main doors. Aranthur was not, particularly, a devotee of the Lady and hadn't been to many chapels, but this one was superb. It was in a wealthy neighbourhood full of judges and lawyers from the Great Hall, the main law court, and the hangings and incense burners and hanging lamps were beautiful.

Drako bought them both sacrificial cakes from a table by the portico and they offered them at a station in the nave. Aranthur knelt and made a prayer, which turned out to be about Dahlia.

Drako was smiling. 'You really are a country boy. Nobody comes here to pray. Good place to make love, though. The Lady never seems to mind. Come on.'

He led the way and Aranthur followed, and they walked up into the sacred area. Aranthur felt vaguely blasphemous.

Drako clearly had no hesitation at all. He passed the rail and led the way through a low door into a room that smelled of incense. He walked to a side door and opened it.

'No noise, now,' he said, and they were back out in the darkness.

They were at a back corner of the temple, and Aranthur could see the square and alley outside as a blur of light. And indeed, two men passed the end of the street, and paused. They were almost close enough to touch.

'They went inside,' said a deep voice.

'I don't work in temples,' said another. 'Bad luck.'

'No shit.'

There was the sound of further footsteps, and then silence.

'We could follow them,' Aranthur said.

'No,' Drako said. 'Too risky. Come.'

They went up the street of tall stone houses. They were close to Master Sparthos' *salle*, a very good neighbourhood. The buildings became shorter, more wood than stone, and the smell of the canal vanished to be replaced with the smell of rotting garbage and human waste.

'Ah, the beauties of the Aqueduct,' Drako said.

'It is very late for the Easterners,' Aranthur said. 'Sasan might be asleep, or full of *bhang* or *ghat* or *thuryx*.' He shrugged. 'Let's try his corner. And I know another man who might help us.'

'In the Pinnacle, after dark.' Drako whistled. 'Well, I wanted a life of adventure.'

The two of them went up the spine of the city until they were at the edge of the Pinnacle. Aranthur went from pillar to pillar, and asked the children about Sasan, but none of them had ever heard of him. Drako offered money, and suddenly they had dozens of people who all claimed to know where to find him.

'Fuck,' muttered the officer. 'I know better, too.'

It took time, and some Armean, to extricate them. Two boys wouldn't leave them; they were small, and both had big eyes that seemed to glitter in the weird torchlight under the great aqueduct.

'Please, syr, syr,' they said, holding out long, narrow hands. 'Please, please. My mother has bone plague, my father is dead. Please, please.'

Aranthur had no money, but he convinced Drako to hand over some obols.

'More, more,' chanted the two boys.

Drako nodded. 'How about I cut off your hands?'

They ran.

Aranthur looked at him by torchlight.

'You're too soft,' Drako said.

'Am I?' Aranthur said. 'I'm really just a farm boy, and an Arnaut. I'm not sophisticated enough for you or Dahlia. And I don't threaten children.'

Drako didn't reply. They had no guides, and it was absolutely dark except where a woman had a small lantern or a man had an open flame. Four men were gambling for bronze obols. A woman was trying to get her children to sleep on the packed dirt with no shelter. Aranthur spoke enough Armean to know that she was telling them that it was all right, an adventure, they were brave little warriors and they would be great men someday.

'We're lost,' Drako muttered.

'Again,' said a voice.

Ulgul, the priest of Apoul, appeared out of the darkness under the arches.

Aranthur embraced him, surprised at his own feeling of affection.

'We're trying to find Sasan,' he said.

Ulgul sounded odd. 'Sasan? Ah, the poet. You know it is the most common name in Safi, eh? Yes, he's back. He tells stories to melt the heart and then takes his fee to buy *thuryx.*'

'I want to take him away to live with me,' Aranthur said.

'You'll have to give him a reason to live first,' Ulgul said. 'Come.'

They walked downhill, to the edge of the Aqueduct. There were huddles of carts and wagons – richer refugees had them, and most had already sold their animals. The carts became homes – better than the gravel and mud under the arches.

'We're being followed again,' Drako said.

Ulgul passed under a torch used by a pimp to display his wares. His slurred voice was explained; his jaw was obviously broken, his face fat with tissue damage, and one eye was closed from swelling.

'Famuz?' Aranthur spat.

'And others. The vermin who prey on these poor souls dislike me. And I revel in it. My god will protect me, though.'

'He's not doing such a very good job so far,' Drako muttered. 'So the two thugs on us are *al Ghugha* soldiers?'

'You know a great deal if you know *al Ghugha,*' Ulgul said. 'Maybe. Maybe just a couple of broken men serving for pay.'

'Or maybe something worse. Aranthur here is always the centre of every fucking discontent. It's his special talent. Here they come.'

Two men emerged into the light of the pimp's torch. They crossed their arms, and one sent a small boy running off.

'Darkness and Light. Well, let's not wait to see who comes, eh?'

Drako walked forward to the two big men. They had strong, harsh faces; one had tattoos up his neck and across his forehead.

Aranthur drew his sword three fingers and followed Drako, painfully aware of the Master of Arts and her order.

'They are just men, like you,' Ulgul said.

Drako's expression was unreadable.

'You wait here,' said one of the men.

Drako nodded. 'I don't think so. And if you try, in any way, to interfere with my business, I'll kill you and your friend and maybe come back and kill a lot more of your type. That would be bad for business.'

'You don't know what you're fucking with, foreigner,' the tattooed man said. He half drew a cutlass from his belt.

Drako killed him from the scabbard, a draw to a rising cut that caught his jaw; the wrist roll put the point through the back of his head. Drako pivoted on his hips, withdrawing the weapon.

'That was unnecessary,' Ulgul said with pleading in his voice.

'Shut up,' Drako said. The second man was backing away.

'You killed one of my people,' Famuz said from the torchlight.

Drako shrugged. 'You need better people.'

Famuz spread his hands. 'I try not to mix in the Byzas world. But you crossed the line, and I will make an example of you.'

There were other men moving.

Drako shrugged. 'I am an Imperial officer, and your threats are wind.'

'The Pinnacle is mine,' Famuz said.

Drako shook his head. 'You live here on the Emperor's sufferance. You are a petty criminal who bathes in the blood of his own people.'

Aranthur caught the move – in the crowd rapidly forming, a skinny young man was moving closer, closer . . .

Aranthur moved, his sword coming from his scabbard.

The skinny man had a pair of daggers.

It was too dark for finesse, and Aranthur cut, a simple, overhand cut.

The daggers rose to guard the man's head. Aranthur kicked him between the legs with all his might – a boyhood trick – and the would-be assassin rolled.

Aranthur's blade caught the man's ear and severed it.

Aranthur heard a puffer's flat crack. The skinny assassin rose, daggers flashing in a butterfly of steel.

Aranthur cut, not very hard, for the man's left elbow, which stuck out at an unnatural angle. The daggers moved, both together, and having deceived both weapons, Aranthur thrust. Skill, and the darkness, and Tyche, put his point in under the man's throat.

The man took a moment to fall. He voided his bowels, and his eyes, full of some drug, were locked on Aranthur in the fickle torchlight as his throat slid off Aranthur's point. It seemed to happen very slowly.

Aranthur's mind closed. It was like a door slamming shut; he was aware of his surroundings, but he wasn't thinking.

The man lay, his heels drumming the packed dirt, and then he gurgled something and stopped moving.

'Any more flunkies?' Drako said, behind Aranthur. He had a smoking puffer in his hand, the smoke lit by the pimp's torch.

Famuz lay on his back, his face ruined by the puffer ball.

Ulgul knelt by the skinny assassin, praying. Then he looked up.

'You bastards,' he said. 'Now I must start trying to earn their trust all over again.'

Aranthur didn't have a thought in his head. He was cold, and empty.

Drako turned to the surviving *al Ghugha* soldier.

'I told you I'd be bad for business,' he said. 'Don't make me come back here.'

He turned to Aranthur. 'Let's find Sasan,' he said wearily. 'I'll have to write a report.' He grabbed Aranthur's arm. 'Come on, lad. Breathe for me. That's right.' He shook his head. 'Bad business.'

He took a short red stick from his belt pouch and broke it in two, and Aranthur felt the burst of *power*. And then a series of pulses – very weak, but persistent.

'Clean-up crew,' he said. 'Let's go.'

He grabbed Ulgul by the hood of his robe.

'They were going to kill you,' Drako spat at him.

'Martyrdom is not so terrible,' Ulgul said. 'Killing them . . .'

'They were vermin,' Drako spat.

'They were men like you,' Ulgul said.

Drako sagged. 'Whatever. Find me Sasan.'

Ulgul led them sullenly along the wagons. No one followed them; the crowd had vanished while Aranthur was unable to function. He kept remembering the dead man's eyes and he shook it off, literally shaking his head, and followed the priest into the huddle of tents beyond the wagon park. A few were lit; most were dark, but in the centre of the tent city was another *agora* and there was light and even music, a very different feel from the area under the Aqueduct. This had once been a temple garden, and the Temple had granted it to the refugees. The smell was better and there was a tang of orange blossom rather than a whiff of faeces.

Aranthur saw the beet seller's cart immediately. And there, sitting on the man's little cart and telling stories, was Sasan. He was high. His hands moved frantically, but his story rolled on, in Armean, and there were a dozen men, a few women, and some children sitting on the dry gravel and listening. Drako and Aranthur joined the little crowd, and when the story drew to a close, some of the people put small coins or glass beads into a cup. One woman, whose hands had no nails, simply bowed deeply, her veil fluttering, before going off.

'You ran away,' Drako said to the storyteller when all his audience was gone. The *labou* seller busied himself with his beets.

Sasan shrugged. 'You don't have anything I want. You want to save the world. I want *thuryx*.' His hands fluttered like moths.

'I have money. And you made a promise,' Drako said.

'My promises are worth less than my shit, which is, itself, good fertiliser, and also has so much smack in it that some people could resell it.'

The addict laughed. His eyes were deeply sunken. His fluttering hands were incredibly frail.

'Sasan,' Aranthur said, 'come and live with me.'

The addict looked at him for a moment. He tilted his head to one side like a very intelligent dog.

'You mean this?' he asked.

Aranthur shrugged. 'Why not?' He found his decision was made. 'I want to save something.'

Sasan bowed from the waist. 'Maybe tomorrow. And maybe I don't want to be saved.'

'Now,' Drako said.

'I don't really want to right now, attractive as a bed might be,' Sasan said. Up close, he smelled of *thuryx* and old sweat.

Drako leant down and lifted the addict on his shoulder.

'I don't really want to carry you five stades,' he said darkly. 'But by the Lady, I'm going to.'

Later that night, when Sasan was cleaner and lying peacefully in the bed that had once been Daud's, Drako sat in the second-best chair with a pipe of stock.

'I don't like all those armed toffs in the street,' he said. 'It is years since we had a House fight.'

'House fight?' Aranthur asked. 'Damn it, Drako, I know nothing. Nothing.' He looked at Drako. 'What is *al Ghugha*?'

'A criminal gang. They pretend to have politics, but all they do is sell their girls as whores and run the *thuryx* trade with Armea.' Drako sighed.

'Why don't you do something about them, you being an Imperial officer and everything?' Aranthur was angry, and drained.

'What do you suggest? Some more judicial killings like tonight? Maybe we'll just wander the streets and kill people who look bad?'

'Someone must know who they are,' Aranthur insisted.

Drako looked at Sasan. 'Someone might. But I'm not...' He paused. 'This isn't my fight. Or my turf. I...' He looked away. 'I can't save everyone and neither can you. And what I'm fighting makes *al Ghugha* look like the fucking amateur thugs that they are.'

'What are you fighting, then?'

Drako was back at the window, looking down at the street, where a dozen bravos in House colours were shouting slogans.

'I'm fighting something that wants to bring about the end of the world,' he said.

'And is *al Ghugha* part of it?'

'*Al Ghugha* is a run-of-the-mill criminal organisation.' He watched. 'I'm more worried by the sudden appearance of all these House colours. And the attempt on the General.'

'Do Houses fight?' Aranthur asked.

'Not in a generation. You know what the Blacks and Whites are, right?'

Aranthur nodded.

'Well. Like that. A House fight is when two of our noble institutions, that is, families, become entangled and the law can't solve it. They fight. They even have the legal right to do so. But the result is somewhere between a riot and a battle, and it's ugly.' Drako shrugged. 'Ugly, but not my problem unless it's connected to the real problem. There's people who watch for such things.'

'That was refreshing,' Aranthur said, taking the pipe. 'You told me something.'

'I didn't tell you much,' Drako admitted. 'I don't really like telling people anything, to be honest. And I'm not honest.' He shrugged.

'Everything you say is a lie?' Aranthur said.

'Pretty much. Now – your report. You saw the armour I was looking for on the backs of a bunch of rebels out west, made the right call, and fetched the General. Is that correct?'

Aranthur took the pipe. 'Yes.'

Drako nodded. 'Well, as best we can tell, now, the Duke of Volta was planning a military coup, much like the one that toppled him. He hired Malconti, who is pretty much the best sell-sword available, and they were to have inside help—'

'What does any of this have to do with the Pure and the Disciples and the Eastern refugees?' Aranthur asked.

'Oho. You do listen when I speak,' Drako said.

'A *sending* tried to kill me in this room.' Aranthur's voice rose when he said it. He hadn't realised how much of that he carried with him until that moment. 'Kati left and never came back. Arnaud died. For something in my travelling case.' He looked at Drako. 'Can I guess? You are looking for a shipment of uncustomed *kuria* crystals.'

Drako looked at him for a long time. 'How did you guess that?'

Aranthur shrugged. 'The price is rising, and you told me yourself that the Disciples use the illegal trade to fund things. Like rebellions, I'm guessing.' He looked out of the window, his mind clear of the dying assassin. 'And maybe the *thuryx* trade, which in fact you'd like to investigate. See? I know when you are lying.'

Drako laughed. He took the pipe, inhaled deeply, and shook his head.

'Damme,' he said in his best upper-class accent. 'Well, guess away, Timos. All I have is guesses. If I could have the Duke of Volta to torture for a day, I'd get it out of him.'

'Torture?' Aranthur said.

Drako shrugged. 'I'm running out of rational, humane options. I don't like what I did tonight. We try very hard not to kill Easterners... One riot there and the fucking Lion aristos will have a House mob slaughtering them. I don't have a clue who my adversaries are, and they are already destabilising the Sultan Beik over in Atti. Around a month ago, as we started planting in the Empire, Armea fell. The last two cities on the Attian border went down. They should have held for years – huge, well-stocked fortresses. I don't even know how they fell. Atti is next, and then us, I guess. I see all the signs that the Disciples are working on us already.' He shook his head. 'I'll tell you this much – the whole crystal thing *makes no sense.*' He whirled the pipe through the air for emphasis. 'No sense. Sure, the crystals would have a street value. A good one. Higher than *thuryx.*' He shrugged. 'But my double agent was a major player, and those crystals weren't worth much more than your family's farm. Maybe two of them.' He shrugged. 'All right, perhaps ten family farms. Still not enough for anyone to die for, or risk an empire or an operation. Yet not only did he die for them, but then they risked their entire covert and arcane structure to search your rooms. Inside the Academy precinct. Every artifact in the Academy was triggered; it was as if the Master meant to announce . . .' Drako paused. 'Meant to announce that he was coming for you. For us. Damn. Maybe that's exactly what he did. I know nothing about him or how he works.' He shook his head. 'Hurry up and learn Safiri so I can take you east.'

'I knew that's where this was going,' Aranthur said.

Drako shrugged. 'I'll be going too. The Sultan Beik has begun what looks like the call up of his feudal levies. Our sources in the seraglio say he's coming for *us*.' He shook his head. 'I know that makes no sense, but the word is . . .' He paused. 'Aranthur Timos, you are too easy to talk to.'

Aranthur laughed. 'I was learning something.'

Drako smiled and smoked. 'I'm tired of being silent, I suppose. Dangerous form of fatigue. I can't share the why, right now, and I beg you not to repeat anything I tell you to anyone, including your professors or even Dahlia or, really, your mother.'

'So dire. The world is at stake and only I can save it? Don't tell my mother?' He shook his head. 'I'm not that much of a farm boy.'

Drako flopped back. 'Timos, the fucking Attians are coming with sabre and drum. In my lifetime,' he said bitterly. 'Why? Why can't they play these games after I'm dead? All I want is to sleep with all the beautiful women and drink all the brandy.' He smiled ruefully. 'This is nice stock.'

'My patur's,' Aranthur said. 'And Iralia?'

Drako shook his head. 'You don't need to know. She does her work and you do yours. I do mine.'

'She invited me to visit her.'

'Go right ahead,' Drako said. 'Don't discuss any of this. Here's ten sequins. Ansu is serious about moving in with you. You know that, eh?'

Aranthur nodded. 'I offered.'

Drako laughed. 'I didn't used to believe in the gods.'

'What does that mean?' Aranthur asked.

'I'll tell you in a year, if we're all still alive. I will come around more often,' he said. 'You really can't be allowed out by yourself, and Sasan needs...'

Aranthur raised an eyebrow. 'You are the one who needs Sasan.'

'True for you. Please be careful, and go armed.' Drako shrugged. 'I'd miss you if you ate a blade. I'll be back tomorrow.'

'Good.' Aranthur rose, and instead of shaking hands, they embraced. 'Despite everything, I like you.'

Drako smiled his crooked smile. 'Count no man happy until he is dead. Despite which, I have done all right by you.' He looked out of the window. 'Fucking Dahlia, though.'

'Is she one of us?' Aranthur asked.

Drako shook his head and suddenly he was sober and his eyes were hard.

'Never ask,' he said.

Aranthur shook his head. 'Damn it, Drako. I've just discovered that we use torture and you're willing to hurt a child to get your way. I don't know enough about our side to play it. What is our side?' Anger coursed through him and he found his fists clenched. 'Am I a government informer?'

Drako smiled crookedly. 'We're a conspiracy to save the world. I wasn't misleading you about that part. We are not a side. I have some pull with the Emperor and General Tribane has more. That's all. We have friends in the Lightbringers and in the Sultan's court, and now, in Zhou.' He shrugged. 'We sometimes do bad things for good ends. I hope they're good. Don't tell me that the Master is right all along, and that he's the one saving the world.'

Aranthur felt his heart beat. 'What?'

'Everyone is the hero in his own romance. Even the Master. Whoever he is.' He shook his head. 'I say again – watch your back for a few days. Those two outside the temple were bravos, but they meant business. Family toughs are better trained than Easterner thugs and you have a surprising list of enemies. I'll ask Verit Roaris to try to get the Da Rosas to take the heat off you. Goodnight.'

'Roaris is... one of us?' Aranthur asked.

'I see you are beginning to understand the politics,' Drako said with an uneasy smile. 'Roaris serves his own ends. As do we all. But he's loyal.'

*

The next day dawned too early and Aranthur's throat burned from too much smoke, but he was in his place at Rasce's stall, wearing his best doublet because Drako, for all his ambiguity, was usually a true prophet.

When Rasce was glossy coated and all Aranthur's tack gleamed with new wax, he heard the inspection party coming along the stalls. He straightened up, coiled his lead rope as the rules insisted, and laid out his tack.

The inspection party was bigger than it had been the last time. When they were looking at a stall almost fifty paces away in the huge barn, Aranthur noted that the General was with them. He spent the next block of time using his neighbour's powdered pumice and some oil to clean – really clean – his arming sword. And then he started on his heavy sword. He was scrubbing at the blade, with its deep brown patina, when he realised that it might have an inlay – a steel inlay in a steel blade.

He was just beginning to doubt his initial observation when Drek Ringkoat said, 'There's a mug I know, General.'

Aranthur shot to his feet and stood at attention.

Centark Equus said, 'Trooper Aranthur Timos, Fourth Tagma, City Cavalry, Selected.'

'Trooper Timos,' General Tribane said. 'You are hereby promoted to the rank of dekark in the City Cavalry.'

Aranthur couldn't help himself. He smiled.

'In addition, for service given freely in a time of emergency, the Emperor has, by purple writ, declared you to be *fideles*.'

The General handed him a tightly rolled scroll of heavy vellum.

Equus nodded. 'Dekark Timos, we would usually conduct this cere-mony on the parade ground, but we have been asked to keep this . . . private.'

Aranthur had an inkling why.

'Stand at your ease, Dekark,' the General said. 'Syr Timos, will you serve on my courier staff? I believe you own two horses?'

'Yes, General,' he said.

She met his eye and his unhidden grin with a slight smile of her own. There was no perfume in evidence.

'You may keep both of them at the Emperor's expense. I regret to say, however, that if you accept the duty, the odds you will be called up are...' She paused. 'Very good.'

Aranthur had to refuse. Being called to active duty would ruin his school career; he'd never catch up with his peers...

'I accept,' he said.

The *Jhugj* laughed. 'Told ya,' he declared. 'Welcome aboard, boyo.'

Ten minutes later he was moving Rasce to another part of the huge stable block, closest to the gate, farthest from the palace itself. It took six trips to relocate all of his equipment. He was issued a breastplate, neatly plum brown and requiring little more than wax to keep it clean, a pair of steel gauntlets and a helmet. The helmet was complex, with a riveted dome, and a long tail like a shrimp or lobster might have that went over his back, and a brim with a nose guard.

A clerk went over his kit. 'Says here you have a *cannone*,' she said.

'Yes, Myr,' he said. 'A *fusil*.'

'In the armoury?'

He nodded.

'Fetch it. You will receive a writ for it and you can keep it with your other gear.' She gave him a grim smile. 'I guess they think you will need it, young man.'

He waited in a line at the armourer's. There were dozens of men and women getting weapons or having swords sharpened, and since he had waited through the line, he had his own arming sword ground sharp while he waited for another clerk to fetch his *cannone*.

The sharpener looked at his sword. 'Too short for horseback. Nah, bud, I'll do it for ye, but we don't usually do non-military crap. Good steel. How sharp?'

Aranthur shrugged.

'Butter knife? Shaving? Butcher knife?'

Aranthur shook his head. 'How would you do it for you?'

The sharpener made a face. 'Depends,' he said, a little annoyed as the line was building up. 'For cavalry fighting, I'd say butter knife, because it won't stick in the wound and it won't get ruined by a couple of hard crosses. Razor sharp is for fools – first good blow and you have a deep nick. Butcher knife...'

'I'll have butcher knife,' Aranthur said.

The cutler rolled his eyes and started sharpening. A page boy brought his *cannone*.

Back at his stall, Ringkoat was waiting.

'You know how to shoot that thing?' he asked.

'Yes, syr,' Aranthur answered.

The bannerman nodded. 'Well, come and show me.'

He led Aranthur to the far wall of the stable block, then through an iron door and along a maze of passages until they could hear both the cough of crossbows and the sharper bark of guns. They went out into the sun, and they were standing behind a long line of un-uniformed men and women with an incredible array of weapons, shooting at distant targets. They had to wait some time for a space on the line. A centark came and led them to a station, which was nothing more than a stone set in the ground with the number 339 carved in it.

'Do not leave this stone,' the man said. 'You may fire at will, but you may not leave this stone until I tell you to. If your weapon points anywhere but down the range, I will warn you once. The second time you will be removed, and punished. If you appear to threaten anyone's life, you will be shot. Is that clear?'

Aranthur felt fear, but the *Jhugj* laughed. 'I know the ropes, Claka. I'll keep him out of trouble.'

Claka shrugged and walked to the next soldier.

Aranthur opened his case and withdrew the weapon. It was well oiled, perfectly polished, and he admired it as he drew it out.

'Whoa!' Ringkoat said. 'Very nice. Where'd you get that?'

Aranthur told the story while he loaded the weapon. He took his time and was careful, and when he was done, he aimed at the distant white sack of sand, and pulled the trigger.

The lock *clatched* and the *cannone* barked instantly.

'Fine,' Ringkoat said. 'Don't make love to it. Load it.' Nonetheless the dwarf leant forward. 'That could even be my people's work.'

Aranthur loaded faster, faster and faster, through ten rounds. But it grew harder and harder to get the round balls into the muzzle as the powder fouling built up.

'Use the hammer,' Ringkoat said.

So Aranthur used the hammer to drive his bullets into the barrel. By the fifteenth shot, he was having to use the little hammer quite hard, actually striking the balls rather than pushing them.

Something inside the hammer rattled, as if something was loose. But

326

the next time he struck a ball, on round seventeen, the whole hammer was like a baby's rattle.

'What's that?' Aranthur asked.

'It's your pretty gun, not mine,' the *Jhugj* said.

He shook the hammer and the tiny rattle was barely audible over the constant pop and cough of the other weapons. He shrugged.

'Handle doesn't seem to be loose.'

Aranthur's heart was beating very fast. He took a deep breath and released it. He had to summon his *will* to stop himself from staring at the hammer. Instead he dropped the thing into his pack.

'So – you are good enough, but you need a lot of practice. Shooting that thing from horseback ... Draxos, boyo, will your horses even accept the sound?' Ringkoat shook his head. 'A lot of horses shy at the bark. I need you to practise. If you are close to me, I don't want you shooting my horse.'

Aranthur nodded. 'I'm —'

'Busy? No, you ain't. This is fucking serious – all that mumbo jumbo at your Academy is not going to get you killed. Figure you have two weeks before you get called up.' Ringkoat shrugged. 'I shouldn't ha' said as much, I suppose.'

Aranthur had the increasingly common sinking feeling that his life was spiralling out of control – that he couldn't do everything: Safiri, leather-work, practical philosophy, the militia ...

Dahlia. Who was gone – whose new coldness was more oppressive than the threat of death.

I am a fool, he thought.

Ringkoat broke into his thoughts. 'Hang your *fusil* in the stall with your charger.'

'Why?' Aranthur asked.

'Start getting the horses used to the *gonne*.' The *Jhugj* laughed. 'We will have some fine times together. You have two weeks. Get ready.'

Aranthur walked home with his arming sword on his hip and the longer, heavier blade on his shoulder, through crowds of people in House colours. There was shouting in the distance: pulses of shouting like the cries he'd heard in the hippodrome at sporting events. Just outside the precinct there was a poster, hand-lettered in paint, demanding the resignation of the Master of Arts. Aranthur couldn't make sense of what it said. It was as if the poster had been painted by someone who didn't speak Liote.

He arrived home that evening to find Drako feeding chicken soup to Sasan. Aranthur loved the smell but didn't have any. Instead he went down all the flights of stairs to get spicy fish stew with squid's ink, because the stupid poster had distracted him from getting food, and then he climbed back to eat it.

'No wonder your legs are so strong,' Drako said, after he'd washed the bowls down in the courtyard. 'Are you still friends with Kallinikos?'

'As far as I know.'

Drako looked out of the window. 'Any stock?'

Sasan laughed. 'And you think I'm an addict.' He was sober and he'd taken food. He was flipping the pages of Aranthur's *Consolations*.

'Can you read it?' Aranthur asked.

The addict shrugged. 'Yes,' he said bitterly. 'My father said that if I didn't learn to read Liote I'd waste my life.'

Aranthur nodded, surrendering. The Safian did not want conversation. He prepared a pipe for Drako and sat opposite him on a stool.

'I think I have something to show you,' he said.

Drako nodded, uninterested.

Aranthur fetched the hammer out of his shoulder bag and handed it over.

'This something you use for leather-work?' Drako wasn't immediately interested.

And then he was. All at once, like a shade being opened to bright sunlight.

'Damme, Timos. This is the hammer from your *cannone*.' He smiled wolfishly. And shook it. 'Damme. Damn my eyes.'

'I was using it today and...'

The spy was already manipulating the hammer, trying various parts.

'...and something gave, and it started to rattle. But you said that *cannone* was not the property of your agent.'

Drako paused. 'No, I said I didn't *think* it was his.'

'I can't feel any *power* inside this.'

Drako shrugged, defeated.

Aranthur looked at it, not as a soldier or a Student, but as a craftsman. After a long minute, he picked it up, turned it over, grabbed the handle, and with a huge effort, unscrewed it from the bronze head.

'It had to be made that way,' he said. 'No other way to put the head on.'

Drako wasn't listening. He was tapping the head on the cutting board, the big board on which Aranthur and his room-mates cut bread and vegetables. He played with his dagger and then with his eating pick. Suddenly, a spill of rainbow light poured out amid the breadcrumbs, and a single, glaring jewel.

'Sun. Light.' Drako shook his head. 'No fucking wonder they killed for it. It's huge.'

Aranthur had never seen a *kuria* crystal so big. Now he could feel the *power* emanating from all of them.

Something was wrong.

'Don't touch it,' Aranthur said.

His tone stopped Drako.

Sasan was looking at Aranthur, and at the breadboard.

'What the hell is that?' he asked.

Drako whistled. 'It is a fortune in *kuria*.'

Aranthur was using his talent. He reached out and tasted his own *kuria* crystal and then . . .

'Ouch,' he said aloud, because the pain was almost physical. 'The big one is charged – it is carrying a heavy *working*. And the little ones . . .'

Drako nodded. 'I feel it too.'

Sasan whistled. 'That's a lot of rock.'

Drako swept all the crystals into a leather pouch with his gloved hand.

'I'll look after these,' he said.

In heartbeats, all they had of him was the sound of his feet pounding down the steps.

Sasan laughed. 'You trust him?'

Aranthur shrugged. 'Yes.'

'Weren't those crystals yours?' the Safian asked.

Aranthur shrugged. His life had become sufficiently event-filled as to seem unreal.

Drako's footsteps grew more distant.

That same evening, Ansu arrived with as little ceremony as he had left. He arrived with two servants, both Byzas. They were palace equerries out of their usual scarlet and blue uniforms, and they carried six heavy cases up the stairs, and then, without being asked, cleaned the whole set of rooms top to bottom. The blond man left while the pale dark-haired man swept and washed, and returned with four sets of magnificent leather and velvet bed hangings and an oil painting of an Arnaut regiment of the Old Empire, all on horseback, breaking into the feared Attian *Yaniceri* infantry.

Aranthur loved the painting at first sight. The servant hung it on a hook already in place. He and his partner hung the bed curtains, and then proceeded to prepare a small dinner of chicken on the hearth.

'Can we keep them?' Sasan said. 'This is better than your magik.'

Ansu chuckled. 'We might perhaps engage them once a week, but this is a favour.'

The blond man bowed. 'It is my pleasure. The Emperor cannot have the Prince of Zhou living in . . .' He looked around.

'Squalor?' Sasan asked. 'Who are you?' he asked Ansu.

'Ansu,' the prince answered. 'And you?'

'Sasan Dhahamet Khuy,' the addict said. '*Thuryx* addict. Former nobleman.'

'Ahh,' Ansu said with interest. '*Thuryx*. Delightful if shared with a sexual partner.'

Sasan threw back his head and laughed.

The next day, Aranthur arrived at the Great Hall to find a student protest in the courtyard. He recognised Sirnan and some of the other Lions, but he pushed through without much trouble and got into Edvin's office by a side corridor, served *quaveh*, and sat to practise his calligraphy.

Edvin was late coming in and had a black eye. He cursed darkly, and drank his *quaveh*. After some furious copying, he looked over his empty cup at Aranthur.

'Did they trouble you?' he asked.

Aranthur shook his head. 'No, I went through them.'

'You know what they want, don't you? The Lions and the Reds?'

'No,' Aranthur said. 'Or yes, but tell me anyway.'

'They want the Master of Arts to resign so that she can be replaced by a male representative of one of their Houses.' Edvin shrugged. 'Don't you follow politics? She has a seat on the Seventeen. She's a non-aristocratic woman. They want her gone.'

'Gods,' Aranthur said.

I already know more than I want to know, he thought.

Edvin shook his head. 'It's the hawks, the same bastards who want war with Atti, or maybe the Iron Ring, or Masr, or maybe all three.' He sighed. 'Bastards like Roaris, who want everything to be run by aristos. I like her. She's stable.'

Aranthur had never imagined the Master of Arts was a political figure, but he realised he was, as usual, thinking like a farmer. Of course she was – she controlled the second or third most powerful institution in the largest city in the world.

'She asked for a larger part of the Imperial budget to raise the number of women who are scholars,' Edvin said. 'How can you not know this?'

'I've been busy.'

Then Edvin fell silent, because the woman in question appeared, seized her magikally hot *quaveh*, and then, a moment later, summoned Aranthur.

'I know all about your crystals,' she said. 'And Drako says you killed again. Let me be brief – it is a good day for everyone having a crisis. I spoke to Drako at length. The crystals are under study.' She shrugged. 'I may not be in this office in a few days, Aranthur.' She gave him a long look. 'I am sorry, what I have to say is hard. If I go, I strongly recommend that you consider continuing your research on the grimoire and on the language of Safi ... elsewhere. Perhaps privately. Perhaps Syr Drako will fund you.' She looked out of her window and then back at him. 'Do you know what I'm talking about?'

Aranthur was busy trying to keep himself together. It was worse than a sword bout with sharps because this had a different reality. In a burst of emotion he realised how much he loved her office, her careful instruction, and even her temper.

'Ma donna,' he muttered. 'How can I continue...?'

She shrugged. 'My successor will not fund any Eastern research, unless it directly supports military efforts against Atti. These idiots think that war with Atti will solve *anything*.' She sighed.

'But the Emperor's manuscript... The magikal reader...' He shook his head.

She raised an eyebrow. 'Officially, the Emperor plays no role in the politics of the City. Unofficially, I believe you will find that you can work in the Emperor's personal library.' She shrugged. 'You may find me there. I will try and get you a writ, today or tomorrow. I believe that's all the time I have. I worry that when the Seventeen know what we are doing here, they might order your arrest.' She rose. 'I have to say, because I am a believer and I believe in the roles of the gods in the lives of people, that you are indirectly responsible for my fall. When you helped prevent the Duke of Volta from retaking his city, you forced him to play different cards. Now he's using the political hawks and religious conservatives to unseat me on his way to forcing us into war with Atti. And my communications with the republican government in Volta are suddenly considered treasonous.' Her amusement was genuine. 'It's never the thing you think. Money to educate women? I could bury them at the Council of Seventeen. But "Foreign Disclosure of Privileged Magik" sounds very like treason.'

'Oh, by the Lady,' Aranthur said. 'That's ... Gods! Terrible.'

She shrugged. 'For what it is worth, I think he meant to bring me down all along, and that he always meant to push us to war with Atti. War with Atti! We haven't faced the Sultan in the field in seventy years. It's insane. Our whole trade is with Atti.' She shrugged.

'I feel I should have been following all this instead of studying Safian magik,' Aranthur said bitterly.

She shook her head. 'Our only hope is to understand the East. 'War with Atti – even Atti seems to want it. They are calling up their militia today, according to Drako. There's a rumour at court that a whole army moved into the Black Lands north of Tanais the day before yesterday, headed here. Can you imagine?' She held out her hand. 'I'm sorry. We live in interesting times. If I am forced to resign today, I'll see that you have a writ on the Imperial library delivered to your rooms. Please do not come back. Please, and I beg you, do not even allow the new incumbent to know what you were doing, or he'll ...' She frowned. 'At best he'll arrest you. At worst ... He'll take you for his own projects.'

Aranthur rose. 'I am *so sorry*.'

'Do not be sorry for me,' she said. 'Be sorry for all the Easterner refugees and all the people in the East who are facing extinction. For the Dhadhi. For the *Jhugi*. The drakes.' She met his eye. 'And *please* stop killing people.'

'I'm not offered a great deal of choice.'

She shrugged. 'It's not a wives' tale. Killing interferes with your *power*. At one level, it clouds the mind ...'

'I've felt that!' Aranthur said.

'At another level, the one absolute requirement for non-*kuria* casting is empathy. Killing erodes your empathy. I know whereof I speak.' She sat, shoulders slumped. 'I wish I had more time. I don't. If this all goes, please work with Syr Drako. If you have a crisis, go see the Lightbringer, Kurvenos.'

'Yes, Magistera.'

She smiled. 'Go with the gods, Timos.'

Aranthur went home to find Sasan sober, and reading. He had all of Aranthur's school books in an untidy stack and he was working through them. Aranthur resented his treatment of the books, which had cost him time and trouble and silver to accumulate, but his irritation was buried by his delight that Sasan was clean and sober.

They went out together, because Aranthur didn't need to work. He took the Safian to the used clothes market on the wharves, and they prowled until they bought the man some clothes: several doublets and pairs of hose, a short cloak. It was Drako's money, and Aranthur didn't count the obols. Boots, a belt, a hat . . .

'I'll be back on *thuryx* before I wear all this,' Sasan said. 'By Rani, I want it now. Every moment.'

Aranthur nodded. 'Well, we should keep walking.'

Sasan was an uneasy companion. He would stop and look at mosaics, or men repainting a building-front fresco; he would stop to urinate in an alley, something Aranthur would never do; he chatted with every Armean or Safian street seller. Now that he was dressed as a tradesman or a Student, the Armeans were surprised at his fluency, and almost distressingly respectful.

He gave one of Drako's silver crosses to a girl with a pox-ravaged face and shook his head.

'Bone plague,' he said.

'What the Darkness is bone plague?' Aranthur said.

He was frustrated at the stops, at the time everything took, at his own fears that Sasan was talking so fast to conceal what he was saying, at his tension over whether they were followed. He saw two men; he couldn't decide if he had seen them at the Academy.

Sasan glanced at him from under his heavy black eyebrows.

'You don't know? Drako thinks you do.'

'Drako is a very strange man,' Aranthur allowed.

'It's fairly new. It only seems to affect the poor. Their bones melt. They soften, their lungs fail and they drown. Sometimes other, worse things happen. Sometimes they rot while they are still alive.' He grunted. 'I'll find you a beggar who has it.'

He began to lead the way up the ridge, towards the Pinnacle.

'No need!' Aranthur said.

Sasan shook his head. 'No, you need to see.'

Aranthur dug in his heels. 'You are going to buy *thuryx*. And I have seen it. I just didn't know it had a name.'

The two young men stared at each other.

'Do you play dice?' Aranthur asked, suddenly inspired.

Sasan raised a black eyebrow. 'I have been known to gamble,' he said slowly. Then he shrugged. 'I do mean to buy *thuryx*.' He raised both eyebrows. 'You know other addicts?'

Aranthur thought of his uncle, and wine.

'Yes,' he said.

He hadn't thought of his uncle for a long time.

Aranthur led the way to a tavern that had dice tables. Sasan looked around.

'Light and Sun,' he said. 'I used to love this kind of place.'

Aranthur took one of the tiny gold sequins and broke it into silver crosses, and then into some bronze obols, and together they approached a table.

'You look like a fuckin' Arnaut to me,' said a big man in a greasy leather jerkin. 'I don't play with fuckin' Souli. Go somewhere else.'

Aranthur had the same feeling of shock and anger that he always had, but he shook his head and went to another table.

'What'd he say?' Sasan asked.

'He doesn't like my kind,' Aranthur said.

Sasan laughed. 'Sunlight! I'm with you, and he doesn't like *your* kind? Best joke ever.'

The end table wasn't so particular. Men were playing for low stakes; a slattern was serving weak beer and showing a shapely belly button every time she swayed.

'I could bring you luck,' she said to Sasan.

He handed her a silver coin.

She smiled up at him, and put the coin on the dirty felt. Dice were rolled.

The coin vanished.

'Dark Night!' she spat.

'Try again,' Sasan said.

'Use smaller coins?' Aranthur suggested.

'Are you always this cautious?' Sasan asked.

Aranthur thought of shooting the bandit. 'No.'

Sasan laughed. 'Damn, I feel alive. Win for me, honey.'

She put another whole silver cross down on a single number. There were six dice. The scores were many and varied and any Student knew how little the scores had to do with the mathematics of the odds.

Aranthur put five obols on a different number. His was a multiple of six. The dice had six sides. It seemed to him that the number eighteen and the odds of rolling six dice were better than the odds charged.

'Now we're playing,' Sasan said. In Safiri, he said 'Let all the Gods witness!'

The dice came up eighteen

The silver cross vanished, but Aranthur's five obols became thirty obols, or three crosses.

'Maybe I'm bringing *you* luck,' the girl said to Aranthur.

'He has plenty of luck already,' Sasan said. 'Help me.'

They put down bets. Other men moved back; in a matter of a few bets, the table was theirs. They played, and the girl, who was clearly very quick, began to follow Aranthur's pattern of betting. The house's odds were out of step with the actual odds, and Aranthur's hurried calculations would lead to his placement. She followed him, a bet or two behind.

In twenty bets they had made a pile of markers. They didn't always win, and an hour later, they lost two thirds of their winnings. Sasan began to bet on his own.

Two big men, both Easterners, came and stood watching, arms crossed.

'Maybe you should not always bet on these numbers,' the shorter man said, very politely, in Liote.

'Maybe you should stay silent,' Sasan said in fluid Armean.

The two bouncers, for so they obviously were, looked at each other.

Aranthur had just won. He'd put down three bets and collected on one at odds of seven to one. The girl had also won. She was positively glowing. Sasan was the calmest that Aranthur had ever seen him – his face still, his hands unshaking.

'Perhaps you should stop playing at this table,' said the tall bouncer.

Aranthur nodded. 'I'll cash out. Let's have dinner.'

Sasan nodded. 'Never count your winnings at the table.'

Aranthur made his way to the change table. He was cautious, but no one accosted him. The bored man at the table changed his pile of wooden beads into bronze and silver, and then into gold – sixteen sequins. And Sasan had more – at least another dozen gold sequins.

'We won too much,' Sasan said at his elbow. 'You know how to fight, right?'

'Yes,' Aranthur said.

'Good, because I'm weak and those two are coming after us. I promise.' The addict sighed. 'Sunlight, once I could have dropped them both. No muscle left.'

'You look good to me, sweet,' the girl said. 'Do I get a tip?'

Sasan handed her five gold sequins.

Aranthur wondered if the young woman was going to faint.

'Oh, Dierdre!' she said, invoking the Iron Ring's goddess of carnality.

'Better come with us,' Sasan said. 'They'll roll you for it, or worse.'

Outside it was dark. Aranthur put his half-cloak on.

'What's your name?' Sasan asked.

'Maddie,' she said. 'I'm from Paona. You know it?'

Sasan smiled his small smile. 'No, honey, I'm an Easterner.'

She laughed. 'Oh, well. Suddenly everyone's an Easterner, right?' She looked back. 'There's only two of them. We could take 'em.'

Aranthur took a breath. 'Canal,' he said.

He looked around – for foot traffic, for a City Militia post, for anything.

Instead, he saw narrow streets in Upper Town, and a beggar. There was a scuffle in the darkness behind them. A shout, and the ring of blades.

'What the seven frozen hells?' Sasan asked.

Aranthur grabbed both of them and pulled them into a stumbling run for the Coryn Steps, the long staircase that wound down the side of the old temple, from the dens of vice down to the respectable canalside neighbourhoods.

He led them into the square in front of the magnificent old temple that rose like a man-made mountain. Below twinkled the lights of the hippodrome, and beyond that the coloured crystal of the spire of the palace. Right before them, beside the temple's massive curtain wall, ran a long flight of steps towards the more prosperous parts of the city.

'Shit,' Sasan said. 'Now there are four of them. What the fuck?'

There were shapes on the stairs, in the dark.

Aranthur took out his knife – a Arnaut knife, longer than a man's hand from wrist to fingertips.

'Know how to use this?' he asked Sasan.

'Like an old friend,' the Safian said, taking it.

Aranthur drew his sword.

Immediately the shapes on the lower steps paused.

The steps were perhaps as wide as four men abreast, and there were sixty or seventy stone steps, with niches meant to house bronze statues – most of them long since stolen – and beautiful cherry trees, almost invisible in the dark. There was a little light: the light of both moons, and the distant twinkle of the lights from the old temple that towered above, and the lights in the hippodrome below, and the starlight that was as bright as late spring could make it.

'Fuck,' Sasan muttered. 'مبهق, ر دام,'

Aranthur glanced back. There were three men up above, crossing the Temple Square with purpose.

'Can we talk about this?' Aranthur shouted.

No one slowed down, above or below.

Maddie, the Northern woman, was made of stern stuff.

'I can handle myself,' she said. 'Let's get 'em!'

'Don't get gutted for a few coins,' Aranthur said.

But these were no common footpads, and the men below them closed first.

Aranthur took a breath to steady himself, and moved. He wanted to talk, but they were coming; the range closed, and . . .

He cut. His cut was deliberately deceptive, from behind his back. He was calm enough. He'd now done this half a dozen times and he didn't pause to think. He flowed along, and then he turned because he'd heard something, and thrust deep into a man's gut. It was the bloody-faced man, from the duel by the canal, which made no sense. He folded over Aranthur's sword and then slid off it.

Sasan had just killed another man, with the knife. The blood was

337

black in the moonlight, and ran down the steps like water over a waterfall. There were still three living men on the steps with them.

Sasan rolled his wrist, flourishing the curved sword he now had in his hand with expert dexterity.

'You never forget,' the Safian said distantly.

The three bravos kept their distance.

'Run away!' Aranthur shouted at them.

One of the downed men was gurgling.

'Dark Sun!' spat Sasan. 'It's a woman.'

She tried to speak and coughed.

The three men in the darkness were talking to each other in accented Liote mixed with Armean.

'I hate hurting women,' Sasan said.

Maddie bent down and stabbed the wounded woman in the temple with an eating knife.

'Let's go,' Aranthur said. 'There could be more. This is quite a wolf pack for a few gold sequins.'

Sasan looked at Aranthur. 'They want you, brother. It's not the money.' He shrugged. 'Or it started as money and now ... They know your name. I can hear them.'

Aranthur led the way down the steps. The two in front of him backed away, and he continued along the muddy upper reaches of the Green Canal. He didn't look back. He watched the men in front.

Then they ran.

Aranthur was fairly sure where they were. On the wrong side of the City from his rooms, with the Academy south and west, and the Pinnacle equidistant to the east. The old temple towered above them, a blank wall of ancient stone rising like a mountain above the long steps.

He looked back. The bodies lay above them on the steps. And now there were other shapes moving – men in cloaks.

Sasan looked back. 'I think we'd better run,' he said.

Aranthur nodded. The three of them ran along the canal, but Aranthur knew he'd end up in the spice market that way – another dangerous area. He certainly didn't want the Pinnacle; that meant doubling back and leading them through the Precinct.

He turned left into a cross street, and then across a narrow bridge over the Blue Canal. Behind them were armed men, swords like pale magiks in their hands, and then they were looking at armed people, men and women – dozens of them in what appeared to be a battle.

Aranthur came to a stop in mid-bridge.

'Who the fuck?' Sasan panted. He was already blown, and he stood and heaved. Maddie was not tired. She looked back.

'Sorry, boys,' she said. 'You *do* know how to show a girl a good time, but I don't want to die with you.'

She flashed Sasan a smile and kissed him on the lips. And then leapt off the bridge into the canal.

Aranthur looked down to see her swimming powerfully, a lithe shape, pale in the darkness.

The people fighting ahead of him were aristocrats. The men behind were growing less cautious.

'Don't kill anyone unless they attack you,' he told Sasan.

He dragged the other man across the bridge while wiping his sword clean with a scrap of linen from his purse. He threw the scrap in the canal as one line of swordsmen broke the other and men and women ran in every direction, including straight at him.

He let the combatants go past – a glint of steel and frightened eyes in the darkness – and Sasan and Aranthur shrank against the stone balustrade of the bridge.

'Come on,' Aranthur shouted when the flood of panicked nobles was past.

He led Sasan along the balustrade at the edge of the canal. It was a good neighbourhood here, and there was a body on the ground.

'What in the Darkness?' Aranthur spat.

'You know what you're doing, right?' Sasan wheezed. But he grinned. 'Hey, it's hours since I thought of *thuryx*. You planned this to get me clean, right?'

Both men grinned.

There was a clack and clash of blade on blade, the swish and swash of a buckler blocking blows off to the right. Aranthur tried to go left, away from the fighting, and found that his guess was completely wrong. Instead of running clear, the two turned a corner under someone's flowering orange tree and ran straight into the back of a chaotic melee. He drew his sword into a high *garde*, parried a blow that had very little intent to it, stepped in and threw the attacker to the ground, and then he and Sasan were in a stone arch, back to back with two other men

339

and fighting for their lives. There were cuts, and more cuts, and a pair of thrusts that Aranthur was amazed he saw, much less parried. He was hit on the thigh and felt the warm wetness that meant blood. He seemed to be fighting automatically, his arm with a mind of its own. It was nothing like fencing – there was no subtlety here. He parried.

Sasan was breathing like a bellows, but he used the hook of his hard-won Eastern sword to cut a man behind his knee and the man screamed and fell. The fight made no sense; the man whose back was a warm presence behind Aranthur was a total stranger, and the two men whose swords he was parrying were equally strange and not in House colours he even knew.

Aranthur crossed his nearer opponent, and, as the man raised his hands, kicked him hard in the crotch. The man fell with a choked sound and Aranthur cut, hard, and a-purpose, into his other opponent's sword from off line. He carried it to the ground, stepped in, and slammed his pommel into the man's head. He was trying not to kill.

The man dropped.

Aranthur turned, but Sasan was already safe, breathing like a race-horse after a race, and he whirled just as the man behind him parried and stepped back.

Aranthur stepped in beside him and the man's opponent turned and ran.

'Damme,' said his ally. 'Thought you was my brother, what?'

The man was wearing a domino, a half mask, with a White badge pinned to it over complex House colours – red and blue. They shone clearly in the torchlight of the gate.

The man laughed with relief. 'Whoever you are, I owe you.'

Aranthur bowed. 'Your servant, syr.'

'Damme,' said the stranger. 'Like a storybook, what?' He had the accent of privilege and money. 'What House?'

Aranthur shook his head. 'Student,' he said. 'Timos.'

'Klinos,' said the stranger. 'Always at your service, syr.' The man, apparently of House Klinos, one of the oldest and poorest, got a shoulder under a wounded companion. 'For the Whites, what?'

Sasan laughed.

'Black or White?' the man asked.

'What is this all about?' Aranthur asked.

'Damned if I know,' the other man said. 'Someone slept with

someone else's wife and there was blood. To be honest, I'm not even sure what side my sword is supposed to back, but I'm sure it's all for honour.' He laughed bitterly.

'I'm neither Black nor White,' Aranthur said. 'And I'm certainly not a Lion.'

'Maybe we should form our own faction, then,' the man said with a bitter smile.

Aranthur shook his head. 'It's all insane,' he said.

He was thinking about the House war and the student protest and the calls for the resignation of the Master of Arts. It was as if the whole world had gone mad.

His new friend hoisted his relative and led him back through the arch and across the bridge.

The men who had been following Aranthur were nowhere to be seen.

'Dark Sun,' Sasan wheezed. He was laughing. 'Damme,' he said, mimicking the accent. 'I might just stay sober, just to see what the fuck you get up to. That was fun.'

Aranthur put an arm around the addict and started him toward the Precinct, and home.

'Fun?'

Sasan panted for a while.

'Yes,' he said. 'Can we go back? I want the girl.'

Aranthur might have laughed, but he was working too hard. He got Sasan around a second riot and began climbing towards the Precinct.

'The girl?'

'I haven't wanted a woman in a year. Oh, by the Twelve.' But he began to walk on his own. 'I'm wiped out,' the Easterner said. 'Sunlight, brother, I don't even like the smell of my sweat.'

Aranthur paused to think and saw a man in a leather jerkin. The torches on the outside of a private home shone on the greasy garment, and Aranthur knew him from the gambler's tavern.

He thought of Drako's words. Two places, well apart, different backgrounds. He wished, very hard, for Drako to appear like a troop of cavalry.

'They're still following us,' he said to Sasan.

He pulled the Safian into an alley as narrow as a man's shoulders, between a tall private house and a glover's shop. It was full of decaying hides, rejects from the glover, and it smelled worse than a jakes.

'Then I'm going to die here,' the Safian muttered. He still had the curved sword in his hand. 'Smells bad.'

'Where'd the sword come from? Aranthur asked, considering his options.

They were below the Founder's Square and from the sounds, the square was full of late-night protestors, or perhaps just revellers. The seriousness of his situation was settling in, but the action had freed something in his head, too. He realised that he had been running for his room as if that would protect him – that he really was half-expecting Drako to appear.

'I took it from the first bastard who jumped us,' Sasan panted. 'Didn't think to take the scabbard.'

'More fool you. They were Easterners.'

'What does that even mean? Easterner? You know, to us, the Zhouians are Easterners?' Sasan breathed in and out, heavily. 'There are quite a few of them,' he panted. 'Four? Six?'

Aranthur made some decisions. 'I'm going to cast a *working* on you,' he said. 'You'll feel better. Fresh. Fast. Strong.'

'You are full of surprises,' Sasan said. 'It sounds like *thuryx*.'

Aranthur had no focus, no talisman, and he was standing in a stinking alley with men hunting him. Luckily he'd had some practice casting in difficult conditions.

He dropped into his concentration routine. He found his crystal wind, and sang to it softly, in Safiri. He pictured the calligraphy, imagined the pen, dipping into the wind of power *and writing on reality in beautiful, sweeping strokes of fire.*

He released his creation: the climax of sex; the moment the sword slid free of a parry and punched into flesh; the moment the dice show the number the gambler chose.

It was, of course, his Safian spell, and it worked.

Sasan's eye almost burned with potency.

'I am the fucking *Sun*!' shouted Sasan. 'Oh, gods, that's a rush.'

The addict charged out into the darkened street, the very last thing Aranthur had anticipated. He followed.

The Safian met the first two pursuers at a dead run. His curved blade cut, was parried, and Sasan's next step carried him past his first opponent even as his sword hand rotated and rose. The curved point rolled in and around his opponent's straight blade and pecked him in the neck. The bravo fell, clutching the side of his throat and Sasan cut back, through the other pursuer's guard and over his hilt. The man dropped his sword and fell to one knee, where Aranthur knocked him flat with a knee to the head.

Leather Jerkin raised a puffer that gleamed malevolently in the darkness, but he miscalculated Sasan's speed. The Easterner slammed into him, knocked him flat, and cut the fourth man in the side before he could draw his weapon.

Sasan shrieked and kicked Leather Jerkin in the head, so that his long puffer skittered across the cobbles. Aranthur pounced on it. It was loaded, but the hammer wasn't cocked.

Aranthur had to guard against a cut. Another assailant had a big sword, a long, two-handed blade, and he cut hard, overhead, whirled it up and cut again, fast. Aranthur tried to make the cover that Master Sparthos taught for this very situation, but the man's blows were so hard he couldn't drop them off his own blade to retaliate. He backed, tripped over the man he'd kneed in the head, and fell.

Long Sword leapt forward, sword rising. Sasan flew in under the blade, close as a lover, and there was the loud crack of a bone breaking. Then a heavy crunch as a shoulder dislocated, and then the long sword clattered in the street. The man bellowed in pain.

Aranthur lay almost still; he'd hit his head on the cobbles and nothing was working.

Sasan stood over him, his *shamshir* dripping blood.

'Coryn's angels,' he said, in rapid Safiri. 'I am like a god of war.'

'We have to follow them,' Aranthur whispered.

Long Sword roared again and Sasan casually kicked him in the head. The kick was too fast to follow, and the man's neck snapped and he dropped, dead. His Lion badge showed on the back of his cap.

Sasan giggled. 'Oops,' he said.

Aranthur muttered.

'Who?' Sasan asked.

'The footpads,' Aranthur said. 'We need to follow them.'

Sasan had a dark eldritch glow about him. 'Whatever you like, master of Dark Arts. If I'd known you could make me feel like this . . . I can conquer the world.'

He gave Aranthur a hand up. Then the two of them went off down the side street, following the running men, leaving the corpses in the street.

The two running men didn't stop until they had run almost to the Lonika gate, all the way along the waterfront. Aranthur had a stitch in his side; Sasan ran as if he could run all night.

'I can run them down,' Sasan said.

'No. I want to see where they go.'

Aranthur was playing a guessing game, running on side streets. At the first canal, he led Sasan north, up the spine towards the western wall of the Precinct, and then across the canal by the upper bridge to come down on their opponents from the north. The two fleeing men were in sight as they crossed the southern bridge and again at an intersection. Sasan moved like lightning and Aranthur moved from shadow to shadow. But at the Lonika Gate, Aranthur lost them; there was a crowd of aristocrats and some soldiers who were clearly disarming them. The two bravos had vanished.

Aranthur stood bent over, panting with frustration.

Sasan smiled. 'Will I pay for all this tomorrow?'

'I expect so,' Aranthur said.

'Best enjoy it, then. Like *thuryx*. I'll see if I can run them down.'

He set off at a sprint; faster than a racehorse, up a side street.

Aranthur went straight across the square, alone. He moved through parked military wagons, avoiding the line of soldiers. It was clear the House fighting had spread to the gate, and that this noble house had tried to block the soldiers from moving the wagons. Then Aranthur was on the opposite side, moving along the broad avenue that ran up the spine under the Aqueduct. He was reasonably sure of his notion that the men were Easterners and lived in the camp on the Pinnacle. It struck him that this was stupid; on the other hand, he'd just escaped death at least three times, and he felt invincible.

But he could not see anything, nor hear anything, to suggest that he was right. With every step he took up the spine, he worried that he was leaving Sasan to his own. So, after listening to the temples ring the hour, he turned back west and retraced his steps. He was coming down the long ramp under the aqueduct bridge when he heard men coming, and ducked behind a buttress.

'Bastard has the luck of the Gambler,' came a disembodied voice.

'Goddess has a thousand hands to chastise,' said the other. 'Be civil and modest, Juwad.'

'What the hells was that thing? It was like a spectre.' He sounded young, and shaken. 'We have lost half an army tonight.'

'It was a man,' said the other. 'Only a man, but the Servant will not be pleased. We were not told . . .' He shook his head.

Aranthur let them go by. They were quite close – perhaps two arm's lengths. But there was not enough light to see them by.

'Will the Servant punish us?' asked Juwad.

The older voice was soothing. 'The Servant only punishes disobedience and heresy, Juwad. We have lost blood in honest war. I do not think we can be faulted.'

Aranthur thought that the soothing voice was trying to reassure itself.

'Yet the thief lives.' Juwad sounded truly regretful.

'Not for many breaths. The Disciple's reach is long, I promise you. And the Master's reach is longer still.'

Aranthur moved as cautiously as he could behind them. They were under the Aqueduct now, surrounded on both sides by hundreds of rude shacks and small clapboard houses, some quite permanent, most terrible in their simplicity. The smell of human waste was overwhelming; the alleys and streets were almost empty.

'Why does the Master not send the Bone Plague to eat him?' Juwad asked. 'By the saints, my hand hurts.'

'Keep your pain inside,' the older voice said. 'We are the strong. We do not whimper.'

'Yes, syr,' Juwad said, as they passed along the long line of sutlers and temporary taverns, all closed and shuttered.

Aranthur had never been under the Aqueduct at this hour. Far from dangerous, it seemed more like a graveyard or an abandoned theatre. He had little cover, though, and he began to fall back, giving them distance, heart beating with excitement.

The two men surprised him by turning north, towards the sea and the spice market. They began to descend from the Aqueduct and the poor neighbourhoods, and they took a winding street like a spiral staircase that wound through a semicircle while going down from almost the Pinnacle to virtually the seaside. Aranthur had never been in the area, but the long crescent was perfect for following them. He could walk carefully and watch his quarry. For their part, they never looked back and both men seemed to feel secure – far more worried about the Servant than about the possibility of pursuit.

'But the soldiers were suspicious!' Juwad hissed.

'They are suspicious of all Easterners,' the older man said. 'As we want them to be. The worse they treat the Armeans, the readier the Armeans will be to our will. How often have I told you this?'

The two men turned into an alley, and Aranthur had to stop. He was under the eaves of a roof, and he realised that there was a fire ladder to an upper balcony.

He threw caution to the winds and climbed. The ladder was a pole with cross rungs lashed on with cord; it was old, and rickety, and the rungs squeaked. He went up as softly as he could.

'Let us in, Carun!' spat Juwad.

'What happened?' asked a deeper voice.

'We failed to kill the Thief,' Juwad said. 'Now what?'

The door closed, and Aranthur heard no more. But he marked the house; it wasn't hard, because even by moonlight, it was clearly the most run-down house in a decent neighbourhood. The door posts were marked with broken crosses, an ancient sign among the aristocratic families.

Aranthur climbed back down his rickety fire ladder. He reached the bottom without mishap, and then something moved and there was a hand over his mouth.

He awoke in mud and darkness. He was icy cold, his bones ached, and he had dirt in his mouth. Nothing made sense to him, including the pain in his head...

'Awake,' a voice said in Armean.

Hollow footsteps above him, and someone with *power*, casting.

'Hello,' said a cheerful voice above him. A candle-lantern appeared hung on a rope, dangling through a trapdoor.

He said nothing.

'Hello,' said the cheerful voice. 'Tell us what we want to know and everything will be easy. Are you Aranthur Timos?'

'Let me kick the shit out of him,' said another voice, in Armean.

'Later,' said Cheerful Voice. 'Are you Aranthur Timos?' He paused. 'Is he unconscious?' in Armean.

'He is awake,' said a woman. She was obviously a caster. She sounded afraid.

'Are you sure? You're such a useless bitch, I'm never sure of anything you say.'

Cheerful Voice said something else, as if he'd turned his head away from the trapdoor. The sound wasn't enough for Aranthur to hear.

He was wondering about sound, and alertness.

They were going to torture him. That was obvious.

'Let me burn his skin,' said the other voice. 'As they burn us with their gunpowder.'

'This has merit,' said Cheerful Voice. 'I ask again: are you Aranthur Timos?' The voice spoke in Liote. 'Only good will come of your answering.'

'Of course he's Timos,' said the would-be torturer. 'Who else would he be?'

'There were two of them, all evening,' said Cheerful Voice. 'And I do not want to summon the Servant and be wrong. Do you? Woman? Can you determine his identity?'

'With study and time to cast,' she said.

'Always time. Always more time. A woman's way. I need a solution now.'

'Cut his prick. I hear it makes a man talk very quickly.' That was Juwad. 'He's the one who cut my hand.' A pause. 'I think.'

Aranthur felt he was going to vomit. The compendium of fears was enormous. His cheek was lying in cold mud and he lacked the will to raise his head.

The trapdoor opened.

A young man dropped through, and cursed as his expensively booted feet hit the mud.

'No blasphemy. Blasphemy is for the weak,' said Cheerful Voice.

One of the boots kicked Aranthur in the head.

Aranthur came to a sort of consciousness of his surroundings very gradually: the commonality of multiple fractal wakenings; the reality of pain; the feeling that the very air he was breathing was fear. He felt fear first, and then pain, and then he gradually became aware of his surroundings – a big room, the walls painted with old, simple geometric frescos. The work had been precise; the diamonds of magenta that ran all along the wall were neat and orderly. They only became misshapen towards the floorboards, where the plaster bulged from some hasty repair a hundred years before. Outside a window it was dark, but the window only had a dozen intact panes, and the rest of the openings were covered in small squares of pasteboard, discoloured by rain, or stuffed with rags.

There was a taste in his mouth – no, in his head. There was a colour in his head.

That wasn't right either. But there was something – a smell or taste or sound at the very edge of his awareness . . .

A *compulsion*.

As soon as he thought it, he knew it. It was very similar in structure to Iralia's *compulsion*, but anchored, as it was, on fear and pain and his captors, he had little trouble shedding it. He was cautious, in fact, about the way he broke it; they had a woman who was a magiker. He had felt her, heard her.

'So,' said an educated Liote voice. 'Who is he?'

'We think he's Aranthur Timos, syr. But we cannot be sure. He will not talk. Lys put a *compulsion* on him; he should want to speak now.' The speaker was Cheerful Voice.

'Give me his purse,' said Educated Voice. 'Ah. A writ permitting the bearer, Aranthur Timos, student of the Academy in Megara, to bear a sword in public. Were you, perhaps, all too drunk to search his purse? Or was it more fun to beat him?'

Silence.

'And your caster is so foolish that she imagines that a beaten man will accept a *compulsion* from his tormenters? Where is she?'

'Lys doesn't like to watch,' Cheerful Voice said.

'That speaks well for her, don't you think?' Educated Voice said. 'Fetch her.'

There was the brush of a shoulder pushing through a blanket. Aranthur couldn't turn his head; something very painful had happened in his right shoulder. He was tied to a chair. The ropes that bound him were pulled very tight and a good deal of the circulation to his hands was cut off.

A man came into his peripheral vision. He pulled up a chair, reversed it, and sat comfortably with his arms on the chair back.

'Aranthur Timos,' he said. 'What a lot of trouble you have caused.'

Aranthur was looking at the husband from Kallinikos' duel. He knew him immediately.

'It is a pity how badly they have beaten you.'

The man had a blond beard and very pale blond hair, but somehow he carried Darkness in him, or so it appeared to Aranthur's sight. His eyes were almost black.

'I don't suppose you'd convert?' The man smiled. 'We don't have many converts in the City, yet, and you are, at least, intelligent. Some of my allies are the merest riff-raff, I must confess.'

Through the parched desert of his mouth, Aranthur managed to croak, 'Convert?'

Darkblond Man steepled his fingers. 'I am a Servant of the Disciples. All of us serve the Master.' He nodded. 'No doubt your so-called friends have told you nothing about us, or spread their lies about our purpose. But we seek nothing less than the salvation of the world. Magik, as we know it, is being destroyed. The winds of magik are seeping away, wasted by little people and little ideas. We would save what is left and use it for the benefit of everyone.'

Aranthur croaked.

'Oh, the magik is very definitely leaving us. Ask anyone. Ask your precious Emperor why the Aeronaut in the top of the palace never flies any more. Men used to *fly*. Ask the so-called scholars of the Academy where their great works of *occulta* are – they fritter their powers on healing and fire-making.' He shrugged. 'But you are peasant born, an Arnaut. Remarkable, for such a mongrel – and I am a realist. I am all too aware that Lys, no matter how blue her blood, is a weak vessel, and you, my robust farm animal, have much better access to *power*. But we have room for you, Timos. My ancestors believed that war and the life of arms can ennoble. The Disciples now teach that the only true nobility is in the access and exercise of *power*. Can you work without a talisman, Timos?'

Arthur shook his head. 'No,' he managed.

He was lying, because he had an idea. And because he'd seldom hated anyone at first sight, but hate was working for him just then.

'Ah, what a disappointment,' Darkblond Man said. 'Then I don't really need you after all, do I? Which is as well, I think. Juwad is almost sexually excited to beat you – depressing, really. And I, of course, view you as an abettor of my wife's fall from grace. Did you ever meet my wife?'

'Yes,' Aranthur said.

Darkblond Man stopped talking. 'You did?' Almost instantly, his face changed; his calm shattered. He stood. 'Did you fuck her too, Arnaut pig?'

His stick, which Aranthur hadn't seen, snapped out like a sword cut and hit Aranthur in the temple.

He didn't quite go all the way out. The pain was remarkable.

'Answer me,' the voice hissed.

'No.'

'But you wanted to!'

Aranthur was struggling to breathe. He began to explore his own body, ignoring the man with the stick. His legs were tightly bound but bound to the chair; his arms, crossed behind him and tied, were also bound to the chair, and the pain in his shoulder was from the bindings.

It was quite clear they were going to kill him.

Desperate moments call for desperate measures.

He had a great deal of trouble making a plan. Nothing came at first; just a broken wagon wheel of thoughts that raced round and round and then changed like the wheel of the heavens on a starry night.

'Where is the jewel?' Darkblond Man asked. His calm was back; it was as if he'd never lashed out with his tongue and his stick.

Aranthur was running through his own mind, looking for phrases in Safiri.

He was wondering about rescue. The odds, it seemed to him, were very low. So that left death.

In a way, the choices were clear, and like all the other choices he had made lately, once he got to a certain point, it was as if something made the decision for him.

Dead, he could reveal nothing. Dead, he could not be abused.

And the whole plan came to him like the unrolling of a large carpet – first nothing, but then, suddenly, everything. Because they would not expect him to plan his own death.

'Where is the jewel?' Dark Man came close, so close his breath was hot on Aranthur's face. 'Did you kill Syr Xenias? You had his clothes. His case. You knew that peasant at the inn. Speak to me, Syr Timos, and perhaps there will be mercy.'

Aranthur was still calculating. Another part of him was running down long corridors, searching for words.

'Who do you work for?' Dark Man asked.

Cheerful Voice said, 'There's another writ in his purse. As a *fideles.*'

Dark Man struck him, almost casually. 'An imperial officer? An *Arnaut* imperial officer? That's beyond belief.'

He was behind Aranthur, and his stick struck Aranthur's bound hands. The pain was remarkable, lancing up from his broken thumb through his wrist and arm.

'You imagine yourself a swordsman,' said Dark Man. 'A little like a fat girl trying to dance, isn't it? A peasant trying to play with *power.* You are really the epicentre of what is wrong with the world, Syr Timos. You are the child of Tirase's revolution, and we need to put you back to your plough so that the rest of us can have a society.'

The stick struck again – no warning. Fire fountained across Aranthur's nerves.

'No swords for you. Breaking your hands is almost a kindness.' Dark Man leant close. 'Where are my jewels?'

Aranthur was whimpering. Tears were flowing down his face, and snot from his nose. He couldn't stop himself.

'Yes, yes, weep all you like, but tell me where my jewels are.' The voice was calm, almost friendly. 'Yes, it is sad, when you realise that all your dreams are gone. You will not live to see middle age – the diminution of every faculty, the decay of your living body, the death of your world, the promotion of your inferiors, the destruction of trust, the treason of your wife.'

The next blow was savage – a blow to the left shoulder.

Aranthur lost the world.

He came back to find that he was soaked to the skin in cold water, his left shoulder broken, his hands savaged, and his head and gut a tissue of ache that was somehow internal. He had fouled himself; he was sitting in a mess of his own fear.

'Ah, Syr Timos. You are back. Juwad is no longer interested in savaging you. I think he and I had different views on savagery. Mine are more professional and less amusing.'

Aranthur couldn't see very well, but he saw that Juwad was standing by the wall, trying to avert his eyes.

'Where were we? Oh, yes. The middle age, that I am sparing you. Come, syr. Tell me where my jewels are, and for whom you work. And then I will let you go. Perhaps Juwad will have the grace to run you through. I doubt Lys has the stomach or the *power* to kill you with sorcery. Myrtis could just shoot you with a puffer, I suppose.'

Dark Man was back on the chair in front of Aranthur.

'You stink like the farmyard animal you are. Where are my jewels?'

Aranthur concentrated everything he had, his entire will, on Safiri verb forms. Nouns.

The words of his incantation, calligraphed across the page in magnificent, flourishing letters. Soon, if he was to do it, he would have to . . .

Have to what?

There was really only pain. He could not fully remember what he wanted to do.

'Jew-els,' said Dark Man in a sing-song voice. His stick, which was ebony, rubbed gently against Aranthur's jaw, like a malevolent caress. 'Jewels. More cold water.'

A bucket was up-ended over Aranthur.

He had a moment of clarity.

'This is taking too long,' Dark Man complained. 'I am going to work him. I'm sorry, Syr Timos, but I must break your will.' He shrugged. 'I don't even *really* need the jewels any more. I have more – they will do just as well. But I would like those as well. And you cost us *months*. And you interfered with my duel. And because of you I was detained. *Detained!* An Uthmanos detained by the Watch!'

A casual flick; an explosion of pain.

'Perhaps I am too personal. Give me the jewels, swineherd. With them all I can restore the Master's confidence in our Disciple. Dull-witted as he is, we need him to succeed. And you have somehow interfered twice. Twice the . . .' He paused. 'What was that sound?'

Aranthur had not heard anything. It was a struggle to breathe.

He had it. The calligraphy. It was clear in his head. Letters of fire.

He sat in his own excrement and had a moment of pride.

Somewhere below them there was a loud snap and a choked scream – a woman's voice. Even Aranthur, in his tormented state, felt the flash of *power*.

He felt the *power* of a vast *compulsion*, and he knew the author.

Dark Man moved to the door, went out into the corridor, and

called back, 'Kill him. Now. Behead him, Juwad. So he cannot be *soul-searched*. Now.'

Aranthur *focused his will. The terrible, beautiful thing was that, instead of being difficult, it was easy, as if his current state was closer to the winds of magik than his normal state.*

He took the wind and wrote, in Safiri, his will upon reality.

The letters burnt much higher than he remembered . . .

Juwad drew his sword. He did it even as Aranthur's *working* became the law of nature, and the sword was, in Aranthur's sight, some logical extension of his *working*, even as his body flooded with *power*.

He pushed to his feet. There was very little pain and Juwad was drawing his sword very slowly. The legs of the chair, and the chair back, gave under the power of his muscles, and he understood why Sasan had said that he felt like a god. The transformation was incredible; he was no longer a smelly, befouled ruin of a human being, but a demigod lit from within by the secret fire of immortality.

Juwad's face was white. His sword was in line, and Aranthur walked onto the point, taking it in his gut because that eliminated it as a threat, and walking down the blade so that the icy thing grated on his ribcage and spine in a way that seemed beautiful and terrible, but Aranthur *knew* with clarity that the window was about to burst open and that he was clearing the way. With his body. Juwad's grip on the sword failed even as Aranthur slammed his swollen forehead into Juwad's nose, even as his knee slammed into Juwad's groin, again and again, almost too fast to follow.

The young aristocrat, his face caved in from the impact, collapsed to the floor, leaving his sword all the way through Aranthur. Aranthur turned. There was a darkness at the edge of his vision, and already his strength was ebbing, but he was still faster then thought. He leapt at Cheerful Voice as the man entered the room – caught the hand holding the puffer unerringly.

Broke the man's hand against the door frame with casual ease.

The whole rotten frame of the window burst in.

Aranthur began to slump to the floor.

In his dream, it was Tiy Drako, a long puffer in one hand, a small sword in the other. He raised the puffer and shot Cheerful Voice – one careful shot, delivered with the deliberation of a champion athlete – and then Drako was looking down into his face and it didn't seem to be a dream.

And there, with but not with them, was Dark Man.

'Stay with me, Timos,' Drako said. 'Darkness Rising! What have they done...?'

Past him, Aranthur saw a flash of light, an almost incredible, blinding flash. Yet, in his current state, or the shreds of that state, the flash was more like a beacon. In it Aranthur thought he saw the Lightbringer, Kurvenos, brushing back a wall of darkness at a superhuman speed and showering Dark Man with darts of *saar*, and Dark Man struggling and then vanishing...

All in half of a beat of a terrified man's heart. Or so it seemed to Aranthur.

'Stay with me,' Drako said. 'Oh, Sun and Light, save this one.'

Aranthur was seeing Drako from very far away, but it meant everything to him that this man had come for him. It made no sense to him, though, that he drifted away – that he could see himself lying in a pool of blood and worse, so that his own blood dripped through the rotting floorboards, and he could follow it into a lower room where two armed men in plain steel armour had the woman, Lys. He could see her terror, could feel the eagerness of one of the soldiers to hurt her.

In another room and an aristocratic Byzas man he'd never seen was begging, begging...

'None of that,' Kurvenos said, so clear that words came to Aranthur even in the very midst of a rising tide of death. 'I will not condone a single act of malevolence.'

Drako spat. 'A little torture now will save a thousand lives tomorrow.'

'So men like you always tell yourselves,' Kurvenos said. 'I taught you better. All you are when you are done is a torturer.'

In another room, Ansu and Dahlia, with bodies at their feet and bloody swords in their hands – Ansu's long and curved, Dahlia's long and straight. Dahlia had a jewel in her hand, and her mouth was moving. Ansu's shoulders had the posture of intent restraint, the very edge of violence.

And in the street, a dozen soldiers, and Ringkote kneeling on a man's back, his victim's arm broken and being used as a restraint. And General Tribane standing with a dead man at her feet, cleaning her sword. Iralia in a swirl of jewelled light – her *compulsion* throbbing like firelight.

And the darkness, all around, rising to take him.
'None of that,' Kurvenos said.
'Stay with me!' begged Drako.
'Damn,' said Sasan, in Safiri. 'Damn.'
Sasan sounded as if he was crying.

Book Two
Master of War

True mastery of the art of war leads not to victory,
but to equitable peace.

Legatus Giorgios

Aranthur awoke.

His first thought was about Sasan, and a host of thoughts tumbled after, and then he realised that he was lying in a white room with hundreds, if not thousands, of incantations, supplications, and other *workings* inscribed on the walls in copper ink.

And then he thought, *Sophia! I am alive!*

The room smelled deliciously of religious incense, and he inhaled deeply, and his side hurt.

A door opened outside his range of vision. He tried to turn, and found that he was restrained.

Kurvenos, the Lightbringer, stood there. He was an unremarkable old man with deep brown eyes and a scraggly grey beard, but in his mind's eye he saw the man in another form – the form with which he'd assailed the Servant. It was difficult to decide which was the true Kurvenos, and that thought disturbed him.

Kurvenos smiled. 'You live,' he said.

'I do!'

Aranthur felt wonderful. He felt elated, light-headed, and yet his thoughts came clearly . . .

'Our chirurgeon burnt a little of your youth to heal you quickly,' Kurvenos said. 'I'm sorry, but it seemed to all of us that you have a great deal of youth.' He smiled.

'Burnt my youth?' Aranthur asked.

Kurvenos shrugged. 'Yes. Literally. There are other, potent sources of *power* besides the winds. Or the talismans.' A shadow fell across his face. 'The easiest *power* comes from within us – our own life force. Especially when used to heal the same spirit that generates the force, it is potent. Puissant, even.' He shrugged.

'What happened?'

'I would like Tiy Drako to explain – mostly so that I could watch him squirm.' Kurvenos did not sound like a nice old man. He sounded like a cynical old soldier. He shrugged. 'But he would attempt all sorts of equivocations, and one of the vows all Lightbringers take is to tell the truth. No matter what.'

'That must be hard,' Aranthur said.

Kurvenos raised an eyebrow. 'So hard.'

He looked around, vanished for a moment, and came back at the edge of Aranthur's vision with a stool. It was a very pedestrian stool – made of wood, not particularly well fashioned, and very much at odds with the room.

Kurvenos sat and crossed his hands on his staff.

'So,' he said. 'Once you asked me if there were Darkbringers. I answered truthfully – within my knowledge – that there were not, but I was wrong. There are, in fact, although I'm quite sure that in their minds they are the saviours of humanity.'

'The Disciples,' Aranthur said.

'There is a great deal more to their movement than the group who call themselves the Disciples,' Kurvenos said. 'But let us lump them all together for a moment. There is a faction, across the known world, who desire to roll back the reforms of Tirase and return magik to the hands of the various old aristocracies who have all clung to power since the Revolution – as much in Zhou as here in the Empire. But this faction has a spectrum of members who are as varied as the colours of the rainbow, from those who merely wish to preserve the traditional wealth and political power of the old aristocracies, across a broad range of beliefs, to those who seek to destroy the non-human races, eliminate the use of magik by those not considered worthy, to hoard all the talisman materials for the use of the "deserving", and even end the worship of Sophia. Many of them believe that magik is quantity, and that each act of *power* diminishes the store. All of these beliefs can be found, sometimes feuding among themselves, sometimes allied.'

'And they are the Darkbringers?' Aranthur asked.

Kurvenos shook his head. 'No. They are merely human, with human frailties and ignorance. Zhou and Atti and the Empire have all held beliefs just as pernicious, and condoned acts as horrible, in their time. But the aggregate – the poisonous brew of aristocratic ideology, anti-intellectual assaults on political power, and a monochromatic view of the multiverse, along with access to the *ars magika* – has created an engine capable of enormous evil. They worship power. Increasingly, we see in their adherents a simple desire for power untinged by any ideology at all. And *the worship of power is close to the worship of evil.*'

Aranthur nodded.

Kurvenos nodded. 'At the heart of this movement is the Master and his Disciples and Servants, and the elite who call themselves Pure. They are now a nation state – they are doing their best to conquer the world. Stated that way, it seems simple, but nothing about this is simple.

'And so, to you. Through no fault of your own, you became entangled in our operation – a relatively unimportant one, or so we thought, to take Syr Xenias and turn him back to our side. We thought he had a connection to the Duke of Volta. Later, when Iralia joined us, we acquired, too late to use it, enough knowledge to understand that the Duke of Volta was our target – the Disciple for the Empire, or so we still suspect. Or one of them . . .'

Aranthur saw them seated in the tavern. 'But . . .'

'Chance always plays a role. This time, chance was a tyrant and Tyche ruled our actions more than Sophia. We had nothing to do with the mercenaries who killed Syr Xenias. We were too slow to understand that he was dead. We had no idea what he was carrying. We were, in fact, far behind in the race.'

Aranthur squirmed and his gut hurt. 'Race?'

Kurvenos put his bearded chin on his hands. 'A race that is not over. Let me continue. Drako searched your gear – in fact, he searched everyone's kit. He found nothing, we dismissed our fears, and we continued west, looking for our man. The rest you know.'

'I don't know anything!' Aranthur said.

'True of most of us. Very well. When you were attacked by the spectre, the *kotsyphas*, we understood that you must be important, somehow, to the other side. And we had some doubts about you. I'm sorry to say that your Arnaut background made it possible . . . This now seems to me merely prejudice, but we suspected you.'

'Arnauts are known to be so violent,' Aranthur said with a smile.

'Yes,' Kurvenos said. 'We are not perfect, you know. Lightbringers. We are human.' He shrugged. 'Anyway, the spectre struck. You lived. We knew you were important. We started searching for Syr Xenias and his belongings all over again. We made another mistake, in not looking for simple, human agency. We looked for a powerful Magos, and failed to find one. We placed one of our own to protect you.'

'Dahlia,' Aranthur said with bitter clarity.

'Yes.'

'Fuck!' Aranthur spat, his mood suddenly darkened.

'She wants to speak to you. It is not as it appears.' Kurvenos shrugged. 'I forget how strong the passions of the young are, but Aranthur, she is – was – quite fond of you. She merely had other duties and you were treating her abominably, using her for sex and ignoring her as a person. How could you imagine that she would feel?'

'I . . .' Aranthur leant back, because the tension in his stomach muscles hurt his wound. 'I . . .' He paused.

'Telling the truth can be quite painful, but I assure you that it has beneficial aspects. For example, your mistreatment of her is banal. It may be an unspoken and shameful thing to you, but to me it is as clear as the nose on your face and I will not hesitate to mention it.'

'But she was only watching me for you!' Aranthur protested.

'Does that justify your behaviour? Spare me your protests.' Kurvenos nodded. 'Dahlia watched over you. Incidentally, we have no idea if the bandits who attacked you on the road were related to this matter – "not every road leads to the City" as Tirase says. Regardless, we now know that you had a fortune in *kuria* crystals all along, shipped directly from the Disciples in Samnia all the way to Volta to avoid our customs and our agents. You had them. The largest of them is a masterpiece of *infusion* and contains *power* meant to be released in a single pulse – a massive wave of destruction that could kill thousands of people. It was meant to detonate on Darknight, in the City.'

'Gods!'

'Well might we all call upon the gods. The smaller *kuria* crystals were, if anything, worse. Your Master of Arts has peeled them like garlic and they hold the seeds of a disease that attacks a person's bones, burning them like a cold fire. Using the *power* of the stone.'

'The bone plague!'

362

'The bone plague, directed against the poorest people, and those with no magikal training. Our adversaries are subtle. They want these people to stop using *power* and they are happy to use terror to get what they want. In fact, I believe it actually *pleases* them to use terror. It speaks to who they are, that they *enjoy* these techniques.'

Kurvenos was silent for a while. 'This place where you were tortured was merely a safe house. It was not their headquarters – indeed, I wonder if they even have a single headquarters. But we found very little of their *kuria*. I am afraid that there is more out there.

'Many of the Easterners you found in the woods were dead from the bone plague. But most died of malnutrition and exposure, because they were not lighting fires or cooking food.' Kurvenos nodded. 'I think you have had enough logic courses to reason out why.'

'Sophia!' Aranthur breathed.

Kurvenos gave a wry smile. 'And all of that is bad. But, largely thanks to you, we found some of the poisoned jewels and now we know what causes the bone plague. There must be other sources – in fact, we know there are. We are riddled with adherents of the Disciples, Aranthur. Some are Easterners, but most of them are our own people. So far, we can't stop the smuggling of *kuria* crystals. We can't even slow it.'

Aranthur frowned. 'So what did you do?'

Kurvenos was silent. He looked at the writing on the walls for an uncomfortable time.

'We used you as bait.' His brown eyes met Aranthur's green eyes squarely. 'I'm sorry. Drako's idea. I gave the order.' He went on remorselessly. 'We have tried following *thuryx* dealers and we've tried raiding houses, arresting couriers – almost nothing. But you ... They wanted you. We tried, very carefully, to put you where they could see you. In positions of prominence, but well protected.'

Aranthur thought about it for a moment, considered anger, and abandoned it.

'It worked,' he said.

'Yes and no. You are not dead. You survived torture and a terrible wound, for which we are responsible. We took a large supply of tainted crystal, and we captured a dozen of their agents – the most we've ever taken. But the Servant escaped. He was too powerful for me to render him harmless and take him. On the other hand, we know who he is. We have his house and some of his documents.'

'He said he'd been detained,' Aranthur put in. 'He told me that. He said it was embarrassing that an Uthmanos had been detained by the Watch.'

The Lightbringer closed his eyes. 'He was detained and I wasn't told? But who would release him?' He opened his eyes. 'We are riddled with traitors,' he said again. 'Well, at any rate, we have set mousetraps on both houses.'

'Mousetraps?' Aranthur asked, still thinking through being the stalking horse for all this.

'A mousetrap is a time-honoured system for catching thieves and spies and political undesirables. When you take a malfeasant, you render his house as normal as possible and set people inside to take anyone who enters. Thus, you take all the fellow travellers, and couriers, and friends. Some will be innocent. Many will be guilty. We have already taken a courier carrying crystal. And we have enough proof of the Servant's murder of his wife to hang him in court.'

'Eagle! What did we find?' Aranthur asked.

'Her mummified head,' Kurvenos said. 'Listen, Aranthur. I am a Lightbringer. I *do not* believe that the end justifies the means. I believe that the means are everything. I do not eat meat, I do not lie, and I do not kill.' He gave a small, bitter smile. 'Actually, though, since becoming a Lightbringer, I have lied and I have caused people to die, and I've had some delicious beef broth.' He shook his head. 'We are men and women, not gods. I ramble. In a moment I'll be confessing my many sins. Let's leave it at this. Your survival and our apprehension of these miscreants owes more to luck than to our brilliant planning. When they attacked the Master of Arts—'

'What?' Aranthur asked.

'Under cover of the House war, bravos attacked the Master of Arts as she walked to her rooms.' Kurvenos shrugged. 'We were warned and she was protected – Drako was there. But no one was watching you when you were attacked, relentlessly, and then when you chose to pursue your attackers...' Kurvenos smiled. 'Sasan saved us all. He went to the soldiers at the gate. The General was nearby, and we were very lucky.' He sighed. 'I am sorry, Syr Timos. We used you, and we didn't even do it well. And now we have hurried your healing in hopes that you will help us again.'

'What was the target? Of the jewel?' Aranthur asked.

'It was to be chosen by the Duke of Volta. Though I can't prove it. Really, you now know a great many secrets.'

'And we will arrest the duke?'

'No. But we are in the process of proving his guilt to his cousin, the Emperor. We took enough, in papers and prisoners, to prove to most of the political factions in the Empire that this threat is real. Now we need to see how deeply the Disciples have penetrated the Sultan's court, and if we can stop a war that can only serve our adversaries. And alongside all that, we prepare for war with Atti, which would be a disaster, but may also be required.'

'The Master of Arts is alive?' Aranthur asked.

'Wounded, but recovering. She is in an Academy facility. Her attempted assassination and the information we gained in the last nine days may save her job. The faction out for her blood is discredited – perhaps temporarily, perhaps forever.' The Lightbringer smiled cynically. 'Probably for about three weeks.'

Aranthur turned his head slightly so that his eyes met the Lightbringer's.

'Syr,' he said. 'Is the iron cold, or hot?'

Kurvenos smiled bitterly. 'You are too astute.'

'Is there a finite amount of *power*? The Servant said there was.'

Kurvenos hesitated.

He seemed to be reading a conjuration off the wall.

'An excellent question. Perhaps. Our adversaries believe in a very simple world – black and white, strong and weak, good and evil, *power* and emptiness. Lightbringers believe in a world as complicated as the very nature of truth. It may well prove that the power of the winds of magik is finite. But there are other sources of *power*, harder to tap, and weaker, but nonetheless *potent*. And their contention that the old aristocracies hold the germ of the true use of *power* is hogwash. They just want to keep it for themselves, like all ruling classes. They would be more ideologically dangerous if they offered a meritocracy of *power*, where only the very best practitioners were allowed access to the purest wellsprings. Regardless, they are correct in their contention that mages before the time of Tirase could draw more *power* and perform feats largely lost to us.' He smiled. 'Hence the Safian grimoire.'

'All *workings* powered from within the target,' Aranthur said.

'And all dating from before Tirase. You know they didn't have as much *kuria* in Tirase's time?' Kurvenos rose to his feet. 'The big sources were only located by the *Jhugi* four hundred years after Tirase died.' He looked away. 'You realise that you, and you alone, have been at the centre of every incident involving the Disciples in the last year? Drako had no choice but to have you watched. I ask that you understand that.'

'Yes,' Aranthur said. 'Yes. I must have looked very suspicious. But I guess we now know why they were always after me.'

Kurvenos made a wry face. 'Perhaps. I still have concerns. I think there is something more to know.' He shrugged. 'I'm going to knock you out for another day. You are healing splendidly. That body of yours is almost superhuman in its healing ability.'

'What if I said that I wanted to be a Lightbringer?'

Kurvenos smiled. It was a different smile, as if the sun suddenly rose.

'That would be wonderful. Although in truth many are called and few are chosen, and all of us are inadequate to the task. We will speak of this again.'

Aranthur awoke, and this time he was immediately conscious of the room.

And of Dahlia.

He knew her scent before he opened his eyes. She was looking at the writing on the walls; he watched her for a while.

He had forgotten how beautiful she was. She was leaning back, so that her back was against the wall and her stool was up on two legs.

He tried to remember why he had been unable to find time for her. He considered how seldom he had asked her anything about herself. He had never gone to her room, met her room-mates, taken her fencing...

'I am an idiot,' he said aloud.

She turned and looked at him, and she smiled.

'Yes,' she said.

'I'm sorry,' Aranthur said. 'I don't even know what to say.'

'It was good in one way. You made my job easy since you never asked me anything about myself.' She sat forward, so that the front legs of the stool snapped crisply onto the floor. 'Listen,' she said. 'I was told to get close to you. There was all kinds of shit between us, really. I'm sorry too.'

When she left, he cried.

*

Aranthur found he had no restraints. He sat up a little and his abdomen didn't protest. The floor was a mosaic – a great sunburst from wall to wall. The sun had a face, a beautiful face like a wise old woman's. It was First Empire work, and he thought he'd seen the sunburst somewhere before.

Tiy Drako came in as if a bell had rung somewhere. He had his tamboura tucked through his sash.

'Are you all taking turns?' Aranthur asked.

Drako smiled. 'Yes and no.'

Aranthur was still experimenting with moving his torso. 'How is Sasan?' he asked.

Drako began to strum his strings. 'Excellent. As soon as it was clear you were going to make it, Kurvenos put him under. He had a week of sleep to help him beat the *thuryx*. And the exhaustion. And Dahlia is with him all the time.'

Aranthur took that in. 'Sasan gets Dahlia and I get you? He was trying to be light-hearted, but his tone was wounded.

'Yes,' Drako said. 'That's about right.'

Aranthur was jealous.

'I hear that Kurvenos has revealed all our secrets.' Drako began to pick out a sad, slow tune.

'I doubt it. He said enough to restore my faith that I might be on the right side.'

Drako smiled. 'Who even knows? But Kurvenos has a point about the end and the means. The Master's people tortured you.'

'And you didn't?' Aranthur asked. 'No, I get it. Spare me.' He was reading some of the writing on the wall. 'Bring me my Safian grimoire. I might as well get some work done.'

'You could learn to play the tamboura. I could teach you.' Drako smiled.

'I'll take the grimoire, thanks.'

The next few days were difficult – detached from reality in many ways. He was very weak and he had difficulty walking. He had to be lifted to stand up and urinating was very painful. Twice, Magi came and worked on him – once with the aid of a chirurgeon, and once just with *power*.

Sasan came with Dahlia. He had more colour than he'd ever had, and

Dahlia looked scared. The two stood very close together, and answered each other's statements.

Aranthur drew his own conclusions from that, and spent more time reading.

After four days, when he was able to walk all the way around the temple without holding on to Ansu's arm, and even to put himself back to bed, Drako came to tell all of them that the Master of Arts had made a complete recovery, and that the Emperor had publicly accused the Duke of Volta of treason.

'Well,' Drako said, waving a hand. 'At least, he hinted at it, which is strong, for the Emperor.'

Aranthur lay in his bed, with Sasan sitting on the chest at the end, a book in his hand, and Dahlia perched on the back of Drako's chair. Ansu leant in the doorway, opening and closing a small steel fan.

'So we've won, and it's over?' Dahlia asked.

Drako sighed. 'It's never over. Even if we have defeated Volta, the Master is still trying to take Atti. We still have thousands of hungry refugees, autumn is coming, the Attian army is marching, and Zhou is under threat.' He shrugged. 'And beyond that, war, pestilence, famine, and human stupidity remain the norm.'

Aranthur laughed, which hurt his gut. 'I think Dahlia means to ask, what's next?'

Drako nodded. 'In that respect, I suppose when you've healed, it'll be back to the world. Aranthur has been called up. The General knows where he is supposed to be, and he'll be on horseback as soon as he's recovered. As for the rest of you – I recommend you consider becoming housemates. Barring all-out war with Atti, the Academy will be back in session in four weeks. I need you to watch out for each other.' He rose. 'Although all-out war with Atti looks fairly likely.'

'And we're dismissed?' Dahlia asked.

Drako shrugged. 'Until the next time.' He smiled at Aranthur. 'We have no legal status, you know. We are not the Watch. We can't make arrests. So our evidence is in the hands of those who can.'

'Damn it! You aren't dismissed. Why us?' Dahlia said.

Drako shrugged. 'You all have other lives. You were essential for this operation, which revolved around Timos. That's done.'

After Drako left, Dahlia shook her head. 'He's so full of shit, his eyes are turning brown,' she said.

*

Dahlia set out to find them a better place to live. After two days of looking she was already frustrated and anxious, and Sasan declined to go out with her again.

'She's impossible,' he muttered.

'Why?' Aranthur asked.

'I'm not from here, but I think I have some notion of what a few silver crosses will buy.' He shrugged. 'She's cheap, and aggressive. It's wearing.'

'You do it, then!' she spat from the doorway.

Aranthur had a notion, and with Ansu's help, he rose from his bed, dressed carefully, and almost gave up. Drako stopped by and encouraged him, and the three of them went out into the late August sun. It was the time of year when new students came to the Academy, when anyone with aristocratic pretensions went to the hills west of the City to breathe cooler air and relax, when every street seemed to stink of dead animals and old garbage, even in the richest quarters. It was, as Aranthur had reason to remember, a dreadful time to be looking for rooms.

Drako winked at Aranthur. 'Will you accept your call-up?' he asked.

Aranthur felt a pang of fear. 'I haven't been home.'

'The General would be happy to have you. I have reason to know. And it might suit me... to have a friend on her staff.'

'Draxos, do not tell me you distrust the General,' Aranthur said.

Ansu relaxed. His hand had gone to his sword.

Drako shrugged. 'Aranthur, you are a little too intelligent to make a good agent. Let's just say there is more – far more – going on than meets the eye.'

'I may follow the General,' Ansu said.

Drako smiled. 'You were the General's lover, old boy. Not quite the same thing, eh?'

With that, he snapped his chamois gloves against his boot and bowed before walking off into the heavy midday traffic.

Aranthur took Ansu to his leather shop first. He noted that Ahzid Rachman's shop was closed tight – odd for the time of day. There was a young man on the step, wearing a sword. He caught Aranthur's eye, as he wore a mask and a sword and looked self-important and very out of place in the Square of Mulberry Trees, where the street traffic was apprentices and journeymen, most of them in a hurry, and some suddenly in uniform.

Aranthur went in, wondering why the young man was masked, and why he looked familiar. But he was immediately greeted like a returning son, and he had to introduce the prince. Ansu made friends by the simple expedient of spending ten sequins in as many minutes on leather – a scarlet belt with a gold buckle and gold studs, and a matching dagger sheath.

'I probably won't be back to work,' Aranthur said sadly. He inhaled the smells of leather and beeswax. 'I'm sorry.'

He bowed to Bajolla, the wheelwright, who was taking *chai* despite her hair being full of wood shavings.

Manacher shrugged. 'We hear you are a famous swordsman now. And the jeweller, Rachman, was asking about you.'

'I still say he's a crook,' Ghazala said. 'Come back any time, my dear. Your name is in the books; you are always welcome in the guild. If you make something nice, bring it to me and I'll see you passed as a journeyman. Your work is good.'

'Is all well with you?' Aranthur felt odd. Distanced from these people, who had helped him and cared for him.

Ghazala shrugged. 'We have a great deal of work, and our best apprentice has abandoned us.'

Manacher shook his head. 'Military orders.'

Aranthur raised his eyebrows. Prince Ansu leant forward.

'It's no secret, at least not in our guilds!' Bajolla said, finishing her *chai*. 'I have to be back at it. Forty pairs of wheels by the end of the week.'

Manacher kissed the wheelwright on both cheeks and then came back to the table.

'War with Atti,' he said, shaking his head. 'A sorry business. Who wants war with Atti?'

'Someone has to stop the flow of Easterners,' Ghazala said, putting her cup down.

'Mama! We're Easterners ourselves!'

'Nonsense. We have been here for generations. We are citizens,' She smiled at Aranthur. 'Nothing against Arnauts, my dear. You have always been an excellent worker and a good man.'

Aranthur bowed, because there was nothing to say. Ghazala went upstairs to her fine-work bench, and Manacher spread his hands.

'You know she is a good woman,' he said.

'I do.' Aranthur kissed the man on both cheeks. 'Never think I'll take offence.'

'But in front of the prince?' Manacher asked, glancing sidelong at the Zhouian.

'He is very difficult to offend,' Aranthur said.

Aranthur asked him about apartments and rooms and Manacher called up the stairwell to Ghazala, who promised to ask her friends. Manacher bowed to Prince Ansu, who returned his bow with one of his own.

'I love such people,' he said when they were in the street.

'You do?' Aranthur asked.

'They make beautiful things that will last a long time. Their friendship for you is as durable as this belt. These are good people. The people that we protect.' Ansu smiled and showed his black teeth. 'And you are a good man.'

'I am?' Aranthur's jealousy of Sasan was overwhelmed only by the pains in his abdomen.

'Yes. These people value leather-work above all things. They see you as a leather-worker and you accept this. You do not press your identity as a Student or a blade. You meet them as a junior leather-worker. This is . . . correct behaviour. Very . . . elegant.'

'Elegant?' Aranthur glowed with praise, and was unsure exactly what he'd done to deserve it.'

'Come on. Let's ask at the Sunne in Splendour.'

The streets were full of militiamen and women – one or two in every shop, buying everything from tooth powder to new scabbards or feed bags or shoes. Aranthur, despite his brief stints of military service, had no idea who they all were. There were red coats and yellow coats and blue coats and black coats, and Arnaut fustanellas and red caps or blue turbans on Byzas clerks trying to look fierce. It amused Aranthur that the Byzas, with all their contempt and fear for his people, put on fustanellas and tried to look like Arnauts when they fought.

The militia did give the streets a feeling of grim holidays, or a military holiday – hundreds of apprentices and journeymen wearing swords, singing, and swaggering. A pair of them bumped Prince Ansu hard; he reached for his sword, and Aranthur put a hand on his arm and smiled at the two men, who were younger than he.

'Save it for Atti,' he said, and walked Ansu away.

Down by the docks and wharves at the ends of every street, there was an even thicker forest of ships' masts than usual. Aranthur led the prince along the waterfront at the foot of the Angel, the Street of the Heralds. There were four military galleys tied alongside the wharf, stacked like dried fish. The same heavy crane that had raised the drake out of the hold of the Zhouian ship was lowering a heavy bronze cannone into the open maw of a round ship.

'You were right,' Ansu said, spitting in the water. 'I should not pick fights with children. Nonetheless, where I am from, one does not behave so.'

'You don't have rowdy soldiers in Zhou?' Aranthur asked.

'Perhaps we do.' Ansu gave Aranthur a wry smile. 'This is a major war effort.'

Aranthur shrugged. 'I suppose. I lack the experience—'

'I don't. I have just seen sixteen heavy cannones loaded into one ship. That's a horse transport – I can smell it. There's a merchant ship – it is loading militia. I see bales of shovels and picks.' He looked at Aranthur. 'War with Atti? It seems . . . insane.'

Aranthur shrugged. 'My understanding is that Atti is attacking us.'

Ansu frowned. 'And instead of mounting a defence, your General Tribane is attacking them?'

'It works in swordplay.'

'It often results in two dead men, in swordplay.' Ansu shook his head. 'Come, let's find some rooms.'

They enjoyed a glass of wine and an excellent meal: pork dumplings for Ansu, shrimp for Aranthur, with beans in garlic and a bowl of excellent fish curry over fine steamed rice. No one on the staff, not even the innkeeper himself, knew of a room for rent. They had a great deal to say about soldiers, though; half of the staff had been called up.

'The city will be empty when the ships sail for Atti,' the innkeeper moaned.

Still, they were well fed by the time they stood in the square where the two of them had met. Ansu had insisted on paying.

'I owe you for rent, too,' he said.

'Yes,' Aranthur said. 'I accept.'

'Are you very poor?'

Aranthur shrugged and thought of Sasan and the men and women under the Aqueduct.

'No,' he said. 'But silver crosses are hard to find. Thanks for dinner.'

'It was quite excellent – the beans were as good as home.'

'Let's ask Kallinikos about a place to live.'

Ansu shrugged. 'He'll be in the hills with his family.'

The sun beat down like an enemy and the canal stank like the bilge-water of an old ship, despite which two boys were sailing paper boats.

'He lives right here. He didn't go home last summer . . .' Aranthur shrugged.

He thought about how long it was since he'd last seen Kallinikos, and how many times he'd knocked and had no answer. Maybe the aristocrat was away for the summer, riding in the hills . . .

'Very well,' Ansu said with a bow

They went up the steps, from terrace to square, and the canals fell away beneath them. Both of them paused to make reverence to Tirase, whose statue gazed east, and then they went along the low street, criss-crossed with walkways and bridges and balconies. Even here there were student militia. A couple were deeply engaged in a farewell kiss outside one door, and a man was stretching his leather belts over another door.

It was cooler, but still unpleasant, and the street smelled musty.

'Need anything from our place?' Aranthur asked as they passed the familiar yellow door. His wound hurt, and he didn't really want to climb six flights of stairs.

'I'll get my pipe,' Ansu said.

Together they climbed all the way to their rooms, which were so hot as to be uninhabitable, and Aranthur swore he could still smell Arnaud's blood.

There was a large pasteboard card on the rug, where it had been pushed under the door; a carefully lettered summons to military service for:

Syr Aranthur Timos, Fideles, Dekark.

Aranthur stood there, looking at the summons. War. And no Academy.

'I suppose I'm well enough to go,' he said. 'I'll have to report.'

'The General is sailing soon. Perhaps even tonight,' Ansu said.

'You know everything.'

Ansu shrugged. 'Let us see if we can find an apartment – although, come to think of it, if you and I are going to war, Dahlia and Sasan can just stay here, can they not?'

'As long as they want to exercise their legs. Let's see Kallinikos anyway. I've been a poor friend.'

They walked down, past Kati's rooms, and all the way down to the street, where two young women in yellow doublets were walking tall horses along the narrow street.

'Everyone is suddenly a soldier,' Ansu said.

They waited for the women to pass and crossed.

'Do you think he'll be here?' Aranthur asked.

'No,' Ansu said, and knocked at the outer door to Kallinikos' apartments. Aranthur was used to it being open.

They waited, and then Ansu went and peered in windows.

'The windows are not shuttered.' He raised an elegant, plucked eyebrow. 'If I went to the mountains for a month, I'd lock my shutters.'

Aranthur knocked again.

The musty smell was stronger here. He sniffed, trying to place it, and thinking of the masked noble outside Manacher's shop.

His mind made no connection. He shook his head.

'He can't be here.'

But Kallinikos' bed, since taking his wound, was right by the window on the street, because the young man liked watching people.

'Make a stirrup,' he said to Ansu.

'I'm not used to being ordered about,' Ansu said. But then he shrugged. 'But, sure. Here.'

The slim Zhouian was very strong, and Aranthur stepped up, his head at the same level as the diamond pane window. It was slightly ajar; he reached out and opened it. The musty smell rolled over him, and he had a sudden vision of the boneless bodies in the winter hovels south of his father's farm.

Ansu let him down.

'What is it?' Ansu could see that Aranthur was rattled.

'Something dead,' Aranthur said. He had to sit on the step and put his head in his hands – a combination of ills. His abdomen was spasming in pain, and he thought that he might be bleeding a little, but the real pain was in his head. 'Sorcery!' he spat, as if he could spit out the taste. It made his head pound.

Ansu went back to the door and pounded on it.

'He rents the whole building?' he asked.

'I suppose.'

Aranthur had no idea who lived in Kallinikos' house, but then, the man was rich, and he had several servants. Aranthur tried to count them in his head: Chiraz, the butler, who was well-spoken and obsequious and sometimes funny; a housemaid . . . another valet? Footman? He'd met Kallinikos' sister once, but she was at the Arsenal, not the Academy. A military engineer.

As Aranthur lived on the top floor of a similar house with three other students, it seemed almost obscene for one student and his servants to use so much space.

'Is the door locked?' Aranthur asked. 'It shouldn't be.'

'Should we be doing this?' Ansu asked. 'I try not to be stuffy about the law, as you Westerners ignore so many of them, but we are breaking into another man's house.'

Aranthur lifted the latch and put his shoulder to the door.

It gave a little, as if pushing against something soft. There was a sudden drone. The door opened a crack, and a dozen big bluebottle flies droned out.

Aranthur thought of stopping, but Ansu changed his mind and put his shoulder to the door. They heaved, and it opened slowly, almost wetly, and something . . .

The corpse was a week old, or more. The bones were rotted away and the flesh was black, more like a sack of rotting garbage from a tannery than a man, an image with which Aranthur was all too familiar.

Ansu swore in his own tongue, at length. He went outside, untied his sash, and tied it over his face.

'A miasma like that can kill,' he said.

Aranthur was less concerned with the astrological and hermetical implications than with the presence of the taint of sorcery – malevolent majik, and recent enough that the stale tang stayed in the air like the smell of old sweat in a brothel.

He really did not want to go in any further. He already knew what he'd find. But the *daemon* was on him, as he now considered the spirit that animated him, and it made him push forward into danger.

He stepped over the corpse-sack and into the front hall. Stairs climbed away ahead of him. He'd never been up them. Kallinikos lived through the door to the left, and the corpse was leaking a terrible brown fluid, mottled and bilious.

'Why do we have to do this?' Ansu asked. 'Oh, fine, then,' he said and shouldered through. He was slimmer than Aranthur and didn't disturb the corpse.

The flies were disturbed again, though, and they flitted and buzzed like insane guardians of the portals of death. Aranthur had a piercing headache.

The door to Kallinikos' outer chamber was closed. Aranthur tried the handle and it opened and slunk back to reveal the handsome room, complete with silk hangings and two fine silver lamps. On the floor between them was another corpse-sack, boneless and leaking onto the Attian carpet. Even with his skull melted and his bones gone, the butler Chiraz's face was recognisable.

Ansu turned away and threw up.

Aranthur summoned his new Safian *working*; a simple casting, much easier than the 'Inner God' spell. He concentrated and worked, writing on the air in front of him in letters of liquid fire – quick, neat calligraphy from right to left.

Instantly, his eyes saw *power*. He had cast the spell the day before, in the Temple, with several amusing effects, including near-blindness from all the radiating artifacts.

In the Temple, the dominant colour represented by the spell had been a golden yellow, with some strong blues and reds and a single loud green.

Here, amid the stench of death, the dominant colour was somewhere between the dark red of old wine and the red-brown of fresh meat, streaked with an ugly, organic grey-brown.

A curse. A deliberate, malevolent curse.

'Don't touch anything,' Aranthur said.

'We're in over our heads,' Ansu managed.

'Yes.'

Yet the daemon that dared him to do things pushed him forward into the whirling maelstrom of the sick red death.

He worked a *purification* from *Consolations*. He did it internally, without touching his crystal, the Safian way. It was an odd amalgam; he wrote on the winds of magik in Safiri calligraphy, but the words were those of a long dead Ellene philosopher.

It worked.

It took a noticeable bite out of the curse.

He paused.

'Do you know what you are doing?' Ansu asked.

'No.'

Aranthur's abdomen was damp and this was foolish, maybe even stupid.

He stepped back and bent by the butler's body. One limp glove held . . .

A *kuria* crystal.

He took his knife out of his neck scabbard and used it to carefully lift the chain on the crystal. He didn't touch it, just dropped it into his purse.

'I have to know if my friend is in there,' Aranthur said.

Ansu grabbed his shoulder. 'No. You don't. In half an hour, we can go in there with Kurvenos. Or the Master of Arts. This is foolish. Listen to me, Timos. You are like a man possessed – you do not have to do this!'

Aranthur started to walk forward into the swirling red curse.

Ansu caught his shoulders and pulled him back.

'No,' he said. 'Out, now.'

Aranthur accepted defeat. He followed Ansu out of the room, back over the first corpse, and out into the comparatively sweet, cool air of the street.

'Go and get help,' Ansu said.

'Why me?'

Ansu smiled. 'I absolutely trust *me* not to go back in by myself.' He winked. 'But not you . . . I think you should get the help.'

Fifteen minutes later, Aranthur found the Master of Arts and Magos Sittar the healer, both drinking wine in the Academy's Senior Mess. Kurvenos the Lightbringer was nowhere to be found.

Aranthur bowed, and began.

'Kallinikos – you know him?' he asked the Master of Arts.

She nodded. 'He's only the richest student—'

'Yes, yes,' Aranthur spat. 'I think he's been murdered. By sorcery. The curse . . . is still live. His butler is dead . . . He was holding a *kuria* crystal and I think . . .'

Sittar reached out with *force* rather than his fingers and took the *kuria* crystal that Aranthur held by the chain.

'Did you touch it?' he asked.

'No,' Aranthur said.

Sittar ignored him and cast something that flashed a deep violet blue as it crossed his *enhanced* vision. Other masters sitting at other tables raised their heads at the open display of *power*; one raised a glowing set of golden shields, insectile and somehow feral despite the healthy golden glow.

'Take us there,' the Magas said.

Aranthur led them at a run back down the hill towards Kallinikos' rooms. He was relieved to see Ansu leaning against the corner of the building in the shade.

'There is a victim of the curse, or of the bone plague, just inside the door,' Aranthur panted.

Sittar threw more *power* in the next three heartbeats than Aranthur had ever seen – a massive and interlocked set of protections and *enhancements*. He summoned, and a small sparrowhawk appeared on his fist, and he threw the little bird through the door. Even as he moved, a set of tiny scales of golden light seemed to spiral out of his hand, growing and spiralling, until he was covered in transparent gold spirals, a sort of flower shape.

Even amid fear and horror, Aranthur took note. He understood the principle well enough. This was a very powerful shield built of hundreds of small, interlinked shields. The failure of one would not lead to the failure of the whole.

The Master of Arts cast once, and Aranthur could not see the outcome of her casting except that she seemed to glow at the edges of his vision.

Sittar went through the door.

The Master of Arts drew a small black stick from her belt-purse and broke it. Then she followed Sittar.

Neither emerged. There was no sound from within, and after the clocks rang for mid-afternoon, a tall, foppish figure appeared, moving quickly but with dignity. It was the man they called Harlequin, and he nodded to Aranthur.

'We meet again. I was summoned,' he said.

Aranthur explained.

'I'll await my comrade,' Harlequin said.

After a stilted pause, there was a sound as if drums were being played, a rush of air, and suddenly a sinuous tail appeared from between the buildings. The dust began to lift from the street before the green drake landed, tail first, hovering low, his wings an angled blur in the narrow street.

'You called?' the dragon said.

Harlequin laughed.

'经扶 Zhu Jingfu!' the dragon exclaimed, and launched into a rapid, liquid language. Aranthur guessed it was Zhouian.

Ansu bowed and responded in the same.

Magas Benvenutu appeared at the door; her hair was wrapped in a turban.

'蟠龍 Pánlóng!' she called. 'By the gods, we need you.'

The drake grinned, a truly fearsome sight.

'Always at your service.'

The drake folded his wings, wriggled, and made it through the door.

'Dissssgusssssting,' the drake said sibilantly, in Ellene.

Harlequin dusted his gloved hands on his colourful hose.

'Ah, well.' He stepped through the door.

A moment later, a dozen armoured figures appeared on horseback. Aranthur had never seen men in full armour on horseback in the streets of the City. He was clearly not alone. Citizens, militia and visiting masters stood as if petrified to watch the armoured figures as they cantered along the streets. The hooves of their heavy horses crashed against the paving stones, striking sparks and sending out a roll of hooven thunder that echoed across the City.

The armoured figures had their visors down.

'I was summoned by the Master of Arts,' said one armoured man, dismounting.

He was big, as tall as Aranthur, and his armour was articulated from his visor all the way to the sabaton on his foot. He was clearly a Magdalene.

'She's in there,' Aranthur said. 'There's been a murder by sorcery – perhaps a curse —'

'You are Aranthur Timos, Student,' said the armoured man. 'Murder. By sorcery. Inside the Precinct.' The man turned to his companions. 'Dismount.'

Five more armoured figures, visors closed, anonymous and somehow like automata, dismounted. The smallest one, who might have been a woman, drew a long puffer from a scabbard on her saddle. The others drew swords – long swords, with simple cross hilts.

'It's sorcery,' Aranthur insisted.

The first knight bowed. 'We're Magdalenes. We can deal with sorcery.'

'There is a drake and three human Magi inside,' Ansu said. 'Our friends.'

'Good to know,' said the faceless woman. 'We'll be careful.'

In the end it proved that three houses were affected by the curse – a dozen people horribly dead, and even then, only a third as many as would have died had the Academy been in session. Aranthur had to be taken back to the Temple and bed, exhausted, before the Magdalenes, the drake and the three Masters emerged from Kallinikos' rooms.

Another day passed and Kurvenos came.

'Young Kallinikos was killed by a *kotsyphas*,' he said. 'A terrible way to die, like slow poison. Worse.'

'Worse?' Aranthur asked.

Kurvenos shrugged.

'Tell him,' said Dahlia. 'Stop hiding these things, by the Light, Kurvenos. Just tell him.'

'It ate his heart,' Kurvenos said. 'A little at a time. After the caster used it as a vector to pervert the house's *kuria* crystals, so that when the butler attempted a rescue, he literally killed himself. Someone's idea of humour.'

Aranthur blinked several times.

'It paralysed him and then ate his eyes and then his heart,' Dahlia said. 'Because the Servant hated him. Or wanted to make an example of him. That's my guess.'

Aranthur blinked, trying to rid himself of the image. The four of them, eating dinner at the Sunne in Splendour. He looked at Dahlia, and she met his eye.

'Because Kallinikos slept with his wife.'

'I know,' she said, and left the room.

Kurvenos shook his head. 'That is one possible reason, but I fear there are others. And now we must investigate everything about him.

Because we need to understand why the Servant did this, if the solution is indeed so obvious.'

'He slept with Uthmanos' wife,' Aranthur said.

Kurvenos shrugged. 'I heard that from Dahlia. But it doesn't seem . . . on the same level . . . as the Servant's long-term plans.'

'I think it was, sir.'

Kurvenos spread his hands, unbelieving. 'This is more complicated than mere sex,' the Lightbringer said.

Aranthur wished he had Drakos there. Drakos would understand; men like the Servant saw no difference between vindication of their own immediate needs and the greater good.

Kurvenos was too naïve. Or so Aranthur thought.

When Kurvenos left, Aranthur sat alone for a while. And suddenly he was crying. He was beginning to wonder if he was cursed. People died around him.

He cried, and was better for it. Sittar, the master healer, came and looked at his abdomen, and cast over him again.

'Was it terrible?' Aranthur asked.

Sittar nodded. He didn't speak until he was washing his hands.

'Yes,' he said. 'A dozen people dead, and for what? One sick bastard's revenge for being cuckolded?' Sittar shook his head. 'Or Kallinikos was one of them, and turned, as some of us now believe?' He sat on the edge of the bed. 'I can't pretend I understand what's going on. It's like trying to find a path in a blizzard.'

'Turned?' Aranthur asked, dumbfounded.

'I'm probably not supposed to tell you this, but Kallinikos may have been one of their junior members. And then he left, or stopped communicating with the Servant. Maybe he changed his mind. Maybe he never agreed with them.' Sittar shrugged. 'The older Houses are all tied up in factions that are too old for we peasants to understand.'

'Draxos!' Aranthur spat.

Master Sittar got up. 'I came from a farm. I'm suddenly tempted to go back to it.'

Kallinikos' funeral was two days later, and Aranthur needed them to recover. He tried a little exercise, practising some of the dances of home, and the 'rule' he'd learned with the *montante*. His dances made him think of Alfia, and home, and a farm.

The factions were obviously there. He could see men in the street with weapons – most of them militia, but others in House colours, and a great many Lions, and some Whites. He saw a man with a white headband, and another wearing a black rag tied around one leg, and assumed they were members of factions. He still didn't even really know what the sides were. He wondered when Nenia was coming. He had the time, so he wrote her a letter. It was long, and it talked about very little: school; the difficulty of finding a place; then, to his own amazement, he found himself writing to Nenia about all the things wrong with his relationship with Dahlia. Foolish as that seemed, he handed the sealed letter to Prince Ansu to be put in the wagons to Fosse.

He walked out with Sasan that afternoon, all the way to the Lonika Gate, and reported to Centark Equus of the Nomadi, because he had tried his City cavalry barracks and found it empty. Equus was the only other officer he knew.

The man was dressed for duty at court, in white deerskin breeches, a scarlet doublet and a small fur hat trimmed in gold. He looked at Aranthur's pasteboard card and tapped it on the table.

A soldier appeared with a pair of long-barrelled flint pistols.

'My lord,' he said.

'Thanks, Gouli,' Equus said. 'Listen, old boy, this is all shockin'ly irregular. You are clearly injured, but you failed to appear when summoned, which makes you a deserter, and then the General wanted you as a staff courier . . .' He shook his head. 'Shockin'ly irregular. Got Tiy Drako written all over it. Do you want to go?'

Aranthur nodded. 'Yes,' he managed.

'Good lad. You were a friend of young Kallinikos, yes?' The guards officer looked at him sharply.

'Yes, syr.'

Equus nodded. 'His sister's military. Know that?'

'No, syr.'

'Going to the funeral?'

'Yes, syr.'

Equus nodded. 'I'll see you there. Until then, if anyone questions you, refer them to me.'

Aranthur and Sasan walked back through streets packed with wagons, a long train of them moving slowly aboard the transports at the wharves.

Aranthur shook his head. 'They have prepared for this for a long time,' he said.

He and Sasan walked up to the Aqueduct, and Aranthur found he was afraid to go into the Easterner areas. He made himself. And later, after a fencing lesson and a hard set of bouts with both heavy and light weapons, his gut hurt. He walked home again with Sasan, aware of the factions still hovering at the edge of something.

The next day, the day of the funeral, he dressed in his best black garments. When he was fully dressed, he reached for his arming sword, but something – some flair for the dramatic – made him buckle on the old sword, despite its being long and heavy. It was a reassuring weight against his hip.

He looked at himself in Arnaud's mirror, and frowned. He was still contemplating what he saw – the marks of pain and recovery – when Dahlia came, and he cornered her.

'This whole city is like a fire, ready laid and waiting for the *kuria* crystal,' he said.

She nodded. 'I know. I just saw the Lion Masks trying to pick a fight with a gaggle of Reds. They used to be allies.'

'Does Drako know?' Aranthur asked.

Dahlia bit her lip. 'We'lll be late for the funeral.' She wasn't a good liar, and her evasion was obvious.

Her sense of time, however, was good, and Aranthur had to hurry. He walked with Sasan, Dahlia and Ansu out into the Precinct and then across the Academy and down into the very nicest part of town, where the nobles had their palaces on the Long Canal. The General had sailed the day before with more than a hundred ships, apparently bound for the coast of Atti, and the streets were still crowded with soldiers and House bravos. Aranthur had a feeling of anticlimax, as if he'd attended an opera with no finale. The General had gone to Atti, the servants of the Pure had been captured, and everyone seemed to have forgotten him. His part of the story was over.

None of the four talked much. It was very hot – so hot that a black wool doublet felt like a suit of armour – and sweat trickled down Aranthur's back and gathered at his waist. But he was happy that walking wasn't so difficult any more, and thanks to some very potent Magi he hadn't lost muscle mass.

'The Master of Arts will return in the autumn,' Dahlia said. 'I'm to see her after the funeral, with Sasan.'

Aranthur nodded. 'Sasan can work the grimoire,' he said, with what he hoped was a selfless attitude.

He didn't mention that he had seen the Master of Arts, however fleetingly. She hadn't said anything to him.

'No, I can't,' Sasan said. 'Nor do I particularly like being spoken of in the third person. No, one talent I lack completely is *power*. But I'm pretty sure I can help you learn Safiri faster.'

Ansu glanced at Dahlia. 'Found us a place to live?'

'No,' she said. 'And why is it my job, anyway?'

Ansu shrugged. 'You're nobly born and local.' He shrugged again. 'All the rest of us are one type of foreigner or another, yes?' Then he relented. 'Aranthur will be sailing with the military expedition. I expect I'll go as well. The last supply ships won't leave for three days, and then you two can have our room. No need to search.'

Dahlia paused. 'You are going with the army? To Atti?'

Aranthur shrugged. 'I'll hear today.'

She sighed, and they started down the long steps to the Embankment, the long park on the south side of the Long Canal. During the First Empire it had been a palace with hanging gardens, but Tirase had given it to the city. Almost three hundred marble steps led from the student houses below the Sunne in Splendour all the way down to the Embankment, and the bronze handrails were polished by the passage of thousands of Students. A magnificent bronze of the sea god, Posedaos, had been touched for luck so many times that his face had developed a noseless smile. The Weaver, sometimes called Tyche by the Byzas, stood opposite. Her robe's folds were almost rubbed smooth.

'You really think that we can just . . . go back to the Academy?' Aranthur asked.

Dahlia shrugged. 'Yes?' There was a question to it, but also an answer. 'Things change. Doesn't one of the pre-First Empire philosophers say something . . . ?'

'One of ours says that there is no constant but change,' Ansu said.

Aranthur thought of his parents; of Alfia; of the Inn of Fosse and the world in which he'd grown to near-adulthood, where everything at least appeared to be the same every day. Cattle and sheep; wheat and millet and barley and oats; stock and grapes and olives.

He thought of Alfia with guilt and worry, and wondered what had driven him to make love to her, and what the result might be. And about the foolish letter to Nenia.

He thought a great many uncomfortable thoughts, descending the long stairs, until Ansu punched him lightly in the shoulder.

'You're not that ill,' he said. 'I count on you to be entertaining.'

'Me?' Aranthur asked.

Dahlia covered a chuckle. 'You do most of the talking.'

Sasan kept going down the steps.

'Don't listen to them.' He laughed. 'Last one to the bottom buys the wine after the funeral.'

'Don't you take anything seriously?' Ansu asked.

'I used to. Look where it got me,' Sasan said.

Aranthur stepped between them and began to bounce down the steps two at a time.

'Bastard!' Sasan shouted, in Safiri.

If the city was like a ready laid fire, the funeral was a tinderbox. The ceremony was long, and very pious: a Sophian funeral in an austere temple of white marble, with no decoration beyond the aesthetic purity of the columns. But the congregation was clearly divided into three sections, and the nobles wore their House colours, and a bewildering variety of alliance tokens. Almost no one from any of the three groups spoke to the other groups. All of them, men and women, were armed.

When the ceremony was over, Kallinikos' father and his younger brother and sister and his mother all stood in a line, receiving the guests, who were ushered into a garden for a meal. Aranthur was behind Dahlia, and Kallinikos' mother embraced her.

'And you were on each other's marriage lists,' she said, with a sob.

Dahlia nodded.

'I am Hangela, of the Coutri. He was such a lovely boy. If harebrained,' she said, and Dahlia smiled. Hangela kissed her on both cheeks. 'You are probably too well-bred to mention that he was involved in theatre.'

Aranthur bowed, and Hangela was just turning to him.

'We were there the night that Mikal and the Emperor provided all the effects for *Niobe*.'

Kallinikos' mother looked at him intently. 'What is this, now? Were you his room-mate?'

'No, my lady. I was a friend. I lived across the street and your son very kindly fed me on many occasions.' Aranthur bowed.

Hangela put a familiar hand on his arm. 'What House are you from, young man?'

Kallinikos' father turned. 'You are Timos? The sword chap?'

Dahlia smiled. 'He is.'

'Oh, Mikal thought the world of you,' Kallinikos Primo said. 'And it is *so* good that he had Arnaut friends. Isn't it? Damme, that we are only meeting you now.'

His tone was false, and his eyes seemed to stare through Aranthur.

'I want to hear this story of Niobe,' Hangela said. 'When we eat.'

At the word 'Arnaut' her look of friendly familiarity vanished.

The line moved on, and Aranthur went in, trying not to feel . . . the vague anger that every Arnaut comment sparked in him.

'That's their palazzo just across the canal,' Dahlia said.

She pointed at an edifice of pink-grey marble with elaborate painted columns between a myriad of arched windows.

Aranthur shrugged. 'I knew he was rich.'

Dahlia laughed bitterly. 'Do you think our precious Lightbringer has even told them how their son died, or why?' She looked around, watched a young man in a red, black, and yellow armband push a tall woman in striped hose – an ungentle shove. She reached for her dagger, and another woman grabbed her arm.

'If someone doesn't stop this, we're going to have blood everywhere,' Dahlia snapped.

She left Aranthur without waiting for an answer, pushing through the crowd of aristocrats towards a woman who could only be her mother – the same hair, the same look of calm intelligence.

There was one man standing to the side: tall, with long, dark hair and a neat beard and moustache, straight as an arrow. He wore red and black House colours with a yellow velvet patch sewn to the breast of his coat. Other men and women who wore twists of yellow and red came and went, paying court to him. Aranthur noted that Kallinikos Primo brought him a cup of wine.

Aranthur turned and took a cup of red wine from a tray and noted that the hired servant was an Arnaut. Their eyes met for a moment and Aranthur allowed himself a small smile, which the other man echoed.

'*Ditë e mirë për ju,*' he said quietly in the language of home, and the man's smile intensified.

'May the Eagle stand with you, brother,' he said. 'They are all crazy, yes?'

Aranthur nodded to the man in the red and black. 'Do you know who that is?'

'Brother, he is the famous Verit Roaris,' the Arnaut waiter said. 'He doesn't like us, give him a wide berth.'

'Many thanks,' Aranthur said. 'May the Eagle bless your works,' he added.

The waiter bowed and moved on.

'Was that Arnaut?' Sasan asked.

'Yes,' Aranthur said. 'At least, my valley's dialect. That gentleman is from over the mountain somewhere.'

Sasan nodded, sipping white wine. He was neatly dressed, and he looked very different – more muscular, less hollow-cheeked. But he appeared as Arnaut as Aranthur, or more so, in tight hose under a fustanella of linen with a magnificent red velvet sleeveless doublet and a turban of silk that changed colour as it caught the light, blue green to gold.

'That's my best turban!' Aranthur laughed, but he was not entirely amused.

'It is very nice, yes.'

Sasan smiled and patted it, adjusting the fringe. He also wore the *shamshir* he'd taken in the fighting, thrust rakishly through his sash, which was, somewhat daringly, in Dahlia's green and gold House colours.

Sasan was exotic and Aranthur could see how handsome people found him.

As if reading his mind, Sasan put his wine cup down on a table and turned.

'She doesn't love me any more than she did you,' he said.

Aranthur wanted to look anywhere but into those black eyes.

'I really . . .'

He didn't even know what he intended to say. *Really wanted another chance? Really cocked up? Really happy for you? Really never knew who she was?*

He shook his head. 'You saved my life.'

Sasan smiled thinly. 'I did, too. And that gives me hope, because I've had a lot of reasons to die and too few to live.' He put a hand on Aranthur's shoulder. 'I—'

'Never mind,' Aranthur said. 'Really. I screwed it up and you... she...'

He flailed about a little, and then he and Sasan were locked in an embrace.

'I could go back to *thuryx* tomorrow,' he said. 'Please help me... so that I do not.'

Aranthur smiled. 'Fair enough.' He shrugged. 'Anyway, it's her choice...'

Sasan grinned. 'Perhaps also my choice, eh?' he asked sharply.

'Fair enough,' Aranthur said.

'Good. Because I want to work with you. Teach my language. Maybe write again. I know... I know she is not for me, but she makes me feel alive, instead of dead. And the other person who makes me feel alive is you. Eh?'

Aranthur snatched a second cup of wine. 'To Dahlia,' he said.

Sasan nodded. 'I can drink to that.'

Then suddenly everyone was kneeling.

The Emperor had come. He was not incognito this time; he was dressed in black and cloth of gold, and wore a sword with a diamond the size of an egg at the pommel. At his side, Iralia shone as brightly as the jewel in the sword hilt. Behind them were twenty Axes of the Imperial Guard. The Axes were supposedly incorruptible and were reputed the best blades in the world.

The Emperor greeted the parents and embraced them, and then spoke briefly to the older son.

'He'll be making his oath of fealty,' Dahlia said. 'All of the heirs must. It's the law.'

'The king is dead, long live the king?' Ansu asked.

Behind him, a noble-born woman in a kirtle of scarlet silk stood close, as if trying to possess the foreign prince.

'That sort of thing,' Dahlia said.

They all sat to eat. Kallinikos Primo gave a short speech, thanking everyone for attending and asking them to sit as they wished, without ceremony, as his son would have wanted. The Imperial Axes circulated, and suddenly the temperature cooled; there were no hands on sword hilts, and very little posturing between the factions.

About the time that Aranthur was finishing his second helping of *polpo*, an octopus dish, the chair behind him moved. He found that Hangela was sitting with him, with his sister, whom he'd met once and seemed familiar.

'Aranthur Timos,' she said. 'This is my daughter Elena.'

The young woman, perhaps three years older than Aranthur, smiled. She had red-brown hair and freckles, and was dressed foppishly in a laced shirt and a long velvet coat.

'We've met,' she said. 'You made my brother a better blade, that's for sure!' She shrugged.

'So tell me this story of Niobe,' Hangela demanded of Aranthur.

Dahlia leant forward. 'We were there as paying guests,' she began. 'We didn't even know that Mikal was participating.'

Aranthur nodded. 'The effects were dazzling. Superb. When Aploun shot his poisoned arrows, they burned with green venom...'

Dahlia laughed. 'Anyway, afterwards I wanted Aranthur to meet some of my friends, and my cousin, and my sister Rose.'

'Ah,' Hangela said.

The small exhalation conveyed a great deal of information about her views on women who became actresses, especially women of noble families.

Elena Kallinikas shot her mother a look of irritation. 'Mater. Women have careers now. *I will be an engineer.*'

Hangela sniffed.

Aranthur went on. 'We bumped into Mikal backstage. We discovered that the magiker was sick, and he had volunteered to do the effects. The Emperor helped him.'

'It's not true,' the Emperor said.

Aranthur shot to his feet.

'Informal!' the Emperor said quietly. 'We are not at court. If we were, I would not be wandering about.'

Aranthur turned to find one of the Axes standing behind him, a hand on Aranthur's dagger.

'Nothing to worry about, laddie,' the man said. 'Just chat. And don't do anything really sudden, like.'

Hangela shook her head. 'What's not true?'

'It wasn't me,' the Emperor said.

'It was me,' Iralia said.

Her smile dazzled, and her web of *power* put her in a haze of *compulsions* and *enhancements*. Hangela reached out, as if against her will, and took Iralia's hand.

'Mikal was a splendid caster and had a fine talent. He just didn't have the store of *power* needed for the whole performance.' Iralia looked at the Emperor. 'I did *so* enjoy working with him.'

'It's true?' Hangela asked. 'Mikal was good at this "effect" magik?'

The Emperor bowed. 'I won't set up as a theatre critic. But he had talent. He was also amusing and *loyal*, a combination one rarely finds these days.'

Aranthur found the emphasis on the word *loyal* to be out of character. Disturbing. As if the Emperor was probing for a reaction.

Hangela excused herself with a deep curtsey. 'The gods bless you, Majesty.'

But her eyes thanked Iralia. She was flushed, and she might even have been angry.

Elena Kallinikas bowed. 'Majesty,' she said. 'I'm due aboard.'

He smiled. 'Myr Kallinikas, I know my city is well defended by the likes of you.'

The Kallinikas woman rolled her eyes.

The Emperor turned, and smiled at Iralia. 'Really, I should reward you for your contributions to the arts.'

'Don't be silly,' Iralia said.

'I could give you the rubies that Volta just gave me to buy off my wrath,' he said lightly.

'He would hate that,' Iralia said with satisfaction.

Aranthur saw Lady Hangela start.

'You could wear them in your hair,' the Emperor said.

He touched her hair, a very intimate gesture that was, at the same time, romantic, and natural.

Then his focus, which was almost as intense as Iralia's, fell on Aranthur like a lens powered by the sun.

He smiled at Aranthur. 'Ah, Syr Timos. How is my reader?'

'Safe and sound in the inner Temple,' Aranthur said. 'Syr.'

The Emperor nodded. 'And this is the Safian?'

'Is there only one of us left?' Sasan asked.

The Emperor winced. 'My apologies, syr. I know Dahlia, and I know Aranthur Timos, and I know Prince Ansu – that leaves you.' He gave an empty smile that in a less practised politician might have been bitter. 'I know what you four did, alongside some other brave souls. I wish to thank you.'

'Don't throw flowers, just send money,' Sasan said.

The Emperor laughed. So did Dahlia.

'It's something my sister says,' Dahlia added.

The Emperor bowed. 'Perhaps an appointment might be made for these four to visit me, with Kurvenos and Drako?'

'I have it,' Iralia answered. She had a rectangle of light between her hands and she wrote with a stylus of ruby light on the shining page of *power*. 'I can bring them in for a private audience after your formal reconciliation . . . tomorrow.'

The Emperor made a face. 'Aphres, is that tomorrow?'

'Yes,' she said.

The Emperor sighed.

Aranthur watched, fascinated. 'Would you teach me to do that?'

Iralia furrowed her brow in mock consternation. 'Don't I ask and ask you to visit me? I sit alone in my tower, waiting, hoping . . .'

The Emperor smiled. 'Now you're in for it.'

He smiled and swept off, and Aranthur felt the slight pressure on his back vanish; when he looked, the Axe was gone.

Dahlia rose and Sasan with her. 'I'm off; meeting the Master of Arts.' She smiled. 'I still can't like your Iralia. She's like a cheap trollop overdone and writ large.'

Sasan shook his head. 'I can't agree. She's . . . remarkable.'

Dahlia rolled her eyes. 'Make-up and *enhancement* and a really fine cleavage, and that's all a girl needs,' she said bitterly. She put a hand on her sword hilt. 'I liked Elena though. Why haven't I run across her before?'

Aranthur felt himself willing Sasan to make some comment – something that would make Dahlia relax.

'I found Iralia extremely attractive,' Sasan said. 'Aranthur, that *goddess* asks you to visit and you haven't been?'

Aranthur didn't look at Dahlia. 'We've been busy.'

Dahlia's eyes were narrowed, but not for long.

'What you need is work,' she said.

She pecked Aranthur on the cheek, which seemed an improvement, and then Aranthur was sitting with Ansu.

Ansu raised an eyebrow. 'He's a fool,' the prince said. 'Actually, almost everyone is a fool.'

Aranthur was just shaking his head when everyone stood to wish the Emperor farewell. There was some jostling; a tide of people who had been waiting to leave went out, and chairs cleared.

A man came and bowed: a man of middling height, in very expensive clothes, a fine dark wool doublet cut to look like an Arnaut fustanella.

'You don't know me,' he said, after a bow to Prince Ansu.

'No, sir,' Aranthur said, rising. And then he did.

'I suppose that technically I could arrest you,' the man said with an easy smile.

'Centark Equus,' Aranthur said, smiling. 'May I introduce Prince Ansu?'

'We've met,' Equus said smoothly.

'Ahh. For a delinquent deserter, you are very well dressed. And you know everyone!' The Centark pulled up a chair and sat with them. 'Drako mentioned you again and stressed that you'd taken a wound in the service. I take it you're well enough to travel?'

Aranthur couldn't resist. He hiked his shirt out of his hose and showed the spiderweb of scar tissue and the slight hole in his abdomen.

Equus whistled. 'Nice. Girls like that sort of thing. Boys too, I imagine.'

He flicked his moustache with his hand and winked at Prince Ansu.

Softly he said, 'The General has marched. I can arrange for you to catch her until as late as Draxday. Then she'll be out of our reach.' He smiled at Ansu. 'And I'll be with her.'

'I need the permission of the Masters of the Academy,' Aranthur said.

Equus nodded. 'First actual military campaign of my lifetime. If you fancy being a soldier, this will be the moment—'

'Unless he dies,' Ansu said.

Equus sat back.

Ansu shrugged. 'I come from a warrior people. War kills.'

Equus smiled his crooked smile. 'Of course it does. Why talk about it?'

The Arnaut waiter poured wine for Aranthur and for Ansu, and Equus waved him off.

'No, no,' he said. 'I can scarcely walk, and there's a young person who seems to appreciate my sense of humour.' He winked, and bowed. He handed Aranthur a brown leather wallet. 'Here are your new orders – you'll sail with me, day after tomorrow.'

Aranthur bowed. 'Thank you, syr!'

'Think nothing of it. Drako and I . . . see some things the same way, what? Birds of a feather, eh? And he does get things done . . .'

Equus stepped back and looked around.

Aranthur turned to speak to Ansu, and he found . . .

Iralia. She smiled. Her *enhancement* was gone. Most of the make-up was gone, and she wore a shorter gown in violet and gold, but nothing as revealing as what she'd had on half an hour before – the sort of kirtle any active woman might wear to a good inn. She was no longer breathtaking, but merely brilliant, which seemed her natural state.

Nonetheless, Centark Equus made a very deep bow before looking for his young person.

'I asked my . . . friend to go on without me,' Iralia said.

Ansu raised his wine cup. 'To you, my lady. Two thousand years of Zhouian poetry cannot do you justice.'

Iralia made a face. 'Haven't you done enough of that?'

The prince took one of her hands and kissed it until she tore it away. 'Really,' she said.

Ansu shrugged and drank more wine. 'You are the *most beautiful* woman I've ever seen. I want to make love to you.'

Iralia leant back, tossed her head, and the Arnaut waiter appeared as if by magic and handed her a glass of red wine. She flashed her eyes at him and he flushed, and she dropped a gold sequin on his tray.

She looked back. 'Am I the *only* woman in the palace you haven't bedded?'

Ansu smiled and his black teeth showed. 'Not quite.' His smile widened. 'Close, though.'

'Don't you think it is more than a little impertinent to proposition a courtesan contracted to the Emperor who is your guest-friend?' she asked, archly, as if she was someone's grandmother.

Ansu folded, as he would with someone's grandmother.

'I mean only to praise you. To be...'

Iralia looked at him steadily. 'You seem to be a very intelligent man. Do you fail to see that the Emperor is not only such in name, but must not be challenged, because he can never compete?'

Ansu bristled. 'No one is above—'

Iralia had a fan, and she snapped it shut.

'My dear man, I am telling you. Are you listening to me?'

Ansu frowned. 'Yes. But he is not *my* Emperor.'

'Bah, it turns out you are just another young man with a high opinion of himself.'

She shrugged, dismissing him. She turned to Aranthur.

'And Myr Tarkas?' Iralia's eyes were on Aranthur. 'She has taken a new lover, I think?'

'Ouch,' Ansu said.

Iralia shrugged. 'Courtesans take love affairs as seriously as soldiers take wounds.'

Ansu almost spat out his wine.

'Are you recovering?' Iralia asked Aranthur.

He smiled, trying not to be entranced. 'Yes. I feel better. I've had all sorts of...' He paused. 'You know all about it. You were there.' Then he smiled. 'Are we speaking of wounds? Or love?'

She smiled. 'Not bad. You are learning.' She glanced at Ansu to indicate that he was now included in the conversation. 'I was speaking of mere bodily wounds. And I was there. If Kurvenos had allowed me, I'd have pulled down the Servant.'

'Allowed?' Aranthur asked.

Ansu leant forward.

Iralia rose. 'I feel like a walk, Syr Timos. Would you be kind enough to escort me?'

'Lucky devil,' Ansu said quietly.

'We're old friends,' Aranthur said.

Ansu shook his head. 'I need more *old friends.*'

It proved that Iralia had changed at the family palazzo; her Eastern *pashmina* scarf was draped over a banister in the *piano nobile*. Both Kallinikos Primo and his wife came to wish her a good evening when the two of them crossed the canal to retrieve it. It was obvious to

394

Aranthur that she'd left it on purpose, to have a chance to speak to the grieving parents in private.

Hangela, Kallinikos' mother, had been crying, but her voice was even.

'It was so kind of you to come, to stay, to tell me such a beautiful thing about my son. The Duke of Volta is *so* wrong about you.'

Kallinikos Primo glanced at his wife, as if concerned with what she'd said. Then he put a hand out.

'Iralia,' he said.

'Yes?'

'You always know everything.'

He was a courtier, but grief had made his face naked; his sadness and his anger were right there.

Very quietly, he said, 'Did Uthmanos really kill my son with sorcery?'

Iralia took his hand in hers. Gone was all sign of seduction or enticement. Her voice held nothing but sorrow and regret.

'Yes,' she said. 'And he will be caught, and questioned, and punished.'

'Not if my House catches him first,' Kallinikos said.

Iralia looked into his face as if reading him. 'That is, right now, one of the worst outcomes the Emperor can imagine. I beg you to help us find him, and to ensure that he goes to trial.'

Kallinikos stepped back, and Iralia released his hand.

'I don't think I could do that,' Kallinikos Primo said.

Iralia managed a smile. 'I wish you would.' She smiled up into his eyes, all her art, all her warmth focused on him. 'And the Emperor wishes it.'

Kallinikos nodded. 'But there is a matter of honour, my dear.'

Hangela looked at her husband, a look that burned. 'What honour? My boy is dead. Iralia, why do you want this man alive?'

'Because he is the key to all of it. The bone plague, the *thuryx* trade, the murders, the attacks on the Academy, and the death of your son. He will be put to the question, and then he will . . .'

Iralia smiled, and Aranthur might have shivered. But he was too busy watching Kallinikos Primo, while Iralia spoke to Hangela. The man's face grew hard; his eyes were haggard.

'No,' he said. 'This is not for the Emperor's justice, but for our own.'

Hangela looked at him with anger, almost rage, unspoken grief and worry. Aranthur was glad not to be receiving it.

Iralia caught his hand and tugged.

A minute later they were walking along the canal. In this neighbourhood, the canal had a full width street running along it, and there was a greensward and cherry trees.

They walked in silence for a little while.

'Potnia *fuck*!' Iralia said fiercely, invoking the Armean Lady of Animals. She stopped, leant against the railing that ran along the canal, and stripped off her magnificent sandals, which were embossed, gilded, and high heeled.

She lobbed them into the canal.

'Littering. A four obol fine,' she said. 'I intend to lead a life of crime.'

Aranthur had no idea what to make of the change that had come over her.

'What's wrong?' he asked.

'Please tell me they will at least sink.' She turned around. 'His son is dead and he wants fucking *revenge*.' Iralia shrugged. 'Is it because I make love for my living that I have a distaste for the ease with which people use violence?' She looked out over the canal. 'Is Kallinikos Primo so rich that he doesn't care about consequences? I was there when the Emperor, in person, told them that the House war was a set-up to cover other activities. If that jackass kills Uthmanos Primo...'

She looked at Aranthur. 'Do you know what I'm talking about?'

Aranthur felt that three cups of heavy red wine might have been too many.

'Yes,' he said.

'And?' she asked, as if she was testing him.

'Cold?' he asked.

'Iron,' she said. 'Cold fucking iron, Aranthur Timos. Drako thinks it's time to move on, to penetrate the court of Atti and fight the Pure there. He is excited to support the General in her war.' She glared at Aranthur. 'I think we have to find the Servant and put him on trial, so everyone knows...'

She looked at him. It wasn't as dark as it might have been; many of the palazzi were illuminated for the evening funeral and dinner, and another house was having a dance.

'Tirase believed that everyone should know everything,' Aranthur heard himself say.

Iralia's eyes were deep and dark, and in the evening light, might have been brown.

'He was correct, and so are you,' she said. 'Drako is a spy, with a spy's sense of secrecy. This is a conspiracy that cannot live in the light. We need to expose it.'

Aranthur nodded.

'The Emperor needs to put this man on trial.' Iralia was speaking less imperiously now. 'The balance of powers is delicate – far more delicate than I imagined before...' She smiled. 'Before I started sleeping with the government.' She turned. They were side by side at the marble railing.

'Why did Myr Tarkas leave you?' she asked.

'I...' Aranthur sighed. 'I treated her badly. And she was only...'

Iralia smiled. 'Only watching over you? Tell me another one. I watch bodies; I watch the way men posture and women manipulate. Dahlia is a very honest young woman and she wanted you.'

Aranthur felt he might choke. 'Well, I didn't talk to her for a few weeks,' he admitted.

Iralia began to laugh. 'Aphres!. You are something, Aranthur Timos. You just... forgot you had a lover?'

'I was so busy...' he began. 'By the Hero, that sounds weak.' He shook his head. 'And foolish. But when I concentrate on something...'

'You do it to the exclusion of all the other things. I know. I've been inside your busy, busy head.' She smiled. 'Let's go somewhere and drink, Aranthur. We're not so different. I, too, push things too far. It's not a bad fault, in a magiker. And I understand you walked down a sword blade.'

Aranthur could still feel it grating along his spine.

'Yes,' he said.

'That's insane. And somehow, beautiful. You wanted to die?'

She had started walking. She was barefoot, but the streets here were smooth marble, the cheaper, heavily veined kind. And very clean.

'I thought it was the only option.' Aranthur shrugged.

'Beautiful. A little over-focused, but that's who you are.' She shrugged. 'Where can I get a drink?'

'Was Mikal Kallinikos really working for the Servant?' he asked suddenly. 'Since you seem to know *everything*.'

He hadn't realised that he was bitter until that moment. Or perhaps he had...

Iralia turned. 'Aphres! Who told you that?'

Aranthur felt a chill.

'Drako?' Iralia asked.

'No,' Aranthur said.

Iralia breathed for a moment. 'Maybe if we showed those papers to his father...' she began.

Aranthur shook his head and caught her arm, in the middle of a marble bridge, just below the Golden Angel that gave the neighbourhood its name.

She turned.

'His father is involved,' Aranthur said. 'I can't prove it, but I watched them. Hangela was... beyond rage. I saw it on her face when she realised that her husband is trying to find Uthmanos and kill him. I think he killed his son to cover something up. Listen – Mikal told me his father would kill him. I thought it was a phrase. And she said...' He put his hands to his temples. 'She said that you were better than Volta claimed... Something like that.'

Iralia turned away rapidly. 'Yes,' she said quietly. 'I caught that.'

'And I saw Siran and Djinar at Kallinikos' rooms. Kallinikos knew all about the Duke of Volta's plans... Damn.' He shrugged. 'He was a Lion.'

'Ah,' she said. 'Of course he was.'

'No. No. Djinar. I just realised that I saw him – two days ago.'

'Tell me,' she said.

His breath was caught in his throat as he tried to organise what he thought that he knew.

'Djinar is a Byzas aristo. A friend of Kallinikos. But he was part of the rising that Volta led—'

'That we're not supposed to discuss,' Iralia said.

Aranthur shrugged. 'Everyone in the West Country knows it happened. Djinar has a tie to Kallinikos and to Volta, and the day before yesterday I saw him...'

He was visualising it: the masked man standing on the step of Rachman's jewellery shop.

Myr Ghazala had said the jeweller received stolen goods and Manacher had said he sold *ghat.*

398

'What?' Iralia asked him.

Aranthur shrugged. 'I want to look at a shop. I will see you tomorrow.'

Iralia laughed. 'See, Prince Ansu would never, ever leave me standing alone in the moonlight to run off and look at a shop,' she said. 'I'm coming with you.'

Aranthur nodded. 'It may be dangerous.'

She looked at him for a moment. 'The implication that I cannot deal with something dangerous is a little patronising,' she snapped.

'That's unfair. You dislike violence,' Aranthur said.

'I know more about violence than most men. I dislike how *easily* the ignorant use violence. But I'm quite fond of it, myself.' She smiled an ugly, tight smile. 'I try to use it for good causes. Where are we going?'

Aranthur took a deep breath. 'I'm sure I'm wrong. But it seems that I know a jeweller whom local people thinks deals in *ghat* and *thuryx*. Who my friends said was deeply in trouble with soldiers a few months ago, and then had no further troubles. And Djinar was on his step two days ago.'

'Aphres!' Iralia said. 'I see it.'

'I see it too, but I am doubtless merely imagining it. We'll have a quick look.' He was already walking rapidly. 'Iralia, what does Kallinikos do? In the government?'

'He has, from time to time, been one of the Emperor's ministers. At the moment he is the commander of the City Watch.'

Iralia, it turned out, could walk as fast as Aranthur.

He led Iralia across the bridge and then through the east bank of the Angel, and along the base of the Aqueduct Ridge, out of the richest neighbourhoods, past where Master Sparthos lived and taught, and then yet further east, where the warehouses lined the waterfront and the better shops crowded at the canal crossings.

He slowed, walking along the Street of Lanterns and passing though the Square of the Mulberry Trees along the wrong side. There was a man leaning against a tree and everything about him was wrong.

Arnathur slipped an arm around Iralia's waist.

She smiled up into his face and kissed him.

It was a wonderful kiss. Aranthur found it very hard to maintain any kind of awareness of the world around him.

They walked past the man, who turned away with the embarrassment of a man watching lovers. But then he turned back, with a leer. He opened his mouth . . .

Squint.

It was Squint, the bandit.

Even in the poor magelight of the square, Aranthur knew the man as soon as he began to turn.

Squint reached for his sword. The recognition had been mutual.

Iralia seemed to burst into golden flames.

Aranthur reached with his left hand, as Master Sparthos taught. Iralia's *compulsion* bought him a heartbeat. He stepped as far as he dared with his left foot as his left hand locked down on Squint's sword hand, pinning it against his sword, still in its scabbard.

Aranthur slammed his forehead into Squint's nose. This was not the method taught by Master Sparthos, who'd probably never been in a farm boy brawl.

Squint had a dagger on his right hip and Aranthur knew he could go for it. Instead, he reached with his right hand, caught the back of Squint's leg, dropped him on the ground and then knelt on his sword hand, while his own hands went to the other man's throat.

Iralia stepped up behind him and uttered one word:

'*Philiax.*'

Squint was gone. His eyes rolled back and he was asleep, or worse.

Aranthur looked up and down the street.

'They will have another watcher,' he said.

Iralia cast, and then cast again. Her *power* rolled out of her like one of the Magi of the Academy, but even faster. Aranthur was almost unable to tear his mind away from the display of her puissance as shields unrolled like awnings in springtime.

Aranthur stepped back from the downed man, rising but trying to keep the fringe of mulberry trees between himself and the other side of the street. He touched his *kuria* and raised the small red shield that he'd learned from the Safian grimoire.

He ran through the second Safian *working*, the one that allowed him to see the colours of magik, and then he cast it. He wrote it in fiery calligraphy, an effect he enjoyed even under stress, and Iralia made a sound of approval.

Ghazala's shop was across the street and perhaps six shops to the north. The jeweller, Rachman, was one storefront closer, and his shop's interior *blazed* with arcane *power* in his *enhanced* vision.

'We have company,' Iralia said. 'I'm calling for help.'

'We can't run – we'll never have this chance—'

She made a face. 'I'm not running.'

She drew a glittering, golden wand from her hair and broke it between her fingers.

Aranthur was still looking at Rachman's shop.

And then he saw a burst of *power* at the edge of his vision.

Iralia had just erected a shield that shone like molten gold in the darkness. A red missile burst on it.

'So much for secrecy,' Iralia said, and raised a hand. A river of crystalline light poured out of her hand.

The other caster was faster than thought. He filled the air with red fire, and moved, passing like music.

Iralia's crystalline eruption seemed to pulse with the movement of the other caster, and every image of the man moving seemed to be outlined in her crystal – all this in a single beat of Aranthur's heart.

'Bitch,' spat the other caster. He was not close – fifty paces away – and he was staggering.

And from Rachman's shop came a dozen men.

'The Lightbringer isn't here to protect you this time,' Iralia said.

Aranthur was already casting his first Safian spell. On himself. This time he was well fed and unwounded, although the wound in his gut immediately exploded in a lightning storm of pain. He staggered back against the tree as the spell racked him. Then the pain ebbed away and left him with the feeling that he was a god.

He drew his sword.

Iralia unleashed a net of white fire, and the Servant was caught. He tried to flee in the *Aulos* as he had the night of Aranthur's wound, but he was caught in her net.

He retaliated.

Iralia screamed and stepped back, her arm covered in worms.

Quicker than thought, Aranthur's sword sliced along the worms and millipedes. They were real, physical, and poisonous, and he cut them away in one precise stroke. Then he pivoted on the balls of his feet and parried the first blow of a bravo behind his head. He reached out, faster than any mortal, took the man's arm and broke it, reversing the bend of the elbow brutally. He snapped his heavy blade around the screaming man's head and into the neck of the next victim, who fell without a word.

Aranthur spun, now in the midst of them. He cut and cut, all his cuts rising from low to high, opening groins and arms and chins – blows that were difficult to follow in the poor light, almost impossible to parry or cover. He left Iralia behind, spun, cut, and then rolled over his own sword. He rose with an up-cut between the legs of his immediate adversary, who fell with a choked scream of horror.

Aranthur was now behind the bravos, and four of them were down. One bravo had received a cut to the chin and was holding his head in his hands.

There was an explosion of light and every pane of glass on the street of shops burst with the scream of a tortured soul as Iralia's next *working* warred with the Servant's.

Aranthur's *enhanced* vision followed the contest even as his *enhanced* body ignored the effects. His sword was relentless, and another adversary went down, his sword hand severed by an impossible stop-cut. Aranthur had time to wonder how many opponents he might take on in this state. The men he was facing seemed reckless, and his luck was running out like sand through a man's hand. There were just too many.

And then Ansu appeared.

The Zhouian had a long blade in both hands, and his first blow beheaded one of Aranthur's opponents. Five heads turned as one fell to the ground.

Aranthur kicked the closest one in the leg. His *enhanced* muscles broke the man's knee, sending him to the ground, never to walk again. Aranthur made a parry too quickly, and took a wound from the slower sword. His ripping back-parry cleared the weapon, and he stepped in, his point over the man's shoulder. He caught it with his free hand and threw the man over his outstretched leg. He turned, but Prince Ansu had two of the last three. The last was running, his sword abandoned.

'You could have just invited me to come with you,' Ansu said with a smile. He seemed to speak very slowly, and Aranthur could just understand him.

'I wish I had,' Aranthur admitted.

Ansu looked as if he didn't understand.

Aranthur glanced at Iralia. She was cloaked in golden smoke. Beyond her, the Servant was cloaked in red. Between them was a bewildering garden of flashing symbols, ropes of colour, and ribbons of other realities. Through this jungle of lethal arcana, pulses of *saar* and *sihr* lost their way, and each pulse seemed to add to the forest of unreality.

At the far end of this bleeding of the *Aulos* stood the Servant. Iralia's white fire net still had him, although there were great rents in it. Iralia was bleeding, and something was wrong with her posture.

Her left hand was a blur of potentialities.

'I go right, you go left,' Aranthur said, as slowly as he could.

Ansu flicked blood off his long sword in a crisp roll of his wrist and turned.

Aranthur moved towards the shops. Although the street had no canal, many of the older buildings had loggia, as if there had once been a canal. Aranthur ran at the nearest, leapt, caught the decorative work at the top of the arch, and swung himself like a gymnast up onto the gallery.

Across the street, Ansu attempted to slip between two of the flickering ribbons, and something brushed him. A talisman at his throat spat black fire, and he was flung five paces to lie at Iralia's feet.

Aranthur ran ten steps along the elevated colonnade and leapt the next gap. The Servant became aware of him and he raised a red hand. The black ball he threw was like velvet on a moonless night, but Aranthur was too quick, and the ball melted the thousand-year-old stonework of the balustrade behind him. He was already past, leaping to the next.

The Servant turned, his head tracking Aranthur. Aranthur guessed he was the target of the next cast, and supernatural speed was not going to get him to his adversary in time.

He threw his sword instead.

It tumbled through the air. The throw was accurate enough, the tumbling of the blade unpredictable, and sword throwing was not something Aranthur had ever practised.

The hilt struck the Servant's arm and the blade clipped his knee. Neither was a debilitating blow, but the man's concentration was ruined. A brief flare of red light marked his wrecked *working* as it imploded in unfinished logic, and Aranthur leapt.

His leap was simultaneous with Iralia's cry of 'No!'

He struck the Servant with his feet, bore the man to the ground, and was surprised by the speed with which the man rolled clear.

Very much like the quickness Aranthur himself was riding. The Servant was *enhanced*, too.

But his arms were moving oddly. Aranthur's leap had broken something – maybe dislocated a shoulder or broken a collarbone.

'You!' Uthmanos said. 'How can you be alive?'

Aranthur threw a straight, Arnaut farm boy punch. Uthmanos was just as fast, but his arms weren't working properly. Aranthur's blow was no fight-ender, but he'd fought often enough. He threw a flurry of strong, simple blows, each one robbing the Servant of a little of his balance.

'No!' screamed Iralia.

Aranthur's hands were going numb. Striking the Servant was like fighting the *kotsyphas*, but the decision point was reached. He brushed aside a late defence, and his fist went past the Servant's head as quick as one of Iralia's crystal lightnings. Aranthur slammed the man into a mulberry tree head first.

The tree cracked.

The Servant's neck was broken. Aranthur could see it.

Uthmanos' hand came up, like a priest of Draxos giving a benison.

'So be it,' he said. 'I am but a servant, and those who come after me will—'

A wall of gold exploded between Aranthur and Uthmanos. It was like a tapestry of transparent cloth of gold, figured with men and women, every one of them apparently alive, illuminated, moving . . .

Aranthur stumbled back, his night vision wrecked.

Iralia caught him. Her face was flayed. Blood ran from her cheek, an ear was gone, and her right arm was swollen and black.

Light was growing in the Square of the Mulberry Trees.

Iralia put Aranthur on the cobbles, turning his backwards stumble into a throw, and she threw herself on top of him.

There was a single pulse of *nothing*. As if the world blinked.

The golden wall held.

Aranthur was deaf, and could not account for the weight on him, or the inability of his eyes to focus on detail. But light was growing around him. Iralia's slight form lay over him; he remembered her throwing him to the ground . . .

Without conscious direction, he reversed their positions, rolling over her.

She screamed when his weight came on her blackened arm.

Had she attacked him?

He didn't think so, and he rolled off her, reaching for her face with his free hand.

She grabbed it with her left.

'Open to me,' he said.

She lay, her eyes locked on his. She blinked once, and then her defences opened. He reached in, just a tendril of *power*, to stop the bleeding from her face and ear. The arm was another matter . . .

Her golden shield was wavering, and the light in the square was brighter than daylight. The other side of the street was on fire; most of the mulberry trees were afire. The one directly by them was half aflame; the half protected by the shield was still immune.

'I can't hold it.' She clenched her jaw. 'Aphres protect your servant.'

Aranthur had passed her *power* before, and now he pushed it down their link, and she took it like a starving mongrel eating meat.

The golden shield wavered and steadied. People beyond it were screaming.

Something exploded.

And then Kurvenos was there. Aranthur looked up and saw the Lightbringer standing by him, his staff moving with inhuman speed, twirling in his hand so fast that it appeared to be a circular shield.

'I have it, Iralia,' he said.

Iralia let her *working* go with a sob of pain.

The golden shield fell, and a burst of light and sound swelled, but Kurvenos' staff was, almost literally, everywhere. The *power* was shepherded, herded, tamed, and reduced. What could not be contained was parried into the wreckage of the six houses across the street, already destroyed and burning.

Iralia lost consciousness.

Kurvenos lowered his hands. 'I told her not to try the Servant in a public place,' he said wearily. 'I wanted him alive.'

'He left us very little choice,' Aranthur said tersely. He grabbed the sword lying under the tree. He could hear a little. 'Can you save her?'

Iralia lay on the ground, her beauty destroyed, ugly with blood and black swelling. The poison had begun to reach her neck.

'I can cut off her arm,' Aranthur said.

Kurvenos turned and looked at him.

'No,' he said wearily. 'I will save her, although others will die. What provoked this . . . ? No, there is no time. I must trust you. Go!'

Aranthur nodded, and ran for the jeweller's shop, which looked like a blinded man, all its glass panes blown in by the combat. Householders and shopkeepers were stumbling into the brightly lit street. Men and women, naked or in simple sleeping robes, were bringing buckets and flinging them on the fires. A cat darted from a burning building, and dogs barked, whined, cringed . . . A man shouted for his daughter; a woman cried. Manacher stumbled from his shop, his mother in his arms. She had a shard of glass in her abdomen, and both of them were covered in blood.

A man appeared at the door of the jeweller's shop, wearing a cloak and a mask. He had a sword in his hand and he swung once at Aranthur, forcing him, even *enhanced*, to make a full parry. Then the man raised a puffer.

The lock snapped, and Aranthur flinched, and then the man was running.

'Aranthur!' shouted Manacher.

The running man . . .

Aranthur pivoted and dropped to one knee beside his friend the leather-worker. He put his hands on Ghazala's temples, and her eyes opened. He went in past her rudimentary defences, reached her blood flow, and steadied it. His own *enhancement* helped him, as everything in her body seemed to be slow and easy to control, but he was calm, icily calm, almost remote from the fire and death.

He lacked the skill to knit her flesh, but he stopped the flow of blood around the wound.

'Straight to an Imoter,' he said. 'My work will hold for perhaps an hour.'

'Gods bless you,' Manacher said.

Aranthur had not time to consider the blessings or curses of the gods, and he launched himself through the door to the jewellery shop. The fleeing man had left it ajar.

A man was stuffing a bag from a set of shelves in the middle of the shop. He turned and shot with a puffer. This time there was no misfire.

Aranthur flinched away, placing a counter between himself and the puffer. The burn of the shot felt like fire along his left side. He rolled over it, landed, and the man had moved. But his movements were slow – he was casting, and Aranthur's cut removed his pointing finger and thumb. And then Aranthur was on him, his hilt in the other man's face, dropping him to the floor.

He heard, or felt, the next man behind him. He turned, his sword rising into one of the simple *breve gardes* as his body straightened. He crossed his new adversary's sword in the middle.

The other man attacked, a simple beat followed by a murderous lunge, hard to see in the flame light of the fires outside. Aranthur managed a crisp circular parry. The two men went hilt to hilt, but Aranthur was faster, catching his opponent's sword hand and pulling as he turned his hips, so that the other man went past him. He should have slammed into the counter, but instead he rolled over it with a lithe expertise that warned Aranthur that this was no bravo.

His expert adversary stood up into the light of the fires outside.

He raised his sword.

'Sorry, old boy,' said Tiy Drako.

Aranthur lowered his blade slightly. 'Drako?'

'I came in the back,' Drako said. 'Iralia called us.'

Aranthur stood in the shop, his feet on shattered glass, and contemplated everything he knew. Or thought he knew. He kept his sword point in line.

'I'm not sure who is on what side, just now, *old boy*,' he said.

'Draxos' hairy dick!' Drako spat. 'I'm your . . . officer!'

Aranthur nodded, backing away slowly. Under the shattered glass were scraps of vellum; an odd thing to find in a jewellery shop.

'If you distrust me, you distrust all of us! Iralia! Dahlia!' Drako sounded calm and rational.

'Just you,' Aranthur said. 'Tell me, Tiy. Did Kallinikos serve the Pure? Does Kallinikos Primos work for them?'

Drako lowered his sword. 'Yes. Your friend Kallinikos . . . came over. To us. But he wouldn't leave the damn woman. And he entangled you.' He nodded. 'You don't need to know. But his sister was always one of us.'

'And his father had him killed.'

Drako shrugged. 'Or allowed it to happen.'

'Or you had him killed to tidy up.'

407

Drako nodded. 'In a way, I like the way you think. But no. I was trying to keep you two apart because I still thought you were one of them. Or he was. Can we put up? I'm bent, but not bad.'

Aranthur thought the mountebank's voice had a ring of weary truth. He *wanted* to believe Drako.

'Why did you tell everyone to back off?' he asked.

Drako was sheathing his sword. 'I didn't, old boy. I simply left you out of an operation. Dahlia and Sasan are in. You were out. Wounded, and personally involved. And meaning no offence, in ten days everyone will know what we're doing, but right now, you don't *need to know*.' He grinned in the firelight and looked like someone's image of evil incarnate. 'Despite which, you smoked out the Servant and Iralia nailed him. And this place . . .'

He was flipping over shards of glass, and he used a *kuria* crystal to raise a magelight. Outside, the Fire Runners had arrived – an elite unit within the City Militia. They brought a water wagon and hundreds of buckets, and the street was full of organised chaos: shouts, orders; a dozen Brown Order nuns ordering women to form a line for medical attention; an Imoter station . . .

Aranthur still had his magik sight on him, although it was tattered by the final exchanges between Uthmanos and Iralia. The sight itself seemed to have furrows burnt into it. But he could see traces of magik all over the shop.

And under the floor.

Suddenly the shop was full of light, as if the moon had risen from under the floor.

Kurvenos stepped in. He was surrounded by light.

'Iralia?' Aranthur asked.

'Will be healed,' the Lightbringer said. 'You still have a sword in your hand.'

'He's not sure he trusts me,' Drako said, holding up a scrap of vellum, neatly cut and folded. 'Occupational hazard of lying all the time, I suppose,' he added, and shrugged at Aranthur.

Kurvenos shook his head. 'Stop it. People are dying out there. A building has exploded in the Angel and a dozen people are dead.'

'Kallinikos Primos?' Aranthur asked.

Kurvenos nodded. And raised his hand.

'They fight among themselves, the Pure. They have factions – some older than their allegiance with their precious Master. The Servant you two defeated was attempting to supplant the Duke of Volta, or that's how we read it.'

'By putting him down, we may just have helped Volta.' Drako shrugged. 'Whom the Emperor, on his name be praise, plans to pardon. See why we didn't want the Servant dead?'

Aranthur sagged.

Kurvenos shook his head. 'No. Victory is still victory, and Iralia paid a high price.'

Drako made a clicking sound with his tongue.

'We certainly have made the Master look this way,' he said, as if this pleased him.

Aranthur had no idea what he meant, as usual. He pointed at the floor.

'There is something redolent with *power* under the floorboards.'

He used his sword blade to pry at them after all three of them cleared the glass and parchment away.

'What is all the vellum for?' Kurvenos asked.

Drako held up the scrap he'd retrieved earlier.

'What does it look like?'

'A paper boat,' Aranthur said.

Drako nodded. 'I thought so too. Or a very small party hat.' He laughed bitterly. 'I'm supposed to be somewhere else doing something else, and I hope none of my spiderwebs unravel. But we're here now, and—'

He whistled. Then he leant down, snapped something metallic, and pulled. The floorboards came up on a hinge, and underneath was a locked door.

Kurvenos went outside and returned with two men in full armour and a third with an axe over his shoulder, wearing a long hauberk of maille and a magnificent golden helmet.

'An Imperial Axe,' Kurvenos said. 'For Iralia.'

Drako held something out. It looked like an iron rose.

All three armoured figures nodded.

'When I open this door, anything could wait beneath it,' he said.

The two Magdalenes closed their visors and took their blades in their hands, ready to fight.

Aranthur was loading the fallen man's puffer. He had the powder

409

and balls in vellum cartridges he wore in a little wallet on his body; Aranthur spanned the lock after priming it. Searching the unconscious man, he realised that this was the jeweller himself: Rachman. He spent a moment stopping the man's bleeding.

'This is Rachman, the jeweller,' he said to Drako.

'You're sure?' Drako grinned like Zanni, the Twelver god of tricks and lies. 'My night is made.'

Aranthur ran his hands over Rachman's figure, over his throat and chest. The jeweller wore a bunch of talismans and a huge *kuria* crystal which, lit by Kurvenos' glow, was rose pink.

There was also a pair of golden keys.

Aranthur used his Arnaut knife to cut the chain that held them, and tossed the keys to Drako, dropping the crystal and the talismans into his own purse.

Drako winked at him.

Aranthur took a breath. The image of the Arnaut thief was one he always tried to counter, but larceny was becoming natural.

Drasko summoned two militiamen to fetch an Imoter.

'I want him *alive*,' he said.

Even Kurvenos spent some *power* on the fallen jeweller. Only when the man had been taken away on a soldier's cloak did Drako cock a puffer.

'Everyone ready?' he asked, and tried the door.

It was locked. It didn't even rattle.

Drako put one key into the lock, grunted, and tried the second.

It clicked. He lifted. The heavy iron door seemed to hiss as it opened.

The two Magdalenes dropped into the darkness and Kurvenos pushed his white light into the lower room.

'Clear,' said one of the Magdalenes in a woman's voice.

The Imperial Axe relaxed.

'I think you need to see this,' one of the Magdalenes said.

Aranthur dropped down after Drako, the loaded puffer in his belt. They were in a long room, a sort of finished warehouse cellar. There was a set of heavy shelving – forty shelves running the length of the basement – and on the shelves were packets, wrapped in *myrta* leaves, of raw *thuryx*, uncut. The black, tarry cakes gave the whole room a scent of cinnamon and ginger.

Drako was standing with a packet in his hands, the *myrta* vine cut to reveal the contents of the leaf.

'Damn, damn, damn,' he said.

At the far end of the basement was a jeweller's bench, lit by a very expensive magelight, itself powered by *kuria*. The shelves above the bench were laden with drawers of *kuria* crystal – hundreds of them, in all sizes and shapes.

Aranthur reached into one, cast, and found it untainted. And another.

But on the bench were three large jewels, and one smaller, that all carried the infusion of *power* that made them lethal.

Aranthur didn't touch them, but he looked carefully at the bench. One of the tainted crystals was dark, blood red – an almost impossible colour for *kuria*, which was sometimes pale blue or rose red, especially from the Imperial Heart, but usually white or pale yellow and never, ever dark red.

He sat in the jeweller's seat and began to open the drawers, and Drako came and stood behind him.

The jeweller's bench was not so different from a leather-worker's bench. Drawers held tools: wax; scribes; a set of small chisels; sharpening stones; a drawer of hammers, most of them very small; a crystal, ground to provide magnification; a large iron bowl of what appeared to be tar.

Aranthur smelt it. 'Pine pitch,' he said.

With his nose close to the surface, he could see that the pitch was pocked with holes; bits of jewellery had been worked on its surface. They looked like rosettes.

There was an iron vice and a set of iron surfaces, a tiny anvil and a larger one. And a single piece of parchment, with odd red marks on it.

Aranthur took the parchment and placed it under the magnifying crystal, very like the Imperial Reader he used to decipher Safiri. Up close, he could see that the red marks were left by something that had been painted.

It was the same red as the tainted *kuria*.

Aranthur turned around. 'Drako, is it possible that the Servant was attacking this place?'

Drako made a face. 'Yes,' he admitted. 'Anything is possible.'

'He certainly didn't come from inside. He intended to prevent

Kallinikos and Djinar and the others from acting. I even know what they planned. I don't know how they came to own the *thuryx* and the *kuria*.' Aranthur shook his head. 'But why?'

Drako looked at Kurvenos. 'No idea. Except that the Pure are very focused on Atti right now, and Kallinikos and his faction care only what happens in the City.'

Kurvenos nodded. 'Volta is young, vicious and arrogant. He cares little for the wider issues . . .'

Aranthur turned to the Lightbringer. 'Volta is going to try and kill the Emperor. Tomorrow, at the reconciliation ceremony.'

Drako looked at him. 'You sound very sure of yourself.'

Aranthur put his hand on the anvil.

'The iron is cold,' he said.

Early morning in the Crystal Palace. The guard changed; the Nomadi went off duty, hurrying to their barracks to prepare for the ships that would take them to Atti. It was an open secret now – the war with Atti had begun, and the General was already in the field.

The Noble Guard had been assigned to guard the corridors of Imperial power, but they did not appear. Instead, the entire body of the Axe Bearing Guard turned out, a once in a lifetime event: five hundred young giants in long hauberks, with axes and glaives and partisans and giant swords, every one of them in a helmet worked in gold filigree and wearing a cloak of Imperial purple and bright red boots. They moved purposefully through the corridors, taking up guard positions outside the Imperial chambers and throughout the audience halls and stables, and even the gardens.

Aranthur was awakened by the sound of crashing feet and heavy armour in the corridor outside his room.

'Time,' came a voice.

He could scarcely move. He felt as if he'd been beaten with an iron club, over and over; there was not a muscle that was not strained or sore.

The Axe opened the door. A servant came in – the blond man who had helped clean the rooms for Prince Ansu.

'Good morning sir,' he said. 'I have *quaveh*, and a masseur waiting outside. And I am to tell you that Dama Iralia will join you for breakfast.'

An hour later, pounded within an inch of his life by a masseur who might have been on the secret list of Imperial torturers, fortified with *quaveh*, and wearing a magnificent scarlet silk fustanella that had been laid out on the bed for him by unseen hands, Aranthur was taken to breakfast by the Axe.

'The Fideles Aranthur Timos,' he was announced.

The Emperor rose from his seat and wiped a bit of egg from his mouth with his snowy white napkin. It was instantly replaced.

Aranthur bowed, his legs creaking with pain.

Iralia was sitting by the Emperor. Her ear was restored, although the left side of her head was an intricate web of white scars and sparkling crystal where an active medical *occulta* from a very powerful Imoter was keeping it all knitted together.

'It hurts to talk,' Iralia said.

'You saved me,' Aranthur said, ignoring the Emperor.

She smiled very slightly. 'We saved ... something,' she said very quietly, her lips scarcely moving.

'What you both saved, is me,' the Emperor said.

The day wore on. Coaches came and went; the Attian ambassador came, and with deadly formality, presented the Imperial Court with Atti's declaration of war. He was received gracefully, and not offered wine.

After the twelfth bell, the Axe Bearing Guard turned out *again*, and every position in every corridor was changed.

Soon after, the Duke of Volta's coach entered the great drive before the palace. He was attended by almost four hundred armoured men on fine horses, in direct defiance of an Imperial edict. Half of them dismounted with him, and the rest remained in the great, ten-acre courtyard under the imposing walls of glass and crystal.

The Duke of Volta's helmet framed the surprise on his naked face as he registered that the Noble Guard were not on duty. Almost equally surprising, the Axe-Bearing Guard made no attempt to stop him and his armed men from approaching the Audience Hall, the very centre of the great crystal lantern that were the main halls of the Imperial Palace. The Audience Hall was over a hundred feet tall, almost nine hundred feet in length, buttressed by white marble like the organically grown branches of a tree, with sheets of clear crystal between them. A thousand magelights burned from the high nave, night and day, so that the palace always shone like a great temple of light. High above them rose the needle of glass that men claimed had once flown, long ago.

The Emperor sat on a low dais. He sat comfortably in an ordinary chair — if a gold and ebony and ivory chair taken from one of the official banquet rooms could be called ordinary. He was not formally dressed, but wore the comfortable linen clothes a prosperous man might wear to go hunting. He wore almost no jewels. He did not rise when the duke was announced. The duke swept down the Audience Hall to the clash and rattle of his armoured bodyguard.

The long hall of glass and mirrors dwarfed the Duke of Volta. It dwarfed the Emperor. It had been built to induce awe in visitors, and that compulsion lingered over the centuries and was only enhanced by history. Above the duke, in stained glass, his ancestors and the ancestors of the Emperor supported Tirase, conquered the North, ended slavery, defeated Atti, and opened the Academy. The coloured light of a hundred generations of governance fell on the duke's white-gold hair as he clashed to a halt at the foot of the dais.

The Emperor was not alone. At his side, with her arm in a sling, was Iralia. She wore a hundred magnificent rubies in a net on her hair, an effect spoiled by the line of her scalp where a third of her hair had been burned away, although the gold wire of the rubies' setting did obscure the lines of crystal that held her face together.

'Bowing is traditional,' the Emperor said, after a pause.

'You didn't even wear a state robe!' Volta said. 'You think I'm some child to be reprimanded! Where is the throne?'

The Emperor put his chin in his right hand and leant back.

'In storage.' His voice changed. 'It is not for you, the throne.'

Volta frowned. Then he glanced at Iralia, and smiled.

'You look good in jewels, whore,' he said.

Iralia smiled very carefully.

Volta smiled back. 'Just exactly as I imagined it,' he said, and closed his visor.

He raised his armoured hand faster than a pair of Imperial Axes could close on him.

'Goodbye, cousin,' he said from within his helmet. He raised his arm.

Nothing happened.

414

Nothing except that two armoured men grabbed him by the arms and flung him to the carpet. Then they stood on his arms.

Behind him, his standard bearer put a hand on his sword, and his men-at-arms pushed forward.

Almost faster than a man could think, the hall was *flooded* with soldiers – not a hundred or two hundred, but almost the whole of the Guard: the Axe Bearers, the Nomadi, the Ferikon, a regiment of mercenary knights from the north and west; Keltai and Ictan barbarians from beyond the Iron Circle. Every door into the hall opened, and in they came, a rising tide of gold armour and scarlet and purple. And over it all, the rush of wings, like the largest hawk or eagle ever born, multiplied fifty times. Aranthur looked up in time to see the drake settle.

Taken at odds of almost twenty to one by the best soldiers in the Empire, the duke's guards gave way. Only his standard bearer drew a weapon. He was beaten to the floor with the hafts of axes, a hail of blows his armour could not fully stop, and knocked unconscious.

Prostrate on the floor, the duke attempted to cast, and found his *power* siphoned away. He screamed as a large, taloned foot pressed onto his back.

The Emperor sighed as the drake ate the duke's *power*.

'He is my cousin,' he said, almost petulantly.

Iralia nodded. 'He must go.'

The Emperor rose to his feet. 'Did he attempt to trigger the jewels?' he asked the drake.

The drake stood with one broad foot on the back of the fallen man and a smug, if reptilian, smile.

'Oh, yessss,' hissed the drake.

The Emperor looked as if he might cry. Instead, he stood up straight. 'Let him up,' he spat.

The Axes very cautiously hauled the duke to his feet.

'You plotted my death,' he said. 'You had these *kuria* crystals turned into a disgusting weapon, and then you disguised them as rubies so that I would wear them. With the robes of state.'

Volta's arrogance was undaunted. 'I am of the Blood. I am beyond accusation or trial and I will have what is rightfully mine.'

'You attempted my death,' the Emperor said.

415

Volta shrugged. 'We will triumph in the end. Your whores and your animals and your peasant mob cannot protect you forever.'

'You are of the Blood,' the Emperor said. He was red in the face, his lifelong dedication to urbanity and good manners gone. He was angry. 'You want to destroy everything we have built. We are servants, not masters, and you are a fool. You are beyond a trial, but this, my dear cousin, is the palace, and I am the Emperor.' He turned to the Axes. 'Strangle him.'

Volta was in full armour and he attempted to struggle. To Aranthur Timos, a few paces away, it was a horrible lesson in the power of training. One Axe raised the haft of his weapon between the duke's knees into his groin, and when he doubled over, the other man fastidiously removed a wire from his mail sleeve and threw it over the duke's head. He crossed his hands, and pulled sharply.

The duke's eyes seemed to bulge out of his head as the wire bit into his neck.

A palace servant appeared with a silk cloth. He stood, wiping the blood from the duke's neck, as the wire bit deeper and the man died.

'No blood has ever been shed in the Imperial Audience Hall,' Kurvenos said at Aranthur's side. 'None must touch the floor, at least.'

The wire went through the man's neck muscles and the Axe pulled it tight, but the duke was dead.

The Emperor exhaled.

'Clear the hall,' he said.

Six of them sat in a magnificent greenhouse garden on the seaward side of the great Crystal Palace. Tiy Drako sat with his legs up, playing his tamboura and flirting with Dahlia. Sasan glared at the two of them with ill-concealed hostility. Prince Ansu tried a courtly attentiveness on Iralia, who had a pair of Imoters *working* on her arm as she listened.

Very carefully, she whispered, 'Perhaps now that my face is ruined, you'll desist?'

Ansu laughed. 'Never. It is not your face, nor your magnificent body, that I *desire*.'

'Come, this is better,' Iralia muttered, with her jaw almost unmoving. 'You have *almost* learned how to flatter me.'

Kurvenos came in, his long grey robe brushing the floor.

'The Emperor,' he said quietly, and everyone, Iralia included, got to their feet.

The Emperor came in, and smiled.

'Sit, sit,' he said quietly.

He looked out of the tall windows at the sea for long enough that Aranthur started to fidget, Ansu to look at his nails, and Drako to tug at his beard.

The Emperor turned back to them.

'The Empire owes you all a debt of gratitude. But because I trust you, I wish to say that today, I feel nothing but anger, and fear, just as my enemies wish me to feel. I have killed my cousin.' He shrugged. 'I will carry that burden all my life – that, and the deaths of every man and woman who has died in this infernal conflict. How many died last night?' he asked Kurvenos.

'Thirty-six,' Kurvenos said. 'So far. The milliner will probably die today.'

The Emperor looked around, as if studying each face in turn.

'Nine of Volta's people died last night,' he said. 'The other twenty-seven were bystanders, local shopkeepers, and their families.'

Iralia flinched. The movement hurt, and she choked with pain.

'I didn't think—' Aranthur began.

Drako stood suddenly. 'With respect, Majesty,' he said, 'Aranthur didn't think of that. If he had, Volta would be in the palace now, and you and Iralia would be dead.'

The Emperor nodded slowly. 'I know. They're still dead.'

'And Kallinikos Primo and his wife and both sons and seven of their servants,' Kurvenos said. 'And we still do not know how it was done.'

'One of the crystals exploded with lethal force,' Drako said. 'Enormous force, exactly as the Master of Arts predicted. But how that crystal reached their palazzo . . .' He shook his head. 'Their line is virtually extinguished.'

'Kallinikas Primo is now his daughter. She's a military engineer training at the Arsenal, and absolutely loyal.' Drako shrugged. 'It is my business to know these things.'

Kurvenos frowned. 'The Academy team says the jewel exploded in a water pipe. How on earth did it get there?'

The Emperor nodded. 'Despite the casualties, we must move on. Aranthur?'

'Syr Djinar escaped. I saw him run.' Aranthur looked around. 'And we don't know what the vellum was for.' He was nervous, speaking to the Emperor. 'They were making something. Something deadly.'

Drako nodded. 'Obviously.'

'Nonetheless,' the Emperor said, turning from the window, 'we must now concentrate our attentions on Atti. We cannot fight this war on the defensive.'

Kurvenos nodded.

Drako bowed. 'I will go with the army, if I may, Majesty.'

The Emperor shook his head. 'No, I want you here. I thought that the brave Syr Timos, as he is already a dekark in one of my regiments, might serve as our courier to the General.'

Drako made a face, and then turned to Aranthur.

'Are you up to a sea voyage and a long ride?' he asked.

Every muscle hurt; it felt as if every muscle in his arms and shoulders had been forced into knots.

'Yes,' he said.

Iralia's eyes glittered.

'I would like to go with him,' Sasan said.

'And I,' Dahlia said.

'And I,' said Prince Ansu.

The Emperor looked around. 'Four good swords,' he said.

'Four sharp minds,' Kurvenos said.

'I can give you perhaps three hours to prepare,' Centark Equus said. 'As you have Imperial orders and you are, by decree, an Imperial Messenger, you could order the ship held for you, but I don't recommend it.'

Aranthur nodded. 'My horses—'

'I'll have them aboard, and all your tack,' the centark said. 'I'll assign you a groom. What more do you need?'

'Swords, armour, pack, feed bag . . .'

'Clothes,' Dahlia said.

'Where are your horses?' the centark said to Dahlia.

She smiled archly. 'In the Imperial stables. The Emperor has given us mounts.'

The centark nodded with the long-suffering patience of an expert staff officer.

'I'll just assign a pair of grooms to get you all aboard, shall I,' he asked. 'You are Myr Tarkas?'

She bowed.

'You are not on my list, more's the pity,' he said with a twirl of his moustache.

'Hmm. Well, they say war is good for courting,' she returned, and Sasan puffed his chest out.

She put a hand on his arm. 'Relax,' she said.

'You should run,' the centark said. 'We are to be aboard IS *Nike*, at the foot of the Street of the Heralds.'

'Two streets past the Angel,' Dahlia snapped. 'I'll meet you there,' she said to Sasan.

They ran. Prince Ansu had the easiest time; he had a saddle and a heavy bow in the palace, and he walked off to fetch them. Sasan had no equipment to speak of. Dahlia owned everything required, but spurned it.

'Let the army provide,' she said. 'I want a copper pot to make *quaveh*, my best sword, and a leather doublet. I'll see you at the ship.'

'We're on the *Nike*, remember,' Aranthur shouted, but Dahlia was already running.

Sasan shrugged. 'I'll come with you. All I own is shirts. I might as well bring them.'

The two young men ran through the streets: across the great marble bridge by the Angel; past the blackened ruin of the Kallinikoi palace and the temple where the funeral had been held just a day before. They ran up the steps, and Aranthur's legs threatened to fail him. They bowed to the statue of Tirase, and ended their odyssey at the top of six flights of steps.

Aranthur had all his equipment to hand. He took the heavy sword he'd purchased so long before, in what seemed like another world, and he took his *kuria* crystal from the window. He thought for a moment, took a quill from the case of cut quills he had, sat at the writing table, and wrote a letter to his father.

He began to fold the paper – good, expensive paper, but nothing like the perfect, creamy vellum they'd found scraps of the night before. He drew and checked his long sword, and he cleaned the puffer he'd taken off Rachman the night before: a long barrel, a snaphaunce mechanism – a particularly fine weapon.

He emptied his purse on the bed, examined the tangle of talismans and *kuria* crustals he'd taken from the drug dealer, and thrust them back into his purse.

'I have about twenty silver crosses,' he said to Sasan. 'Here's ten.'

Sasan smiled. 'You are a good friend.' He thrust the curved sword he'd taken the night of the House fight into his sash and put a leather sack across his shoulders. 'I have a copper pot and two clay cups.'

Aranthur was in his red military doublet, and he pulled the breastplate on over it and Sasan buckled his straps.

'Easier than carrying it,' he said.

He put the rest of his kit in a leather knapsack, started down the steps, remembered the carbine strap he'd made himself and ran back and found it hanging behind the door. He started down the steps again and remembered the letter he'd written to his father. He turned for the door and caught the sword in the door jamb, just as he had more than a year ago.

He followed Sasan down the stairs. A hasty bow to Tirase, and he found a waiter he knew standing outside the gate of the Sunne in Splendour, smoking his pipe.

He handed over a silver cross. 'I need a favour,' he said. 'Put this on the mail coach for Soulis?'

The young man bowed. 'My pleasure, syr.' Then he grinned. 'Aranthur! Didn't know you in all the iron.'

Then Aranthur and Sasan went down the steps to the canal, where small boys were staging a regatta with paper boats. They crossed at the Angel and walked quickly down to the head of the street.

Nike wasn't alongside the pier. It was on a single cable, two hundred paces off the wharf, with small boats around it.

There was not a gondola in sight.

'Boat here,' Aranthur yelled.

A fisherman raised his hand. 'Where to, Syr?' he called.

'*Nike*, there.'

'Two silver crosses,' called the fisherman, and they dropped into his boat.

The man rowed them with long, careful, professional strokes, and he kissed alongside the round merchant ship without touching her paint, despite the calls of the bosun above him.

'Up the side,' the fisherman called.

Aranthur put his two silver coins, plus two bronze obols, on the seat, and the fisherman nodded, not having a hand to take them. The harbour was choppy and he had to work to keep his little shell of a fishing boat in the lee of the round ship.

Sasan took a deep breath and leapt for the lines that hung over the side. He caught one but not the other, and swung for a moment in the gentle swell.

'Get yer arse up the side o' my barky and don't scrape me paint!' yelled the bosun. 'And you, squidee, clear off. There's a gent coming in.'

'While I have a passenger yet,' called the fisherman, none too pleased at being called 'Squidee'.

Sasan got one hand above the other, then got a hand on the ship's rail and vanished over the side.

Aranthur wished that his muscles didn't hurt so much. Or perhaps that he had never *enhanced*.

'On the rolls, syr, if you please,' the fisherman said.

Aranthur wasn't seamanlike enough to know what he meant, but he saw his moment and leapt as high as he could manage. He got a hand on the rail and another on one of the dangling lines, and then his leg was over the rail.

It was an odd moment to have a galvanic revelation. But it hit him – a cascade. Folding the letter to his father; the vellum on the floor of the jeweller's shop; the boys sailing paper boats; the ruin of the Kallinikoi palazzo, which he could see from the deck of the ship.

'You made jolly good time,' Centark Equus said.

Aranthur saluted, for perhaps the third time in his life.

'I need to get a message ashore,' he said. 'Life or death, Imperial business.'

'You are an exciting lad,' Equus said. 'We have pigeons who go straight to the palace.'

Aranthur wrote out a message, explaining how paper boats could carry explosive jewels through the Aqueduct and water pipes.

'When you are done with that,' Equus said, 'I'd be very pleased if you'd teach my mages what you know about Safian *occultae*. Especially the shields.'

'Safian?' Aranthur asked.

Equus shrugged. 'Humour me.'

*

An hour later, as Aranthur fought seasickness and tried to explain the way in which the Safian grimoire summoned *saar* and built *occultae* to three junior military Magi, there was a loud sound of feet on the deck above, and the ship seemed to boom with activity.

'Pass the word for Timos!' came a roar from the deck.

'Apologies, friends,' Aranthur said.

He stood up and slammed his head into a beam. The deck was very low.

Sailors laughed.

He made his way up into the fresh air and light of the open deck to find Centark Equus with Sasan and Dahlia. She was flushed.

'Are you all right?' she asked. 'Did someone hit you?'

Aranthur shook his head. Which hurt.

Equus nodded. 'They're securing the Aqueduct and all the access to the water pipes,' he said.

'There's no proof yet,' Dahlia said. 'But I'm sure you are correct. So is Drako.' She squeezed his hand. 'Good one.'

Sasan shook his head. 'I'd like to understand.'

Aranthur pointed at the massive aqueduct, high above them on the central ridge that dominated the city. Seen from the water, the ridge seemed impossibly high, and the hanging gardens of the upper city and the tall tenements built out from the bare rock looked as if they were balanced on air.

'You make a little boat out of parchment,' he said. 'You put an explosive *kuria* crystal into the boat. You drop it into the Aqueduct – perhaps as far away as Dharg in the hills.'

'Gods,' Sasan spat. 'And the little bombs just float along into the system.'

Dahlia nodded. 'With a nudge of *saar*, a Magas can control them. They're very light. Choose which pipe they enter...'

They landed just after first light, four days later, after sailing through the islands as if on a pleasure cruise. The beaches of Atti looked very much like the beaches of home: long, golden white in the sun, and for the most part lined with deep groves of pine. Most of the Imperial Fleet was there. The Attian fleet had not made an appearance or contested their landing. Further down the beach there was a small fishing village. The whole beach was filled with men, wagons, and neat piles of everything from boards to spare wheels.

The Nomadi landed their horses by swimming them ashore, something they did with great expertise. Aranthur and his friends followed along, swimming cheerfully in the warm water, holding the manes of their mounts.

'Did you bring a towel?' Dahlia asked.

Sasan shook his head.

'Men. A towel is the first thing you pack,' Dahlia said, and threw her lover a fine cotton towel.

The Nomadi formed up with military precision in less than an hour, drew a supply of oats for horses, biscuit and sausage for the troopers, and two guides. Equus ordered red doublets out of his *banda* stores and gave them to Dahlia and Sasan and Ansu.

'Wouldn't want you chaps to be mistaken for Attians,' he said.

Sasan raised an eyebrow. 'Meaning me, no doubt.'

There were two City Militia regiments watching the anchorage, and they'd built a star fort of newly cut logs and sand shovelled into wicker gabions. It all looked very professional.

'I'm still a little surprised we haven't been attacked,' the militia colonel said.

Equus smiled. 'The General moves fast. I'll wager they don't know what she's up to yet. Confused command is divided command, what?'

The Vanax nodded. 'She's three days ahead of you, Equus. Don't get snapped up. I have a note that you are to take a supply convoy.'

Equus laughed. 'I'd hate that. First war in my generation – captured in my first action?' He shook his head. 'Yes – the convoy – that's our part in the schedule. I have sixty wagons.'

'More now,' the colonel said.

Sasan turned aside. 'What a buffoon,' he muttered.

Aranthur shook his head. 'I think Equus only *acts* the courtier.'

An hour later, all four of them were helping bored Nomadi troopers to dig. They spent four hours filling gabions along the edge of the beach fortifications.

'War is so glorious,' Dahlia said, looking at her red hands.

Prince Ansu sighed. 'Well, that was a new experience.'

Sasan looked at the trees. 'This is not Atti.'

'What?' Dahlia asked.

Sasan put his pick carefully in the pile where two militia dekarks pointed, and a third motioned for them to proceed to a mess line to be fed.

'This is Armea,' Sasan said. 'My homeland is about six hundred leagues that way.' He pointed east.

They marched with almost a hundred wagons, and the Nomadi regiment was spread out over the whole column – a vanguard, a rearguard, and flank guards. Every wagon was a rolling fort, with huge rear wheels and smaller front wheels, the body of the wagon six feet off the ground, pulled by eight horses. A third of the wagons carried the fodder to feed the thousand or more horses in the column.

The Nomadi were an odd regiment – a holdover from a former time when the Empire had itself spread north to the farthest shores of the Sea of Moros. There, on the steppes, were dozens, if not hundreds of tribes of nomads: Pastun and Monul and Turuq and Kipkak and a hundred others, with their vast herds of sheep and cattle and their incessant pursuit of the *Wyldakind*. They tended to be small, and dark, and women served as freely as men; they travelled from the steppe to the City to volunteer. They wore khaftans of scarlet cloth, and had baggy fur hats lined in blue, and every man and woman had three horses. They carried curved swords like Sasan's, a few had bows, and most had *gonnes*. Their Byzas was stiff and formal, and Aranthur was surprised to hear the centarch, Equus, speaking easily to one of his Nomadi troopers in Pastun.

They rode up the steep ridge off the beach and immediately entered a different world: fertile land instead of sand; oaks and beech and maple instead of pines. There were farms, with terrified farmers. In the first hour they passed a small village with its temple and tall whitewashed tower crowned with a pointed dome, unlike the square towers and round domes of home, and the vanguard brushed aside a mob of refugees fleeing from the east and south.

'Anyone speak Armean?' Equus asked.

'Not well,' Aranthur said.

Sasan raised his hand, and they found the local innkeeper, purchased all of his oats, and rode on.

'Some of those people on the road were Safians,' Aranthur said.

Sasan nodded.

'We are being very polite to the locals,' Aranthur said to Equus.

'Purchase, no thievery, and no interference whatsoever with the locals,' Equus said. 'It's a strange sort of war, but I'm ordered to publicly execute any soldier who disobeys.'

They made camp forty leagues from the coast, with a range of tall, white-capped mountains now visible in the east. The troopers had no tents, but they picketed their horses and made themselves comfortable by destroying a few leagues of fencing while their dekarks looked the other way.

In the morning two of the regiment's horses were too lame to move. Equus took them to the farmer in recompense for his fence line.

They rode on, with a dozen scouts out in the first dawn light and a strong rearguard. Twice they had to stop to work out where they were. The roads were far more primitive than in the Empire, just deep slashes of rock and old wagon ruts across the irrigated plain, The countryside was full of people moving; tens of thousands of refugees fleeing, although no one in the column could see any sign of war – no columns of smoke, no burning villages.

The villages were almost empty. The farmers had run for the fortresses visible on the highest hilltops, or so the soldiers guessed.

They climbed all day, up ridges and down the far side, but always ending higher than they had started. Afternoon, and two solid hours of driving rain, which cleared off as suddenly as it had come, and then they made camp again, with sentries and fires and a hasty fortification thrown up at either end. The troopers lay in clumps to sleep, and no one undressed.

'More digging!' spat Dahlia. 'My sword hand is ruined.'

Aranthur was a soldier, on the rolls, unlike his companions. Equus put him on the watch bill, so he stood a midnight watch and rather enjoyed it, as did Rasce, as they moved carefully around the perimeter of the camp in the moonlight.

And then, with only an hour's sleep, he was being awakened by Dahlia.

'Move in one hour,' she said.

He couldn't get hot water to shave, so he boiled his own, shaved, and drank some acceptable *quaveh*. They were mounted and moving again with the sun just a smear on the eastern horizon. In fact, the mountains towered over them now, and the sun took its time cresting them. Still they rode east to meet it, until by midday the column halted to allow the troopers to don their cloaks. Sasan and Ansu didn't have heavy cloaks, but Equus shared out spares.

Aranthur took advantage of the break to ride up to the cavalry officer.

'I can't help but notice we're riding east,' he said. 'But Atti is north.'

Equus was looking at the mountain pass visible ten switchbacks above them – two leagues of hard riding, and only six hours of daylight left.

'Very perceptive, young Timos,' he said.

Neither of the guides, both Black Lobsters of the General's guard, said anything.

Aranthur turned Rasce and rode back to his friends.

'No idea what we're doing,' he said.

Two hours after midday Aranthur's part of the column crested the high pass and suddenly he could see the plains of Armea laid out before him like a cartographer's map. He felt as if he could see for a thousand miles.

He could see a river valley far away, at the eastern edge of his vision, and a ribbon of water, and low hills almost at his feet . . .

'*Hereketsiz qalsin!*' shouted a dekark.

'He's telling us to keep moving,' Sasan said with a smile. 'In strong language.'

'You speak – what was that, Pastun?' Aranthur asked.

'Kipkak,' Sasan said. 'Or close enough. All these people are from the lands north of Safi.'

The ride down the pass on the far side was more difficult and slower than riding up had been, and they were forced to keep moving even as the sun crept down the sky. Equus was everywhere, up and down the column, encouraging, jostling, joking, and even threatening.

'We can't make camp up here,' he said. 'Move it.'

Aranthur looked back, and there, silhouetted against the afternoon sky, were the last troopers in the column. He adjusted his carbine strap for the three hundredth time, because the weapon kept sliding off his shoulder, and leant back as best he could to help Ariadne as best he could. Rasce was already back with the remounts, exhausted from the climb.

It was still light in the pass when they reached the plains below, but it was dark at the foot of the mountains, and they were ordered to camp without fires. The watch was doubled, which halved Aranthur's sleep. His friends had no watches and were inclined to linger, lying on their saddles.

'Some of us have to get up in two hours,' he snapped.

'Oh, the army life,' Prince Ansu said, but then they were quiet.

A cold morning, and no fires, no *quaveh*, and no food. Aranthur knew it might have been worse; on his watch in the very early morning, forty troopers and a dekark had been sent east and north to look for the General, with one of their Black Lobster guides.

The whole column was moving before dawn, which was much earlier this side of the mountains. It was all too clear that it was going to be hot. The plain seemed virtually waterless, and before ten bells of the morning, there were heat shimmers in the distance and horses started to walk with their heads down.

A handful of scouts returned as the sun reached zenith above them. The column turned sharply north at the next crossroads, threaded its way through a veritable maze of stone walls, collected a herd of sheep, and disgorged into a gully that led them to a deep, clear river.

Aranthur was happy – inasmuch as he was anything but exhausted – to be with veterans. They knew how to water horses carefully and the whole column proceeded carefully. Aranthur was sent out on Rasce to be a guard, so he sat on his horse in the shade of a pine grove on a very slight hill and watched the road to the south.

Dahlia rode up to him. 'I'm bored,' she said.

'Me too,' Aranthur said.

'Peace?' she asked, and handed him a piece of hard bread and a chunk of sausage.

'Of course.'

She smiled. 'You have any water?'

'No.'

She gave him a mouthful of water, lit a pipe, and they passed it back and forth.

Somewhere between one puff and another, a little dot of dust had appeared on the south road.

'Ride back behind the hill and tell the dekark "alarm post four",' he said.

Daliah didn't argue. She handed him the pipe and led her horse over the low hill and then he heard her riding away.

The dust was moving straight for him. Aranthur had the usual reactions, including relief that he hadn't made the whole thing up. Nonetheless, it seemed a long time until Equus rode over the hill, dismounted, and shook his head.

'I can far-see,' Dahlia said.

'If you please,' Equus said.

Dahlia cast, and the dust cloud seemed to move towards them.

'From the south,' Equus said.

His officers were coming up the hill.

'My horse hasn't had water,' Aranthur said.

Equus nodded sharply. 'See to that. Tell Anda Qan that we'll form up facing south.' He looked at his wagon master. 'Hitch up and go north. The General can't be more than two hours away.'

'Yes, syr.'

Aranthur rode down to the river, handed Rasce to one of the Nomadi grooms, and mounted Ariadne. He had the sense to move his puffer from the holster on Rasce to the holster on Ariadne's saddle, and then he passed on the centark's orders.

Dekark Anda Qan was the Nomadi's senior dekark; he looked around.

'Form four deep on me, facing south, on my word.'

He walked his horse cautiously up the embankment, looking right and left, studying the ground, until he was satisfied. Dekark Lemnas, a tall woman, spurred her horse up the embankment and then began to count off distances as she rode away from Anda Qan.

The troopers stood by their mounts, perfectly silent.

The military wagoners were rehitching their teams. They were garrulous – a little afraid, louder than the troopers. Still, the wagons were getting hitched and were moving out, headed north, a long line of dust rising into the bright white sky.

'Carabiniers on me,' Lemnas said.

Aranthur pulled at his reins and trotted to the dekark's side.

The dekark glanced at him. 'Ain't you the Messenger?'

'Yes, Myr.'

'I didn't mean you,' she said in good Byzas, but then she shrugged.

'But I'll take you an' all yer friends. We're going to take them in the flank, if it's a fight.'

Equus stopped at the top of the bank.

'Listen up, lads and lasses. There's about half again our numbers. They don't look like regulars and they have an odd white and red silk flag. Our orders are not to engage, but there's nothing we can do to avoid this – I have to cover the wagons. So listen up! This is the order: not a shot, not a blow, until you hear my trumpet.'

The two dekarks nodded.

Lemnas looked over the rest of her mounted carabiniers: men and women with rifles, as opposed to simple muskets.

'On me. Across the water, and up the bank.' She looked around. 'And you'll shoot when I say so. Centark didn't mean us.'

There were just twenty of them, with Dahlia, Sasan and Ansu. They crossed the cold water, and their mounts powered them up the stony bank. The river was lined in trees, tall cedars unlike the trees of home. The dekark stayed among them, watching the water now five paces below her, rocky and impassable to horses.

'Damn,' she said. 'Damn and damn and damn. I need to cross back. This is already taking too long.'

She stood in her stirrups. Peered ahead under her hand, and then glanced back at Aranthur and Ariadne.

'That's a good horse. You stupid, lad?'

'No, myr,' Aranthur said.

'Good. Go ahead, find me a place to cross back.' She pointed. 'Don't die, don't take a risk. Go and look. Wave if you find a ford.'

Aranthur looked back at Sasan and then trotted ahead. After a few paces he gave Ariadne her head and she ran, as if happy, despite the heat, to have a clear run on the good ground.

As Aranthur cleared the end of the trees, he could see the Nomadi forming off to his right, across the river, a long ribbon of black armour and red khaftans and fur caps.

Ahead of them, to his left, was a column of horsemen in flowing robes and fur-lined khaftans; the predominant colour was a dusty red, and most wore maille. Many of them had pointed helmets and looked like the figure illustrations in his Safian grimoire, except that these were quite colourful.

The distant enemy began to loose arrows. A spattering of *emanations* flew from their ranks – *workings* of *power*. A dozen shields appeared along the Nomadi line.

A handful of the enemy had musketoons; puffs of smoke appeared along their line.

A scarlet khaftan went down among the Nomadi. Another screamed. A riderless horse burst from the Nomadi ranks.

'Steady,' called Equus clearly. His voice carried hundreds of paces. *Augmented.*

Aranthur was riding at a canter along the stream, wondering how he came to be in a battle. Everything seemed dangerous.

He could see a farm path or a cart track, and his heart rose. As he came abreast he could see that it continued on the far side of the river, marking the ford.

He turned and galloped for the dekark, and waved. Then she had seen him, and the twenty troopers with carbines came trotting along. Aranthur reined in, checked the priming of his weapon, and watched the Nomadi regiment move forward. He and the carabiniers were well past the Nomadi, and the red-robed horsemen were moving past them. Some turned their heads and looked – two hundred paces away across the river.

Some of the enemy archers loosed another storm of arrows and trotted away. They were just about level with the cart track when a storm of red lightning played over the Nomadi shields. One went down and there was a choked scream.

'Dismount,' the dekark said. 'Horseholders.'

Aranthur slipped to the ground. Dahlia took his reins.

'Mark a target. Fire as you will.'

Aranthur was kneeling. Aimed . . .

The carbines cracked. The range was short – perhaps seventy paces – and the enemy horse archers, broadside-on, made an easy mark against the light sky.

Aranthur fired, and loaded, and fired again, his mouth full of the salt-sulphur tang of powder as he bit the back off his paper cartridges.

An arrow landed almost at his feet. Another struck the ground nearby and exploded, bits of the cane shaft spraying around him. A third skidded along the ground just a few paces to his right.

Without preparation, he flicked a *working* out of his head – a much less effective shield than Iralia's, but enough for arrows. He fiddled with it for a moment, and it covered the little skirmish line of carabiniers, and Dahlia added a roof.

'They will charge us, I think,' Ansu said. 'These are not Attians. These are the soldiers of the Pure. Look at their banner.'

Indeed, the banner was all white.

Aranthur spared a glance for the enemy. More than a dozen were down, and suddenly, like a bolt released from a machine, the Nomadi drew their swords, like the sparkle of a thousand meteors falling to earth, or the flash of a hundred mirrors in the brilliant sunlight.

'Mount,' the dekark ordered.

The enemy riders coming to face the carabiniers were not as decisive as their officer wanted them to be. They were riding for the ford, but they were aware that none of their shafts were striking home. They were all too aware that the Nomadi trumpeter was blowing and a long line of red was moving across the stubble of the gleaned fields.

They were going to be cut off.

'Can you maintain those shields while we ride?' the dekark asked.

Aranthur tried to shrug, but the straps of his breastplate cut into his shoulders.

'Never tried, myr.'

'Try now,' she snapped. 'Move!'

The carabiniers formed up close. Aranthur had trouble managing his simple shield, but Dahlia did not, and another flight of arrows tumbled harmlessly to the ground. The enemy riders coming to face them looked very human. Fifty paces away, they were dispirited by the lack of effect of their bows, and their faces showed it. One man had a modern carbine. He aimed, and Aranthur wanted to flinch. He fired, the crack audible over the distant sounds of battle, and a carabinier fell with a grunt. Aranthur's heart seemed to lurch.

Among their immediate opponents, a single figure in a flowing red robe dismounted.

'Ware!' called Dahlia. 'It's occulted!'

Sasan bit his lip. 'I've seen that before. It is one of their "Exalted".' He looked around. 'It can kill . . . It will move faster than a wolf, faster than an antelope.'

'Then we'll shoot it,' the dekark snapped. 'Anyone loaded? Good lads. Take aim!'

Aranthur sighted down his carbine, Ariadne perfectly still between his legs.

The *Exalted* began to move. It was like a red streak, almost too fast to follow, except that it came straight at them from eighty paces away.

'Fire!' the dekark screamed.

Aranthur's carbine went off simultaneously with both of Sasan's puffers and Ansu's magnificent matchlock jezail.

The scarlet streak staggered; despite its speed, they'd hit it, and it slowed.

Dahlia's puffer snapped, too close to Aranthur's ear. He flinched, and his horse half-turned, and then half a dozen other carbines spat. The scarlet *Exalted* came on, into the little group of cavalry, and behind it came the enemy horse archers.

Dekark Lemnas put the muzzle of her carbine against it as it cut at her and pulled the trigger. It had been hit multiple times, and it was no longer particularly fast; the last shot rolled it back into the dust.

Sasan shot it again, even as the rest of the enemy struck them, catching their horses at a stand. There was a flurry. Aranthur found that he had a cut along his forearm, and his arm was tired, and they were gone, running back to their own lines.

'After them!' the dekark sang out. 'We're not going to walk or trot. On my word.'

She drew her sword.

'Charge!'

Aranthur was so surprised by the riding skills of the men and women around him that he was left behind. Twenty horses went from a gentle walk to a gallop in a pace or two, and the only one of the four friends to keep up was Prince Ansu, who rode like a centaur.

Aranthur cursed. So did Sasan, who also rode well and had hesitated.

Aranthur left him and went forward.

The mailed enemy fled. Most of them tried to shoot back over the cruppers of their little saddles, but they were too slow, and the lead carabiniers caught them; the Imperial horses were better to start, and fresher.

The enemy lost a dozen men in seconds and their controlled flight became panic.

Aranthur was behind, but Ariadne bore him nobly, opening out into a gallop. He passed a pair of armed men, and then he was in a dust cloud. He made an unconscious parry with his heavy sword as steel came at him out of the dust, as if the sword was thinking for him. He had the impression of a beard, teeth, a pale horse and black robe, and then he was fighting for his life, first on one side, then on the other, the heavy sword in both hands, in one hand, pressed horse to horse and flank to flank, so that he thought he might lose his leg. He had his long sword by the hilt and his left hand at mid-blade, and he was jamming it into another man's maille as if he was using a spike to break ice. A heavy blow to his head, turned by the helmet, and one to his shoulder that felt cold, and then . . .

It was over. There were men on the ground, and his horse trotted a few paces, head up, stopped without a signal from him and she put her head down and bit something.

Aranthur turned her, got her head up. He could see Dekark Lemnas to his left and he rode to her. The whole line of the regiment had passed them, though, and they were out of it. Off to their left, there was a sudden whirl of dust, like a storm cloud. Then the red-clad troopers were forming on their standards and a bugle was sounding recall.

Aranthur trotted back along the line of their very small charge. There were men in dusty red, in green, in black on the ground – some wounded, some dead. Sasan was kneeling by one.

He looked up, and there were tears running down his face.

'My people!' he railed. 'We are killing Safians! I am helping kill my own people!'

He turned his face away.

Aranthur went to fetch Dahlia.

Prince Ansu came back, shaking the blood from his long sword, a broad smile on his face. Aranthur intercepted him, took his bridle, and led him away.

Equus didn't stop to interrogate his forty prisoners, although he did order his Imoters to work on their wounded.

'You are not surprised,' Dahlia said.

Equus turned and looked at her. 'They attacked us.'

'You expected to meet Safians,' she said.

Equus turned his horse. 'Not my place to say,' he snapped. 'If your young gentleman would keep them calm, though, I'll see them well treated.'

Further back in the column, Dahlia shook her head.

'He knows something he's not saying.'

Sasan shook his head. 'We have headed east from the beginning. I know the mountains. We're only four hundred leagues from my home – perhaps less.'

Aranthur was surprised to find his friend in mail, with a spiked helmet.

'They are the Pure,' Sasan said bitterly. 'Whether they volunteer or are driven like cattle. But it hurts.' He touched his heart. 'They are the very tip of the spear. They know we are here – they know all about the Empire invading Atti. Even now, they mock us. One boy says they have *thirty thousand* cavalry.'

Prince Ansu whistled. 'My arm could get tired.'

'Don't be thoughtless,' Dahlia spat, before she leant over and kissed Sasan.

Aranthur rode away, and found a place with the carabiniers, who were happy to have him. In fact, Lemnas gave him an extra ration of wine at dinner.

'Neat trick, that shield.'

'Happy to have you any time there's iron in the air,' said another man, in stilted Byzas.

They weren't allowed fires, and most of the troopers spent the night with their mounts, rubbing them down, keeping them warm. Aranthur stood his watch, smoked Dahlia's pipe because he'd forgotten his own, and fell into a sleep troubled with dead men, and jerking recollections of the combat.

He was up before dawn, and the centark had ordered just enough fires that everyone could have hot *quaveh*. No one had shaved for days. Even under the red khaftans, the troopers looked dirty. Most of them had so much dust on their faces that they looked like revellers wearing masks.

'That's the last of the sausage and the wine,' Equus said to Aranthur. 'My compliments to your friends. They were... very useful.' He nodded at Sasan, who was sitting with two prisoners. 'Tell Myr Dahlia that I was rude and I'll apologise if she insists.'

Aranthur forced a laugh. 'I guess you had other things on your mind.'

The centark glanced at him, and just for a moment, Aranthur

appreciated what the other man had experienced: command, and loss; fear, and victory.

'Someday, perhaps, some history will say I only lost six,' Equus said. 'But I knew every fucking one of them.'

He turned away, spat, and looked back with his usual face of bland gentility.

'No more of that, what?' he said. 'Let's ride.'

In early afternoon, they found the Imperial Army. The Imperials were camped on the western slope of a long, shallow ridge, facing south, with a pair of redoubts being dug to cover their flanks, and an impressive dust of cavalry screen to the south and east.

Equus rode down his own column, as soon as watchwords had been exchanged and thumbs came off snaphaunce hammers. He found Aranthur with Sasan.

'You are Imperial Messengers, and I'm your escort,' he said. 'We'll try not to mention how I used you as flankers in a desperate skirmish, what?' He pointed up the long ridge. 'General's up there. We should go. Immediately.'

Aranthur was on Rasce, but he switched to Ariadne and the five of them cantered away from the column. Aranthur found his messenger's wand and waved it at the mounted sentries as they went up the hill. About a hundred paces from the summit, they were surrounded by the Black Lobsters, and there was Jeninas, and there, under the Black Rose banner, was the *Jhugj*, Ringkote.

'Now we're in for it,' Ringkote said hollowly. 'Timos the raven is here.'

Some of the troopers laughed.

Alis Tribane emerged from a huddle of officers. She wore a black coat and a white shirt, and she was tanned and didn't look as if she'd been in the field for a week.

'Companions,' she said with a smile, using an old word, a military word. An Ellene word: *Hetaeroi*.

Equus saluted, and Aranthur, who'd grown more accustomed to life in the army in five hard days, also made a passable salute.

'Syr Equus,' the General said.

He swept his hat off his head. 'I fought an action yesterday. Red-clad Safians and some Armean light horse. A vanguard – refugees

435

everywhere, and perhaps as many as thirty thousand horse coming at us from the south. A vast army.'

'Excellent.' The General smiled with what appeared to be satisfaction. 'Aranthur Timos. You do appear in the most unlikely places.'

'Majesty,' he said.

'Speak!' she ordered.

'My lady, the Emperor has executed the Duke of Volta. I was to tell you this first.'

Her head flashed around, and shock was writ plain on her face.

'Where? When?' she asked.

'He attempted to kill the Emperor by means of sorcery. I was there.' He handed her the Imperial Message.

'Gods, what an idiot,' the General said. She straightened up. 'Anything else dire?'

'The Emperor was concerned lest . . .' Equus glanced at Aranthur. 'Lest some of your troops or officers had . . . other loyalties.'

'I appreciate the Emperor's concern,' she said. 'But no one here will have time for mutiny.'

'I have dispatches, and Myr Tarkas has a whole bag of military—'

'Good. And mail?'

The General snapped her fingers, and servants ran.

Prince Ansu nodded. 'Two bags.'

'Excellent,' the General said. 'So – we are still on schedule. Syr Timos, my mages will want anything you can tell them about Safian casting. I believe you have been working the *Ulmaghest*?'

'Yes, ma'am.' Aranthur was stunned.

'I knew you were the right person for this. Well done, Centark. Still on schedule.'

'I brought you sixty wagons of food and powder—'

'Schedule?' Aranthur asked, feeling stupid.

Tribane smiled. 'The war. We have a schedule.'

'With Atti?' Aranthur asked before he could clench his teeth on his questions.

'They don't know,' Equus said.

'Quite right,' Tribane said. 'But Aranthur and I are old friends, and I know the prince all too well, and Dahlia is family. Sasan and I have stood together as sword companions, have we not? So let me show you all something.'

436

She had a white baton in her hand, and she waved it at her officers, all of whom were on horseback. A groom handed her a helmet of gold with a single, tall black plume. She put it on, and made her horse rear to the cheers of soldiers nearby.

She trotted up the hill, posting occasionally, and Aranthur followed her with his friends.

As they crested the ridge, the breath left him as if he'd been punched.

Laid out on the other side of the ridge were hundreds of silk pavilions, and a mile of horse lines, and a long, deadly row of bronze *cannones*. Big men in turbans stood guard.

The Attian army.

Aranthur had trouble controlling his horse.

'Draxos!' spat Dahlia. 'But we are . . . at war . . . with Atti.'

'I'm so pleased you are surprised,' the General said. 'In the morning, we'll see how surprised the Master is.'

Her grin was feral.

Down in the Attian camp, a magnificently mounted man waved, and then he and his jewelled companions began to ride up the slope.

'We're not going to fight Atti?' Aranthur said.

'No, my dear,' the General said. 'We have lured the Master, or one of his senior servants, onto a battlefield with most of his forces. He thinks he will face a divided Atti and a handful of Imperial cavalry, while his pawns topple our government.' She waved her arm. 'He's not omnipotent. And we had to keep his eyes focused elsewhere.'

'The City,' Aranthur said.

The General nodded. 'All those busy plots . . . We will not win by defending ourselves. We will triumph by destroying the Master.' She waved her baton over the plains of Armea. 'And we will start here, tomorrow.'

The End

Of 'Cold Iron' Book One of Masters and Mages

To be continued in Book Two and completed in Book Three.